"An action-packed and intriguing look at the world leading to WWII that will be enjoyed by all those who like suspenseful political stories. The authors bring to life multiple historical figures and create a narrative filled with interesting anecdotes and asides even as the race to stay alive is vividly depicted." [*Amazon* review]

The Liebold Protocol

"A fast-paced historical thriller with a strong female lead... Extremely well-researched and intriguing to the last page. [*Mobius* review]

The DeValera Deception

"Crisply written and meticulously researched, *The DeValera Deception* is a remarkably well-crafted adventure story." [*Mysterious Reviews*]

"A fast-paced historical thriller. The historical aspects of the novel are especially true to life, giving a strong factual feel to this fictional story." [*Suspense Magazine*]

The Parsifal Pursuit

"Evocative of Ken Follet and Steve Berry at their best, *The Parsifal Pursuit* is a thrilling ride through pre-World War II Europe, a masterful page-turner that packs a wallop you won't soon forget!" [D.E. Johnson Author of the historical mysteries *The Detroit Electric Scheme* and *Motor City Shakedown*]

"Vivid portrayal of Churchill and unusual insights into Hitler's character, a fast-paced thriller that is hard to put down." [Richard Langworth, Author of *Churchill By Himself*]

The Gemini Agenda

"A thick and rich tale that is impossible to put down, So many twists and turns and the ending is gripping...This book holds its own with the best historical fiction." [*Goodreads review*]

"An excellent read and brilliant follow-up to *The Parsifal Pursuit*. The thought-provoking issues raised will question your beliefs and touch your emotions." [*Beck Valley Books*]

"A novel with crackling suspense and amazing characters. Better than a semester-long history class about Europe's twisted doings during the 1930s. The character of Winston Churchill is a delight." [Les Roberts, *Past President, Private Eye Writers of America* and *The Crime Writers League*]

Literary Awards and Praise
for Mattie McGary's Adventures
with Winston Churchill

Three-Time Grand Prize Winner Fiction,
Next Generation Indie Book Awards

Three-Time Thriller/Suspense Book of the Year,
ForeWord Reviews

Two-Time Historical Fiction Book of the Year,
ForeWord Reviews

Two-Time Historical Fiction Honorable Mention
Reviewers Choice Awards

Two-Time Historical Fiction Winner
Next Generation Indie Book Awards

Appointment in Prague

"A thrilling historical novel with a no-nonsense heroine is what you'll find... Wow! This is an action-packed, intense story that brings the reader right into the world of WW II espionage. Well-developed characters, a tough heroine, and great attention to detail fills these pages." [*The Book Connection* review]

"Mattie McGary was easily my favorite character and I loved how the authors made her into a strong female character with a very real personality. So many times strong female characters end up feeling almost unrealistic and that was not the case with Mattie." [*Books for Books* review]

The Berghof Betrayal

"Mattie McGary is what every woman wants to be: strong-willed, the ability to take care of herself, and who doesn't take crap from anyone." [*Goodreads* review]

"I've read and enjoyed all of the books in this series and I vote this one as the most exciting yet, full of twists and turns and I really cared about what happened to the characters. It was a most believable page-turner right to the very end. I can't wait for their next book. "[*Amazon* review]

"This series of books is fantastic—as good as any New York Times Best Seller. Anyone who likes a thriller but appreciates an accurate historical background would like this book. I look forward to the next in the series." [*Amazon* review]

"One of the best thrillers I've read in a long time. It's detailed, nuanced and beautifully written. Historical fact and fiction were so seamlessly woven together that I wasn't sure which was which!" [*Amazon* review].

The Silver Mosaic

"This is a well-written historical novel that stays true to the time period and keeps its historic facts accurate. I really liked how the authors immersed me in the time period right from the first page." [*Amazon* review].

"Historical fiction which excels. I immediately became involved with both the characters and plot which took on a life of their own. I have read much shorter books that have seemed far longer than *The Silver Mosaic*." [*Goodreads* review].

The Prussian Memorandum

A Mattie McGary + Winston Churchill 1930s Adventure

by

Michael McMenamin & Kathleen McMenamin

The Prussian Memorandum
A Mattie McGary + Winston Churchill 1930s Adventure

Copyright ©2020 Michael McMenamin & Kathleen McMenamin

ISBN 978-1506-912-09-7 PBK
ISBN 978-1506-909-06-6 EBK

LCCN 2020907884

June 2020

Published and Distributed by
First Edition Design Publishing, Inc.
P.O. Box 20217, Sarasota, FL 34276-3217
www.firsteditiondesignpublishing.com

To Carol and Walter,
the loves of our lives

In the early 1930s, Nazi lawyers were engaged in creating a race law founded on anti-miscegenation law and race-based immigration, naturalization and second-class citizenship law. They went looking for foreign models and found them—in the United States of America.

James Q. Whitman
Hitler's American Model,
The United States and the Making of Nazi Race
Law

Part I

Washington D.C. & Berlin,
4 October 1933—6 October 1933

Inside, Franklin Roosevelt was the coldest man I ever met. He didn't care about you or me or anyone else in the world on a personal level.

Harry S Truman
April 1970

American jurisprudence would suit us perfectly, with a single exception. Over there, they have in mind, practically speaking, only coloreds and half-coloreds, which includes mestizos and mulattoes; but the Jews, who are also of interest to us, are not reckoned among the coloreds.

Roland Freisler
State Secretary, German Ministry of Justice
5 June 1934

1

That Goddamned Little Fairy

The White House
Washington, D.C
Wednesday, 4 October 1933

FRANKLIN DELANO ROOSEVELT finished stirring an ice-filled pitcher of martinis in the Oval Office and placed it back on the drinks trolley beside his custom made wheel chair. It was of minimalist design—a plain, straight back wooden chair with no arms or legs placed on a base between two large rigid black spoke wheels. Behind the seat were two smaller spoke wheels that turned 360 degrees so that the chair could go in any direction the polio-crippled Roosevelt desired. The two large wheels did not extend above the chair's seat so that the overall effect of the chair was not to draw attention to itself, but rather to its occupant whose massive chest and broad shoulders conveyed an image of strength, not weakness, and belied his shriveled legs below the wheels.

Roosevelt carefully poured the icy liquid from the pitcher into two stemmed glasses and, after popping an olive into each, handed one to the man who sat in a maroon leather club chair on the other side of the drinks trolley. He raised his glass. "Well Louie, to our good health and the consternation of our enemies."

Louis Howe lifted his glass and lightly touched it to the other extended glass. Howe was Roosevelt's right hand man—Secretary to the President—and had been FDR's fixer while he was governor of New York as well as his unofficial campaign manager both for the nomination and general election in 1932. In contrast to Roosevelt who had a handsome face topped by wavy silver brown hair, Howe was short, dark and ugly with large, bulging, bloodshot eyes and an emaciated frame. Roosevelt thought he looked like death warmed over. Still, he was the most astute political operative Roosevelt had ever known and the President was going to ride him as hard as he could until his health—and luck—ran out. He only hoped that Howe would last until his re-election campaign in 1936.

"Speaking of enemies, Louie," Roosevelt continued, "what did J. Edgar say he wanted to discuss with me in our meeting tomorrow morning?"

"Beats me, Boss," Howe replied after taking a sip of his martini. "All he said was that it involved 'intelligence matters' that would be an embarrassment to the country, to your administration and to you personally if it ever became public knowledge."

"Interesting. Do you suppose he's going to try and blackmail me again about Lucy?"

"Not a chance, Frank. You remember when, after your election, he showed me photographs of Mrs. Rutherford entering your private railcar in Chicago while you were there to accept the nomination and I told him it would be most unwise were he to make them public?" Howe asked, referring to Lucy Mercer Rutherford who had been Roosevelt's long time mistress both before he contracted polio and after she married the aging socialite Winthrop Rutherford. Howe had arranged to have her there in the railcar in Chicago as a reward for Roosevelt when he returned from giving his acceptance speech at the convention.

"Of course," Roosevelt replied and took a sip of his martini.

"I don't believe I mentioned this to you at the time, but that goddamned little fairy actually blushed when I showed him *our* photographs of *him* with Clyde Tolson's cock in his mouth," Howe continued, Tolson being Hoover's #2 man at the FBI with whom he lived. "So, don't worry, whatever he wants to talk about tomorrow, all he's doing is sucking up to you—pardon the expression—and trying to get on your good side."

Roosevelt laughed and drained the rest of his martini. "I would have loved to have been there to see that. Remind me, is that the photo where he's wearing a woman's frilly dress?"

Howe shook his head and finished his martini also. "Nope, he doesn't know we have that one."

Roosevelt laughed again. "Well, it's good to know we have something in reserve if what he's going to tell us tomorrow is going to embarrass me and my administration. Another martini?"

Howe nodded and placed his stemmed glass back on the drinks trolley. Roosevelt stirred the martini pitcher again and once more filled their glasses.

The White House
Washington, D.C
Thursday, 5 October 1933

ROOSEVELT WATCHED the FBI Director walk across the carpet in the Oval Office, followed by Louis Howe, until he reached the President's desk. Dressed in an immaculate Brooks Brothers suit, he thought the short, stocky man's face really did resemble a bulldog. "Edgar! How good to see you again," he boomed in a loud voice and extended his hand.

Hoover grasped it. "Thank you for seeing me on such short notice, Mr. President, but I thought this was of such importance that it could not wait."

"Take a load off your feet, Edgar, and tell me all about it," Roosevelt said and placed a cigarette in a silver holder and lit it.

Hoover took a seat in one of two straight-backed armchairs in front of the President's desk and Howe sat in the other. Hoover frowned and glanced disapprovingly at Howe.

"This is a most sensitive matter, Mr. President."

Roosevelt laughed. "Don't worry about Louie, Edgar. He knows *everything*."

"Very well, Mr. President, you're the boss."

Yes, I am, Roosevelt thought, and don't you forget it.

Hoover took out a slim folder from his briefcase and began to talk. "This is based on interviews my agents have had with the commanding officer of the US Army's Military Intelligence Division (MID) Major General Leonard Marlborough, his immediate predecessor Brigadier General Ralph Van Deman, the Harvard Law School Dean Roscoe Pound..."

"Roscoe?" Roosevelt said, interrupting. "The devil you say! How is the old rascal?"

"He's fine, Mr. President. He was most cooperative. We also have had interviews with six former MID agents, all lawyers, who were selected by Dean Pound to perform under his supervision certain legal research for a foreign power."

"A foreign power, eh? Which one?"

"Nazi Germany, Sir."

"The Nazis? Really? You have my attention, Edgar. Let's hear it from the beginning."

"Well, Sir, it began with information from a wiretap of General Leonard Marlborough's office and home telephone lines. Based on that, I ordered an investigative file opened and sent Special Agents into the field for interviews with all involved."

Roosevelt was surprised at this, but said nothing. Was the sonofabitch tapping White House phone lines as well? He made a mental note to have Louie find out. If he was, then it was time they showed the little bastard the photo of him in a woman's dress. Meanwhile, the President listened with growing horror as Hoover told his story in a dull, dry-as-dust monotone.

"In June, acting on behalf of the Nazi's German Commission on Criminal Law Reform which was contemplating racial laws which would make Jews and gypsies second class citizens and prohibit sexual relations and marriage between Aryans and Jews, Gypsies and other non-Aryans, Wilhelm Krueger, an SS officer and a political attaché at the German Embassy, approached General Marlborough to commission and pay for confidential legal research into American race laws on miscegenation they could use as models to do the same to

Germany's Jews. We learned from other sources that Marlborough was an anti-Semite like many other MID officers. In fact, Marlborough admitted to us he didn't like or trust Jews and that this was why he readily agreed to the request. He also told us that he recognized how politically sensitive it might be. So he farmed it out under a Black Drape using secret MID contingency funds to retain RVD International, a private security group named for and headed by Marlborough's predecessor at MID, retired General Ralph Van DeMan. RVD frequently had been given government subcontracts by MID and employed many ex-MID agents."

FDR did not like where this was going, but he decided to keep quiet until the little bastard finished. The faint odor of blackmail trailed Hoover like the scent of a skunk.

"Once Marlborough told Van Deman what kind of research the SS wanted, they both agreed that the most qualified—and sympathetic—person to supervise the research was the Dean of the Harvard Law School, Roscoe Pound. He was known to be a Nazi sympathizer and had publicly accepted an honorary degree from the University of Berlin personally presented by Hans Luther, Nazi Germany's Ambassador to the US."

"The head of Harvard Law School? Old Roscoe?" Roosevelt said almost reflexively.

"Yes sir." Hoover said and then continued "He and the whole Harvard Law faculty attended a Nazi luncheon on the university's campus"

Roosevelt wished he was surprised but he wasn't. He could tell Hoover was waiting for some kind of reaction but he wouldn't be getting any. Roosevelt stared at him and said nothing. Finally, the ugly little toad started speaking again, the air firmly vacuumed from his sails by FDR's silence.

"Uh…well in the late summer of 1933, RVD hired Pound with secret MID funds to sift through personnel files of former MID agents with law degrees to find the six best men for the job. Pound then supervised, also under a Black Drape, these six ex-agents who performed on the ground research in law libraries in thirty states whose laws in 1933 prohibited marriage between whites and assorted 'coloreds' and Asians."

FDR just shook his head as Hoover read off the thirty states. He had known the Deep South prohibited interracial marriage, but was mildly surprised at all the western states that did so as well—Alabama, Arizona, Arkansas, California, Colorado, Delaware, Florida, Georgia, Idaho, Indiana, Kentucky, Louisiana, Maryland, Mississippi, Missouri, Montana, Nebraska, Nevada, North Carolina, North Dakota, Oklahoma, Oregon, South Carolina, South Dakota, Tennessee, Texas, Utah, Virginia, West Virginia and Wyoming.

Hoover paused after reading off the names of the states as if to ask if the President had any questions. Roosevelt gestured for him to continue. "Go ahead, Edgar, and get it over with."

Hoover did. And, to FDR's dismay, it got worse.

"While they have no such laws today," the FBI Director continued, "an additional seven American states once enacted laws against interracial marriage during the 19th century and later repealed them: Illinois, Iowa, Ohio, Massachusetts, Michigan, Rhode Island and Washington. Oh yes," Hoover added, "the District of Columbia once had laws like that as well."

Exactly, Roosevelt thought, courtesy of those idiot Democrats in the U.S. House of Representatives before the Civil War. One of the few decent things the Republicans did after the Civil War was to repeal those laws. The last piece from Hoover, however, was the goddamn spoiled cherry on top of the whole rotten cake. Even savage Indians— the Cherokee Nation in 1824 and 1839, the Cree Nation in 1839, and the Chickasaw Nation in 1858—prohibited marriage and sexual relations with Negroes!

"In September 1933, Pound compiled the resulting research and delivered it to Wilhelm Krueger, the SS officer at the German Embassy who commissioned it. RVD was then reimbursed for its expenses by the SS and, after taking its cut, in turn passed it back to MID to replenish their secret contingency funds. The SS officer later told Pound that he had sent it on to Berlin where, after translation and removal of his name, they were calling his report the 'Prussian Memorandum'. The SS officer also told Pound that many members on the German Commission on Criminal Law Reform were relying on it to advance their arguments that German Jews should be stripped of their citizenship and that marriage between Aryans and Jews, gypsies and other non-Aryans should be criminalized. Pound reported all this to the FBI agent with no small amount of pride and gave him a copy of Pound's original memorandum."

After Hoover finished, Roosevelt sighed. What complete idiots! It's not that he didn't understand what had motivated Marlborough, Van Deman and Pound. After all, he privately had informed more than one Catholic or Jew reluctant to do his bidding that this was a Protestant country; that the Catholics and Jews were here on sufferance; and that it was up to them to go along with anything he wanted. Well, make that a *white* Protestant country as well and Negroes better do what he wanted also. And what he wanted was for all of them to vote in large numbers and elect more Democrats in the mid-term elections next year, not to mention his own reelection in 1936. But these were not things he could say publicly. To have it known that the Nazis were using openly racist American laws to craft their own laws against Jews would not play well among Jews or Negroes. And while he needed the larger Negro vote, he also very much needed campaign contributions from the Jews who would not understand that some politically tone-deaf idiots in his Administration had gone off the reservation without his knowledge.

"Thank you, Edgar. I appreciate your bringing this to my attention. I will take care of it. I assume that folder you've been occasionally reading from is for me?"

"Yes, it is, Mr. President."

Roosevelt held out his hand. "Good, I'll take it." Hoover handed the folder to him. "I want any copies of this file in the FBI classified as 'TOP SECRET' and I don't want this appearing in any of Drew Pearson's 'Washington Merry-Go-Round' columns in the *Post*. Understood?"

"Perfectly, Mr. President."

"Fine. Louie will see you out."

Moments later, Howe returned. "What were those morons at MID thinking?"

"Who knows, but have the fannies of Marlborough and Van Deman sitting in those two chairs," Roosevelt said, pointing to the two armchairs in front of his desk, "first thing tomorrow!"

"You got it, Boss," Howe said and turned to leave.

"One more thing, Louie."

"Yes, Frank?"

"This is political dynamite and absolutely cannot get out. I don't trust Hoover. Call him sometime in the next few hours; re-emphasize to him the importance of keeping this quiet. Tell him I want all FBI records on this destroyed. He'll agree, but he'll keep one copy for his personal blackmail file anyway," Roosevelt said and then paused. "Also, tell him I want the names and personnel files of the two agents who conducted the investigation on my desk by the close of business today. Then, have someone check them out. Make sure they're good Democrats. If he is at all reluctant, this may be the right time to mention the photograph of our top cop in a dress."

2

Hanna Raeder

Reichsmarine Officers Club
Berlin
Friday, 6 October 1933

THE WIFE of Admiral Erich Raeder, Commander-in-Chief of the *Reichsmarine*, was usually so bored that this was the most exciting part of her week. Hanna Hindermann Raeder held her Walther PPK automatic pistol in two hands, arms extended, forming a triangle with her body, and fired three quick shots. The smell of gunfire lingered in the poorly ventilated basement, but she always felt powerful and calm after target practice, even if the world around her was making that feeling very difficult to maintain.

She pressed a button beside her and the paper target, hanging 20 yards away on a wire, began to move towards her. The target showed a tight group of three holes in the middle of the bulls-eye. She tore it off the wire and placed it on top of five other paper targets, only one of which had a single shot outside the bulls-eye. That annoyed her. It rarely happened. She sighed and looked at her watch. It was 11:30 a.m. Time to go anyway. She took out a new paper target and ran it down the line; placed her five targets in her purse and left by the way she had entered—the servants' entrance.

Hanna hated having to use the club's target range, not least because women were officially not allowed on its premises. For the wife of the Navy's Commander-in-Chief, however, an exception had been made so long as she used the servants' entrance. Unfortunately, using this target range was necessary because, ever since the Nazis took power, they had closed all the private rod and gun clubs in the country, including the one with a shooting range to which she had belonged since 1921. It was just one slight among many since the Nazis took power. While Berlin in the twenties was a dangerous place with constant battles between left wing and right wing gangs, the events of the last few years were much worse. She was glad she'd learned how to protect herself in her own twenties, and these days she was glad for the release of anger that target practice provided. Besides, as a former criminal defense lawyer, it never hurt to have a weapon handy.

Outside the club's servants' entrance, her husband's *Horch* and their chauffeur Heinrich were waiting to take her to their home in the suburbs of Berlin. This luxury made her uncomfortable, reminding her of the growing inequities in her country. But the driver was her husband's price for being able to use the basement target range. And if her husband knew who she was meeting for lunch today—a one-time lover—and why, he might not approve that she was taking the *Horch* out on her own.

While her independence, sharpshooting, and accomplishments as a trial lawyer were something that had attracted Erich to her, they were now merely amusing anecdotes she told at the endless parties the Commander-in-Chief of the *Reichsmarine* was expected to host. She loved her husband and, if she had to say so herself, she did an excellent job chatting up and charming her husband's allies and enemies. That was because all good trial lawyers had to be good actors and she had been a very good trial lawyer. In fact she'd managed to keep practicing law even after she'd produced a male heir and a spare, but, by 1928, when Erich became the head of the Navy, she just couldn't successfully juggle all her roles. And Hanna did nothing if not successfully.

Hanna didn't regret that stepping away from practicing law had given her more time with her sons these past five years, but she did mind her being 'on stage' as her husband's hostess. Hanna looked the part, tall and blonde, and, at 38 years old, the much younger and second wife of the head of the German navy. Naval officers sucked up to her because she was the wife of their boss. They were boring. Politicians and diplomats couldn't help it. They were inherently boring. After Hitler became Chancellor, it got worse. The Nazis were vulgar as well as boring.

The *Horch* pulled up to her beautiful house and she let out a breath of relief. It was still here. The best perk of playing the hostess. It was built in 1907, designed by the then-unknown 21-year-old architect Mies Van der Rohe and she had spent the last five years lavishing large amounts of attention on it. After 'retiring' as a lawyer, she really had no idea what to do with her idle time. Erich had bought it because he knew how much she admired the *Bauhaus* school. In fact she would have been quite happy in a little cottage, envious of the simple lines of the house Erich had shared with his first wife and child. It wasn't the house of the head of the Navy, whereas her grand *Bauhaus* home most certainly was.

Erich had even allowed her to decorate his study with actual Mies Van der Rohe furniture even though it was too sleek and black for her taste, but once the Nazis took over and made it clear they hated the *Bauhaus* school, she was glad it was only Erich's study that contained the objectionable furniture. Indeed, after Nazis began outnumbering naval officers at her cocktail parties, she had put the Van der Rohe furniture in storage as Erich had asked. Lots of things were going in storage these days. Like the rule of law.

Once in her bedroom, she took off her jacket and pants that reeked of the shooting range even more now that they were in the confines of her perfumed boudoir and lay them on a tufted ottoman that stood in the center of her dressing room.

The shower was warm and strong. Van der Rohe was a stickler for modern American plumbing and she relished it. Wash away all the stress of the last few years. 1933 was supposed to have been her time. The boys were both away at boarding school now and she was back in the courtroom, doing what she did best. Hanna sometimes wondered if she was more angry at what the Nazis were doing to the country or what they had done to disrupt the new frisson of excitement in her life that going back to being a lawyer had done for her. She loved her two sons dearly, but how had she ever thought that running a house, hosting cocktail receptions, presiding over formal dinners and taking care of children could ever be as exciting and fulfilling as coming up with precisely the right argument that would persuade a judge. She had just that month begun to work again when Adolf Hitler was appointed Chancellor on 30 January 1933. She successfully defended two burglaries the following month. She was getting her feet wet again and feeling fulfilled in a way she hadn't felt in years. Then came 27 February and 28 February. After that, nothing was ever the same.

Hanna stepped out of the shower and grabbed a bath towel to dry off, reflecting on those two days and their aftermath. First, in the early morning hours of 27 February, arsonists set the *Reichstag* ablaze, completely gutting it. The Nazis blamed it on the Communists and a Dutch pyromaniac with a room temperature IQ. Hanna and almost everyone else in Berlin who wasn't a Nazi thought the Nazis had done it. Next, on 28 February, President Hindenburg signed a decree drafted by her former lover and the Minister of Justice, Franz Gurtner, and grandly titled *Suspending Constitutional Rights and Instituting Other Measures*. In it, all the Weimar Constitution's protections for freedom of speech, assembly, unionization and compensation for expropriated property were suspended "until further notice" as was the right to be free from arbitrary search and seizure.

What had Franz been thinking? How could he have gone back on all his principles so quickly? When he did not resign, but meekly acquiesced in the Nazis taking away the basic rights of every German, she lost all respect for him. She was angry that someone whom she had always admired, who stood up for the rule of law, for the German Republic, would so quickly buckle under to Nazi thugs. No, that had been madness and she had refused to go quietly.

Hanna picked one of her better trial dresses, a suitably demure, but fitted deep blue dress that accented her waist and collar bones. When going into battle, the better you looked, the more confident you felt and therefore the more persuasive you could be. And she expected an argument today at lunch with Franz because nothing he did now could change the moral cowardice he had shown on 12 March.

Emboldened by the Nazis' victory in the 5 March 1933 general election, the Ministry of Justice had circulated an Official Memorandum on 12 March to all German attorneys over Gurtner's name specifying that, when it came to attorneys defending political crimes, "Only such attorneys can be considered whose attitudes prove beyond doubt that they fully approve of the political plans of the State and of the ideological aims of the movement." Worse, the ugly memorandum went on to say that defense lawyers were to assist in the process of deciding whether their clients were guilty and that "whoever is not ready to accept this ought not to don the robe of a German lawyer nor take a place at the defense counsel's bench."

Hanna still couldn't believe it, not really. And it was written under Franz's name! How could he go along with it? Until the advent of Hitler, she had counted on Gurtner as an ally; someone who would make sure the German judiciary would remain free and independent from political pressure. It was why release of that memorandum was such a body blow to her. If Gurtner was signing his name to such things, justice in Germany was on life support.

Hanna thought her position as the wife of the Commander-in-Chief of the *Reichsmarine* would insulate her from any judge tossing her off a case. Nevertheless, even if she believed her clients were guilty, she was *never* going to "assist in the process" by saying so. On the day of that odious memorandum, she wrote a short note on her personal stationery, attached it to the memorandum and sent it by messenger to Franz Gurtner:

Dear Franz,

You used to have a spine. Apparently you have misplaced it. Let me know if you ever find it. Until then, I quit. Take me off the rolls of actively practicing attorneys.

H.

Over six months had passed since she sent the note with no reply or acknowledgment from Franz. Yesterday, she received a handwritten note:

> *Dear Hanna,*
>
> *I've found it. Will you join me for lunch tomorrow, 1:00 p.m. at the Ministry? I'll explain then. Please destroy this note for the same reason I destroyed yours.*
>
> *Franz*

The German Reich Ministry of Justice
Wilhelmstrasse
Berlin
Friday, 6 October 1933

EXCEPT FOR the fact that his full, once dark brown, mustache was now a snowy white, Hanna thought the 54-year-old Franz Gurtner closely resembled the 39-year-old Gurtner, their brief affair in 1919 occurring a year before she married Erich in 1920. A little under six feet tall with a solid build, his rimless spectacles, closely cropped hair, and a three-piece suit over a starched wing-collar shirt and tightly-knotted dark blue tie completed the picture.

"Hanna, so good to see you again," Gurtner said as he rose from behind his desk and walked around it to greet her, taking her hand in both of his. "Thank you for accepting my invitation. Come, let us repair to my private dining room."

The dining room was smaller than Gurtner's formal office, but the décor was the same. Dark walnut wainscoting, cream colored walls and dark, heavy wooden furniture designed in the 19th century. Like his office, the windows looked out on the bustling avenue that was *Wilhelmstrasse*.

"I apologize for subjecting you to food from the Ministry's kitchen," Gurtner said as they took their seats in wooden armchairs across from each other at a round table that usually accommodated up to six people, "but it is the only place where I am confident no one else will be listening to us. I know that Göring has wiretaps on my home and office telephones and, I imagine, any number of listening devices in popular public restaurants."

Hanna nodded her understanding, but otherwise did not reply. She had no intention of engaging in polite small talk, let alone Berlin gossip about wiretaps. She was not going to make this easy for him. Soup, a clear consommé, was served, but Hanna declined a glass of Reisling.

"Let me clear the air," Gurtner began. "I know, from mutual friends, that you believe I should have resigned in protest when Hindenburg suspended the Constitution after the *Reichstag* fire. I considered doing just that, but if I had, then that Nazi bastard Roland Freisler, who had just been appointed Director of the Prussian Ministry of Justice, would likely have been appointed as my successor. If that had happened, he would have gutted the judiciary and replaced as many judges as possible with Nazi stooges. You may not agree, but in the past eight months, I've had a lot of political pressure put on me to appoint Nazi party members as judges, but so far I've been able to resist. The only judges I've had to replace were the Jewish ones."

Again, Hanna nodded, but did not reply. Franz made a good point, but until she learned what the purpose of the meeting was, she would wait in silence. Unless and until the Ministry rescinded that 12 March Memorandum, she was *not* going to resume the practice of law.

"I don't think my doing that was 'spineless'," Franz said, "but I can see your point of view. Something new has arisen, however, on which I seek your advice and, I hope, your assistance."

A waiter returned, took away their soup tureens and replaced them with medallions of veal, sauerkraut, and potato pancakes. After Hanna declined a glass of Bordeaux and the waiter had left, Gurtner resumed talking.

"Last June, I was directed to create a commission on criminal law reform to study and make recommendations to the *Reichstag* on how to change our criminal law to more closely conform to Nazi 'ideals', whatever the hell that means. I also was directed to make Freisler the

Commission's chairman. I did both of those things, but that's all I did. I think the criminal laws we have on the books today are fine."

"I agree, but what exactly does that have to do with you locating your misplaced spine?"

Gurtner paused, took a deep breath and smiled nervously. It was obvious he was not used to being questioned. Good, she thought, get used to it Franz. She was just getting started.

"I'm coming to that. What I did was appoint as many top-flight legal minds to the new Commission who share my views as I could. With them, I hoped to stop or dilute the more radical Nazi proposals."

"So, in effect, you wanted them to keep you in touch with the spine you recovered?"

Gurtner shook his head and smiled. "Yes, my dear Hanna, I suppose you could say that. Georg von Dohnanyi of the Ministry of Justice and Werner Kramer at the *Reichsbank* agreed to serve. Joseph Weber also agreed to serve, but he died last week from a heart attack. I was hoping you would agree to fill his vacant seat on the Commission and help keep me in touch with my recovered spine."

To say that Hanna was shocked by the offer was an understatement, but she was good at keeping her emotions hidden. She had always excelled at playing poker in the boys' club that was the German legal profession. Inwardly, she was flattered. It wouldn't be the practice of law *per se,* but it would put her in a position to stymie the Nazis. She relished the prospect of being able to fight them. It would give her something more important to do than passing canapés to boring politicians and vulgar Nazis.

"Why me?" she asked. "Weber was a good man although he could be too pedantic at times. I, on the other hand, can be somewhat, ah, antagonistic, especially when it comes to Nazis."

Gurtner laughed. "You don't have to remind me of that. My spine still bears the scars. Your potentially antagonizing Roland Freisler is one reason I'd like you on the Commission. More importantly, you are one of the finest criminal defense lawyers I know. Further, you have Jewish friends. I've met them at your dinner parties," he said with a smile and paused, "at least when you were still inviting me to those parties."

"Why does my having Jewish friends matter?"

"Freisler and other radical Nazis on the Commission are proposing a new law that criminalizes marriage and sexual relations between Aryans and Jews and strips Jews of their German citizenship. They commissioned legal research in America where many states have passed miscegenation laws regarding whites and non-whites. They call it the 'Prussian Memorandum' and they want to use it as a model for Germany in treating our Jews in a similar fashion."

"What?" Hanna said much louder than she would have wished, and without the restraint she'd shown thus far through the lunch. She scolded herself, but Gurtner reached across the table and put his hand over hers in comfort and shook his head in agreement.

"I know. Himmler and Goebbels are pushing this and I don't think I'll be able to stop them. What makes it worse is that the radical Nazis want to go back four or five generations to define who is a Jew."

Hanna's stomach dropped. For the first time since all this began she felt real fear. She couldn't remember if Franz knew about her family tree. Erich knew. They had discussed it quietly before their marriage and decided that his position in the Navy protected her. With her blonde hair and blue eyes, no one would suspect Hanna on sight, but God knows what kind of access the Nazis had to records and if those records would show her lineage. But this was the first time that someone had said out loud what she had been fearing since these Nazi thugs had come into power in January.

"The radicals want to define someone as a Jew if they have a single great grandparent who was a Jew. That definition is something I believe the Commission can stop, but we can only do that if it has people like you, Dohnanyi and Kramer to help me. Please say you'll consider accepting an appointment to the Commission."

Hanna hesitated. A law that criminalized marriage and sexual relations between Aryans and Jews and stripped Jews of their German citizenship was insane! So too was defining a Jew as someone with only one Jewish great grandparent. Franz may think he's not able to stop the former, but that didn't mean Hanna was going to roll over and let the Nazis have their way. So, yes, she very much wished to accept an appointment to the new Commission, but there were other considerations than her wishes.

The German Navy, for one. Just as Gurtner—who wasn't a Nazi—had been kept on by Hitler as the Minister of Justice, so too had her husband—who also wasn't a Nazi—been kept on by Hitler as head of the *Reichsmarine*. Another consideration was the possibility that her great grandmother had been Jewish. It was only family lore because her great grandmother had been a practicing Lutheran all her adult life, but it was possible there was something on paper. She needed to find her great grandmother's marriage certificate and see if it indicated her Jewishness. Germans were rigorous, methodical record keepers and, if family lore was true, it might prove embarrassing to both her husband and Franz Gurtner. Hanna felt the need to fight rise up in every molecule of her being. She tried to keep the emotion out of her voice when she replied to Franz, but it was difficult.

"Franz, I'm flattered, but I need to think this over. I share your concerns and, if it were just me, I would be inclined to accept. I cannot do so, however, unless my husband agrees. The future of the *Reichsmarine* depends upon Erich's vision and leadership and I won't do anything to jeopardize that. Only Erich is in a position to decide if my becoming a member of your Commission will do that. I will talk with him this evening and let you know what he decides."

Gurtner smiled. "Well for the sake of my poor spine—which needs all the help it can get—I sincerely hope he says 'yes'."

And, for the first time that day, Hanna actually smiled back.

Haus Raeder
Spitzweggasse 3
Potsdam-Neubabelsberg, Germany
Friday, 6 October 1933

HANNA HAD cocktails ready on the veranda at the side of their home in Potsdam by the time Erich arrived. He was a good-looking man in his late 50s with glossy black hair and clear blue eyes and looked much younger than Gurtner. He had changed from his crisp

Navy blues into his at-home uniform, a cream-colored turtleneck submariner sweater and dark blue trousers.

Hanna had changed out of her blue suit dress. Like her husband, she needed to shed her work disguise when she came home, but she didn't opt for her usual home outfit – sailor pants and silk blouse topped with a comfy and warm sweater. Nope, she wanted very much to be on this Commission and she needed her husband's permission. While he loved her for her style and intelligence and biting wit, he also loved her for her legs. She was wearing his favorite dress—last year's birthday present—when Erich greeted her on the veranda, took his drink in hand, and gave her a warm kiss.

"Don't ask about my day," he began…

"I wouldn't dare," she said with a smile, knowing full well how trying his days had become after the Nazi takeover of the government. Landmines everywhere…and Navy men didn't do well with those. For some reason, Hanna was reminded of a simpler, less stressful time on an evening in late 1928 when, wearing the same sweater and slacks, he told her that, after much intrigue and internal in-fighting, the Defense Minister Wilhelm Groener had appointed him Chief of the *Reichsmarine* and promoted him to full admiral. She had been proud of his accomplishments and proud he was her husband. She hoped she would still be proud when this evening was over.

Despite the fact he had agreed to her resuming her law practice earlier this year, Hanna had no idea how her husband would react to her being appointed to the German Commission on Criminal Law Reform. Gurtner clearly wanted her on the Commission to stand up to the Nazis and, while Erich wasn't enamored of them, he had to live with them in order to protect his precious navy. He had made clear to Hanna from the outset that the *Reichsmarine* was the most important thing in his life and his wife and children were, respectively, second and third in the hierarchy. While some wives might object to this, it gave Hanna comfort knowing where she stood. She had been grateful that he understood her need to resume her legal career now that the boys were away in school.

"You look especially lovely tonight."

"I try," she said, smiling again and taking in his appreciative smile. Erich always looked 20 years younger when he smiled. When he didn't, which was most of the time these days, he looked like the head of the navy. His large blue eyes were weary and hooded, his usually full lips set into a stoic grimace. When he was home, especially on the veranda and in their bedroom, most of the stress of the last eight months fell away and she would see that twinkle in the eyes that drew her to him. This quiet and stalwart man, whose presence was meant to terrify all the young sailors in his command, still intrigued her. After first meeting him, no one could tell her anything about him. Even his best friends seemed to know little about him. It wasn't until she had accidentally gotten him alone at a party by speaking her mind about the general failure of the German elite in the Weimar Republic that he leaned in close and whispered "You know you could just ask to speak to me alone. You don't have to alienate the whole of German society to do it."

Hanna was almost instantly smitten. So she wasn't concerned when Erich's silence was a bit longer than usual after she told him about her lunch with a former lover and his request that she become a member of the Commission on Criminal Law Reform. He remained silent when she told him her worries for what this might mean for the Navy as well as the family lore about her great grandmother. Nor was she that surprised by his first question.

"You once were involved with Franz Gurtner?"

"Yes."

"You never told me about him."

"I thought we agreed never to speak about former love affairs."

Erich took a sip of his Manhattan. "This is excellent my darling," he said by way of silent apology.

"I'm sorry I didn't tell you about the lunch with Gurtner, but I received his note after you left this morning."

"What? Oh don't worry about that. You know I trust you. And you're right, I never need to know that kind of thing. But all the same, thanks for telling me. No, I'm not worried about any impact on the Navy of your being on the Commission, especially since you'll be listed as Hanna Hindermann. What I'm worried about more is …"

"Evelyn." She said referring to her British-born great grandmother.

Another sigh. "Before you say 'yes' to Gurtner, we need to make sure either that the 'family lore' is inaccurate or that there are no records if it's true. Otherwise…"

"It might come back to bite us in the ass."

Erich opened his eyes wide. Her salty comments startled him, but they inevitably made him smile after the mild shock wore off. He did not smile. "It's worse than that."

"That's why my being on this Commission is so important. Someone has to stand up to them."

"I know my dear. You have no idea how much I know. I've even received subtle and not so subtle hints from the SA leader in Berlin about terminating the commissions of those naval officers with a Jewish background even though none are practicing Jews and many are devout Christians. I told him to go to hell and had two strong young ensigns throw his sorry, brown-uniformed ass out onto the street."

"Good for you!" Hanna said and laughed. "I'll look into those records tomorrow."

"You'll be discreet?" Erich said, finally smiling.

Hanna smiled back at him and took his hand. "Let's just say that if, by chance, there are any *unfortunate* records at the *Rotes Rathaus*," she said, referring to Berlin's 19th century red brick town hall, "they won't still be there when I leave. The same will be true of any, ah, *misleading* marriage records at the *Kaiser Wilhelm Gedachtniskirche*," she said, referring to the memorial church on the *Kurfurstendamm* built in the 1890s by Kaiser Wilhelm, II, and named for his grandfather, Kaiser Wilhelm, I.

Erich took her hand warmly. "Even in the Navy, if you can imagine, records are often lost or misplaced. Why should the town hall or a church be any different? I know you'll do a good job on the Commission. If the day comes—and it may—when I am compelled by the *Reich* government and not the SA to terminate Jewish naval officers, I want to lose as few good men as possible."

Hanna relaxed. She'd thought he'd say yes as he almost always did, but because of how taciturn and unsmiling he'd been these last few months, she'd felt less certain of him. Now, she felt pride in the fact that, rather than embarrass him and his career, he thought her work on the Commission might actually help their country and his precious Navy by allowing him to retain more naval officers than he otherwise would if the radical Nazis were allowed to define who was a Jew by going back four generations. Nothing was certain anymore, but it wasn't just about his career, it was about their country, and their place in it. She was still proud he was her husband.

3

Have You Completely Lost Your Minds?

The White House
Washington, D.C
Friday, 6 October 1933

HAROLD HUDSON CANFIELD, III, a trim, handsome man with dark blonde hair in his late 30s wore a navy blue pin-striped suit tailored at Hawkes & Co. in London's Savile Row, the same bespoke establishment where his father and all the other Canfield men had their suits made. He stepped from a long black Cadillac limousine into the shade of the White House portico followed by his companions Generals Leonard Marlborough and Ralph Van DeMan. A graduate of Princeton and Harvard Law, Canfield was not looking forward to meeting this afternoon with the President of the United States. He couldn't *stand* Franklin Roosevelt.

That much and a lot more he shared in common with his first cousin, the late Theodore Stanhope Hudson, IV, who had been killed earlier this year on a secret MID assignment in Germany. Both had been U.S. intelligence agents during the war and after, Ted in Military Intelligence—MID—and Harry in Naval Intelligence—ONI. For another, the cousins grew up together in adjacent estates on Long Island Sound. Ted's father was very close to Harry's mother, Elizabeth Hudson, who married a Canfield and insisted that her trust fund husband build her an estate right next to her brother. As a consequence, the cousins—both trust fund babies themselves with a net worth well into eight figures—were close as well and remained so into adulthood.

Given their wealth, both cousins were able to pursue careers in public service. When Harry served in the ONI during the war, he specialized, as did Ted, in counter-espionage against Imperial German agents operating in North America. And, from time to time, each had been an assassin, systematically eliminating Americans who too actively opposed the war. After the Bolsheviks took Russia out of the war in late 1917, the deadly cousins also eliminated Americans who too actively supported the Bolsheviks, which to Harry's mind meant Jews. In his experience, scratch a Bolshevik and underneath you usually found a Jew. Happily, President Woodrow Wilson had agreed. Just as Wilson re-segregated the District of Columbia's restrooms and drinking fountains for the coloreds after twelve years of desegregation under the Republicans Teddy Roosevelt and William Howard Taft, Wilson also expected 100% Americanism from the Jews, the Irish, the Dagos, the Polacks and other lower forms of life.

Now, if you believed the scuttlebutt in Washington—and Harry did—FDR was determined to establish diplomatic relations with the godless Soviet Union as soon as next month. It was a damn shame, he thought, that his cousin Ted Hudson had come oh so close to ending the crippled bastard's life back in February with a well-aimed rifle shot at the President-elect from the window of a high-rise apartment building in Miami.

That aging pimp Louis Howe had disclosed to Marborough and Van Deman that FDR wanted to discuss the Nazi legal research project Roscoe Pound had supervised over the summer for RVD International. Van Deman had hired Harry away from the ONI in the early 30s —where he had been the adjutant to the Director of ONI, Captain Hayne Ellis. He had been the one who urged a skeptical Van Deman to have RVD take on the assignment from the Nazis and he also suggested that his former Harvard Law School professor and dean, Roscoe Pound, should supervise the research. As a consequence, Harry became the liaison between RVD and Pound. While he had no desire to meet with Roosevelt, he reluctantly agreed to accompany Marlborough and Van Deman to the White House today because he literally knew more about the project than anyone except Pound himself.

"LEONARD, RALPH! How good to see you both again. It's been too long," FDR said as Louis Howe escorted Generals Marlborough and Van Deman into the oval office. "And who is this handsome young man behind you?"

FDR was dressed in a conservative, gray chalk stripe suit with a blue and white striped tie. He wore rimless pince-nez glasses and his trademark silver cigarette holder was clenched between his teeth and pointing upward at a jaunty angle, a big smile on his broad, patrician face. He was sitting behind his desk, however, so his crippled legs were hidden from view. Harry had no intention of waiting like a schoolboy to be introduced to the headmaster, however, so he strode forward, pushed between the two generals and extended his hand.

"Harold Canfield, Sir. Formerly adjutant to Captain Welles at ONI and now Executive Vice President of RVD International."

"Navy man, eh?" the President said as he grasped Harry's outstretched hand in a surprisingly firm handshake. "What was your rank?"

"Commander, Sir."

"Well, welcome aboard, Sailor. All three of you take a seat on the sofa. Louie will now give you each a copy of a report I received yesterday from the FBI. Louie, give Commander Canfield my copy. I expect he's here because he knows something about this. I don't imagine Leonard and Ralph thought they needed a bodyguard while they were here in the White House."

There were appropriate chuckles from Marlborough and Van Deman as Harry took the proffered copy from Howe and began to read along with the other two men. The report was thorough and accurate in a pedantic, bureaucratic FBI sort of way, but hardly worth a summons to the White House. It wasn't a big deal. The Nazis simply had wanted research done on American state race laws that they could use as models to do the same to Germany's Jews. So what? Harry didn't blame the Nazis. He thought it was a good idea, one that America should adopt for its Jews once Germany showed the way.

When all three men had looked up, an indication that they each had finished reviewing the contents of the FBI folders, FDR spoke. "Now, gentlemen, is the FBI report accurate. Leonard, you first."

Marlborough cleared his throat. "Well, Mr. President, I think that, as far as it goes…"

Roosevelt cut him off in mid-sentence. "Come, come, General, a simple 'yes' or 'no' will suffice."

"Then, uh… yes," Marlborough stammered.

"And you, Ralph?"

"I don't necessarily think it's wrong, but…"

Again, Roosevelt interrupted. "Yes or no, General."

"Yes, it's accurate, but…"

"No 'buts', General. I'm satisfied with your 'yes'. Now, you, Commander Canfield?"

Harry had enjoyed watching FDR make the head of MID and his immediate predecessor squirm. He never had a high opinion of Military Intelligence in the first place, especially compared to Naval Intelligence. Sure, there were exceptions at MID, his cousin Ted Hudson being one of them and their boyhood chum, Sebastian Slade, another. But he owed nothing to Marlborough and Van Deman needed him more than he needed his position at RVD International.

"Absolutely, Mr. President!" Harry replied. "The FBI has done their typically fine job in preparing this report. There is one minor inaccuracy, however, but it does not detract from the overall excellence of the report."

"Really?" FDR asked. "What was the inaccuracy?"

"Dean Pound didn't deliver the final research to the SS *Obersturmfuhrer* at the German Embassy. He was reluctant to put it in the mail and he didn't want to travel all the way from Cambridge to deliver it so personally. He said he had more important things to do with his time than be a messenger boy. I said I agreed and volunteered to deliver it myself. Which I did."

"I see, Commander, thank you for that correction. I always enjoy an opportunity to tweak Edgar when he gets something wrong," FDR replied. Then he sat back, steepled his fingers and focused his gaze directly on Marlborough and possibly Van Deman as well. It wasn't difficult for Harry to tell that the two generals were about to receive a stern Presidential dressing down. He wondered if they realized this. Regardless, it was clear the President wasn't looking at him when he spoke so he took no offense at what FDR said next.

"Have you two completely lost your minds? If this gets out, Jewish campaign contributions for the 1934 midterm election and my re-election in 1936 will dry up. Do you really want the Republicans—whose Smoot-Hawley Tariff helped prolong, if not cause, the world-wide Depression—in power once again?"

"No, Sir." Marlborough and Van Deman replied in unison. Harry didn't reply. The tariffs hadn't hurt his investment portfolio or his rather larger trust fund, so what did he care? He had gotten out of the market anyway before the crash in 1929. Those who didn't were fools and damn well deserved what happened to them.

"Even worse," FDR continued, "I was the first Democratic candidate for President ever to pry away a majority of the Black vote from the Republicans, the party of Lincoln who freed the slaves. Hell, even though I was the Democratic vice-presidential candidate in 1920, we got thoroughly licked and lost the Black vote because the idiot Democrats in the South began a rumor that the Republican Harding, because of his naturally darker complexion, had Negro blood! So, now do you understand why what you have done is so stupid?"

"Yes, Sir," the two generals replied again in unison. Once more, Harry didn't reply. Who gave a flying fuck if the Negroes didn't vote for the Democrats or the Jews stopped their campaign contributions? His own low opinion of FDR just went lower. A typical goddamned politician.

"So, gentlemen, here's what you're going to do," FDR said, with more than a trace of menace in his voice. "I want all evidence of this sorry arrangement destroyed from the first Nazi contact with General Marlborough right through all the research, including Dean Pound's compiling the research and its submission to the Germans. Director Hoover will do the same with his boys. Their field reports as well as the final FBI report I've shown you will be destroyed. I want this buried forever. No loose ends. Is that clear?"

"Yes, Sir, Mr. President," both men replied. Harry remained silent. He had a copy of Pound's final report which he would dutifully turn over to Van Deman for destruction, but not before he made a photographic copy. That was a no-brainer. If this report would be as devastating politically as Roosevelt claimed, it never hurt to have an ace in the hole when he needed one. He really couldn't stand FDR.

Just then, a door behind Harry opened and he heard a female voice. "Yes, Mr. President, you buzzed me?"

"Yes, Missy, thank you," FDR said over their heads to his long time secretary, Missy Le Hand. "These gentlemen are leaving. Please escort them to Mr. Howe's office." He then looked at the two MID men. "Excellent, gentlemen. I'm pleased we see eye-to eye on this. Thank you all for coming to see me. I need a word alone with Louie. After that, he will brief you on how I want this to be carried out so it never sees the light of day."

LOUIS HOWE closed the door after the three men had left. "What do you think, Frank? Can they be trusted to keep their mouths shut?"

FDR looked at his watch. It was only 4 pm, an hour early for cocktails, but he needed a drink. He held up his hand. "In a moment Louie, but first, we're going to begin our attitude adjustment hour. Let them cool their heels in your office while I tell you what I want done."

With that, Roosevelt's powerful arms quickly propelled him across the Oval Office to the drinks trolley. There he filled a glass pitcher with ice, six jiggers of Beefeaters' London Dry gin, two jiggers of Noilly Prat French vermouth and began to stir it vigorously with a long silver spoon. Two minutes later, he popped two olives into stemmed martini glasses, filled them with the icy liquid and handed one to Howe.

FDR took a sip of his martini and looked at Howe. "Can they be trusted? For Marlborough and Van Deman, I think so, yes. The ex-ONI guy, certainly," the President replied. "The same goes for Roscoe. I want you to see Pound personally, though, and have him turn over all his files on this. Tell him I have classified everything about the project TOP SECRET PRESIDENTIAL."

The President took another sip. Damn! Was that good or what? "What concerns me more are the six former MID agents who did the research. They're no longer under military discipline, so can they be trusted to keep their mouths shut or are they loose ends? I don't know them like I do Marlborough, Van Deman and Pound. For all I know, they could be Republicans just itching to deliver all this to Drew Pearson! Tell those two idiot generals to make sure their agents understand the critical need to keep their mouths shut. If there is the slightest doubt about any of the six agents, then that's a loose end that must be tied up. Tell them I don't want any slip-ups. Make that crystal clear to Roscoe as well."

"Okay, Frank, I'll take care of it," Howe said, drained the rest of his martini and stood up.

"Wait a second, Louie, I'm not finished," Roosevelt said and held up his hand. "We need to do something about the Germans. It's none of our business what they do to their own citizens, Jewish or otherwise. It's why I've refused to support the Jewish boycott against German exports. And if they want to use the laws of some of our more backward states as a model for their own laws that discriminate against the Jews, I can't stop them. But I damn well don't want them making it a matter of public knowledge that this is what they're doing. So, when you talk to Marlborough and Van Deman, I want you to task that ONI guy Canfield with going back to the SS man at the German Embassy and deliver a private message from me for his masters. He is to warn them in no uncertain terms that if a single word ever gets out that the Nazis are using American laws as models for anti-Jewish legislation, I will officially support the Jewish boycott of German exports. Got that?"

"You bet, Boss."

HAROLD CANFIELD watched as Van Deman pushed a button that raised the glass partition in the Cadillac limousine to seal off the driver from the conversation in the rear as they pulled away from under the White House portico. For a good five minutes, no one said anything about the just-concluded meeting.

"I'm not entirely certain just what the President wants done here," Marlborough said.

"Yes," Van Deman agreed. "Howe was certainly vague, if not opaque."

For God's sake, Harry thought, what part of tying up a loose end wasn't clear? They were acting like a couple of prissy old ladies rather than two legendary American intelligence chiefs. He couldn't imagine any ONI agent being this obtuse.

"Don't worry about it," Harry said. "It's just the President's way of saying 'Will no one rid me of this troublesome priest?' The President is being something of a pussy on this. I don't believe it's nearly as bad politically as he thinks, but he's the boss and this is my responsibility, Ralph. I persuaded you to take it on when Leo brought it to us and I'll take care of it. I'll see SS *Obersturmfuhrer* Krueger at the German Embassy personally and deliver Roosevelt's threat about supporting the anti-Nazi boycott if they leak anything about using American laws as a model for their new anti-Jewish legislation. Then, I'll visit all six former agents and confiscate their research. I'll explain it's been classified as TOP SECRET PRESIDENTIAL. If—to quote FDR's bagman Howe—I have the 'slightest doubt' that any of them are a 'loose end', I'll have Leo advance the necessary funds from one of MID's black accounts. With that done, I'll fly to New York and give a list of the names and addresses of these 'loose ends' to Owney Madden. He'll make sure they're tied up. Permanently. Nothing will be traced back to us. Okay?"

"Owney Madden? Isn't he…" Marlborough began, but Harry cut him off.

"Yes, he's the head of the Irish mob in Hell's Kitchen on the west side of Manhattan. I've used him before. He's one of the most ruthless bastards I've ever met, but he's also the most dependable. If he says he'll do something, you can take it to the bank. Okay?"

The other two men each gave him a curt nod.

What the two men didn't know was that Louis Howe—and, by implication, FDR as well—was worried about more than those six ex-

MID men for, after Marlborough and Van Deman had left his office, Howe had grabbed Harry's arm. "A moment, please," he asked.

Harry turned to face Howe. "You made a good impression on the boss today," Howe said. "He wants you to check out the two FBI guys who conducted the investigation. We don't want them to be a loose end either." With that, Howe handed him two manila FBI personnel folders that Harry put in his briefcase.

Harry knew he would have to take out the two FBI guys himself. For one thing, most FBI agents were straight arrows, the very definition of a loose end. For another, Owney had a strict policy about not ordering hits on FBI agents or—with rare exceptions—cops. It didn't matter, Harry thought, because he was a ruthless bastard himself. It was just two more troublesome priests to add to the list. He hadn't done anything like that since the twenties and he was kind of looking forward to it.

Part II

Ireland, England, United States & Germany, 5 September 1934 —12 September 1934

Dr. Mobius: *I am reminded of something an American said to us recently. He explained, "We do the same thing you are doing. But why do you have to say it so explicitly in your laws?"*

State Secretary Roland Freisler: *But the Americans put it in their own laws even more explicitly!*

Transcript of 5 June 1934 meeting of German Commission on Criminal Law Reform

It shall be unlawful within this state for any white person, male or female, to intermarry with any Negro, Chinese, or any person having one fourth or more Negro, Chinese, or Kanaka blood, or any person having more than one-half Indian blood; and all such marriages, or attempted marriages, shall be absolutely null and void.

Oregon Statutes, 1930

4

Mattie McGary

Offices of the Army Comrades Association
Galway, Ireland
Wednesday, 5 September 1934

IT SEEMED like a good idea at the time, Mattie McGary thought as she looked out a window to a spectacular view of Galway Bay. Spend August in Europe interviewing the heads of fascist political parties in countries other than Germany and Italy for a story she was doing for the Hearst newspaper chain. She traveled first to Belgium, the Netherlands and Portugal. After that, it was on to Austria, Hungary, Romania and Poland. She had saved Ireland for last both because it was her home base for the summer and because she wasn't positive that General Eoin O'Duffy—the tall, handsome man sitting across from her behind a large desk in front of that window overlooking Galway Bay—and his Blue Shirts were really fascists. If they weren't, they did their best to imitate them, what with the Roman salute of the Nazis and light blue shirts and black trousers, mimicking the Brown Shirts of Hitler's Storm Troopers.

It had seemed like a good idea because she had been depending on her husband, Bourke Cockran, Jr. to help her prepare for the man's interview. As a journalist, Cockran had covered the Anglo-Irish War of 1920-22 and was a conduit between Winston Churchill and the Irish leader Michael Collins that led to the negotiations creating the Irish Free State. It gave Ireland her freedom from Great Britain and was overwhelmingly approved by the Irish people in an election. Cockran knew O'Duffy from that war and became involved in the subsequent Irish Civil War launched by Eamon deValera in the wake of the creation of the Irish Free State. Specifically, Collins had dispatched Cockran to America to assassinate the three IRA paymasters who were supplying the funds for deValera's wounded ego revenge. No one could better prepare her for an interview with an old colleague of Michael Collins like Eoin O'Duffy than her husband.

Alas, Cockran had sailed for the U.S. a week earlier with his 14-year-old son Patrick in tow. One of his best friends, Timothy O'Hanlon, a colonel in the U.S. Army's Military Intelligence Division (MID), had asked Cockran to undertake an investigation of the mysterious deaths last year of six former MID agents, two of whom were close friends of O'Hanlon. Even though Cockran had been planning to spend all of August and most of September finishing his book on political assassinations, he had promptly secured yet another extension from his publisher and agreed to seek his law firm's consent to take the case. As he had explained to her, he owed Tim more than one big favor.

Mattie was disappointed for she was in Budapest at the time and hadn't been able to make it back to Ireland in time to see him and her stepson off. She hadn't complained, however, because she also owed Tim an equally big favor. In March of 1933, in the wake of a failed assassination attempt on Adolf Hitler with whom she had just finished an interview, she had shot and killed one of the failed Hitler assassins, Ted Hudson. One of her former lovers, he was an ex-MID agent who was about to execute Cockran in an Austrian ski chalet until six shots in his chest deterred him. Later that year, Sebastian Slade, another ex-MID agent and close friend of Hudson, had stolen her Walther PPK. Then, he had it tested by an independent laboratory against one or more of the six bullets she had fired into Hudson's chest that the Austrian police had given to Slade. The bullets matched her PPK and, thanks to a black bag job by Tim, her weapon and all six bullets were currently residing at the bottom of the Potomac River.

Without Cockran to help, most of what Mattie knew about Eoin O'Duffy she learned from the clippings on him in the many Hearst newspapers. He had joined the Irish volunteers in 1917; rose rapidly through the ranks; was involved in the first capture of a Royal Irish Constabulary barracks in his native County Monaghan; and was later enrolled in the Irish Republican Brotherhood by none other than the 'Big Fella' himself, Michael Collins. After the formation of the Irish Free State, O'Duffy became the youngest general in Europe and was instrumental in the defeat of the IRA in the civil war that followed the Treaty with England. After the civil war, O'Duffy had been appointed the head of the *Garda*, the Free State's police force where he served for over ten years, creating and maintaining a highly respected, non-political and unarmed constabulary. When that black-hearted villain, de Valera—Mattie embraced her husband's views on him—had been elected in 1933 ousting the pro-Treaty party led by Michael Collins' successor, William Cosgrave, he fired O'Duffy.

Confirming Mattie's views that he was a villain, de Valera promptly unleashed the IRA to attack rallies of Cosgrave's party under the slogan "No free speech for traitors". O'Duffy had formed the Army Comrades Association—later renamed the National Guard—in response to the IRA violence to serve as the party's muscle to repel the de Valera-directed attacks. It was all too reminiscent to Mattie of the armed clashes between Communist and Nazi thugs in Weimar Germany in the late 20s and early 30s.

Unfortunately, O'Duffy had his 'Army Comrades' adopt the straight-armed Roman salute and dress in dark trousers and light blue shirts with a wide red 'x' over the left shirt pocket, which was what O'Duffy was wearing now along with a navy blue beret. He was only 44, but he looked ten years older, his hair more gray than brown. Jowls and a double chin were beginning to form on his still good-looking face.

"Thank you for taking time out of your busy schedule to see me General O'Duffy," Mattie said with a smile. "May I take your photograph?"

"Of course, Mrs. Cockran," O'Duffy said and stood up. He placed both hands on the desk and leaned slightly forward with a determined look on his face, his head raised, his double chin having disappeared.

Mattie's *Leica* hung on a strap around her neck and she picked it up and quickly took four shots. She always liked to take photographs of her interview subjects before she began. After she finished, many were no longer willing to accommodate her. Based on Mattie's experience interviewing other fascist leaders in Europe, her style was to immediately go on the offensive, yet O'Duffy wrong-footed her from the beginning.

"Ah, Mrs. Cockran," he said with a broad Irish brogue after serving her tea, "and sure wasn't I looking forward to meeting the woman who married our 'Last Apostle'."

It wasn't so much being called 'Mrs. Cockran' even though Mattie had not changed her name for professional reasons and had scheduled this interview with her maiden name. It was the reference to Bourke as the 'Last Apostle', a name she had never heard associated with that big, beautiful Irish bastard she had married. The confusion must have showed on her face because O'Duffy continued.

"That's what the 'Big Fella' called him the only time we ever met. It was in the summer of '22 right after the civil war began. We were in the back room at O'Dade's Pub in Dublin—Mick Collins, Joe O'Reilly, Bobby Sullivan, me and your man. Mick gave him three names and addresses—the IRA paymasters in America—and a Webley revolver. Afterwards, right before he died, Mick said it was a toss-up between the two of us as to who would be responsible for the Free State winning the civil war—me for creating the strategy of seaborne landings of the Free State Army into IRA-held areas or your husband for knocking off those three IRA bastards in America and shutting down any arms coming from there."

Mattie knew all about 'The Apostles', Michael Collins' personal hit squad during the Anglo-Irish war of 1919-1921, so named once their number reached twelve. The British called them a 'murder gang' and they weren't far wrong. On a bright Sunday morning in November 1920 in Dublin, the Apostles had executed 14 British secret agents and informers. The fact that Michael Collins had called Cockran his 'Last

Apostle' was interesting. That Cockran had never told her this was not surprising. He never talked about his time in the Great War either. She knew that Cockran had assassinated three IRA paymasters in 1923. He told her that five years ago when they first met in 1929, but in terse words with no detail. That same summer of '23, the IRA had kidnapped, raped and murdered Cockran's first wife Nora, the mother of his son Patrick. Cockran's desire for revenge that summer was overwhelming and Collins had promised that the Apostles would find and execute the IRA men responsible for his wife's death, a promise unfulfilled until the summer of 1929 when Cockran and Michael Collins' most feared Apostle, Bobby Sullivan, tracked them down and killed them all.

Mattie was not going to let this reference to her husband throw her off her game. Social chit-chat was over. Time to go back on offense. "I'm sure you both played your part," she said and smiled sweetly. "Bourke really isn't that good a shot, you know. I'm much better. We sometimes practice together on the shooting range he has on his estate in Long Island and he never wins. Now, tell me how someone who was close to Michael Collins and who opposes deValera, that man who once said 'the Irish people have no right to be wrong', came to think Adolf Hitler and the Nazis are the proper path for Ireland?"

"Isn't it obvious?" O'Duffy said, his blue eyes flashing. "There is one nation alone, the German nation—which at present is again subject to the slanderous press campaigns of the British-Jewish propagandists—that has never concealed its sympathy for the Irish people and their just cause. Hitler has done more for Germany than any other leader in the world. He is a model for what I want to do for Ireland."

"Let's go into detail on that," Mattie said and for the next hour she walked him through the nine points in the constitution of the National Guard. After she finished, she certainly thought he sounded like an Italian fascist if not a German National Socialist. The uniforms, the salute and the anti-Semitism completed the picture and, in Mattie's eyes, passed 'the Duck Test'—if it looks like a duck, walks like a duck, flies like a duck and quacks like a duck, it bloody well *is* a duck.

Mattie was ready to wrap up the interview with the question she had saved for last. She took a sip of tea. "General O'Duffy, last year in August, the National Guard planned a parade of 30,000 Blue Shirts in Dublin in honor of Michael Collins, Arthur Griffin and Kevin O'Higgins that was to end on Leinster lawn in front of the Irish parliament where you and others would make speeches. De Valera banned the parade and sources have told me he did so because he feared a *coup d'etat* and he was unsure whether the Irish Army would obey his orders to put it down. You accepted the ban then, but I am hearing persistent rumors that you plan another parade in Dublin this month and you won't accept being banned this time around. Any truth to those rumors?"

O'Duffy flushed. Then he stood up, placed both hands on the desk, his tall body outlined by the afternoon sun glancing off the waters of Galway Bay, and, in Mattie's opinion, lied through his teeth. "Absolutely not! Wherever did you hear such nonsense?"

"I can't disclose my sources, but I wouldn't ask if I didn't think they were credible."

O'Duffy's eyes narrowed and his voice was low and cold. "Be very careful, Mrs, Cockran, before you publish such nonsense. I fear you would very much come to regret it."

Outside Sligo, Ireland
Wednesday, 5 September 1934

THE LONG BLACK Bentley motorcar began following Mattie as she left the town of Sligo in the early evening on her way to their Irish home, a Martello Tower on the 1,500 feet high Cliffs of Slieve League that Cockran had renovated for her as a wedding present.

After Mattie spotted the Bentley, she altered her speed—faster, slower, and then faster again, but each time she did, the Bentley stayed the same 40 yards behind her. She didn't think the Bentley could really keep up with her at its top speed so, when Mattie hit a deserted straightaway with Donegal Bay to her left, she floored the pedal on her new Scottish blue 1934 MG roadster. Equipped with the same supercharged, four-cylinder, overhead cam engine as the MG Q-type racing car, Mattie quickly had the MG up to and then over 100 mph.

To her dismay, she saw the Bentley in her rear view mirror easily match her acceleration. Damn! It must be a Bentley 8 Litre, she thought, and that meant it could match if not exceed her top speed of 120 mph. She tapped the brake and downshifted as she approached a sharp curve to the right and away from the Bay, but that bloody Bentley just came on coming! She was into the curve now, slowing down to 35 mph and couldn't accelerate away from the big motorcar now looming large in her mirror. She felt a thump as the Bentley hit her rear bumper and the MG lurched to the right into the opposite lane on the narrow road. Mattie fought to bring the roadster back into the left lane when the Bentley rammed into her rear once more, hitting her harder than before. She lost her grip on the steering wheel as the MG again veered into the opposite lane. This time, she could not bring the car back under control and it headed off the road. Mattie braced herself for the impact and braked hard, but she was still thrown forward as the MG hit a drainage ditch with a loud bang as the right front tire blew and the car came to a halt.

Mattie hit her head at the top of the windscreen, momentarily shaken. She reached to her forehead that was sore to the touch, but not bleeding. Ahead she saw the brake lights of the Bentley as it came to a halt. As it began to back up, Mattie reached for the shoulder bag on the passenger seat, but it had fallen onto the floor. She reached down, pulled the bag up and extracted her Walter PPK. She checked the magazine, released the safety and chambered a round. Keeping the pistol in her right hand, she leaned forward onto her left arm curving around the steering wheel and feigned unconsciousness. She heard the Bentley come to a halt, the engine turned off and doors open. Then she heard one of the men speak.

"No, we can't just leave her here without checking. O'Duffy said to scare her, not kill her. If she's dead, we'll leave her. If she's not, we'll stop at the next town and anonymously place a telephone call to the *Garda.*"

Keeping her head cradled on her left arm, Mattie could see the two men were less than ten feet away. One was short with black hair, the other was tall and slender with light brown hair. Both looked to be in their twenties. She was not surprised to see they were dressed the same—dark trousers and a light blue shirt. Bloody Blue Shirts!

"Miss, Miss, are you hurt?" she heard a voice ask, the same one as before. Then, she felt a hand lightly touch her shoulder.

Mattie instantly sat up, brushed the arm aside with her left hand and aimed the PPK at the man's forehead, the taller of the two. "Hands up! Don't move or you're both dead men!"

The two men startled, their eyes growing wide.

Mattie motioned with the PPK. "Up! Now!"

Both men slowly raised their hands.

"That's better. Clasp them behind your head."

Both men did.

"Good," Mattie said. "Here's what's going to happen next. I'm going to reach behind me and open the door to my car. After that, I'm going to back out and you're going to remain perfectly still. If you don't, the man who moves gets a bullet in his kneecap. Understood?"

"Yes, M'am," each man said with an affirmative nod.

Mattie reached for the door handle, opened the door and carefully got out of the car, never taking her eyes off the two men. She motioned with the PPK once more. "On the ground. Sit there with your hands under your bum."

They sat down and did as told.

"Who sent you and what were your orders?"

"Bugger off! We don't have to tell you nothing!" the short, dark-haired man said.

Mattie fired a single shot, two inches from Shorty's knee. "I won't ask again, so don't test my patience or my marksmanship. Your kneecap is next."

The taller man gulped. "General O'Duffy. He said we was to scare you."

"By running me off the road?"

"No, that was Seamus's idea," Slim said, nodding over at Shorty. "He was the one who was driving."

"You bastard!" Shorty said with a scowl at Slim.

Mattie then walked around the MG, her PPK trained on both men as she did so. The only damage appeared to be the blown right front tire.

"Gentlemen, you are in luck. The only damage to my new car appears to be the right front tire. You two lads appear to be strong enough so the first thing you're going to do is push my car out of the ditch and back onto the apron of the road. After that, you're going to release the spare tire fastened on the outside of the boot; open the boot and take out the jack; use the jack to raise the right front of the car; remove the blown tire; and replace it with the spare tire. When you're finished, you put the jack in the boot and fasten the blown tire onto the boot. Then you're free to go. Right? So hop to it and get busy!"

Mattie leaned against the Bentley's boot as Slim and Shorty did their work, her PPK still in her hand, dusk beginning to fall. Several times, she shifted the weapon to her left hand and lifted the Leica with her right to take photographs of the two men at work. Twenty-five minutes later, they were finished. She pushed away from the Bentley. "Excellent work, Gentlemen. If you would be so kind as step into the back seat of your motorcar, I'll be on my way."

Slim and Shorty were sitting in the back seat of the Bentley when Mattie started the MG and turned on its headlights. She pulled onto the road and stopped opposite the Bentley. Then she picked up her PPK and, with a broad grin, fired two shots, the first into the left rear tire and the second into the left front tire. Both men had ducked at the sound of the shots and slowly sat back up when they realized the shots were not directed at them. Still grinning, she took several photos of Slim and Shorty staring out at her with open mouths, gave them a salute and the MG sped away, kicking up a spray of gravel.

Slieve League
County Donegal, Ireland
Wednesday, 5 September 1934

MATTIE TURNED off the road onto the crushed stone driveway that led to their home, a restored Martello Tower overlooking Donegal

Bay. The sun was very low on the horizon, a beautiful sunset slowly sinking. The tower was at the end of the driveway, a good half-mile away and invisible from the road. Beside the tower, ropes anchoring it down, was *The Celtic Princess,* Cockran's personal PCA-2 Pitcairn Autogiro that she had used to fly all over Europe last month interviewing fascist party leaders.

Martello Towers were built during the early 19th century throughout the British Isles, mostly as a defense against an invasion by Napoleon. Theirs was an early one for it was square whereas most of the Martellos were round. It was two stories high with a flat battlement on top. Typically, a Martello Tower had eight-foot thick granite walls and one gun that could fire in all directions. One officer and 24 soldiers manned them. They were patterned after a similar fort on the island of Corsica that the Royal Navy had thought impressive. Over a hundred were built in England and over fifty in Ireland. The Corsica fort was located at Mortella Point, but somehow the English managed to misspell it as 'Martello'. As a Scot, she wasn't surprised. In her experience, most English weren't all that bright. That certainly wasn't true of her godfather Winston Churchill, but he was half-American so, to her, that explained it.

Mattie reached the back of the tower where there were no windows on the ground floor, only a small, polished wooden door. Above her, there were four windows on each side of the tower, two to a floor, all had glass in them and they all glowed with light, which meant that their cleaning lady, Meg Feeney, had been there during the day and had left the lights on in anticipation of Mattie's return. She fished out a key, opened the door and stepped into a long, whitewashed hallway that led to stairs at the front of the tower. There were electric sconces as well as framed pictures along both sides of the hallway. Halfway down were the doors to two rooms that originally held gunpowder and supplies, but now were bedrooms, each with a full bath and shower. The Tower had its own gasoline-powered generator for electricity that lighted the place and ran a water pump that took water from the tower's original cistern and sent it to the bath and up to the kitchen, which was on the roof level. There was an internal drainage system on the roof that captured rainwater and refilled the cistern every time it rained which, being Ireland, meant every day.

Mattie walked up the stairs that led to the flat top floor of the tower—the battlements. Two-third's the length of the top floor had been enclosed to form a combination kitchen and dining room complete with sink, stove, refrigerator, fully-stocked bar and a long refectory table seating eight. And it really did have a thatched roof over it. It also had a spectacular view of the Atlantic Ocean in three directions. The roof soared up from the back wall; the sidewalls had large windows extending above the stone battlements; and the front wall was entirely glass in the middle of which was a wood-framed door that led to the terrace beyond.

Mattie opened the door and walked onto the terrace where there were two weathered Adirondack chairs and a matching table between them, identical to the ones Cockran had on the lawn at their country home, The Cedars, leading down to the beach on Long Island Sound. She went past them to the four-foot high stone parapet and rested her arms on it as she looked out to sea. What a perfect little house, she had thought when Cockran first brought her here last year after their marriage. And it was still perfect. She missed her husband and she missed their evening ritual of martinis on the terrace watching the sun set over the Atlantic Ocean.

Nevertheless, Bourke's absence wasn't going to deter her from enjoying an evening martini in the dying light of the sun. After a day spent with O'Duffy and then with his thugs Slim and Shorty, she deserved it. She returned to the house, found the martini shaker and filled it with ice, gin and a capfull of vermouth. She popped an olive into the stemmed martini glass and shook the shaker vigorously for precisely 21 shakes. She had started to return to the terrace when she noticed a white envelope on the refectory table.

There was nothing written on the outside of the envelope, but she assumed it had been left by Meg. She picked it up and walked outside with the martini glass and shaker. She poured her martini into the stemmed glass and was pleased to see that little ice crystals had formed in the liquid. Perfect! She hadn't lost her touch.

Mattie sat in the Adirondack chair and raised a silent toast to her absent husband. After a first sip of the icy drink, she placed it down and opened the envelope.

Mattie,

> *Mr. Churchill called this afternoon. I told him you wouldn't be back until late this evening, but he asked that you return his call no matter how late it was. He said it was a matter of great urgency involving Germany and the Jews. He wants you to come visit him in England this weekend.*

> *Meg*

Mattie sighed and took another sip. Ever since her godfather had fallen from power when the Tories lost the 1929 election to the Socialists of Ramsay MacDonald's Labour Party, he had been the source of some of her best stories, including the ones that resulted in not one, but two, Pulitzer Prizes this year. The problem was that, for every good story he sent her way, at least five more were total busts! Winston was a journalist himself—indeed a far better paid one than her—and while he did recognize a good story, if his sources were suspect—as they frequently were—the 'good story' soon disappeared.

Mattie drained her martini and poured another. She looked at her wristwatch. It was nearly 11:30. The sad thing was that Winston would be wide-awake right now. After all, when you took a two-hour nap in the afternoon, as he regularly did, you could stay up working and writing into the wee hours of the morning. Mattie had never been able to afford that luxury. Besides, she had a new E. Philips Oppenheim novel to begin, *The Gallows of Chance*. Whatever Winston had for her could wait until the morning.

Perhaps she might call him at 6 a.m. and wake him up! "I'm sorry to call so early, Godfather, but your message said to call you when I got in, no matter how late it was."

Mattie smiled, walked over to the telephone and placed a trans-Atlantic call to her husband in New York where it was early evening. She couldn't wait to tell Cockran her adventures that day. Before their marriage, they had frequently quarreled over what Cockran thought—with good cause, she admitted in hindsight—were the unnecessary risks she took on her assignments in the field. Compared to almost falling off the top of the *Graf Zeppelin* into the Atlantic Ocean below as she took especially dramatic photographs, however, today was a walk in the park. And she had the photographs to prove it.

Once she finished her call to her husband, Mattie picked up the Oppenheim novel and walked down the stone steps to their bedroom.

5

Winston Churchill

Chartwell
Kent, England
Wednesday 5 September 1934

STATE ATTORNEY Dr. Georg von Dohnanyi of the German Ministry of Justice and a member of the German Commission on Criminal Law Reform was having second thoughts as the taxi that he had taken at the Tunbridge Wells train station pulled up in front of the country estate of Winston Churchill. He placed his hand on the door handle and hesitated. Other than his niece, Greta Mayer, who had accompanied him today, the only person to whom he had confided his plans was his brother-in-law, Dietrich Bonhoeffer, a well-known anti-Nazi theologian. Dietrich, of course, had encouraged him to see Churchill, but then he would, wouldn't he? After all, as he had said in April of last year about Nazi persecution of the Jews, "It is not sufficient to bandage the victims under the wheel, but to jam the spoke in the wheel itself."

That was why Georg was here today. He didn't want to bandage victims; he wanted to jam the spoke in the wheel that was the German Commission on Criminal Law Reform before it could change German law to reflect the radical ideas contained in that damnable Prussian Memorandum. Exposing it to the sunlight of public scrutiny in

Germany was impossible, but if Great Britain and the rest of Western Europe could learn what the radical Nazis on the Commission were advocating, the weight of world opinion might make a difference. And Churchill was just the man to generate that publicity. He reminded himself that he wouldn't have another chance like this. Attending a legal seminar in London seemed to him the perfect cover to visit England, something he couldn't repeat without drawing suspicion to himself. He drew a deep breath and opened the taxi door and stepped out on the crushed stone driveway.

"Why did you hesitate a moment ago, Uncle Georg?" Greta asked.

Dohnanyi looked down at his lovely niece. She had just turned 21. Blonde, beautiful and glowing with the health of the athlete she was—an Olympic-class sprinter—she exemplified the ideal of the perfect Aryan woman so frequently touted by the *verdammt* propaganda of that crippled Hitler acolyte Joseph Goebbels.

"Today is a big step for me, Greta. Others might think me a traitor."

"Nonsense, Uncle! You are as courageous as any man as I know. I've listened to some of these radical Nazis prattle on at the Commission meetings about following the 'one drop of blood' rule from some of the American states. They're all quite mad, you know. It's just like Uncle Dietrich says, we've got to jam the spoke in the wheel itself to stop them."

Dohnanyi squeezed his niece's hand. "Thank you, Greta. Your support means a lot to me." They reached the front door and he pressed the buzzer. Was he being a traitor? To the Nazis? Perhaps. To Germany? Never.

WINSTON CHURCHILL was in his study working in front of a stand-up desk whose surface slanted up at a 20% angle, galley proofs marked with red corrections in front of him, when Dr. Georg von Dohnanyi and his niece, Greta Mayer, were announced by Inches, Churchill's butler, who handed him the lawyer's business card and carefully pronounced the man's name as "Dock-non-yee". An unlit Havana in his mouth and a crystal tumbler of whisky and soda on a short round table beside him, he walked over to the man and shook his hand. "So good of you to come Dr. Dohnanyi. Welcome to Chartwell."

"*Herr* Churchill, it is an honor to meet you. May I present my niece Greta Mayer? She is a graduate student at Heidelberg, but she is taking time off to work as an apprentice stenographer for the German Commission on Criminal Law Reform."

Churchill grasped the young woman's extended hand. "Welcome to you as well, *Fraulein* Mayer," he said. Then he turned and pointed to a large, chintz-covered sofa across from his desk and beside the fireplace. "Please, have a seat."

Dohnanyi appeared to be in his early 40s, Churchill thought, with a handsome face, dark blond hair neatly combed, and round wire-rimmed spectacles. He wore a dark blue three-piece, well–tailored suit and his black shoes were polished to a high gloss. His niece was blonde, beautiful, and nearly as tall as her uncle. She wore a dove gray skirt and a navy blue cardigan over a crisp white blouse, her only jewelry a single strand of pearls.

"Might I offer you a drink?" Churchill asked.

"Yes, please, *danke*. Whisky," Dohnanyi replied.

"Mineral water and a slice of lemon, please," Greta Mayer said.

Inches went over to a sideboard, poured mineral water into a tall glass, and added a slice of lemon. Then, he poured two fingers of whisky into a crystal glass identical to Churchill's and added a splash of water. He walked over and placed both drinks down on a low table in front of the sofa.

"Thank you, Mr. Churchill, for agreeing to see me," Dohnanyi said, taking a small sip of the whisky. "As I told you on the telephone, I am a State Attorney in the German Ministry of Justice and a member of the German Commission on Criminal Law Reform. I don't have much time as I must be back in London for a late dinner with my German colleagues who are attending the legal seminar I used as an excuse to come to London. So, let me get right to the point. It is not widely known, but the Commission is secretly considering drastic measures to deny German Jews their German citizenship and to criminalize marriage and sexual relations between Aryans and Jews. I have brought with me something called the 'Prussian Memorandum' which the radical Nazis on the Commission are utilizing to justify their position."

Dohnanyi reached down and picked up the leather briefcase at his side. He unfastened the two straps and pulled out two folders. He handed them to Churchill. "The first folder contains a photocopy of the German translation of the Memorandum which is the only one the Commission members have seen. The second folder contains the original English version of the Memorandum from which the German translation was made."

Churchill was surprised. "The original is in English? Why?"

"All the legal research was done in America by Americans whom the SS retained for that purpose."

"Who were they?"

"We don't know. The Chairman of the Commission refuses to say."

Churchill opened the second folder and began to read. He had to admit he was surprised—if not shocked—by what he read. His mother had been an American, so he was half-American. He had made speaking tours of the United States in 1929 and 1932. From having given speeches in Richmond, Virginia and New Orleans, he was aware of the state laws on segregation of white and blacks in the Deep South. He was not surprised, therefore, to see that those states had laws prohibiting marriage between whites and blacks. He was very much surprised to learn from the Memorandum, however, that these laws were not confined to southern states. Over 60% of the American states, fully 30 of 48, had laws prohibiting marriage and/or sexual relations between whites and other races ranging from Negroes and mulattoes to Filipinos, Chinese, Japanese, Koreans, other Asians and American Indians. Assuming the memorandum was correct—and Churchill had no reason to think it wasn't—states from California and Oregon on the West Coast through North Dakota, South Dakota and Indiana in the Midwest to Maryland and Delaware on the East Coast had laws prohibiting miscegenation.

Churchill didn't understand. The United States was, like the independent countries of the British Empire, a white man's country. Yet, with the single exception of South Africa, no member state of the

British Empire had ever enacted such barbarous laws. Even South Africa was not as bad as those 30 American states. It did prohibit marriage between whites and blacks, but it did not, unlike those American states, prohibit marriage between whites and 'coloureds', those with a mixed racial heritage.

Churchill put the photocopy back in the folder and placed it on his desk. "Well, Dr. Dohnanyi, I confess much of this is a surprise to me. I had no idea such laws were so widespread in the United States. And you say what you call 'radical Nazis' on your Commission want to use these laws as a model for Germany to do the same to Jews?"

"That is correct, Mr. Churchill."

"Why bring this to me? What do you want me to do with it?"

"You're well known as a friend of the Jews; someone who supports Zionism; someone who helped organize a world-wide boycott against German exports…"

Churchill interrupted. "A boycott, I'm afraid, that largely failed thanks to the Transfer Agreement between the Nazis and Jewish Palestine as well as the *Concordat* between Hitler and the Pope in 1933."

Dohnanyi's eyes brightened and, Churchill thought, he began to show some animation. "That's not true, Mr. Churchill. The boycott may not have driven the Nazis from power, but it accomplished several important things. First, Hitler issued a directive to the SA and its brown-shirted Storm Troopers to cease any actions like boycotts against the mostly Jewish-owned department stores and their suppliers. He even authorized a loan to a Jewish Department store that was close to bankruptcy. Hitler likely did it to keep thousands of Aryans off the unemployment rolls if any department stores had to close their doors because of brown-shirt bullying, but he still did it and those stores remained open and prospering."

Dohnanyi paused and took a sip of whisky. "The second thing Hitler and Göring did in response to the boycott last year was even bigger. They forbade all violence against the Jews that the SA had been committing without authorization of the government. The penalty for doing so is, at a minimum, confinement to a concentration camp or, at the other end, death. Violence against Jews has practically disappeared, especially in large cities where most German Jews live. I think the boycott deserves the credit for forcing Hitler's hand to issue those decrees."

"I take your point, Dr. Dohnanyi. I had hoped to push the German economy over a cliff and Hitler with it. We failed at that, but those are positive developments that you cite. Still, what do you want me to do with this Memorandum?"

"Make it public! Use your position to let the world know what the Nazis are trying to do to the Jews!"

Churchill shook his head. "It's not as easy as that. Goebbels will simply denounce it as a forgery. It will be, at best, a one-day story and, as my anti-Nazi views are well known, many will discount the story because of that. I expect American journalists might suggest it was a forgery as well. I could identify you as my source to the journalist to whom I give the Memorandum, but I assume you don't want that. Otherwise, you would not be meeting with me secretly. Correct?"

"Yes, Sir. At a minimum, I would lose my place on the Commission. I might even end up in a concentration camp."

"So, is there anything more you can give me? Something to corroborate what you're telling me? Are there transcripts of the Commission meetings where this Prussian Memorandum has been discussed?" Churchill asked, placing his cigar on a crystal ashtray, and taking a sip of whisky.

Dohnanyi frowned. "Well, we certainly discuss it privately among ourselves, I mean the moderate Commission members do, and I've even discussed it with some of the radical members. I believe the subject of the Jews was discussed at a Commission meeting in June I was unable to attend, but I don't know if the Prussian Memorandum itself was specifically discussed. The transcript would show if it was discussed or not, but there is no way to get you a copy. The transcripts are classified 'Top Secret' and the only copies are kept under lock and key in the office of Roland Freisler, the Chairman of the Commission and State Secretary of the Reich Ministry of Justice. Any member of the Commission may review the transcripts, but only in Freisler's office."

Dohnanyi's niece, who heretofore had sat silently beside her uncle, spoke for the first time, her blue eyes lighting up. "I think there might be a way to do it, Uncle. You're correct that there was an all-day session of the Commission on the subject of the Jews that went into the evening hours on Tuesday, 5 June. I was there for training purposes as a stenographer, not to be the official recorder. I wasn't present the entire time, but when I was there, the Prussian Memorandum was discussed extensively by most of the members, both the radicals and those opposed to using the memorandum and American laws as a model. At that meeting, it was clear that the more moderate members want a narrow, precise definition of who is a Jew so that the new laws will apply to as few people as possible. The radical Nazis argued for a more expansive definition and are relying on US race laws to support their position that anyone with even a single Jew in their family tree going back two, three, even four generations will be deemed a Jew and deprived of their German citizenship and forbidden to marry or have sexual relations with an Aryan. It will be difficult, but I believe I can make a copy of the verbatim transcript of the meeting. The transcripts of the meetings may be 'Top Secret' and kept under lock and key, but the official stenographer's stenotype notes are not. I know where she keeps her notes. I believe I can 'borrow' her notes without her knowledge and by comparing hers with mine, I can create a new transcript. Would that help?"

"Yes, *Fraulein* Mayer, a transcript where the Memorandum is discussed and debated would go a long way to establishing it is not a forgery," Churchill said and looked at Dohnanyi. "But since it will not be an official transcript, it will be necessary, Doctor, for you to arrange interviews for my journalist with several other members of the Commission who share your views to confirm the accuracy of the new transcript."

"I can't, not if their names are to be published. Like me, I don't think any of them are that brave."

"No, of course not. The journalist I have in mind for breaking this story would agree to keep their names confidential."

"Can this journalist be trusted to do this?"

Churchill smiled. "I, for one, would trust her with my life. After all, I've known her since she was in nappies. She's my goddaughter; she speaks fluent German; and she won two Pulitzer Prizes last year for her articles on Nazi Germany."

"You mean Martha McGary? Your goddaughter is Martha McGary? I've read her stories in American newspapers!" Greta exclaimed.

"They aren't generally available in Germany," Dohnanyi explained. "Dr. Goebbels would never permit that, but the Ministry of Justice has subscriptions to a wide range of foreign newspapers and I pass them on to Greta."

"Yes, Mattie McGary is my goddaughter. Now, Mr. State Attorney, how soon can you and your niece arrange to have that transcript prepared and delivered to me?"

"It will take me at least a week to re-create the transcript," Greta said. "It was an exceptionally long session."

"I can't come to England again," Dohnanyi said, "but I have a conference to attend in Amsterdam in two weeks. If Greta can prepare it before then, I can deliver it to you in Amsterdam. The conference runs from Saturday 15 September through Monday 17 September. If you could be there on any of those days, we could arrange a safe place to meet and I could bring you the transcript."

Churchill reached across his desk and opened a leather bound appointments book. He quickly scanned its contents and then looked up. "I can be in Amsterdam on any of those dates," Churchill said and reached for a pen. Unscrewing the cap, he wrote quickly on a sheet of paper and handed it to Dohnanyi. "If we come, this is the hotel where Mattie and I will stay in Amsterdam. How much longer will you be in London?"

"I fly back to Berlin on Friday in the early evening."

"Good. That will give me time to contact my goddaughter and ascertain if she will be available to come with me to Amsterdam. Call me here at Chartwell from a public telephone on Friday afternoon and we can finalize a date and place to meet in Amsterdam and receive the transcript. If Mattie cannot come to Amsterdam on any of those dates, you and I will have to arrange another mutually convenient time and place. Meanwhile, leave with me the names of any members of the Commission who you believe will be amenable to meeting with Mattie on a confidential basis."

"Yes, Sir," Dohnanyi said as he reached for the briefcase by his side, opened it and extracted a single sheet of paper that he handed to Churchill. "I anticipated you might want that so I prepared a list of members who I believe would be willing to do so."

Churchill took the sheet, looked at it briefly and placed it on his desk. "Excellent. Thank you. You'll arrange to confirm their willingness to do this and give them Mattie's name?"

"Yes, of course," Dohnanyi replied.

"Now, as to the Americans who prepared this Memorandum, is there any possibility you can ascertain their names?"

Dohnanyi frowned. "I think that possibility is remote. The Commission Chairman Roland Freisler is the one who refused to identify the Americans. He joined the Nazi Party ten years ago and is in the SS. His immediate superior is the Minister of Justice, Franz Gurtner, but he is not a Nazi and does not like to confront Freisler when they disagree. Gurtner believes that Hitler will come down on Freisler's side if there is any unresolved disagreement between them. Gurtner wants to preserve the independence of the judiciary so he bends over backwards to please Hitler. Hitler did keep him on as Justice Minister despite being appointed by Hitler's predecessor."

"Interesting. He's not a Nazi yet Hitler let him stay as Justice Minister. Why do you suppose he did that?" Churchill asked.

"That's likely because Gurtner was Minister of Justice in Bavaria during the twenties. He obtained Hitler's early release from Landsberg Prison for his role in the 1923 *putsch*. Earlier this year he's the one who drafted 'The Law Regarding Measures of Self-Defense' that retroactively legalized all the SS killing during The Night of The Long Knives."

Churchill laughed. "That is *really* bending over backwards."

"Exactly. You'd need someone as powerful and influential with Hitler as Göring to pry the identity of the Americans from the SS."

AFTER DOHNANYI left, Churchill retrieved a small wooden box from underneath his writing desk. Inside of the box was a small Bakelite Dictograph receiving device with a wire-recording spool. A thin electrical wire usually connected the device to a rubber disk approximately an inch wide and a quarter inch thick that was concealed in the base of a lamp on his desk. Scotland Yard's Special Branch had placed it there a year ago at the direction of one of Churchill's political opponents, the Chancellor of the Exchequer, Neville Chamberlain. Churchill had his own friends in Scotland Yard and they had quickly discovered the device. They had offered to remove it, but Churchill declined. It was useful to know your political enemies were listening because it offered untold opportunities to feed them disinformation. Today, however, was not one of those days. So, as he had been taught, Churchill earlier had disconnected the wire between the rubber disk and the receiving device. He only did this for important conversations or telephone calls. Otherwise, he left it in full operation. If Neville wanted to know all the boring details of his daily life, then more power to him. It simply gave any disinformation he wished to feed to the Chancellor that much more weight. Today, however, he did not trust Neville with the information that a German government official was delivering confidential documents to a foreigner. Neville was just daft enough to pass it along to the German Ambassador!

Churchill summoned his secretary to his study. "Mrs. P, would you be so kind as to ring up my goddaughter at her Martello Tower in Donegal, Ireland?"

Moments later, at Mrs. P's signal, he picked up the receier. "Mattie? It's Winston. Oh, she's not in. When do you expect her? I see. Well, please give her a message for me."

6

Bourke Cockran

The Chrysler Building
New York City
Wednesday, 5 September 1934

"FOR STARTERS, Tim, Donovan doesn't like the nickname 'Wild Bill'," Bourke Cockran, Jr. said, referring to William J. Donovan, the Managing Partner of Donovan & Raichle, the New York and Washington international law firm where Cockran was a partner. "Start out with 'Colonel' or 'Mister' and see how it goes. He has a soft spot for Regular Army guys so, if you two hit it off, he'll be asking you to call him 'Bill' in no time."

Like Cockran, Colonel Timothy X. O'Hanlon was in his late 30s. He was a compact 5' 9" with glossy black hair, bright blue eyes and a quick mind. He wore the standard full dress Army Officer 'pinks and greens', a dark jacket over lighter tan trousers. Cockran, by contrast, was an inch or so over 6' with unruly sandy hair, hazel eyes and a cleft chin. His wife, to his embarrassment, insisted he looked like the western movie actor John Wayne. His uniform of the day was a chalk-striped gray suit from Henry Poole & Co. of Savile Row, the tailor for both his father and Winston Churchill.

The two men were in Cockran's office in the Chrysler Building with a view south toward the tip of the island and the canyons of lower

Manhattan. They were in front of Cockran's desk, which faced away from the window. Sitting in two green leather armchairs placed against the wall opposite the window, a small table between them on which sat a yellow and green Tiffany lamp, they had a splendid view of the morning sun glowing over the city's skyscrapers. They had met during the Great War when both were in the same training course for MID Counterintelligence Agents and had been best friends ever since. Cockran left MID after the war because he was fed up with the anti-Semitism and Bolshevik-under-every-bed mentality of its leaders, General Ralph Van Deman and his successor General Leonard Marlborough. O'Hanlon stayed, telling Cockran that someone had to be there to keep the bastards at the top in line.

William Donovan may not have liked the nickname 'Wild Bill', Cockran thought as he prepared his friend for their conference with his boss, but he had come by it honestly and it fit his personality perfectly for his hard charging, damn the torpedoes, full-speed-ahead style that had won him the Congressional Medal of Honor during the war. Tim didn't have the Medal of Honor, but, like Cockran, he had the Silver Star and other impressive ribbons on his chest that showed where he had been and what he had done. Cockran hoped Tim and his service record would impress Donovan because the case he wanted Donovan & Raichle to take on—and for which Donovan's consent as Managing Partner would be needed—was not exactly up the alley of a major corporate law firm.

Criminal defense work at Donovan & Raichle was always farmed out to lawyers who spent their days in criminal court. While Tim didn't have a criminal defense case, *per se*, he did want Cockran to conduct a criminal investigation into the deaths late last year of two former MID agents who were close friends of Tim as well as four other former MID agents who turned up dead at year's end as well. Cockran had no experience in criminal investigations. For a few years after the war and his resignation from MID, however, he had been an investigative journalist and then a foreign correspondent for Hearst's *New York American* so he was no stranger to investigations. It was a testament to their friendship—and to the fact he owed Tim several large favors—that Cockran had cut short his summer holiday with his bride of barely a year and asked for yet another extension from his publisher on his book in order to sail to America and help Tim persuade Wild Bill Donovan to allow his law firm to take on the case.

COCKRAN INTRODUCED O'Hanlon to Donovan and they shook hands. Cockran had known him since his tenth birthday party when Donovan, then-quarterback for Columbia University and a friend of his father, had been a special guest. Donovan was a big man, a few inches shy of Cockran, with a broad frame, expensively barbered brown hair, and a perpetual smile on an Irish face marked by sparklingly clear blue eyes.

Donovan's office was twice the size of Cockran's and was decorated in the same style as the law firm's walnut paneled reception area. The dominant features of both were brass lamps, old oil paintings and tasteful oriental rugs selected by Donovan's wife, Ruth. Four maroon leather club chairs were set around a low table containing a silver coffee service, three china cups and saucers and assorted Danish pastry. Donovan bade them to sit down and help themselves to the coffee and Danish.

During the war, Donovan had been a colonel and commanded New York's 69th Regiment, 'The Fighting 69th'. Cockran, then a captain, had been Donovan's chief intelligence officer, but a leg injury from a shell fragment after only five months in the trenches had sent Cockran back to the states for a long rehabilitation and an eventual assignment from MID as a Counterintelligence Agent.

After the war, Donovan rose to be head of the Antitrust Division of the Justice Department in the Coolidge administration. In the waning months of Silent Cal's second term in office, Donovan became acting Attorney General. Donovan declined Herbert Hoover's offer to be his Vice-Presidential running mate in 1928 to attract the Irish-American vote and served instead as his campaign manager with a promise to be Hoover's Attorney General. Elected in a landslide, Hoover promptly reneged on his promise to Donovan. Anti-Catholic feelings against the Democratic candidate Al Smith were so strong among Hoover supporters that the multimillionaire engineer didn't think it politic to appoint even a *Republican* Irish Catholic to his otherwise all-white, male and *Protestant* cabinet.

After that, Donovan formed what he termed an international law firm for American business with offices both in New York and Washington. He had invited Cockran, then a tenured professor at Columbia's law school, to join the firm as "Of Counsel," which meant that Cockran took on his own cases or assignments from Donovan on an *ad hoc* basis. That had changed three years later in 1932 when a wealthy divorcée client of Cockran—Ingrid Johansson—purchased Freedom House Publishers from the proceeds of her late husband's estate. She promptly hired him as its General Counsel, making Freedom House one of Donovan & Raichle's largest clients, and, in turn, Wild Bill had offered Cockran a full partnership in the firm.

After all three men had served themselves coffee, Donovan placed his hands on his knees and looked at O'Hanlon. "Okay, Colonel, Bourke was fairly close-mouthed on exactly what you want our firm to do for you, but let's get the important things out of the way. We may not be a white shoe firm, but we charge our clients like we are. I'm afraid our fees may be a bit steep for an Army colonel's's salary."

O'Hanlon laughed. "Not a problem, Colonel Donovan. My two brothers and I own O'Hanlon Lines, the largest trucking and shipping company in New England. We have over-the-road trucks, cargo vessels and oil tankers. My brothers run the company, but we inherited equal shares of the business from our father. My brothers are patriots and they approve of my service in MID so we all take the same salary. I've explained to them what I want Bourke to do for me and they agreed to run the expense through the company and to begin sending other legal business to your firm if you agree to take on this case."

Cockran smiled. He had been left well off by his father—a 5th Avenue townhouse, a 300-acre estate on the Gold Coast and a hefty bond portfolio—but, in contrast, he knew Tim was seriously rich. He and his wife lived in a mansion in the Kalorama neighborhood of Washington, D.C and had a weekend home on Chesapeake Bay where their 75 foot motor yacht was anchored and used for cruises to their winter home on Jekyll Island in Georgia. Tim had not told him, however, that he planned to send their company's business to

Donovan & Raichle as an inducement to persuade Donovan to let Cockran take on Tim's case. Well, Tim *was* really smart and he knew he wouldn't have had to do that to secure Cockran's agreement. Springing it on Donovan now was the best way to go.

Cockran said nothing, but watched Donovan closely to see what effect it had. He was a fairly good poker player, but Cockran caught a tell. Wild Bill *had* been surprised. Still, that only meant Donovan would listen to Tim's story with an open mind.

"Okay, Colonel. I'm glad we got that out of the way. Tell me what your problem is and why you think our firm can help."

"In some ways, my problem may involve a matter of national security and, since Bourke is a former MID agent who once had a Top Secret clearance, I want someone who knows the importance of keeping secrets. You've held high government office yourself so you can appreciate why I want someone like him. So, let me begin at the beginning. Last June, my boss General Leonard Marlborough came to my office and gave me an unusual assignment."

Cockran grabbed a Danish, refilled his coffee cup and listened to O'Hanlon for the next half hour as Donovan did not interrupt and occasionally made a note on the legal pad in front of him. Tim's assignment was to review the personnel files of all former MID agents who had a law degree and give the files of the twelve best to Marlborough who would have a legal scholar winnow the number down to six and supervise their research.

"I asked him why," O'Hanlon said, "and he told me I didn't need to know. He said he chose me for the work because I had a law degree from Harvard even though I've never practiced law. All I needed to know, he said, was that the entire operation was under a Black Drape. So I did what I was told. I checked all the personnel files and pulled those with law degrees. Then I selected the 15 men whose law school grades were highest. After that, I gave a greater weight to the Ivy League law schools—Harvard, Penn, Yale and Columbia—and rearranged the order. I packaged the personnel files of the highest twelve and delivered them to General Marlborough."

O'Hanlon paused, took a sip of coffee and continued. "Two of the twelve were close friends of mine, Joseph Carmody and Henry

Sandler. Both were in my wedding, Hank was my Best Man. I sent them each a note saying I had given their personnel files to Leo Marlborough for some hush-hush project. Joe was in charge of litigation for a small business law firm in Pittsburgh, but Hank was in private practice in Cleveland as a sole practitioner. Maybe six weeks later, I received a call from Hank.

" 'Thanks a lot Buddy for sending my name on that MID project to that Ivy League fascist,' he said. I could tell he wasn't happy. I asked him what the MID project was and who was the 'Ivy League fascist'. 'You mean you don't know?' he asked. I said I didn't. He said that he didn't like what he was doing, but a Black Drape was a Black Drape and he couldn't tell me what he was doing or who he was doing it for."

Cockran thought, as he knew the whole story, that Tim was taking too long to get to the point. Then he did. Dramatically. "I learned from his wife Alice this summer that Joe died in Pittsburgh in mid-November. The police ruled it a suicide since he jumped off a bridge with a note in his pocket saying he was sorry for some case he had lost. Then my wife heard a week later that Hank was stabbed to death and his wife Doris raped by a thug in a home burglary in Cleveland Heights in late December. I smelled a rat. I don't believe in a coincidence like those so I called all the other ten agents whose files I had delivered to Marlborough."

"Good move," Donovan said and made a note on his legal pad.

"Right. That's why I want to hire Bourke and your firm. Six of the ten were fine. The other four were dead. All in November or December—a mugging; a hit and run; a hunting accident and a drowning. So, six of the men on my list were dead and Hank's phone call to me suggests they were the six on the list of twelve agents I had given to Marlborough that were eventually selected for a Black Drape operation. I put this all to Marlborough and he told me to forget it. It was a Black Drape and that was all I needed to know. Well, screw that! Two of them were my friends, Goddamn it! I want to know who killed them and why!" O'Hanlon said, pounding the arm of his leather club chair.

Cockran was taken aback. Unlike him, O'Hanlon was a devout Catholic and rarely swore.

"Why do you think Bourke or our firm will be able to help you accomplish this?" Donovan calmly asked as he placed down his coffee cup.

O'Hanlon laughed. "Actually, I'd prefer his wife to either you or any of your lawyers, but Bourke told me she's in the middle of a big story that she wouldn't stop for anything. So I said 'What the hell, bring in the junior varsity'."

Cockran winced and Donovan chuckled. "You make a good point. Mattie's stories over the past two years have hinted at an uncomfortably close relationship between our MID and the Nazi SS. I can appreciate their mutual antagonism to the Bolsheviks, but that business with the kidnapped American twins was beyond the pale."

"That it was, but I want Bourke because I want a quiet, off-the-books investigation. I'm working within MID to get a peek at what's behind the Black Drape and I have a few leads. If he can find out anything from the widows of these agents, we can link it to what I learn."

O'Hanlon stopped, finished the rest of his coffee and poured another cup. He looked directly into Donovan's eyes and spoke in a low voice. "Once I know who is responsible and why, then I can decide what to do next. Believe me when I say, Colonel, that I have more than enough agents loyal to me to carry out whatever I decide should be 'next'."

Donovan did not reply. He put his fist under his chin, and stared silently at Cockran, then at O'Hanlon, and finally back to Cockran. After a long minute of silence, he spoke to Cockran. "How do you propose to staff this case if I agree to let you take it?"

Cockran was elated. They had won! "Bobby Sullivan and the O'Driscoll brothers."

Donovan rubbed his eyes and sighed. "The Angel of Death and the Twins of Doom? May I assume you have green cards for the O'Driscolls as well as Private Investigator licenses?"

Cockran nodded.

Donovan turned to O'Hanlon. "Well, Colonel—Tim if I may—I'll probably have to go to Confession over this, but you've got yourself a law firm."

"Thank you Colonel—Bill—I appreciate it."

"Uh, Bill," Cockran said with a grin, "the odds against my being in St. Patrick's any time soon are pretty long. Nonetheless, I'd appreciate it if you'd give me a heads-up when you go for your next Confession. I'd not like to be there when the walls come tumbling down."

"Bastard!" Donovan said with a laugh. "I don't know what Mattie sees in you."

"A lapsed Catholic. The same thing your Protestant wife sees in you, Bill. Or so Mattie tells me. The girls do talk, you know."

7

Kurt von Sturm

Villa Goebbels
Inselstrasse 10
Schwanenenwerder Island, Germany
Wednesday, 5 September 1934

SILENTLY SLIPPING out of bed, Kurt von Sturm, the commander of the *Graf Bismarck* airship, looked over at the naked body of *Frau* Magda Goebbels, the blonde and beautiful wife of Nazi Propaganda Minister Joseph Goebbels. Lying face down, she was sleeping soundly, her body still pink and flushed from a spirited late afternoon tryst. Sturm dressed and made his way downstairs to Goebbels' study. There were no servants around as they had been given the day off. Magda would sleep for at least an hour and that was all the time Sturm needed. Fun and games were over. It was time to go to work.

Their affair had begun in early June at the behest—on Sturm's part at least—of his immediate superior at the Air Ministry, *Reichsminister* Hermann Göring, who was also President of the *Reichstag*, Prime Minister of Prussia, and *Reichsjagermeister*, Chief Huntsman of the Reich. Göring had directed him to seduce *Frau* Goebbels because her husband was a political enemy and "I damn well want to know what that *verdammt* clubfooted dwarf is doing to screw me over *before* he does it!" Fortunately, her husband bragged to her about all his political machinations and Magda told them to Sturm before and after their lovemaking. Sturm passed it all on to *Unser* Hermann—'Our Hermann' as he was affectionately know to the German public—who was quite pleased with the intelligence he received.

While most affairs of married women take place outside of the home they shared with their husbands, Magda was an exception. She was a most unhappy woman whose husband bedded every new starlet the German film company UFA hired. As a consequence, when Sturm suggested that carrying on their affair in the homes she shared with her husband would serve him right, she readily agreed. Goebbels had three homes. So far, they had made love in two of them—the Propaganda Minister's Official Residence at 20 *Hermann-Göring-Strasse* near the Brandenburg Gate in central Berlin and Goebbels' country house in *Bogensee*. At Magda's insistence, they always did so on Joseph Goebbels own bed in the separate bedroom he maintained adjacent to hers in each house. "After all," she had told him, "if those beds are good enough for him to screw that Czech whore from UFA, Lida Baarova, then they're good enough for you to do the same to me."

Today was their first visit to Goebbels' lakeside house on *Schwanenenwerder* Island. Hitler's architect Albert Speer had a home here and it was rumored that Hitler owned property on the island also, but had yet to build on it. Göring was satisfied with the intelligence Sturm had supplied from the affair so far, but Sturm wanted more. He wanted Joseph Goebbels' diaries.

It was well known that the vain little Nazi kept a daily diary because, earlier this year, he had published excerpts from it—*From the Kaiserhof to the Reich Chancellery: A Historical Account from the Pages of a Diary*—covering the period from January 1932 to May 1933. Sturm had made an extensive search of the Official Residence and his country house, but had not found the diaries. He hoped the third time would be the charm for if they weren't here at the lakeside house, then they could only be at the Office of the Propaganda Ministry on *Wilhelmstrasse* and not even Magda could get him in there.

Sturm was in his late 30s. A tall man and trim, nearly six feet two inches and 180 pounds, it was the same weight he had carried for the past 20 years. With blond hair and a classically handsome face marred only by a prominent two-inch scar on his left temple he knew, to his dismay, that he looked like a damned SS recruiting poster. Sturm wasn't happy about that because, while he had been a Nazi party member himself since 1923 and was once an admirer of Adolf Hitler, he had nothing but contempt for the SS and its leader Heinrich Himmler. The final straw had been his own experience during the summer of 1932 where he and his friends Mattie McGary, Bourke Cockran, and Bobby Sullivan had discovered and sabotaged gruesome SS medical experiments on kidnapped American twins, their purpose being to unlock the scientific secrets to producing a master race.

Sturm further had been appalled by the spontaneous violence that had erupted all over Germany against Jews, Communists and Social Democrats by the Nazi Storm Troopers of the SA after Hitler became Chancellor on 30 January 1933. He once had thought Hitler would be Germany's savior and, in fact, the *Fuhrer* had long held Sturm in high personal regard and not only because he had saved him from an assassin's bullet five weeks later. Hitler had never uttered a single anti-Semitic comment in Sturm's presence, but Hitler had surrounded himself with fanatical anti-Semites. These included the late and unlamented Ernst Rohm, head of the SA, the Nazis' private army of two million Storm Troopers whose murder a few months ago Hitler had personally ordered along with several hundred other enemies both inside and outside the Nazi Party. Other anti-Semites included Heinrich Himmler head of the SS, Hitler's elite, black-clad bodyguard who had carried out the murders and the Nazi propaganda chief, Joseph Goebbels. All this had given Sturm second thoughts about Hitler as well.

Notwithstanding his reservations about the Nazis, Sturm had accepted an invitation last year to serve as a special adviser to the second most powerful man in the New Germany, Hermann Göring. His Air Ministry in the new Nazi government was in charge of both civil and military aviation and Sturm had become Göring's chief adviser on airships. Technically, the Versailles Treaty denied Germany military aircraft, but it was an instrument more honored in the breach by Germany in the 1920s. Göring was a Great War flying ace, a genuine hero who had taken over the squadron of the legendary

Manfred von Richthofen after the famed Red Baron had been killed. Like Sturm, who had commanded naval airships in the Great War, Göring had been awarded the Blue Max, Imperial Germany's highest military decoration.

Of the men Sturm knew to be close to Adolf Hitler, Göring was one of the few for whom he had some respect. In fact, Göring had played a major role last year in helping Sturm and Mattie McGary uncover a conspiracy between the SA and a prominent member of the Jewish Authority in Palestine to murder wealthy German Jews married to Gentile women and cheat them of their inheritance and line their own pockets in the process. True, Göring's motivation had been to embarrass an internal enemy, the late SA leader Ernst Rohm, rather than any sympathy for the dead Jews or their widows. Nevertheless, the five SA Storm Troopers who had castrated their Jewish victims were still dead courtesy of Bobby Sullivan. And Sullivan had been given Göring's more or less official sanction to avenge his sister, whose Jewish husband was one of those killed.

Magda was not the first, nor would she be the last wife of a high level Nazi Sturm had seduced either on his own or at Göring's suggestion. Sturm had another motive for seducing the wives of high-ranking Nazis, one that, had he known, Göring would not approve. In the summer of 1932, in the wake of rescuing kidnapped American twins from captivity at an SS medical clinic, Sturm had been persuaded by the out-of-office English statesman, Winston Churchill, to serve as a member of the informal intelligence network he had assembled throughout Europe. Mattie McGary was the go-between for his reports to Churchill. Sturm didn't think that this made him a spy for the English because Churchill was only a member of Parliament and held no position in the British government. Moreover, Churchill had made clear that Sturm was a free agent who would only tell the Englishman what the Nazis were doing when he, as a German patriot, thought their schemes were not in his country's best interests. Like the SS using kidnapped American twins as human guinea pigs in 1932 or Goebbels coming up with a fake Hitler assassination plot in 1933 as a pretext for banning the Communist and Social Democrat parties and imprisoning their leaders. German rearmament in violation of the

Treaty of Versailles? Never. Sturm made it clear to Churchill that it was off-limits as were any efforts Germany made to reclaim lands taken from it by the same treaty. While Sturm was persuaded that he remained a true German patriot because of this and the fact he received no money from Churchill, he knew that Göring would not agree. Nor would Hitler who still thought that Sturm, the man who had saved his life last year, could do no wrong.

Sturm was no stranger to saving lives. In that summer of 1932, he had saved the life of an American, the very blonde and very beautiful Ingrid Johansson, when her then-husband, Wesley Waterman, III, had taken out a contract to have her killed before she took half of his assets in a messy divorce proceeding. In the process, the two had fallen in love. What Ingrid didn't know was that Sturm had killed Waterman himself because he thought that was the only way to keep her husband from taking out another contract to kill her. Ingrid thus inherited her late husband's considerable holdings in I.C.E.—International Calculating Equipment. Now with a net worth in the low eight figures, she promptly liquidated her stake in I.C.E. and purchased Freedom House Publishers, which she quickly turned into one of the world's leading anti-Fascist, anti-Nazi publishing companies. Prior to being recruited by Churchill, Sturm was on the verge of resigning from the Nazi Party and proposing marriage to Ingrid. Once he agreed to work for Churchill, however, he did not resign. Rather, he and Ingrid had become secretly engaged until such time as Churchill no longer needed him, which meant until the Nazis were no longer in power. It promised to be a long engagement.

Sturm's work for Churchill had Ingrid's enthusiastic approval right down to Sturm seducing the wives of high-ranking Nazis whenever it was required. When Sturm first had tentatively broached the subject, her reply had been along the lines of 'If it hurts the goddamned Nazis and helps you find information for the good guys, I don't give a damn how many of their wives you screw. The more the merrier.' They had otherwise promised to be true to one another and it had helped that, whenever the *Graf Bismarck* made one of its regular flights to America, Ingrid would join him in the *Deutsche Zeppelin Reederei* company's suite at the Plaza hotel for the duration of his layover that, depending on the weather, could last anywhere from two days to a week or longer. When it was longer than two days, they frequently dined with their good friends Mattie McGary and Bourke Cockran.

STURM COMPLETED his search of Goebbels study and found no sign of the diaries. As he had in the other two houses, he then searched the rest of the rooms in the house from attic to basement with no luck. After that, he returned to the study to see what else he could find. In the far corner of the book-lined study with two windows overlooking the Havel River, he saw a four-drawer wooden filing cabinet. The top drawer was labeled 'UFA/Riefenstahl', the second '*Reich* Chamber of Culture', the third 'League of Nations' and the fourth 'Commission on Criminal Law Reform'.

The first two drawers made sense to Sturm as they were within Goebbels' jurisdiction. So did the third as Hitler had sent Goebbels to Geneva a year ago to one of the League's plenary sessions where he had behaved himself and spread the party line that Hitler—and therefore Germany—had only peaceful intentions. Nevertheless, Sturm carefully went through all the files in the first three drawers, but found nothing that would be of interest to Göring.

The fourth drawer was curious. Why did the Propaganda Minister have a file drawer on Criminal Law Reform? That was within the exclusive purview of the Ministry of Justice and *Unser* Hermann might well ask the same question. Sturm decided to take special care in reviewing these files. As he leafed through the files, the first folder that caught his eye was 'The Prussian Memorandum' because Göring was Prime Minister of Prussia, Germany's largest state. Inside the folder, he was surprised to find versions of the memorandum in both English and German. That was curious, but Sturm, while fluent in English, found it faster to read in German. He was mildly surprised to find that so many American states had laws prohibiting marriage or sexual relations between Whites and Orientals, Blacks and other non-Whites. The implication of this to Sturm was clear. The damned Nazis were about to do to Jews what the Americans had already done to their minorities. Would *Unser* Hermann be interested in this? He bloody well would!

Sturm placed each page of the Memorandum in bright sunlight and took photographs with the miniature MiniFlex 16 mm camera that Mattie had recommended he purchase for this purpose. No longer than his index finder, it took high-quality 13x16 mm images lengthwise across the width of the film. The Memorandum was 20-pages-long and he took ten minutes to finish the job. Then, he went back to the file cabinet and struck gold! Two for one! Correspondence between Himmler and Goebbels!

There were a total of five letters, three from Goebbels to Himmler, two from Himmler to him. Sturm looked at his watch. Magda would be awake soon, so he quickly took photographs of all five letters without reading them. After photographing the fifth letter, however, the first sentence caught his eye and he began to read.

> *31 July 1933*
>
> *Dear Heinrich,*
>
> *I am pleased that you, Freisler and I are agreed on three matters to be considered by the new Commission on Criminal Law Reform.*
>
> *First, we are agreed that the SS engage the American MID to locate American lawyers who can perform for us the necessary legal research in American state laws that we can use as a model for stripping Jews of their German citizenship status and forbidding them to marry or have sexual relations with Ayrans.*
>
> *Second, at a minimum, we are agreed upon a definition of who is a Jew, i.e., anyone who has even one great grandparent who was a Jew must be classified as a Jew. Moreover, I am confident that research into American laws will support an even stricter definition of a Jew that will allow us to go back several more generations.*

Third, we are also agreed that sexual relations between Jews and Aryans, inside or outside of marriage, must be subject to criminal punishment. Personally I favor two years hard labor for Jews and Jewesses and something less for the Aryans involved, perhaps six months? Your suggestion that Jews and Jewesses be allowed to choose between prison or castration for men and sterilization for women has much to commend it so long as the Protestant and Catholic bishops do not protest too loudly.

Finally, this will confirm my oral promise to you when last we met that the Propaganda Ministry will pay for half of the costs of the American legal research out of its special contingency accounts.

Heil Hitler!

As ever,
/s/ Joseph

cc: State Secretary Roland Freisler

After he finished reading the letter, Sturm went back and looked at the other four letters. Freisler had been copied on all of them. Interesting. The Chairman of the Commission was in it up to his neck with Goebbels and Himmler. Sturm smiled, recalling what Hitler had said to him after the publication of Goebbels diaries earlier in the year. "Take my advice, Kurt, and never keep a diary like our Joseph. In fact, never put in writing what you can say to someone face-to-face," Hitler had said. "I did this both before and after I became Chancellor. It gives you maximum flexibility when something goes wrong and they claim they were just following my orders. Hah! I laugh in their face and tell them they obviously misunderstood what I said because the *Fuhrer* doesn't make mistakes. 'Pay closer attention next time!' I order them."

Yes, Sturm thought, if Hitler had given that advice to Goebbels, the dwarf should have followed it. *Unser* Hermann was going to be most interested in what Goebbels and Himmler had been up to with the Americans, not to mention State Secretary Roland Freisler.

8

Wouldn't *That* Be Nice?

Slieve League
County Donegal, Ireland
Thursday, 6 September 1934

IT WAS a beautiful late summer morning as Mattie walked onto the terrace carrying a pot of Irish Breakfast tea to the small work table where she had placed her *Imperial 'Good Companion'* portable typewriter. Beside it were photographs she had developed earlier that morning of O'Duffy in his crisp Blue Shirt uniform standing behind his desk and his two henchmen perspiring heavily in their sweat-stained Blue Shirts, sleeves rolled up to their forearms, as they changed Mattie's tire. Mattie smiled at the memory as she sat down and began to type her notes from the O'Duffy interview. Perhaps, she thought with a wicked grin, she should send the photos of Slim and Shorty to O'Duffy along with a thank-you note for their kind assistance.

Mattie had been working for several hours when she heard the telephone ring. That must be Winston returning my call, she thought, as she rose and walked inside. She had been surprised that he was not in when she called him that morning after developing her photographs. Out for a morning ride on horseback with his daughter Mary, Mrs. P had informed her.

"Mattie McGary," she said into the receiver.

"Please hold for Mr. Churchill," Mrs. P said.

"Mattie. How have you been?"

"Just fine, Winston. And you?'

"Couldn't be better. Staying out of trouble on your holiday in Ireland?"

Mattie chuckled. "Not exactly a holiday. I've been working on that story I told you about on fascist parties in European countries other than Germany and Italy. And not exactly staying out of trouble, either." Mattie then went on to fill him in on her interview with O'Duffy and the aftermath with the two Blue Shirt goons he had sent to follow and teach her a lesson.

"Well, my dear Mattie," Churchill said when she had finished, "I daresay the Blue Shirts have learned their lesson."

"What's that?"

Churchill chuckled. "Never cross swords with a Highlander, especially their women."

Mattie laughed. Churchill never missed a chance to remind her of the ferocity of the Scots. "You got that right. So why have you called?"

"I received a visit yesterday from Dr. Georg von Dohnanyi of the German Ministry of Justice and a member of the German Commission on Criminal Law Reform. He had an interesting story to tell and I think it is one in which you and Mr. Hearst might have an interest. It seems the Nazis are contemplating laws to render German Jews second class citizens and forbid marriage or sexual relations between Jews and Aryans."

Mattie interrupted. This was definitely *not* a story that would interest her or Hearst and if she didn't stop him now, Winston's monologue would go on for who knows how long. "No, Winston, I'm not surprised that the Nazis are contemplating this, but their anti-Semitism is well known and hardly front page news."

"Ah, but what if the Nazis were basing their anti-Semitic laws on American state laws prohibiting marriage and sexual relations between whites and other races?"

"Really? I didn't know that about American laws, but that still doesn't seem like a big story."

"There's more." Churchill said. "All the legal research was done in America by Americans whom the SS retained for that purpose. It's all there in something Dohnanyi called the 'Prussian Memorandum'."

Okay, Mattie thought, now it *was* getting interesting. Not interesting enough for a story. Not yet, but it was worth finding out more. "Who were the Americans?"

"Dohnanyi doesn't know. He asked, but the SS man on the Commission who is its Chairman refused to say. There must be a reason why they're keeping the identity of the Americans secret and that, I daresay, could be a big story."

"Alright, Winston, this might be worth looking into. Tell me what you learned from this guy."

Churchill did and by the time he finished, Mattie still was not persuaded the story was worth pitching to Hearst unless, of course, Winston had already done so. It was his typical approach. He would talk to Hearst about a story, get him on board and then hint to her that it would be right up her alley.

"Have you talked to W.R. about this?" she asked.

"No. I thought it would be better if it came from you after you've read this Prussian Memorandum. How soon can you come to Chartwell? You really must read the Memorandum."

"Yes, I agree, but I'm in the middle of finishing that story on fascist parties in Europe. I've spent two months on it and I know he'll want me to do that first. For all I know, he may already have a new story for me to investigate. I'll place a call to the Chief tomorrow; tell him what you've told me; and see if it's okay for me to check it out. I may have to go to Germany to find out the identities of the Americans the SS hired to do this. I'll let you know what he says."

"Excellent, my dear. Thanks very much."

Mattie walked from the living room back into the kitchen, poured a glass of *Pinot Grigio,* made a small Caesar salad and took them back onto the terrace. As she ate, she pondered what she had learned from her godfather and what it meant for her. She couldn't reject the story out of hand. At least she couldn't until she reviewed this 'Prussian Memorandum'. Winston was right that it seemed odd that the Nazi chairman of the Commission was keeping secret the identities of the

Americans who had done the research, but how could she discover who they were and why the secrecy? Would Sturm know? Or could he find out? Would that SS puppy dog Walter Schellenberg—who looked after her safety when she was in Germany earlier this year year working on her Great War trading with the enemy exposé—know? Or find out?

Even if either man could, she still would have to decide whether it was worth her time in two weeks to travel to Amsterdam with Winston to receive and review a transcript of the German Commission's meeting on 5 June. She would also have to decide whether a trip to Germany was necessary in the interim to interview the more moderate members of the German Commission and see if any of them knew the identity of the Americans who the SS had hired.

It was ironic, she thought, that the Nazis and Adolf Hitler had made her reputation as a journalist. From her coverage of the Munich Beer Hall *Putsch* in 1923 to her exclusive interview with Hitler in July of this year about the 'Night of the Long Knives' on 30 June where Hitler's SS had rounded up and executed over 200 of his political enemies, her stories about the Nazis had brought her several Pulitzer Prizes. The irony was that she loathed the Nazis and all they stood for, yet that interview last July with Hitler where he justified his bloody purge had restored her reputation, in Germany at least, as 'Hitler's favorite foreign journalist'. One reason she was intrigued by the story Winston proposed was that if the 'Prussian Memorandum' was sufficiently embarrassing to the Nazis, she might well fall out of favor with Hitler. If she did, then maybe Hearst would not call on her to cover new stories in or about Germany. She took a sip of wine and smiled. Wouldn't *that* be nice?

9

Bobby Sullivan

The National Arts Club
15 Gramercy Park South
New York City
Thursday, 6 September 1934

BOURKE COCKRAN sat at a corner of the dark wooden bar looking out on the Dining Room of the National Arts Club as he sipped a dry Plymouth martini while waiting for Bobby Sullivan to arrive. A Tiffany stained glass chandelier hung over the bar and the Dining Room beyond had a multi-colored stained glass ceiling and a brass chandelier hanging from its center. Illuminated oil portraits and glass-fronted bookcases lined the polished mahogany walls.

The National Arts Club was founded in 1898 and its early members included Theodore Roosevelt and Mark Twain. Woodrow Wilson—who Cockran despised for his racist views and his dismal record on civil liberties—had also been a member, but Cockran had not held it against the club. It was one of the few private New York clubs that had admitted women from the outset. In fact, in recognition of her accomplishments as a photojournalist, his wife Mattie became a member in 1926, before they first met in the summer of 1929. Cockran had not joined until 1928, but his and Mattie's paths had never crossed in the club.

It was only 6:45 p.m. and Cockran was uncharacteristically early, having told Bobby to meet him here for dinner at 7 p.m. He knew Sullivan would be on time because during June, while the two of them were in Germany arranging to ransom three Jews and two Social Democrats from an SS concentration camp, his widowed sister Mary had sublet the Upper East Side apartment on Park Avenue where she and Bobby lived. Then she had taken out a lease on the entire top floor of a four bedroom, two-and-a-half bath penthouse at 7 Gramercy Park West, a new apartment building that had opened in 1930.

Sullivan had not been reachable when his sister was making this change in their living arrangements and she had presented him with a *fait accompli* upon his return to New York from Germany. He had no real objection because, prior to his sister coming to live with him after her Jewish husband had been brutally murdered last year by Nazi Storm Troopers, he had lived in a walk-up cold water flat in Hell's Kitchen on the West Side. When he asked why she had moved their abode, her answer had been plain and straight to the point.

"I didn't like our neighbors always looking down their noses at me," Mary had said. "And there wasn't any real sense of a neighborhood. It was just a concrete canyon of apartment buildings and no real interaction with your neighbors even if you ran across them during a walk in Central Park. A friend of mine at the settlement house where I work in Greenwich Village lives on Gramercy Park. She invited me to a luncheon one Saturday and took me into the beautiful little private park right in the middle of all the homes and apartment buildings. It was wonderful. It seemed like everyone knew everyone else. So I checked out the rent and found a penthouse apartment on Gramercy Park that costs less than the rent on our Park Avenue flat."

When Cockran asked him why he had new digs, Sullivan had merely shrugged. "Nothing's too good for my big sister. Besides, what else am I going to do with me money?"

Cockran knew Sullivan wouldn't be late because his new flat on West Gramercy was, at best, a two-minute walk from the club on South Gramercy. And, at 6:55 p.m. Sullivan arrived in his standard dress-up outfit, a tan Irish tweed jacket, brown corduroy trousers and a cream colored Irish fisherman's sweater knitted by his sister. A little over six feet tall, Sullivan had curly black hair, cold blue eyes and a nose that had been broken more than once. As a teenager, he had been the most feared assassin in the Irish rebel leader Michael Collins' squad of 'Apostles' during the 1919-1921 Anglo-Irish War. Sullivan had killed ten men before he was 19.

Sullivan had visited America in 1929 at the behest of Winston Churchill where, along with Cockran and five of the former Apostles, they had foiled an IRA plot to stage a *coup d'etat* in the Irish Free State by destroying a huge arms shipment assembled in Long Beach California. After that, he decided to stay in America and, as a result, the two became friends. Cockran helped Sullivan become a licensed private investigator in the State of New York where he earned a decent living. Cockran strongly suspected, however, that Sullivan's income as a private investigator was not sufficient to afford either an apartment on Park Avenue or Gramercy Park. Rather, he knew from hints dropped by Sullivan that he was tight with the Irish mob—the 'Westies'—led by Owney Madden that controlled all the rackets on New York's West Side and that he performed occasional jobs for the Westies when someone needed to be taught a lesson or the Irish mob needed payback to be administered or when Owney hired Sullivan out to third parties who required the services of a professional hit man.

"Another martini and a Jameson on the rocks," Cockran said to the bartender as he rose and shook hands with Sullivan. "Did you talk to Sean and Seamus?" Cockran asked, referring to the O'Driscoll twins, both former Apostles who Cockran had hired the year before as bodyguards for an assignment he had in Europe. They once lived in Donegal Town, less than an hour away from Cockran and Mattie's home on the Cliffs of Slieve League, and now lived in New York where they were the "associates" in the detective agency known as Sullivan & Associates.

"Aye, they jumped at the chance to make as much money as you paid them last year. But tell me more than you have. 'Solving a murder mystery' is a wee vague, wouldn't you think?"

"Actually, it's *six* murder mysteries," Cockran said with a laugh. "Let's go over to our table and we can talk more privately there."

Cockran led them over to a table in a darkened far corner of the dining room where none of the tables near them were occupied. After they took their seats, and he leaned his head close to Sullivan. "I asked the head waiter to give us as much privacy as he could for as long as possible. That and the twenty bucks I slipped him should guarantee we wouldn't be disturbed.

"Our client is Colonel Tim O'Hanlon of the U.S Army's Military Intelligence Division in Washington. I may have mentioned him to you in the past. He's an old friend and we've known each other since our days together in intelligence training. He's done Mattie and me more than one big favor in the past few years and I owe him. I had enrolled Paddy at a local school in Donegal and we had planned to spend most of the fall there while I finished my book, but then Tim called me, explained his problem and I changed my plans. Paddy and I caught the next ship to America. That's how important Tim is to us."

The two men both ordered rare strip steaks and, while they ate, Cockran told Sullivan O'Hanlon's story leading up to the deaths last December under various circumstances of the six former MID agents with law degrees whose names Tim had supplied to the head of MID.

"So what's your plan for solving these mysteries?" Sullivan asked.

"Well, there are six deaths to investigate and our first order of business is to find out why MID had Tim do all this research. One thing they have in common is they're all lawyers. Another thing is that Tim put their name on a list for some unspecified project about which his boss told Tim he didn't have a need to know. Well, now we have a need to know because whatever they were working on is a third thing they have in common. I figured you and I would check out three of the names, including the two who were Tim's close friends. We'd give the other three names to Sean and Seamus."

"Okay. Sounds good to me," Sullivan said. "When do we begin?"

"When will the O'Driscolls arrive from their holiday in California?"

"They caught a train today. They'll be here Saturday. I'm not sure when."

"We'll brief them after they arrive," Cockran replied, "and then head out on a night train Monday."

"Where will we be going first?"

Cockran reached inside his suit coat and handed a folded sheet of paper to Sullivan. "Those are the names and addresses of the six men."

Sullivan took the sheet, unfolded it and scanned its contents. He looked up at Cockran, his face suddenly pale. "We need to leave. *Now.* Let's go back to my flat for a nightcap and I'll explain everything."

"Why? I don't understand?"

"You will. I've seen all these names before."

7 Gramercy Park West
New York City
Thursday, 6 September 1934

COCKRAN HAD not been to Sullivan's new flat and he was impressed by his sister's good taste. They were sitting in the book-lined library and he wondered if it was Mary or Bobby who had decorated the room. The walnut bookshelves were built in; and brass sconces provided the light. There was a small desk and two green leather club chairs that resembled the ones Cockran had in his office.

Sullivan fixed them both Jameson on the rocks. He had not spoken a word since they left the club. He placed his hands on his knees and looked at Cockran.

"Would I be correct in thinking that in America, whatever you tell your lawyer is confidential, just like a priest?"

"Yes," Cockran replied, "it's called the attorney-client privilege."

"Good, because I want you to be my lawyer for the rest of this conversation," Sullivan said and put a $20 bill on the table between them.

"You don't need to do that. If I agree to be your lawyer, money doesn't need to change hands."

Sullivan waved his hand. "Keep it. Consider it my contribution to our dinner and drinks tonight. Now, you know that I occasionally do work for Owney Madden?"

Cockran nodded.

"I've never told you what that work entails, but it generally involves ending the lives of people Owney wants ended. Owney pays well for that, but I don't take every job he offers. He must tell me what the target has done and why he deserves to die. If it's another gangster, I generally have no problem. They're all scum, Owney included. I probably turn down more jobs from him than I accept, especially when the target is not a gangster. Do you remember the murder in broad daylight last year of Heinz Spanknobel? He was the head of the Friends of New Germany."

"Yes, I do," Cockran said a took a sip of his drink. "It was front page news and I don't think the cops ever found out who did it."

"Aye that's true. Do you know why he was killed?" Sullivan asked.

Cockran shook his head 'no'.

"The Nazi bastard had ordered two of his thugs to rob the Hell's Kitchen branch of the American Union Bank. That was a mistake because American Union was paying protection money to Owney to make sure something like that never happened. Owney explained all this and hired me to send a message to the Friends of New Germany not to do that again. I did. I used a baseball bat to kill the two thugs and my Colt .45 on *Herr* Spanknobel."

Cockran assumed this had something to do with Sullivan having seen all the names of the former MID agents before. Truth be told, what Bobby had just said didn't surprise him, but now was not the time to interrupt and begin cross-examining his friend.

"I told you I've seen all those names before. At the Cotton Club in Harlem last November on a sheet of paper Owney Madden showed me. There were six names and addresses and he said I had thirty days to take them out. The fee was 60 G's, 30 up front and 30 after the assignment is complete. Minus Owney's 10% of course."

Sullivan paused, took a sip of whiskey and continued.

"Unlike before, Owney wouldn't tell me why the targets had been chosen or what they had done. He said he didn't know. Said all he knew was that he'd accepted work from the client before when he was with the government and that all the guy told him was that the targets posed a threat to national security."

"Did Owney say just what this threat to national security was?" Cockran asked.

"Nope. Said he didn't ask and didn't care. All he cared about was that the man had always paid on time."

"So the man's no longer with the government?"

"Yep. That's what Owney said. I told him I was going to pass on this one. You know I'm happy to kill people, but only if in my opinion they need killing. For that, I want more facts than what Owney was giving me. Six people? National security? That sounded like a conspiracy. Spies even. If so, why didn't the client just say that? This one just didn't smell right."

Cockran thought about this. A former government man ordering hit jobs on six former MID agents. Would it help to know who that man was? He didn't think so. Even if they did know and confronted him, it's unlikely he would disclose the reason for the hit jobs without torture. While he knew Sullivan wouldn't agree, Cockran's experience watching others use torture with interrogation rarely resulted in accurate information.

"I know who probably did the work," Sullivan said.

"Who?"

Owney told me he was going to offer it to Nicholas Carson. 'Nick the Killer' is not picky about who he kills."

"Who is this Nicholas Carson?" Cockran asked.

"A trigger man for the Black and Tans during our war with the English. He was high on Mick's list," Sullivan said, referring to Michael Collins. "I just missed him on Bloody Sunday, and he just missed me a few weeks later. He free lances for Owney now and I suspect his assignments are either the ones I turn down or the ones Owney knows I wouldn't accept."

"This is useful, Bobby, because it gives us a place to begin. Clearly, the victims were all working on a project either involving the government or impacting it in some way. We need to interview their wives, friends and colleagues to see what, if anything, they said to anyone about their work. Other than the identity of the man who hired him, do you think Owney knows more than he's telling you?"

Sullivan took a sip of his drink and paused as if gathering his thoughts. "He might, but I don't think so. If the money is good, Owney's not too fussy about who he takes out. He only draws the line when it comes to law enforcement and even then, he'll make an exception if it's a dirty copper who didn't stay bought. Still, I could ask him if you want. It's been almost a year since I turned down the assignment and Owney knows he needs to stay on my good side."

Cockran shook his head. "No. Don't. He might tell the client of our interest in these murders and I don't want to advertise what we're doing."

10

Hermann Göring

Karinhalle
Friedrichwalde, Germany
Thursday, 6 September 1934

STURM'S BMW roadster pulled up to the main door of Hermann Göring's country estate several hours outside Berlin. A servant was there to open the motorcar's door. As Sturm stepped out, he reached into the space behind the driver's seat to retrieve his briefcase containing the photographs he had taken the day before at Goebbels' lakeside villa. When he turned back toward the house, *Unser* Hermann was there to greet him in full Air Minister mode, a pale blue *Luftwaffe* uniform with a wide dark blue vertical stripe down his trousers that were tucked into polished black leather knee high boots. You could never predict, Sturm thought, how the man would be dressed. The last time Sturm had seen Göring at *Karinhalle*, he was decked out as a country squire in a double-breasted brown tweed jacket with a velvet collar over matching tweed plus-fours and light tan knee high socks, topped off by a snap-brimmed hat with a colorful feather jutting up from the hatband.

"Kurt!" Göring boomed as he grasped Sturm's hand and pulled him into a bear hug. "So good to see you. Thanks for coming all this way. I arrived less than an hour ago from Berlin and I haven't had the opportunity to change into more comfortable clothes. I wanted to start the weekend early or I would have met you at the *Reichspresident's* Official Residence. Come, let's go to my study and let me see what treasures you've brought me from the crippled dwarf."

Göring and Sturm walked into the house through the foyer and into the Great Hall. It ran the entire length of the front of the house with a high, peaked cathedral ceiling, eight massive wooden beams between which were hung three equally massive chandeliers. Enormous open fireplaces, eight feet high, were at each end of the room. Maroon leather armchairs lined the walls and conversational groupings of chintz-covered chairs and sofas were spaced throughout the room. Deer heads and antlers hung above each window that looked out on the courtyard while tapestries lined the wall opposite.

"So, tell me Kurt, is the fair Magda keeping at least your, ah, spirits up, if nothing more?" Göring asked with a laugh."

"It is not the most unpleasant assignment you have given me, *Herr Reichsminister,*" Sturm replied.

Göring laughed again. They reached his study through a large dining room with a vaulted mahogany ceiling and a long polished walnut table seating twenty. In contrast, his study was far more modest. His desk was a comparatively small, five-foot wide worktable with two small lamps at either end. Behind it was a leather desk chair and Göring settled his large frame into it. Above and behind him was the room's only decoration, a large, framed portrait of a beautiful, blonde-haired woman, Göring's late wife, Karin.

Göring gestured for Sturm to sit in one of the two armchairs in front of his desk. "Now, let's see what you've got."

Sturm unfastened the straps on his briefcase, reached inside, pulled out a file folder of photographs and slid them across the desk to Göring. "The first five photographs are correspondence between Goebbels and Himmler concerning the Commission on Criminal Law Reform created last year. The next 20 photographs are a translation into German of something called the 'Prussian Memorandum' which consists of legal research into American laws that the SS and Propaganda Ministry paid American Military Intelligence to conduct."

"*Prussian*, you say? Why haven't I heard of this before? After all, I'm the *Prime Minister* of Prussia!"

Sturm watched as Göring spent the next half hour carefully reading each photographed page, occasionally scowling. Finally, he finished and looked up at Sturm.

"Goebbels and Himmler are fucking idiots!" he said, loudly slapping his desk with a big hand. "They see a Jew under every bed. Incredible! Imagine going back four or five generations to find a single Jew in the woodpile! For God's sake, Jews have been here in Germany for centuries! Many of them converted to Christianity and changed their names. Who knows how many Jews there would be using that definition? It might make over half of Germany into Jews!"

Göring closed the file folder, opened a drawer on the side of his desk and placed it inside. "Don't get me wrong. Now that we've forbidden random violence against the Jews by the SA and others, we need new laws that put the Jew in his place because…"

Sturm was not conscious of doing so, but he must have frowned or otherwise silently telegraphed his disapproval because Göring promptly stopped in mid-sentence.

"Yes, yes, I know you don't approve, Kurt, but I'm President of the *Reichstag* and you're not. As I was saying, we need these laws because we need more scapegoats. Now that we've exiled or put in camps all the prominent Social Democrats and Communists, we can't keep blaming them when bad things happen. The Jews are perfect for that."

"So why are Himmler and Goebbels idiots?" Sturm asked.

Göring laughed. "For one thing, it's because they actually believe all that crap about a world-wide Jewish conspiracy, Protocols of the Elders of Zion and the rest."

"And you don't?" Sturm asked and instantly regretted it.

"Of course not. Do you think I'm stupid, Sturm?" Göring asked with a hint of menace in his tone of voice.

"No, *Herr Reichsminister*, naturally not. What are the other reasons for those two being idiots?" Sturm asked, hoping to shift Göring away from him and back to Goebbels and Himmler, but luck was not with him.

Göring smiled. "Good, because I know you're not stupid either. What do you think the other reasons are?"

When in doubt, Sturm thought, tell the truth. It was, after all, why he had joined the party eleven years earlier. "I don't see how new laws targeting the Jews will put Germans back to work, rebuild our armed forces, repudiate the Versailles Treaty and regain German lands taken from us by that treaty."

Göring clapped his hands. "Excellent! It's a matter of priorities and the Jews aren't one of the more important matters on our plate. The radical ideas those two idiots are proposing for defining Jews will actually hinder our achieving the goals you list. Do you know why?"

"Well," Sturm began, "I think it may…"

Göring cut him off. "It will give new ammunition and new life to that Jewish-inspired world-wide boycott of our exports that I spent so much time last year crushing. If our exports decline, unemployment will go up, foreign reserves will dwindle and rearmament will accordingly be delayed. As you well know from the other work you are doing for me, if we can't rearm as quickly as the *Fuhrer* and I wish, that means repudiating Versailles and retaking our stolen German lands will be delayed as well."

"So what can be done to stop them?" Sturm asked.

"We fight back. Thanks to you, it is clear I have not been paying proper attention to the Commission on Criminal Law Reform while Goebbels and Himmler have been paying far too much attention to something that is beyond their writ. They need to stay in their lanes. Inasmuch as I am President of the *Reichstag* and any new laws on the Jews or anything else must be approved by me and enacted by it, I am appointing you today as my personal liaison to the Commission. Introduce yourself tomorrow to Roland Freisler, the Chairman of the Commission, and have him give you access to all the records of the Commission's proceedings. Then keep me informed after that of everything the Commission is doing, including identifying all who support the ideas of those two idiots and the ones who oppose them. As I said earlier, I don't mind enacting new laws against the Jews that enable us to make them scapegoats, but it must be done in a common sense, reasonable way. That means we can't define everybody and his brother as a Jew!"

Sturm stood to take his leave, but Göring motioned him to retake his seat.

"There's one more thing. Earlier this year—I'm not sure exactly when—Schellenberg of the SD asked for a wiretap on Freisler's office telephone. As you know, I don't trust anyone who works for Heydrich, so I had one of my adjutants ask Schellenberg why he wanted the wiretap, especially since he's head of the SD's Foreign Section. He told my man that Freisler was in regular contact with foreign nationals so I gave the go-ahead. Now that we have this 'Prussian Memorandum', I can see that Schellenberg was right about Freisler's foreign contacts so, beginning today, the Brown Pages on Freisler will go to you as well as Schellenberg."

DRIVING BACK to Berlin that evening, Sturm pondered supplying Churchill with a copy of the Prussian Memorandum and the Goebbels-Himmler correspondence. He went through the pros and cons and eventually came down on the side of doing so. That issue decided, the next question was how and when to do it. Usually, he would deliver the information to Mattie McGary after completing a *Graf Bismarck* flight to America. His next scheduled flight was Thursday next, a week away. Mattie, however, would not be there. He knew she and her husband were spending the month of September at their new home in Ireland.

Perhaps, Sturm thought, it would be more expeditious to send it to Churchill directly along with a typed, unsigned note explaining its significance. That was something that he could not do from Germany. He would have to go to another country to do it and that meant Switzerland was his best bet. Well, that shouldn't be too difficult. He would take the night train from Berlin to Friedrichshafen tomorrow; inspect on Saturday the *Graf Bismarck* which was in residence there being prepared for his next voyage; take a ferry early Sunday across Lake Constance to Switzerland; mail the package to Churchill from there; return to Friedrichshafen; and take the night train on Sunday back to Berlin.

Reich Ministry of Justice
Berlin
Friday, 7 September 1934

STATE SECRETARY Roland Freisler's office was small and unimpressive, looking out onto an enclosed courtyard rather than the skyline of Berlin. Nor did Freisler cut an imposing figure. To Sturm, he seemed the model of an officious, faceless bureaucrat. He had a slender body, maybe 5'9' in height and looked to be in his mid-40s with dark brown hair wrapped in a horseshoe around the sides of a head that was nearly bald. His small dark eyes were close set with a beak of a nose sticking out over thin, humorless lips. He wore a dark suit, a tightly knotted tie and a haughty expression on his face. According to Göring, he had been a member of the Nazi Party since 1925, which meant that Sturm, who had joined in 1923 before the failed Munich *Putsch,* had more seniority in the party. He also had been a Russian prisoner during the Great War and was placed in charge of his prisoner-of-war camp by the Bolsheviks when they took over the government, giving him the title of 'Commissar', something others in Berlin called him behind his back.

Sturm wore his *Deutsche Zeppelin Reederei* airship commander's uniform of dark navy blue with gold trim which he thought to be much more stylish than the black and silver of the SS. It gave him an air of authority, which he was about to display should Freisler give him the opportunity because he didn't like that face or its haughty expression. As State Secretary of the *Reich* Ministry of Justice, Freisler presided over the Commission on Criminal Law Reform where he may have had considerable influence, but Sturm decided that he was going to establish from the outset who had the higher standing and the upper hand in their relationship.

"*Herr* Freisler, *Reichspresident* Göring has appointed me as his personal liaison to the *Reich* Commission on Criminal Law Reform," Sturm said as he pushed over Freisler's desk the letter containing his appointment signed by Göring on embossed *Reichstag* stationery. "I will require immediate access to all Commission files, including minutes, transcripts, exhibits, documents and correspondence on all the Commission's activities so that I can properly brief the *Reichspresident*."

Freisler wrinkled his nose and frowned. "Well, *Herr* von Sturm…"

Sturm stopped him in mid-sentence. "That's *Fregattenkapitan* von Sturm."

Brought up short by Sturm pulling rank, Freisler paused. "Yes, well, *Fregattenkapitan*, I'm not sure I understand why the *Reichspresident* needs a liaison to the Commission."

"You don't need to understand why. You simply need to follow orders. If you think you *need* to understand, I suggest you take it up with the *Reichspresident* directly. In my experience, he rarely explains why he is doing anything unless, of course, the *Fuhrer* asks. But be my guest. Try your luck and ask. There's a first time for everything."

Freisler visibly blanched. "What would you like to see first, *Fregattenkapitan*?"

"Correspondence. After that, transcripts of Commission meetings."

"Very well. If you will allow me several hours, *Fregattenkapitan*, I will have all the records moved to a conference room where you may examine them at your leisure."

STURM RETURNED after lunch and was given a small, windowless conference room. He groaned when he saw it contained ten four-drawer wooden file cabinets. He walked over and looked at the labels for each one until he came to the file cabinet with the caption 'Correspondence'. The Commission had been created on 1 July 1933 so there were fourteen months of correspondence to review. The files were organized by month and contained letters to and from Freisler as well as letters on which he had been copied. He pulled out the July 1933 folder, took it back to the table in the middle of the conference room and began to leaf through it.

Sturm placed the July folder back on the table and sat back. Had he made a mistake? He didn't think so. Perhaps he might have missed one letter. But five? No, he would not have missed five. Nevertheless, he reopened the folder and carefully went through it a second time, page by page, until he was satisfied. The Goebbels-Himmler correspondence on race law and the Commission on which Freisler had been copied was not there. Why was that? Should he confront Freisler and ask him? He briefly weighed the pros and cons and decided not to. It would unnecessarily tip him off that someone had intercepted the mail of Himmler, Goebbels or him.

Sturm put the July 1933 correspondence file back in the file cabinet. If that file had been cleansed of the Goebbels-Himmler correspondence, he doubted he would find anything else as incriminating in the other correspondence files. Instead, he went to the two file cabinets containing verbatim transcripts of the Commission's monthly meetings and spent the rest of the afternoon skimming through them. The Commission met on the first Monday of each month and he was surprised to find that none of the meetings concerned defining who is a Jew, 2nd class citizenship for those defined as Jews and the prohibition of marriage or sexual relations between Jews and Aryans.

The file folder labeled 'June 1934 meeting', however, was empty. This was something he could ask Freisler because at the end of each meeting, the topic for the next meeting would be announced and duly recorded by the stenographer. The May transcript clearly stated that the next meeting would be about 'Jews: Citizenship of and Marriage with Aryans'.

"The June 1934 meeting? I believe it was cancelled." Freisler said after being questioned by Sturm about the empty folder with no transcript.

"Why?" Sturm asked

"I don't recall precisely," Freisler said, steepling his fingers and looking at the ceiling as if the answer might be found there. "I don't think we were going to have a quorum. Some members were on holiday; others were ill; others were travelling on business."

"So you've had no meeting on the announced subject of the June meeting 'Jews: Citizenship of and Marriage with Aryans'.

"Not yet. I'm sure we'll get to it before year's end."

"I'm told many states in America have laws that prohibit marriage between whites and various non-whites. Do you think they will be helpful?"

Freisler laughed. "Oh my heavens, no. Some American states do have laws like that, but all of them consider Jews to be white. Can you believe it? No, America is no model for us."

Given the many lies Freisler had just told him about the Prussian Memorandum, Sturm wondered if he had lied about the cancellation of the 5 June Commission meeting. It would be easy enough to find out simply by talking to the other members of the Commission. When, later that day, Sturm reported by telephone to Göring, his reaction was immediate.

"You were right not to disclose that we have a copy of the Memorandum. We're going to give those lying bastards with their Jew-fetish enough rope so they can hang themselves," Göring said as he pounded the desk so hard that Sturm could hear it over the telephone. "We cannot allow them to stand in the path of Germany's return to one of the world's leading powers. We must continue rebuilding our economy if we ever hope to achieve military parity with France! Those idiots who want to give the Jews more ammunition to build support for their boycott of our exports are idiots! Idiots!"

"What more do you wish me to do about this *Herr Reichspresident*?" Sturm asked.

"Beginning today, the *Forschungsamt* will have a wiretap on Freisler's home as well as his office telephone lines. Apart from me, you will be the only authorized recipient of the 'Brown Pages' that result from the wiretap on his house. I want you to review both wiretaps daily and keep me informed of their contents, especially any contacts Freisler has with Goebbels or anyone else from the Propaganda Ministry and with Himmler or anyone else in the SS."

After his appointment to Göring's staff at the Air Ministry, Sturm had quickly learned that the *Forschungsamt* or FA, its literal translation being 'Research Office', was the most significant of all the many agencies under Hermann Göring's control. In a very short time, it had become Nazi Germany's most effective intelligence agency because it intercepted all international cables that crossed Germany and adjacent waters. In addition, over 500 telephones in Berlin alone were tapped, all of them approved personally by Göring who had a monopoly on wiretaps. Only the FA could install wiretaps and if any other entity such as the SS, the *Gestapo* or even the *Abwehr*—military intelligence—wanted a phone tapped, they needed Göring's written consent.

A vast army of civil servants worked on a 24-7 schedule transcribing all intercepted cables and recorded telephone conversations onto brown sheets of paper, hence 'Brown Pages'. Copies of these reports and transcripts went to the person requesting the wiretap as well as Göring himself. The Brown Pages were conveyed only in red double thickness envelopes inside locked pouches handled only by special FA couriers and signed for in triplicate by authorized recipients. Recipients, regardless of rank, had to return each and every Brown Page intact to the FA.

"Excellent. I will visit *Schillerstrasse* at the end of each day," Sturm said, referring to the four granite-faced, three-story high, turn-of-the-century apartment buildings in Berlin's *Charlottenburg* district that housed the FA offices.

"Good man," Goring said. "Give Magda my personal regards. Tell her I said she is far too beautiful for that ugly little dwarf and that she should divorce him and marry you!"

11

When I'm Bad, I'm Better

Department of War
Munitions Building
Constitution Avenue, N.W.
Washington, D.C.
Friday, 7 September 1934

MAJOR GENERAL Leonard Marlborough looked white as a ghost, Harry Canfield thought as he entered the large corner office of MID's commanding officer who sat at a desk behind which were three windows commanding a view of the Capital Building in the distance.

"Sorry I couldn't make it over here sooner Leo," Canfield said, "but with Ralph in Europe, I've got my hands full at RVD. So, what's the problem?"

"Colonel Timothy O'Hanlon, one of my top aides, is the problem," Marlborough replied and stubbed out his cigarette in the large glass ashtray at the right side of his desk. "He's too much of a straight arrow. I've never kept him in the loop over our projects with the SS for that reason. On Tuesday, he asked me for three days of personal leave. I asked him where he would be and he told me was going to do some fishing at the Maryland shore through the weekend. Yet, on Wednesday, I passed the desk outside his office and overheard his secretary tell someone on the phone that they could reach O'Hanlon at the Waldorf-Astoria in New York. That seemed strange, so I sent an agent from our New York office to tail him and give me a report on where he went and whom he met. When he did, my suspicions increased because he had dinner at The 21 Club on Wednesday evening with Bourke Cockran and then spent all Thursday morning at Wild Bill Donovan's law firm where Cockran is a partner."

"Why is that suspicious?" Canfield asked.

"Cockran is a former MID agent who resigned in the early 1920s over Ted Hudson's interrogation of a Bolshevik baker. Ted sliced his ear off, stuffed it into the little Jew's mouth and told him to call if he heard anything," Marlborough said and lit up another cigarette.

Canfield laughed. "I remember Ted telling me that story at one Thanksgiving. Still, why is O'Hanlon meeting Cockran suspicious?"

"For the past two years, Cockran's been a thorn in MID's side. He messed up that operation we had going with the SS in 1932 where we provided them with American twins for some Eugenics study the Krauts were conducting in Bavaria. He did the same last year on a special assignment we had from FDR to shut down that anti-German boycott the Jews were organizing to stop German exports. So, once I was told that O'Hanlon's reservation at the Waldorf extended through Thursday night, I had our New York man get a wiretap warrant on O'Hanlon from a friendly judge and he served it on the Waldorf's manager late yesterday afternoon. We've made recordings since then of all his phone call. Here," Marlborough said as he pushed several sheets of paper across his desk, "is the transcript of a telephone call between him and his wife last night."

Canfield picked up the sheets and began to read.

O = *Timothy O'Hanlon W = Wife Cynthia.*
10:15 p.m. 6 September 1934

O: Hi, Sweetie, how was your day?

W: Well, for starters, your son and namesake is a holy terror. Otherwise, it was a good day. How did things go with Bourke? Is he going to help find out who killed Joe and Hank? We owe it to Alice and Doris. It's so horrible that both couples were in our wedding.

O: Yes, he agreed, both Joe and Hank as well as the other four agents. His firm's Managing Partner is Wild Bill Donovan and he approved taking on the case this morning. Bourke will handle it personally along with a team of private investigators. The lead investigator is Robert Sullivan who Bourke knew from Ireland. They've worked on a number of cases together and Bourke said he's the best. There are two other investigators, brothers and also originally from Ireland. It's funny, he didn't say why, but Donovan called them 'The Angel of Death' and 'the Twins of Doom'. I asked Bourke about it afterwards, but he said Donovan just had a strange sense of humor.

W: When will you be home?

O: In time for lunch. Then, as soon as Timmy is home from school, we'll go fishing on Chesapeake Bay like I told Leo we were.

W: Sounds great. I'll see you then. I love you.

O: Love you, too. Kiss Timmy goodnight for me.

W: Will do. Bye

O: Bye.

Well, well, Harry thought, Joseph Carmody and Henry Sandler had been buddies with this O'Hanlon. "How did O'Hanlon know about the other four agents?"

"I'm not sure, but it was O'Hanlon who gave me the list of twelve lawyers to send on to Dean Pound who selected the six we eventually used," Marlborough replied, nervously inhaling and then blowing smoke before stubbing his cigarette out and lighting another.

"Wait a minute," Canfield said, shaking his head in disbelief. "You just said you never kept O'Hanlon in the loop over our projects with the SS. Yet he's the one who selected the lawyers for the research the SS wanted done?"

"Uh…" Marlborough said and hesitated. "Well…he wasn't in the loop. Not really. He had no idea why I wanted him to pick twelve lawyers. I just told him that since he went to Harvard Law, he was better qualified than me to pick the twelve best lawyers."

Canfield shook his head again in disbelief. He hoped America's enemies didn't know what a buffoon it had running Military Intelligence. Now, Marlborough wanted Harry to pull his chestnuts out of the fire for him just as he had done last year by hiring Owney Madden to take care of the six lawyers. He would do it, of course, but first he was going to make this fool jump through several hoops.

"Okay, so this O'Hanlon has hired a big New York law firm to investigate the murders of those lawyers. So what?" Canfield asked.

"None of this can ever come out in public. FDR made it clear—or at least Louie Howe did on his behalf—that those six lawyers were loose ends that needed to be tied up. Permanently. That's why we agreed to have you engage that New York gangster, uh…"

"Owney Madden."

"Yes, him, to take care of them," Marlborough concluded.

"Which he did. Six different deaths, no two alike. What makes you think this Cockran is going to be able to find anything?"

"I don't know. Even if he doesn't find out who the killers were, he might discover what kind of work the lawyers were doing. I just know that FDR will have my head on a silver platter if it ever gets out we were doing this kind of legal research for the Nazis. I can't take that chance."

Marlborough opened a side drawer in his desk and pulled out a bottle of Cutty Sark whisky and two short glasses. "I know it's only 3 p.m., but the sun should be over the yardarm somewhere in the world and I need a drink. Care to join me?"

Canfield declined and watched as Marlborough poured three fingers of Scotch into the glass and took a healthy gulp. "So, what do you think we should do?"

Oh no, Harry thought, you don't get off that easily. "No, what do *you* think we should do?"

"Do you suppose Madden would be willing to accept another job, say taking care of Cockran, his lead investigator Sullivan and possibly even O'Hanlon? You know, cutting off the head of the snake, so to speak?" Marlborough asked a he took a swallow of whisky and lit another cigarette.

"For the right price, I imagine Owney would agree to have most anyone killed, but it's going to cost more this time than $10K per head once I tell him the connection between these three and the six earlier hits. Probably $15K. Is there enough in your black accounts to cover that?"

Marlborough downed the rest of his drink. "Sure."

"Okay. Good. Now have your New York man go back to that same judge and get wiretap warrants on Cockran's residences. I know from my late cousin Ted that he has a townhouse on Fifth Avenue and I'm fairly sure he has a country home somewhere. Once your man finds the actual addresses, have him drop those off at RVD's Manhattan's office. I'll have some of my RVD guys plant recording devices inside both places tonight. Meanwhile, arrange for a black bag wiretap on O'Hanlon's home and office phones. Keep me posted on anything new you learn."

After receiving Marlborough's assurances he would get right on it, Canfield left. In the lobby of the Munitions Building, he stopped at the row of telephone booths. He entered the last one on the right, after making sure the booth next to it was empty. He called The Cotton Club in New York and asked to be put through to Owney Madden's secretary, Ruth Johnson. He was surprised, therefore, to be greeted by a throaty voice that definitely was not Ruth.

"Mr. Madden's office," Mae West answered.

"Mae? Is that you? This is Harry Canfield. Why are you answering Owney's phone?"

Mae West chuckled. "Well, Harry my love, he *is* backing my new Broadway play and when the telephone woke us both up at 6:00 a.m., we learned that poor Ruth was in the hospital from an auto accident she was in last night. Owney couldn't make arrangements for a substitute on such short notice, so I volunteered to take her place for a day. Hell, I'll try anything once, twice if I like it, three times to make sure."

Canfield chuckled. "Is Owney in?"

"No, He's not in today. He told me he would be in by mid-afternoon tomorrow."

"Can you squeeze me in to see him tomorrow evening? Half an hour, tops."

"Why not? How about 9 p.m.?"

"Sure. Say, who's the headliner this week?"

"Billie Holiday."

"Great. Reserve my usual table and have her sent over once her set is finished."

"Billie Holiday? *Her*? Really? You can do a lot better than that Harry. I'm in the penthouse at the Waldorf. After you see Owney tomorrow, why don't you come up and see me?"

"Why Mae, are you propositioning me? I'm shocked," Canfield replied.

"Honey, those who are easily shocked should be shocked more often. Speaking of which, how did your wife take to those two new tricks I showed you in Beverly Hills in May?"

"Camilla thought the first was fine, but the second not so much. She's getting used to it, though. She still squeals, of course, just not as loud as that first time."

Mae laughed. "Harry, you're a bad man and I'm a good woman for a bad man. How about ten o'clock tomorrow night? I'll show you something I guarantee both you and Camilla will love. You know me. When I'm good, I'm very, very good, but when I'm bad, I'm better."

Canfield laughed. "Of course you are. See you at ten."

As Canfield walked out of the Munitions Building and began a walk back to RVD's Washington offices, he reflected on the fact that it was that fool Marlborough who had caused this new problem by involving O'Hanlon in selecting the lawyers to do the legal research for the SS. There was no similar problem with the two FBI agents whose folders Louis Howe had given him last year at the White House. That's because Harry handled those two personally. One look at their personnel folders told him all he needed to know. Both were fucking Boy Scouts and both had to die.

Just because gangsters like Owney and other mob bosses decided FBI agents were not to be touched, the two Boy Scouts thought themselves invulnerable. They thought wrong. Harry had lured one of them with a tip to a seedy hotel room in Southeast D.C. where he knocked him out, stripped him of his clothes, emasculated him and stuffed his genitals into his mouth while he bled out. His partner arrived an hour later thanks to a similar tip. Harry sapped him out cold also and hung him with his own tie from a once ornate, but still sturdy, chandelier. It was a classic homosexual lovers' quarrel, which quickly had been swept under the rug by the FBI.

Marlborough was so incompetent, Harry thought, that he really ought to be replaced. He wondered if there was a way to let Louie Howe and, through him, FDR know just how well Harry had done in having taken care of the six ex-MID agents and the two FBI agents and how that idiot Marlborough had placed it all in jeopardy. He would have to think about that. He knew that he was never going to be head of Naval Intelligence. It's one of the reasons why he left the Navy. But head of MID? That might be even better. Canfield already had lots of irons in the fire, both here and abroad, but running your own government intelligence agency might really come in handy one day.

12

Off the Record?

The Tiergarten
Berlin
Friday, 7 September 1934

"HANNA! WAIT!"

The voice came from behind her and Hanna Raeder turned to see who it was. The weather had been so beautiful this morning that she decided to pack a small picnic lunch and take it into the *Tiergarten* rather than visit one of the many restaurants within walking distance of the Justice Ministry. The spacious grounds of Europe's largest metropolitan park—formerly the hunting grounds of Prussian kings— was in the center of Berlin, but its size—2.5 square kilometers—made it seem isolated from the city. She had just passed the *Siegessaute,* the Victory column at the open center of the vast city park, when someone had called her name. To her surprise, she saw Georg von Dohnonyi rapidly closing the distance between them.

As usual, Dohnanyi's dark blond hair was neatly combed and he wore a dark blue three-piece suit with highly polished black shoes. He was out of breath.

"I looked for you in your office, but your secretary said you had gone for a stroll in the *Tiergarten.* I wanted to ask you to lunch, but the *Tiergarten* might be a safer place for us to talk, certainly safer than your office at the Ministry. May I walk with you?"

Hanna was bemused. It had been a year since she'd joined the Commission and Georg was a good friend and one of the good guys on the Commission in that he opposed making Jews 2nd class citizens. The icing on the cake was that, unlike some of the radical Nazis on the Commission who thought they were God's gift to women, Georg had never made a pass at her.

"Sure. It's such a nice day that I decided to have my lunch *al fresco*. What did you want to talk about that couldn't be said inside the Ministry?"

"First, what I'm about to say is in the strictest confidence and can never, under any circumstance, be repeated to others. If you decide not to help, I'll understand, but I want your word that it will stay strictly between us."

Hanna was intrigued, but why was Georg was acting so paranoid. Well, after the Night of the Long Knives two months ago, she supposed everyone was entitled to be paranoid.

"Of course I agree, Georg, but what the hell is this all about?"

"Have you heard of Winston Churchill?"

"Vaguely. Erich mentioned him once or twice as Great Britain's First Lord of the Admiralty during the Great War."

"He's a still a Member of Parliament, but he has no position in the government. He's a strong friend of the Jews and has been most critical of Hitler and Germany's treatment of Jews. I was in England earlier this week and my niece Greta and I went to see him at his country home."

"Why?"

"I gave him a copy of the Prussian Memorandum."

"For goodness sake, why would you do *that*?"

"To expose what the radical Nazis on the Commission are trying to do. The Commission is meeting behind closed doors to consider measures against the Jews and Goebbels won't permit any German newspaper to publish stories about what we are doing. If our proceedings stay secret, the radical Nazis on the Commission may well prevail and people with a single Jewish great grandparent will be classified as Jews. We need to publicize what the Nazis are trying to do and the only way we can do that is through foreign newspapers."

"How can this Churchill help?" Hanna asked. They had turned off the main gravel path onto a smaller path and stopped at a park bench where Hanna took a paper sack from her purse. She pulled out a liverwurst sandwich and offered half to Georg, but he turned it down as well as one of the two plums she had packed.

"His goddaughter is the Hearst photojournalist, Martha McGary. She's won several Pulitzer Prizes for her reporting from Germany. Mr. Churchill thinks she will be interested in covering the story because of the angle of the Commission using American laws researched by American lawyers to apply to German Jews."

As she chewed thoughtfully on her sandwich, Hanna could see Georg's point. The Commission's work *was* secret and what the Nazis were proposing *was* outrageous. Exposing it to negative foreign press coverage would be a good thing. It could hardly make things worse.

"You might be right, but why are you telling me all this?"

"The transcript of the 5 June 1934 meeting where the Prussian Memorandum was discussed—you were there, but I wasn't—is missing. Mr. Churchill thinks that without the transcript, it will be too easy for Goebbels to denounce the Prussian Memorandum as a fake, a fraud."

"It sure as hell wasn't a fake! I spent over six hours on 5 June arguing with that weasel Roland Freisler over those barbaric American state laws," Hanna said and took a bite from a plum. "Are you sure you won't have a plum? They're delicious."

Georg again declined. "I know it's not a fake. That's why my niece Greta is attempting to recreate the transcript from the original stenographic notes as her own notes. Meanwhile, Mr. Churchill says that *Frau* McGary will want to interview, off-the-record of course, moderate members of the Commission like you who can tell her what went on in the 5 June meeting and confirm the accuracy of the transcript of the meeting."

"Off-the-record? What's that mean? Hanna asked.

"According to Mr. Churchill, it means your name would not appear in the newspapers and *Frau* McGary will never disclose your name to the German authorities or anyone else."

Hanna was torn. Georg was right. Publicity in the foreign press was the only way to fight the radical Nazis. On the other hand, an interview with a foreign journalist, even off-the-record, was dangerous and, if it became known, might hurt her husband. She'd made enough enemies among the radical Nazis on the Commission, starting with Freisler. As a rule, her husband didn't trust reporters, or, at least that's what he said to her. Hanna didn't know any reporters except Bella Fromm whom she thought she could trust. Bella was a diplomatic reporter and Hanna had confidentially passed along several juicy, but relatively harmless, tidbits to her with no adverse consequences. She wondered if Bella knew the McGary woman, but it didn't matter. If she asked Bella if McGary could be trusted, that would practically be a confession that she might be a source for her. She liked Bella, but not enough to trust her with a confidence like that which was on a level much more serious than diplomatic gossip.

Hanna weighed the pros and cons as she ate her plum. The real battle on the Commission, the one they had a chance of winning, was defining a Jew. Her husband wanted, like Hanna, for the definition to be as narrow as possible so as to limit the number of naval officers he would have to dismiss. The best way to do that was to expose to negative foreign publicity what the Nazis were doing. On the other hand, Erich was sufficiently risk-averse that he might not give his consent to her giving an interview to a foreign journalist. Still, if she gave the interview and things blew up in her face, she could ask his forgiveness and tell him she did so thinking it was the best way to look out for the Navy's interest to dismiss for being a Jew as few naval officers as possible.

Hanna finished the plum and put the paper sack back in her purse. "Alright. I'll do an off-the-record interview with *Frau* McGary. Do you have my home telephone number to give her?"

"I have it," Georg replied, "but I'll give it to my niece Greta. She will be the go-between you and McGary in setting up the interview. I fear your telephone may have a wiretap as well given your husband's prominent position so she will meet with you and McGary separately to make the arrangements for the interview."

Hanna stood up. "Well, we both should be getting back to the Ministry. I will wait for a message from her. Let's hope this works."

13

First Things First

Slieve League
County Donegal, Ireland
Friday, 7 September 1934

MATTIE WOKE at dawn and, after a breakfast of soft-boiled eggs, bacon and Irish soda bread, she set to work arranging her interview notes into a story outline. While Ireland and O'Duffy had been her last interview, they were going to be the lead. Or rather, the two Blue Shirt thugs who ran her off the road at O'Duffy's direction were going to be the lead. She knew the Chief loved "Hearst Reporter in Peril" stories and she had given him more than her fair share of them over the years.

It was a beautiful late summer day. Mattie worked all morning on the terrace under a cloudless deep blue sky until the sun was directly overhead. She took a break for lunch—cold chicken, a salad and a glass of *Pinot Grigio*—and then, rolling a sheet of paper into her Imperial 'Good Companion' portable typewriter, she began to write the article. By 2:30, she had finished Part I of the story—O'Duffy and his Blue Shirts. She looked at her wristwatch and, since it was 9:30 a.m. in New York, she decided it was time to call Hearst and pitch Winston's German story idea to him.

Mattie rang up the local telephone exchange and placed a person-to-person trans-Atlantic call. She wasn't surprised when the operator told her it would take at least an hour to make the connection. As it happened, it took two and a half hours before her call went through. In the interim, she was able to complete the Portugal portion of the article and had made a start on the Netherlands and Belgium. Having begun her story in Ireland, she had decided to go from West to East in covering the countries she had visited.

Mattie soon discovered, as she picked up the telephone receiver, just why it had taken over two hours to reach Hearst. He wasn't in New York! Or California! He was in Wales! At St. Donat's castle, his third castle-like home. It had taken that long for Agnes Murphy, the Donegal telephone exchange operator, to track him down.

"Chief," Mattie said, "you gave me your itinerary and you weren't scheduled to be in Wales until the middle of next week."

"I know, and I apologize. But Marion was with me on Long Island," Hearst said, referring in his high-pitched voice to his long-time mistress, the Hollywood actress Marion Davies, "and Mildred returned from Bar Harbor much sooner than expected. Marion thought it the better part of valor if we sailed for Britain a week early."

Mattie chuckled. Mildred was Hearst's wife, a former Zigfield Follies dancer, and she lived on the East Coast, the unspoken agreement between them being that Hearst would not embarrass her by appearing in the same state as her with Marion on his arm. As Mildred was the mother of his children, Hearst had always gone out of his way to adhere to this custom even though Marion was the true love of his life. Mattie knew both women and she and Marion were good friends. Not so much with Mildred who was jealous of any woman close to her husband, romantically or not.

"A wise decision, Chief," Mattie said. "Marion always knows what's good for you. Listen, why I called is that Winston has put me on to what may be a big story and I wanted to run it past you before I did anything more."

"Winston has a good nose for stories. Tell me about it" Hearst replied.

Mattie did so for the next ten minutes and was pleasantly surprised at his response.

"Great story idea! Let's do it. It's always been the policy of the Hearst papers to deplore any race prejudice and to promote good feeling among all creeds and classes," Hearst said and then paused. "It's very important, for the *New York American,* especially, to have the support of the Jewish people in New York. A story about Nazis prohibiting marriage between Jews and non-Jews will help in that regard. To be able at the same time to bring sunlight into all those crazy race laws in southern and western states is icing on the cake. How soon can you go to England to see Winston and check this out further?"

"Hold on a second, Chief," Mattie protested. "First things first. For over two months, I've been investigating my story about fascist movements in Europe other than Germany and Italy. I've been working on that all day."

Hearst sighed. "Yes, I let you talk me into doing that one, but frankly that story won't increase our Jewish and colored readership. Nazi Germany using racist American state laws as a model for discriminating against the Jews will. When can you start on this new one?"

"Relax, it won't be long until I'm done with the new fascist threat in Europe. It's a four-part story, 2,500 words for each part. I begin with two very Catholic countries, Ireland and Portugal; then Belgium and the Netherlands; followed by Austria and Hungary; and concluding with Poland and Romania. I've worked on it all day and I'll finish it tomorrow. Then I'll fly to London on Sunday. Once I land, I'll airmail the story to you in Wales and to Joe Willicomb in New York before I go down to Chartwell to see Winston. After I read this so-called 'Prussian Memorandum' and discuss in more detail with Winston what that German member of the Commission told him, I'll let you and Joe know if I think it's worth my while to go to Berlin and Amsterdam to pursue the story."

"Excellent! Good news. I look forward to reading the story. Have a safe journey."

Slieve League
County Donegal, Ireland
Saturday, 8 September 1934

MATTIE McGARY finished writing her "New Fascist Threats in Europe" articles by mid-afternoon. After a late lunch, she packed her suitcase and stowed it in the luggage compartment of their Kelly green Pitcairn PCA-2 autogiro. She topped off the fuel tanks and began her walkaround of the aircraft, meticulously checking everything from the Wright Whirlwind rotary engine and its wooden propeller to the landing gear to the steel tripod between the front passenger compartment and the pilot's cockpit behind it to the four long rotary blades on top of the tripod that provided the aircraft's lift.

At last satisfied with the autogiro's airworthiness, she slipped on her lambskin leather-flying jacket followed by her white leather flying helmet and climbed into the cockpit. She adjusted her flight goggles over her eyes and fired up the Wright Whirlwind engine that powered the propeller and gave an initial boost to the rotary blades. The aircraft moved forward and leaped into the air in less than twenty yards. Once she reached a cruising altitude of 500 feet, she cut the power to the rotor blades that now auto-rotated on their own as the aircraft's propeller pulled them forward.

Mattie's destination was the *Baldonnel* Aerodrome south of Dublin where she planned to spend the night in a nearby inn and catch an early—and the only—Imperial Airways flight that day to Croyden Aerodrome in London. As she flew, her thoughts drifted ahead to the Prussian Memorandum. What the Nazis had in store for the Jews based on racist American laws frankly surprised the Scottish-born journalist. She enjoyed finishing a big story like the one today on the new Fascist threats to Europe, but this was the part she liked best, the start of a new adventure where she didn't know what would come next. All she knew was that she couldn't wait for the adventure to begin. She made a mental note to call Cockran tonight and fill her husband in on where she would be and what she would be doing.

14

Cut the Crap, Edgar

The White House
Washington, D.C
Saturday, 8 September 1934

WHAT IN HELL did Hoover want now? Louis Howe wondered as he lit a new Lucky Strike from the old one between his nicotine-stained fingers. Hoover had been cryptic on the telephone, obviously disappointed when Howe told him the President's schedule did not have an opening for the next two weeks. That was a lie, of course, but that's what FDR expected Howe to do—keep undesirables away from him. And FBI Director J. Edgar Hoover was about as undesirable a person to FDR as they came. All Hoover would say to Howe was that it was related to the matter he had discussed with the President last fall.

Howe knew at once what Hoover meant. He also knew that FDR would want him to handle this personally because it might adversely affect the mid-term Congressional elections coming up in November if it ever became public that American military intelligence had done legal research for the Nazis to use as a model for treating their Jews the same way that many American states discriminated against non-whites.

When Howe's secretary ushered Hoover into his cramped office a few doors away from the Oval Office, the contrast between the two men could not have been greater. Both were short but Howe had an emaciated frame over which was draped a rumpled suit with cigarette ash on its lapels. Hoover was stocky and wore a well-cut, navy blue Brooks Brothers suit with a maroon silk tie and matching handkerchief tucked into his breast pocket.

The two men met in the middle of Howe's office and briefly exchanged handshakes that could only be described as perfunctory. "Good to see you, again, Edgar," Howe lied.

"The same here, Louie," Hoover lied back. "I appreciate your seeing me so early in the morning on a weekend. You're looking well."

"Cut the crap, Edgar! I look like hell and you know it. So, take a seat and tell me why you're here."

Hoover sat down in a chair opposite Howe's desk and reached down to the briefcase he had placed beside the chair. He opened it, reached inside and pulled out a manila file folder that he handed to Howe.

"Once Hearst began opposing the Administration's policies in his editorials, we thought it prudent to determine how best to keep track of what he was doing. We decided wiretaps were the best way, but Hearst has so many residences, it was impractical. His mistress has a large beachfront mansion in Santa Monica where he sometimes lives. Then there's his castle at San Simeon in Central California and a Bavarian Village at Wyntoon in Northern California. On the East Coast, he has a castle-like mansion on Long Island as well as a full floor apartment in Manhattan. Finally he has a castle in Wales. We just don't have the manpower to cover wiretaps at all those places."

Howe drummed his fingers and then lit another new cigarette from the old one and stubbed it out in the overflowing ashtray on his desk. Would Hoover just get to the point? After all, Howe didn't need to know how a watch was built in order to tell the time.

Apparently his impatience was showing for Hoover quickly got to the point. "After interviewing a number of former Hearst employees, we learned that we only needed wiretaps on the office and home phones in Manhattan of Joe Willicomb and that file contains the transcript of a trans-Atlantic call yesterday between him and Hearst."

"Who the hell is Joe Willicomb?"

"He's Hearst's personal assistant and chief troubleshooter. He was a colonel in the Army and Hearst does nothing without running it past him. He is literally the most important man in the Hearst Empire other than Hearst himself. He can usually be found at the *New York American*'s offices in Manhattan."

"So, you got a judge to sign a warrant to wiretap this guy?"

Howe smiled as Hoover's face reddened ever so slightly. "Uh...not exactly. On matters that are politically sensitive or involve national security—rather than criminal activity—all that is required is the Director's approval. Otherwise, I'm not typically involved in securing your run-of-the-mill wiretap warrants."

I'll bet you're not, Howe thought as he opened the folder and pulled out ten typewritten pages stapled together. "Okay, Edgar, I'll read this with care later before I give it to the boss. Meanwhile, just give me the shorthand version of the call and why you think the President should be concerned."

"Well, you remember that so-called 'Prussian Memorandum' the President was so concerned about last fall, the one compiled by former American MID agents at the behest of the Nazis?" Hoover asked.

"Yes, yes, of course. What about it?" Howe replied.

"It seems a member of the German Commission on Criminal Law Reform has given a copy of the Memorandum to this British MP Winston Churchill who's been in contact with a Hearst reporter named Mattie McGary and he's going to give it to her tomorrow. Worse, this German has told Churchill that Americans hired by the SS prepared the Memorandum."

This was definitely bad, Howe thought. FDR was not going to like this. "Do they know who the Americans were?"

"No. This German guy—we don't know his name—told Churchill that the 'radical' members of the Commission were relying on the memorandum and said the SS had refused to tell them who the Americans were."

Thank God for that, Howe thought. Still, the SS man at the German Embassy to whom Harold Canfield of RVD International had delivered the Memorandum was the one who had contacted MID's General Marlborough to arrange for the research in the first place. *There* was a loose end, at least here in America, which should have been tied up, just like the six ex-MID men and two FBI agents who had met untimely ends last year. Hoover, of course, didn't need to know that. There were those in the SS in Germany who knew, of course, but they had no direct knowledge of who did the research and hence no credibility. If it came out, the White House could credibly deny everything, but that was not the optimum outcome FDR would want.

"Okay, Edgar, I appreciate your bringing this to our attention. We'll take care of it from here," Howe said. He could tell Hoover didn't like being dismissed so peremptorily, but he didn't care.

"Very well, Louie," Hoover said as he closed his briefcase and rose from his chair. "Please let me know if there is anything else the FBI can do to assist the President in this matter."

"Of course, Edgar, you may be assured of that."

After Hoover left, Howe pondered what to do next. Tell FDR? No, he knew what the Boss would want. Kill the story. Any way he had to. He lit another Lucky Strike and stubbed out its predecessor. He punched the intercom. Have the idiot responsible for this clean up his own mess.

"Yes, Mr. Howe?" his secretary's voice rose from the intercom's speaker.

"Lucille, call General Marlborough at the Munitions Building. Tell that idiot he has an appointment with me at the White House in precisely 45 minutes. If he objects, tell him the President is ordering him to clear the decks; to kick whoever he's seeing out of his office; and to get his sorry ass over here pronto! Or words to that effect. Clean up my language. You know what I mean."

"Yes, Sir. I do." Lucille replied with a smile.

15

The Last Musketeer

Department of War
Munitions Building
Constitution Avenue, N.W.
Washington, D.C.
Saturday, 8 September 1934

"WHAT IS so fucking important, Leo," Harold Canfield asked, "that I had to drag my butt over here for the second day in a row because you couldn't tell me on the phone? I've got a 9 p.m. appointment tonight at the Cotton Club to take care of the matter we discussed yesterday. It's 1 p.m. now and I've got a 5 p.m. Eastern flight out of Washington-Hoover to New York."

"One reason, dear Harry," General Leonard Marlborough replied, "is that we don't receive our weekly phone check for FBI wiretaps until tomorrow. A second reason is that I've just returned from the White House where I met with Louie Howe and received one royal ass-chewing over that goddamn Prussian Memorandum you talked me and Ralph into undertaking."

"Louie is an old woman. What's his problem now?"

"William Randolph Hearst. Specifically, one of his reporters is going to receive a copy of the Prussian Memorandum tomorrow. Worse, Hearst knows Americans performed the legal research and he thinks it will be a big story. He thinks it will increase his newspaper circulation among the Jews and Coloreds."

"How does Louie know all this?"

"The FBI has a wiretap on Joe Willicomb's office and home phones. He's Hearst *major domo* and Hoover gave Howe a transcript of a transatlantic phone call between Hearst and Willicomb where all this was discussed. Howe let me read the transcript, but he wouldn't let me have a copy."

"Okay, but how does he know Americans performed the work?"

"A member of the German Commission on Criminal Law Reform gave a copy of the Memorandum to Winston Churchill…"

Harry interrupted. "The British politician or the American novelist?"

"The Brit. Anyway, the German told Churchill that the SS arranged for Americans to do the legal research, but they refused to identify the names of those who conducted it."

"That's because I put the fear of God into Willy Krueger at the German Embassy last fall when I told him if anything leaked about MID's role in researching and creating the Memorandum, the US would begin to support the Jews' anti-Nazi boycott and I would personally make sure that his superiors knew he was responsible."

"Be that as it may," Marlborough said, "Howe says that's not good enough for the President now."

Harry sighed. As if he didn't have enough reasons to despise FDR. "Alright, just what *is* 'good enough' for that fucking cripple in the Oval Office?"

"He wants the story killed."

"Swell. And just how are we going to do that when we're here and the Hearst reporter is in England and maybe going to Germany next?"

"Louie said they didn't care how we did it just so long as the story doesn't see the light of day. He's also concerned that the German at the embassy…"

"Wilhelm Krueger."

"Yes, he is the only 'loose end' left in America."

Well, Harry thought, he had to admire the crippled bastard's ruthlessness if nothing else. It had been the same thing last fall when

FDR learned what MID had done for the SS. Six ex-MID and two FBI agents were now dead as a result, the last two by Harry's own hand. Tomorrow he was going to add the lawyer Cockran, his investigator Sullivan and that deputy of Marlborough's, Tim O'Hanlon, to the list. Tacking on an extra Kraut embassy official wouldn't trouble Owney.

How to kill the story? That was entirely different. For starters, of course, he'd place the problem in the Nazis' lap. He'd have Krueger alert his SS superior in Berlin and tell him that if they wanted the United States to continue opposing the Jewish boycott of Nazi Germany's exports, they only had two options with respect to any Hearst reporter who came to Germany to investigate the Prussian Memorandum: assassination or indefinite detention in a concentration camp, preferably the former.

"The SS guy at the German Embassy is no problem. I'll add him to Owney's list tonight," Harry said. "I'll put a week-long delay on killing Krueger to give him time to contact Berlin about the Hearst problem. Who's the reporter on this? I'll need that before I see Krueger today."

"Martha McGary. She knows Germany well. She received two Pulitzer Prizes earlier this year for her reporting from Germany. Plus, Hitler gave an exclusive interview to her in July where he justified the killing the SS did on the Night of the Long Knives. Our military attaché in Berlin says she's known there as Hitler's favorite foreign journalist."

"Okay, good to know. Thanks," Canfield replied, his face expressionless. Inside, he struggled to keep a grin from spreading across his face. Damn! Mattie McGary! It was the same broad who had killed his cousin Ted Hudson over a year ago last March in the Austrian Alps. After he took his leave of Marlborough and walked in the bright September sun over to the German embassy, he began to form a back-up plan in the event the Germans did not take care of McGary.

Harold Canfield had finalized his back-up plan by the time he reached the 70-room red brick Victorian mansion that housed the German Embassy. Marlborough's mention of McGary brought back to him 'The Three Musketeers' and the fact that, with Slade having been killed in Berlin during the Night of the Long Knives this year and Hudson in Austria the year before, Harry was the last Musketeer standing. Harry, Ted Hudson and Slade grew up together on Long Island in their respective mansions where they had first dubbed themselves 'The Three Musketeers'. They had all gone to the same prep school and then on to Harvard although Harry suspected that, with Slade's grades, his father had been required to give a larger donation to Harvard's trust fund than did either Harry's or Ted's fathers. Harry and Ted had stayed close over the years because they were family, but he and Slade had drifted apart, mostly because Harry was ONI and Slade was, until last year, MID. Then, he and Slade had lost all contact once Slade went to work for the Ford Motor Company as head of its Foreign Intelligence Department.

The mention of McGary brought back memories of 'The Three Musketeers' because Harry knew Slade believed he had ballistics proof—since disappeared—that McGary had killed Hudson in Austria and he had been determined to avenge his best friend's death. Harry also knew that Slade had unsuccessfully attempted to kill her in Scotland on her wedding day last year and later on her honeymoon flight to Ireland. Harry never understood that. Sure, Ted Hudson was family, but anyone who let himself be killed by a broad probably deserved to die. As a consequence, Harry would not even cross the street to kill McGary if the opportunity presented itself. Hell, Hudson would still be dead. If killing her was the fortuitous by-product of killing her story, however, Harry would be only too happy to oblige.

So, if the Krauts were unable to kill the story, Harry would do it using ex-ONI agents he had recruited to RVD International. They were so much better than the ex-MID agents that Van Deman had hired prior to Harry coming on board a few years back. There were six in Europe right now, but he figured that, with him, it would take only two of them to do the job. And since McGary would be reporting on her investigation to Hearst or Willicomb, the FBI's wiretaps should let him keep one step ahead of her. His agents would stay in the shadows, but they would watch her. The Krauts would be given one chance to take her out or toss her into a concentration camp. After that, Harry would head to Germany and activate the back-up plan.

SS-OBERSTURMFUHRER Wilhelm Krueger looked to Harold Canfield like he was straight from Central Casting when they asked for a model SS poster boy—a tall, blond, fit 25-year-old wearing an immaculate black with silver trim SS uniform and gleaming, knee high black leather boots. "Welcome, *Herr* Canfield. *Heil* Hitler! To what do I owe the honor of this unexpected visit?" he said as he sat down behind his desk.

"You guys screwed up, Willy! We've got a problem and it comes from your end. You've got a big mouth loose on your damned Commission on Criminal Law Reform," Canfield replied as he declined Krueger's invitation to sit down. Then he gave him chapter and verse on what they had learned from the FBI wiretap of Hearst and Willicomb.

"The bottom line, Willy," Canfield concluded, "is that if this story ever appears in the Hearst papers, the Roosevelt Administration is not only going to deny it, but the President personally will announce his support for the Jewish boycott of German exports."

"I agree this is most disturbing news," Krueger said. "What would you like us to do? We certainly don't want your government to support the boycott."

"Two things. First, find out where the damn leak came from and plug it. Permanently. Two, and much more important, kill the story!"

"How?"

"The name of the Hearst journalist who is investigating the story is Martha McGary. We expect her to be in Germany soon. Be on the lookout for her. Then arrange for her untimely death, preferably an accident. Can you do that? Or should I go to the Ambassador?"

"No, no…" Krueger replied nervously. "He can't help you. I must report this to my immediate superior in the SS. Only the SS can do what is required."

"And who is this superior? Is he placed high enough to accomplish what we need?"

"He is the *SS-Sturmbannfuhrer* in charge of the Foreign Intelligence Section of the SD, the Security Service of the SS."

"And who does he report to? Himmler?"

"No, no…" Krueger again replied nervously. "Even better. Himmler never involves himself in operational details. My boss reports directly to *SS-Obersturmbannfuhrer* Reinhard Heydrich, the head of the SD and the #2 man in the SS. Only *Reichsfuhrer-SS* Himmler is higher."

Okay, Harry thought, that appeared to be high enough up the SS ladder for them to take care of the McGary woman. If they didn't? Well, that was why he had a back-up plan. "Tell me Willy, when are you going to report this to your boss? And just who is this boss?"

"I will send him an encoded cable today, immediately after you leave."

"And who is he?" Canfield asked with an edge in his voice.

"A brilliant man. He's only my age, but he's the fastest rising officer in the SS."

Jesus Christ! Harry thought, it's like pulling fucking teeth! "His name, Willy! Tell me his goddamn name!"

"Schellenberg. *SS-Sturmbannfuhrer* Walter Schellenberg."

The Cotton Club
142nd Street and Lenox Avenue
New York City
Saturday, 8 September 1934

HAROLD CANFIELD first met Owney Madden in 1932. Acting on instructions from Van Deman, he had hired some of Owney's men to accompany MID agents and assist in the kidnapping of American twins for medical experiments that the SS were conducting in both the United States and Germany. It was an operation in which his cousin Ted Hudson played a major role. Harry had not expected to like the little gangster and was surprised to find he owned, among other things, a string of nightclubs in New York, the most famous being the Cotton Club in the middle of Harlem. Billed by Owney as providing "authentic black entertainment to a wealthy, whites-only audience", it was Harry's favorite nightclub even if Langston Hughes' description of it as "a Jim Crow club for gangsters and moneyed whites" was probably more accurate. The musicians were superb and included Louis Armstrong, Duke Ellington, Count Basie, Fats Waller, Cab Calloway and the Mills Brothers. The women were even better, all beautiful, light-skinned blacks like Billie Holiday, Lena Horne and Dorothy Dandridge.

Owney was a dapper dresser who wore perfectly tailored suits and always sported spats over his shoes and a tiepin under his shirt collar. For an Irish gangster, he didn't have an Irish accent as he had been born in England before he emigrated to America at the turn of the century. He didn't have a posh English accent, but it wasn't Cockney either. He and Harry hit it off immediately. He had a great sense of humor, but the fact that his nickname earlier in his career was Owney 'the Killer' Madden allowed the two men to see each other as kindred spirits.

Canfield was in Owney's lavish office upstairs at the Cotton Club. The mob boss was sitting behind a desk the size of a small aircraft carrier and Harry sat in an armchair beside the desk, an open bottle of champagne in a silver ice bucket on Owney's desk accessible to both. Owney poured champagne into two flutes.

Owney raised his champagne flute and tilted it toward Harry who did the same with his flute and they lightly touched. "So, Harold, my friend, to what do I owe the honor of your presence in my establishment? Other than the fact that both Louie and the Duke are playing tonight."

Harry reached inside his suit coat, pulled out a letter size sheet of paper folded into thirds and slid it across the desk. "There are three names and addresses there. As a matter of national security, they need to be disposed of. They're investigating the six hits I paid for last November. We don't want them to do that. The first two names are the ones conducting the investigation; the third is the man they're working for.'

Harry reached again into his suit coat and pulled out an unmarked white envelope and pushed it over to Owney. "There's $15,000 in there. The usual terms. Half now, the other half when you deliver to me obituary notices for each man from his local newspaper or photographs of their dead bodies."

Owney picked up the sheet of paper and looked at the names, a surprised look on his face.

"Is something the matter?" Harry asked.

"You might say that. Cockran and O'Hanlon are no problem. Robert Sullivan very much is."

"Why?"

"Have you ever heard of 'The Angel of Death'?"

"Can't say as I have."

"Sullivan is my best free lance hitman. He's worth a lot more to me than ten grand."

"How much?"

'Fifty.'

"As in thousand?" Harry asked in an incredulous tone of voice.

"Take it or leave it. I'm not giving up my best hitman for a penny less."

"But it's still ten each for the other two?"

Owney nodded.

"Okay. I don't have that much on me. Keep the fifteen. I'll go back to our office for the other twenty and have one of my men deliver it to you tonight. Also, once these three are dead, there's a guy at the German Embassy I may want taken out also. Will that prove a problem?"

"Nope." Owney said and picked up the envelope, opened his center desk drawer and placed the envelope inside without checking the contents. "As always, a pleasure doing business with you, Harold. Anything else I can do for you?   Billie Holiday is our headliner tonight."

"Thanks, but I'll take a rain check. I have a date with Mae West."

Owney chuckled. "You always did have good taste in women, Harold. Give Mae my love."

"You bet, Owney. Thanks, I appreciate your taking this on."

16

Let Owney Be Last

The Çedars
Sands Point, Long Island
Saturday, 8 September 1934

BOURKE COCKRAN, JR. watched his 14-year-old son Patrick take the saddle off his horse, Lancelot, and begin to brush the stallion's coat after their morning ride on the beach of Long Island Sound. Patrick was a tall lad, nearly six feet, with an unruly shock of red hair inherited from his late mother, Nora, who the IRA killed during the Irish Civil War in 1922 when Paddy was only two. Nearby, Jimmy McDermott, their Irish-born chauffeur and stable hand, did the same with Cockran's horse, Galahad. Jimmy would gladly have done both horses if asked, but Paddy made his own bed and groomed, fed and generally looked after his own horse. Cockran's father had done the same with him and he thought it a good idea for his son to be self-reliant as well.

Jimmy was a nephew of Paddy's maternal grandmother, Mary Morrisey, who came to America after her daughter's death to help raise her grandson. She served as as the housekeeper of both his Fifth Avenue townhouse and his country estate and Jimmy was happy to have a good paying job when so many others were without one during the worldwide depression. While Cockran employed two live-in maids—one in each of his two homes—for his mother-in-law to supervise along with Jimmy and a kitchen helper who travelled with Mary between the two homes, making her the housekeeper was not his idea. He would have been more than happy to hire someone to do the job, but Mary would not hear of it.

"And what else would I be doing all day?" she had said back in 1923. "No idle hands for me, Bourke. This is what God made me to do. I take care of houses and babies. Leave it to me. Thanks to my husband, may he rest in peace, I live upstairs now, but my parents lived downstairs. I learned from them how to run a house."

When he had married Mattie last year, Cockran wasn't sure if she would want to have a say in how their many households were managed, but Mattie laughed, her own shock of red hair shining in one of the many sunsets on their honeymoon, "Oh Cockran, if you married me for my housekeeping skills or my ability to cook anything more complicated than a steak or an egg, you are going to be sorely disappointed!"

So Mary remained in charge of both residences and was a little put out that she wasn't officially managing their Martello Tower in Donegal. "It's my homeland Bourke," she had said, "and I still have many friends there who would know how to get the right help." So Bourke hired a girl from Donegal Town whom Mary recommended to come in once a week to clean and do the laundry.

When they came into the house from the stables, father and son sat at the large butcher-block table in the center of the large kitchen where Mary and her kitchen helper had prepared a large breakfast of scrambled eggs, country ham, orange juice, toast and Irish Breakfast tea. After breakfast, the two went into the library, a large room with high-ceilings and built-in bookshelves lining three walls. The front wall, with tall windows and French doors, looked out onto a flagstone patio and Long Island Sound beyond. The back wall had a small fireplace nestled in among the bookshelves with four green leather club chairs, two on each side of the fireplace with a butler's table in between.

Cockran went to one of two large mahogany, leather-topped writing desks facing the front wall while Patrick went to the other desk that technically belonged to his stepmother, Mattie, but that he had permission to use when it was otherwise unoccupied. Each desk was equipped with a large Remington typewriter and two brass lamps patterned after the ones in the New York Public Library's reading room.

There were several volumes of *The World Crisis* by Patrick's godfather, Winston Churchill, on his desktop along with a volume of Theodore Roosevelt's autobiography that Cockran's own father had edited. Paddy was working on a term paper comparing the records of both men, Roosevelt as assistant Naval Secretary at the outset of the Spanish-American War and Winston as First Lord of the Admiralty in the first years of the Great War. He watched with pride as his son opened one of his godfather's books and began to write in his notebook, tucking a lock of his red hair behind his ear in an unconscious imitation of his mother. Cockran was often struck these days as Paddy grew older how small gestures like that reminded him of Nora and how proud she would be of the fine young man their son had become.

Cockran's desktop was occupied by six files Tim O'Hanlon had furnished on the six ex-MID agents who had died or been killed last year during the last two months of the previous year. He had briefly read them all yesterday evening after he, Paddy and his grandmother arrived from Manhattan. Now, as he went through them one-by-one, the pattern wasn't difficult to discern. The deaths began in Philadelphia on November 10 and ended on December 15 in Cleveland. In between were deaths in Atlanta, New Orleans, Chicago and Pittsburgh. Give or take a few days either side, each of the deaths was roughly a week apart. That meant that whomever Owney Madden had hired after Sullivan turned him down could easily have killed all six. A week gave the assassin more than enough time to conduct surveillance on each victim so as to find the right time and place to kill him.

Cockran had no illusions that they would ever identify, let alone prove who the killer had been. Tim would have to be satisfied that it was a hit job arranged by someone through Owney Madden. His job was to find out why. And for that, he needed to find out what each man was working on for MID. He looked at his watch. 11:30 a.m. Bobby and the O'Driscoll twins would be here at 1:00 p.m. for him to brief them and give them their itineraries.

SEAN O'DRISCOLL took a sip of his Guinness as he sat at a round glass-topped table on the patio outside the library with his brother Seamus, Bobby Sullivan and Cockran, the remains of their corned beef and cabbage lunch in front of them.

"Was Owney angry you turned him down?" Sean asked Sullivan.

"Not especially. T'was not the first time I said no to him."

"Who do you suppose he got in your place?" Seamus asked.

"Can't be sure," Sullivan replied, "but the name he mentioned to me was Nicholas Carson."

"Nick the Killer? We should have shot that Black & Tan bastard on Bloody Sunday like we did the others," Sean said, referring to that infamous Sunday in November 1920 during the Irish War for independence when the 'Apostles', Michael Collins squad of twelve assassins, including Sullivan and the O'Driscoll brothers, tracked down and killed fourteen British agents and informers.

"Aye, that we should," Sullivan said, "but I think one of our own tipped him off."

"Really? And who would that be?" the O'Driscoll twins simultaneously asked.

"Can't be sure, but my money is on Dev," Sullivan said, referring to Eamon deValera, current head of the Irish government.

Cockran smiled as he rose from the table and walked over to the French doors of the library. "Curse his black Spanish heart!" was one of the less profane epithets uttered at the table by the 'Angel of Death' and the 'Twins of Doom'. He knew that at almost any pub in Ireland today, you could still pick a fight by cursing either Michael Collins, 'the Big Fella', or deValera, 'the Long Fella'. Cockran knew whose side these three were on because he was on the same side himself. One man, Mick Collins, risked his life to win Ireland her independence. The other was a coward who safely sat out the war in America raising funds for the rebellion, the vast bulk of which mysteriously never made its way back to Ireland.

"Paddy," Cockran said as he opened the French door and walked inside. "Please tell your Grandma that Molly can clear the table now. Your Uncle Bobby and I still have business to discuss with the other men, but you and I can still play a couple sets of tennis after that."

"Sure thing, Pop," his son replied as he put down the book he was reading and headed off toward the kitchen.

Cockran went over to his desk and picked up the six manila folders he had reviewed that morning and walked back outside to the table. He handed three folders to Sean, the older of the twins by twenty minutes.

"Sean, these are the three victims whose next of kin you and Seamus will be talking to in Philadelphia, Atlanta and New Orleans. Bobby and I will take the other three in Pittsburgh, Cleveland and Chicago. Everything we know about them, and it isn't much, is in those folders. My secretary Alexis has scheduled appointments for you with all three widows. The dates and times are in the files. All she told them was that I was a former MID agent and that a high official in MID hired my law firm to investigate the circumstances of the victim's death. If anyone asked, Alexis said she was not at liberty to disclose who had hired us, only that MID wanted to be sure the death was unrelated to any aspect of MID's operations.

"Any questions so far?" Cockran asked, but they all shook their heads 'no'.

"Good. Now what we want to find out is what legal work each of them was doing for MID after they were selected from the list O'Hanlon prepared. Talk to their widows first and act as if you already know what they were working on, but you want to make sure they told no one else. If a widow knows what her husband was doing and can tell you about it in detail, fine. Move on to the next widow. If they were never told or only have a general idea of what their husbands were doing, ask them for the names of any good friends who their husband might have confided in. Check out all those names as well and ask them for any other friends in whom the victim may have confided."

Sullivan took a sip of his Guinness and raised his hand. "And wouldn't I be having a question for you now?"

Cockran nodded and Sullivan continued. "I know you said not to ask Owney who hired him for the six hits because he might tip off his client. But if I explain to Owney how, uh, *disappointed* I'd be if he did that, I think he'd keep his mouth shut. Then once we know who hired Owney, all we have to do is find him. Once we do, just give me thirty minutes with him, maybe less, and he'll be singing like the proverbial canary."

Cockran shook his head and laughed. "No, Bobby, I don't think that's the best way to proceed. You can't be sure Owney will stay quiet and it may be more difficult to find his client than you think. We'll learn more undercover. After we've done that and interviewed all the victims' wives and friends, we'll evaluate what, if anything, we do with Owney. But, in any event, let Owney be last."

Sullivan just shook his head and smiled. Cockran and the O'Driscolls knew it was a smile, but only those who knew him well would recognize it as such. Most would think it a grimace, a warning that this was a man perfectly capable of tearing your heart out with his bare hands.

"Okay, okay," Sullivan said, "we play it your way. I understand what you're saying. And I thank you for not invoking Aquinas to support you."

Cockran smiled. When the two worked together on other assignments, Cockran had frequently quoted St. Thomas Aquinas and his concept of a just war to restrain the more violent impulses of Michael Collins' most feared assassin. Sullivan was not only an eye-for-an-eye, Old Testament man, he also believed in a pre-emptive strike. Raised by a father who was a pacifist lawyer and being a lawyer himself, Cockran believed in the rule of law. Except in self-defense, violence was not acceptable in most situations. Of course, there were exceptions to this rule. Where others did not play by the rules, especially in the gangster state of Nazi Germany, Cockran gave his violent friend free rein.

"Bobby, you and I are on a early morning train to Pittsburgh on Monday. We'll be at the William Penn. Then it's Cleveland on Thursday at the Alcazar Hotel. After that, it's Chicago on Sunday at the Drake. I'll call Tim from each city with what we've learned. The

O'Driscolls will be calling me with what they learn in their cities so I'll keep Tim posted on their progress as well."

Cockran saw Sullivan and the O'Driscolls off and had no sooner closed the door when Patrick came running out of the house and breathlessly said "Dad, it's Mattie! She's on the telephone. She's calling from Dublin!"

Dublin? What the hell was she doing in Dublin, Cockran thought. The last he heard, she was still working on the other fascist parties in Europe story back at their home in Donegal.

"Hi, Mattie, what's up? Why are you in Dublin?"

They hung up twenty minutes later and Cockran shook his head. The Prussian Memorandum. Leave it to Winston to come up with a story like that. And leave it to the damned Nazis to be drafting laws to criminalize marriage and sex between Gentiles and Jews. And to add insult to injury, the bastards were using the laws of racist Southern states as models. He had to admit, however, that, unlike Mattie, he had been all too aware of how many other states had similar statutes. They were mostly in the Mid-West and the West and they weren't just limited to prohibiting marriage between blacks and whites, but whites and just about any other race, yellow, brown or red. Many of these were the same states that had passed laws calling for compulsory sterilization of 'mental defectives'. Why did God create so many ignorant bigots and how the hell did they get elected?

17

An Assassin's Life Isn't Easy

The Cotton Club
142ⁿᵈ Street and Lenox Avenue
New York City
Sunday, 9 September 1934

NICHOLAS O'NEILL CARSON—aka 'Nick the Killer'—liked Owney Madden despite the fact he was an Irish Catholic. For one thing, he wasn't actually *from* Ireland, having been born in England and grown up in Liverpool. For another, they had the same nickname, 'the Killer', that had been honestly earned by both. For Owney, he'd earned it as a hit man early in the century for the Gopher gang on the West Side of Manhattan known as Hell's Kitchen. For Nick, formerly from Belfast, Northern Ireland, he'd been a member of the Black and Tans in the 1919-1921 Anglo-Irish War. The Black & Tans were all hard men, but Carson stood out. Not only was he willing to kill the families of known IRA members and sympathizers, he took cruel pleasure in doing so.

The Black & Tans specialized in burning and sacking Irish small towns and villages, killing the men and raping their women. His immediate commander had been David Brooke-Smythe, code-named 'Blackthorn', who was something of an Old Testament fundamentalist. Blackthorn taught him that any good leader, intent on maintaining morale, should always selflessly share the spoils of war with those serving under him and, in wartime, it meant women were fair game. More than maintaining his men's morale, Blackthorn had told him, violating the fair sex was a key tactic for demoralizing the enemy. Better still, the Bible mandated rape. "Target their women, Nicholas. Turn them into trollops. Return them as damaged goods. The Bible says so. The Book of Deuteronomy. The women of your enemies are the spoil of war delivered by God, which He *commands* you to enjoy. All is fair in love and war. Supply the lasses with a generous sample of both and boast about it in their pubs. Make their menfolk hang their heads in shame as they face the proof their precious IRA can't even keep the honor of their wives and daughters unstained." Carson and his men enjoyed those gifts God had delivered.

Carson was a beefy man, six feet tall, 200 solid pounds, with a florid face and a balding head topped by close-cropped red hair. Not only did he like Owney Madden, he also liked doing business with him. The pay was good—$10,000 for each hit—and Madden placed no limits on how he carried it out. This pleased Carson because it allowed full rein to his creativity as a professional assassin. Thanks to his tour of duty with the Black & Tans, he was an expert marksman with both a sniper rifle and a handgun, just as he was equally skilled with his Fairbairn-Sykes fighting knife. And in his training for the Black & Tans, the knife's inventor, Captain Bill Fairbairn of the Shanghai Police himself, had taught Carson at least five different ways to kill a man without a gun or knife.

Those skills had come in handy for fulfilling his last assignment from Owney Madden that he completed last December. Six men to kill in six different cities. No timetable, but each kill had to be different. It was a challenge, but Carson had been more than up to it. He had crippled one victim with a kick to his knee, stuck a typed suicide note in his pocket and tossed him off a high level bridge to train tracks below. Another had been a hit and run victim. A third had been pheasant hunting and Carson had blown a hole in his head from 300 yards away in the woods adjacent to a farmer's field where the victim had just flushed and shot a rising pheasant. A fourth had 'accidentally' drowned in Lake Michigan. He had been fishing alone in a secluded location when Carson knocked him unconscious with a sap and held his head under water until he died. A fifth had his throat slit by a Fairbairn-Sykes fighting knife in a downtown St. Louis garage and his wallet stolen. The last had suffered a similar fate during a home invasion and burglary.

"Nicholas, how good of you to come on such short notice," Madden said from behind his enormous walnut desk and pointed to a silver bucket filled with ice on the corner of the desk. "Please accept my apologies, but I only heard from our client a few hours ago. Help yourself to some champagne."

Owney's office was impressive with dark, wood-paneled walls and oil paintings in massive frames. Sitting in an armchair beside the desk, Carson waved his hand with a casual 'it's nothing' gesture and filled his flute with champagne.

"This new assignment," Madden said, "is related to the last job you did for us."

Interesting, Carson thought. "You mean the six?"

"Yes, the same. It seems someone is investigating those kills in an effort to find a common thread. Our client doesn't want that to happen. He wants it stopped. Initially, there are three people he wants eliminated. With them gone, he believes that will be the end of it. Interested?"

"Maybe. Who are they and where do I find them?" Carson asked.

"The first two he wants gone are a New York lawyer named Bourke Cockran and a private dick who works for him, Bobby Sullivan. The third is a federal employee in Washington named Timothy O'Hanlon, but you're to save him for last after you've taken out the other two."

Bobby Sullivan? Really? This was too good to be true, Carson thought. Still, no need to let Madden know he'd take out Sullivan for no charge. He had been #1 on the Black & Tans' hit list during the insurrection in Ireland and a lot of good men, friends of Carson, had died at the hands of Bobby Sullivan—'the Angel of Death'—and his bloody twin Colt .45 automatics. Carson had tried, but failed to get the bastard himself because he had eyes in the back of his head. Even so, shooting Bobby Sullivan in the back was the only sane way to take out the Angel of Death.

"Sullivan, eh? I knew of a Sullivan back in Ireland when I was with the Black & Tans. He was a hit man for Michael Collins. We called him 'The Angel of Death'. Any relation?"

Owney hesitated and Carson saw that he was about to lie. "I don't really know. Might be. Might not be. Why? Does it matter?" Owney asked.

"It sure as hell does matter. If it really is 'the Angel of Death', it's going to cost you a damn site more than the standard ten Gs. Robert Michael Sullivan is a pro. By reputation alone, he's in the same league as me."

"How much?"

"Twenty large, no deductions for your share. Add on an extra two K if you want your cut."

"Okay, done. But the standard for the other two?" Owney asked.

"Nope. Look, taking out those six last year was a piece of cake. They didn't know it was coming. I'll get Sullivan first, but that will tip off the other two. Fifteen large, no deductions, for each of the other two."

That's pretty steep," Owney said.

"Take it or leave it. Good luck finding anyone else willing to take on the Angel of Death at twice that price. I'm giving you a bargain."

Madden sighed. "Okay, Killer, I'll meet your price." Madden reached into a drawer, pulled out a stack of crisp $500 Federal Reserve notes and counted out twenty five thousand dollars and pushed it across the desk. "There you go, Nicholas, fifty William McKinleys. The other half will come upon completion of all three assignments."

Carson smiled as he took the fifty notes and placed them in an inside pocket of his blue herringbone suit coat. "Where do I find Sullivan and Cockran?"

Madden opened his desk drawer and pulled out a sheet of paper and slid it across the desktop to Carson. "This is their itinerary. Both are going to interview widows in Pittsburgh, Cleveland and Chicago. The dates for the interviews are on there along with their hotel in each city and the names and addresses of the widows."

Damn! Carson thought. Cleveland again? This really *was* his lucky day! He looked at the paper. Yep, there it was. Doris Sandler, widow of the late Henry Sandler who had been Carson's last victim of the six he had been hired to kill. And the address was the same. A big house on North Park Boulevard in Cleveland Heights. Oh my, Carson thought, he still had vivid memories of an intimidate interlude he had shared with Sandler's blonde and beautiful wife.

Peter Luger Steak House
178 Broadway
Brooklyn, New York
Sunday, 9 September 1934

THAT EVENING, as Carson tucked into his rare porterhouse steak and took a sip of *Bordeaux* from the crystal wine glass on the immaculate white tablecloth at his table in the back corner of Peter Luger's dark wood-paneled steak house, he marveled at his good fortune. He was being paid to revisit the scene of one of his most perfectly designed operations and, as a bonus, renew his acquaintance with the victim's widow.

The plan in retrospect still seemed every bit as flawless now as it had then. Burglary and rape would mask the real purpose—the murder of Henry Sandler. The passing pleasure of a romp in the hay with the man's sexy spouse was not the point. What mattered was the part it would play in the plan's success. After all, apart from masking the real purpose, Sandler had been a former MID agent, a potentially dangerous man. Discovering his naked wife bound and gagged on their bed would surprise him and put him off his guard, rendering him less dangerous. The only supplies Carson had needed were rope, three large white bandanas and his Fairbairn-Sykes fighting knife.

While Carson worked at his really excellent porterhouse and the side of asparagus with Hollandaise sauce, he relished recalling in detail just how perfectly his plan had unfolded.

Jimmying the back door of the large Sandler residence and placing the contents of the silver chest and the wife's jewelry box in two pillowcases had been easy. Subduing the wife easier still, the back door having offered more resistance. In fairness, there was not much Doris

Sandler could do, coming home after lunch with the ladies to be confronted by a large, well-muscled man, six feet tall and over 200 pounds with a white bandana covering his lower face and a Fairbairn-Sykes fighting knife with its seven-inch, double-edged, pointed blade in his right hand.

Offered the option of stripping herself or having Carson cut her clothes off with the knife was all the persuasion Doris needed to disrobe. In no time, she was naked and lying face down on their bed, a gag around her mouth, while Carson tied each of her wrists to a bedpost with the clothesline, her arms stretched out above her head. In his mind's eye, he could still see the late afternoon sun streaming through the leaded glass window in the bedroom, creating a pattern of diamonds over her pale body and its bare and beautiful backside. It took all his self-control not to sample her charms right then and there, but he was a professional. The plan came first.

His steak and asparagus finished, Carson drained the last glass of wine. Then he ordered Bananas Foster and coffee. Once the flames from the dessert died down, he took a bite and resumed his recollection of that winter day's events.

Having previously observed the couple's evening ritual of martinis followed by their making love, Carson had gone downstairs and mixed a pitcher of martinis. He left it and a single stemmed glass on a table in the foyer with a typed note: 'I'm upstairs. Interested?' He then waited in the bedroom, figuring that, at the least, Sandler would be carrying the martini glass as he entered the bedroom, leaving him vulnerable with only one hand free when he saw his spread-eagled wife with her wrists tied to the bedposts. In the event, it was even better. The poor fool had been carrying both the glass and the pitcher of martinis.

"Doris! What the hell is ..." Henry Sandler had sputtered at the sight of his naked wife tied to the bed right before Carson hit him at the base of the skull with the brass pommel of his knife and he fell to the floor with the pitcher, ice, glass and liquid flying out in front of him. He then lifted the unconscious man into a chair at the foot of the bed and bound him hand and foot. Next, he wrapped a bandana around her husband's mouth to muffle his fury once he was conscious and discovered, to his horror, he had a ringside seat to see his spouse serviced by a masked stranger.

After taking the last bite of Bananas Foster, Carson signaled the waiter for a brandy and coffee. He swirled the brandy when it arrived, inhaled the aroma and again began to revisit what transpired next in the couple's bedroom.

With Sandler secured, Carson had thrown a glass of water in his face. "Who are you? What's going on?" the man asked, blinking his eyes at the impact of the water.

Hearing, but not able to see, her husband, his wife's eyes went wide. "Hank!" she pleaded in a muffled voice through her gag before it slipped down and her voice was clear. "Do something!"

Carson had laughed. He climbed onto the bed, knelt between the woman's legs, pushed them wide and effortlessly hoisted her hips high in the air. It had been quite a sight, one he easily recalled now as he took another sip of wine, for it brought back memories of his days with the Black & Tans and the many unwilling Anglo-Irish wives and daughters forced to bend over before him in the same tempting position—on her knees, her shoulders flat on the bed, her wrists tied and arms stretched above her head in a large V, her back arched in a concave curve and, best of all, her seductive, shapely tush perched right up there, pretty as a peach, unprotected and ripe for the taking. As his old Black & Tan commander Blackthorn would have said, it was the 'spoil of war delivered by God which He *commands* you to enjoy'. Carson wasn't much of a religious man, but by that point, he wasn't about to disobey the Word of the Almighty, especially when his plan and God's plan were one and the same.

Carson had looked back over his shoulder and smiled at her husband who was straining uselessly against his bonds, his words unintelligible through the gag. "Yes, Henry, your wife wants you to *do something*," he had said in a mocking voice while he unbuttoned his fly to free himself and clamped his big hands almost completely around her small waist. Then, he slowly drew her body back until it was snug against his. "Sadly, you don't seem to be in a position to *do* anything. I tell you what; let's not disappoint her. Why don't I *do something* instead? Watch."

Without a further word and in full view of her husband, a sudden surge forward had easily carried Carson completely inside the other man's helpless spouse, her startled gasp and a scream greeting that first solid thrust. As he continued his assault, giving no quarter, the woman's increasingly sharp cries were joined by loud, stifled protests from her hapless mate. The lengthy chorus of the couple's marital duet grew in intensity and was still rising toward a crescendo when, at last, the inevitable convulsions of his climax had cut it short.

The Lord's command to enjoy the spoil of war had been well and faithfully obeyed that winter's night, Carson thought, as he took another sip of brandy. He paused and withdrew a large Havana cigar from inside his suitcoat and unwrapped it. Looking over at his waiter, he signaled for a light that was quickly produced. He took a puff on the cigar and another sip of brandy. To be sure, he had enjoyed shagging the man's wife, but the best part of the plan was still to come.

Tugging free from the woman, Carson had stood and faced her husband with a satisfied smile as he carefully tucked himself away. As she continued to kneel there, gasping for breath, exhausted from her ordeal, he walked over behind Sandler where he clasped the man's shoulders with both hands. He leaned over and put his face close to him, pointed his finger at the man's recently ravished wife and chuckled.

"Boy, your broad sure is one hot little number, isn't she? Look at her. Our little tryst has left her all played out. You know, it's funny. I don't think she was into it all that much at first, but it didn't take long for things to change. It's like I was priming the pump or something because, all of a sudden, your wife started to become all slick inside. After that, I think she sounded like she was really liking it, don't you?" He then laughed and patted the man on his back. "C'mon, of all people, you should know better than anyone. Isn't that what she sounds like when you're in the saddle?" Sandler's angry reply through the gag was incoherent, the humor of the situation apparently lost on him.

Carson chuckled again as he continued to smoke and sip his brandy. Well, 'like' probably wasn't the right word, he admitted, as any sensations Sandler's wife experienced were clearly as involuntary as her participation. Besides, he really didn't care what she felt. It wasn't personal. She was simply one part of his plan. He took another sip of brandy, a puff on his cigar and once more savored the best part, the irony of his plan's fatal parallel.

Having just impaled the man's wife, Carson next impaled the man himself with a single thrust from a rather more lethal weapon. He placed his left arm around Sandler's neck and, with his right hand, shoved all seven inches of his Fairbairn-Sykes fighting knife between his ribs and up into the man's back where it pierced his heart. Keeping the knife firmly in place until his spasms ceased, Henry Sandler was unconscious in less than ten seconds. Three minutes later, he had no pulse. Removing the bandana from the man's mouth and the knife from his back, Carson had wiped his blade clean. He prided himself on his work and it had been, in his professional opinion, a quick, clean and relatively painless death.

As he had walked past Sandler's newly widowed wife, now prone and sobbing face down on the bed, he paused to caress her smooth bottom and give it several affectionate pats for having played her part in his plan to perfection. "Thanks very much, my Dear, for giving me such a nice ride," he had said. "And a fine fit you were. We should do it again sometime."

Yes, they should, Carson thought, and now, thanks once more to Owney Madden, they would. He took a puff from the Havana and blew a splendid smoke ring that rose up into the hazy interior of the steak house. People didn't realize that an assassin's life isn't easy. Apart from being paid, the kill itself, of course, was the ultimate rush, but sometimes there were other benefits as well. Shagging Doris Sandler in front of her husband on that cold winter's eve was certainly one of them. Leaving Peter Luger's, he whistled as he walked to his 1933 Cord Cabriolet. He knew Pittsburgh was his first stop before Cleveland, but even if he were successful in making the two kills in Pittsburgh, he was definitely going to Cleveland for an encore performance with the desirable Doris. Who knew? Maybe this time, she really would like it.

18

A Remarkable Coincidence

Chartwell
Kent, England
Sunday 9 September 1934

CHURCHILL'S CHAUFFEUR, Samuel Howes, was waiting for Mattie at the gate in the Croyden Aerodrome when her flight from Dublin arrived. She gave him a receipt to secure her luggage while she found the familiar red Pillar Box of the Royal Mail and dropped into it large envelopes containing her European Fascist story addressed to Joe Willicomb in New York and William Randolph Hearst at his castle in Wales.

Traffic was light on a late Sunday morning and Howes made good time on the trip from Croyden to Chartwell in Churchill's Daimler Landaulette motorcar. Mattie knew this had been a gift two years earlier from a group of Churchill's friends to celebrate his return from America where an auto accident had hospitalized and nearly killed him during a speaking tour of North America. The group had been organized by Churchill's close friend Brendan Bracken and contributors included Charlie Chaplain as well as Bourke Cockran.

Churchill greeted her warmly upon her arrival with both a kiss and an embrace. "I'm so pleased you could come today, my Dear. Clemmie and Mary are visiting Goonie," referring to Gwendoline

Churchill, his brother Jack's wife, "and I feared I would have to dine alone. Come, let us have a glass of champagne while the maid sets another plate for luncheon."

Their meal, by Churchill standards, was simple, a clear chicken consommé, trout, asparagus and a shoulder of lamb followed by chocolate éclairs for dessert with champagne served throughout. Churchill drank an entire Imperial pint, a 20 oz. bottle, while Mattie was only able to manage half of that, knowing that Winston would be treating them each to a snifter of brandy after their lunch.

They had their brandies upstairs in Churchill's book lined study below a wooden-beamed cathedral ceiling. Mattie sat in a chintz-covered armchair beside a large fireplace reading the English language version of the Prussian Memorandum, while Churchill stood at a rough-hewn stand-up writing desk correcting pages for his latest newspaper article.

By the time Mattie finished reading, she had also finished her brandy. She held out her snifter for a refill. "I've worked for an American newspaper chain for ten years and now I'm married to an American I've known for five years. Yet, I've obviously got a lot to learn about America. I mean I know that Britain abolished slavery in the Empire in 1833 and that slavery was not completely abolished in America until 1865 after a bloody Civil War. I also know that in the Deep South today, Negroes are still subject to abominations like the Jim Crow laws and segregation. But, my God, a majority of American states—30 out of 48—still prohibit marriage, sexual relations or both between whites and other races? That's horrible and now the bloody Nazis are using those laws as a basis for their doing the same to the Jews? What a black eye for America."

"I share your feelings," Churchill said as he refilled Mattie's glass. "That's why I called you about it. Do you agree with me it has the potential for a good story? More importantly, do you think Mr. Hearst will agree?"

"You bet! On both counts. The Chief was enthusiastic about what little I could tell him on Friday. Once I tell him in more detail what this memorandum covers, I'm sure he'll approve. I'll give him a call tonight after dinner. Meanwhile, I recall you saying your sources won't have a transcript of the June 5 meeting of the Commission where the Prussian Memorandum was the subject of debate for another six days. Correct?"

Churchill nodded his agreement.

"Do you have the names of any of the so-called 'moderate' members of the Commission who might be willing to talk to me in the interim if I promise to keep their names confidential?"

"I do. Dr. Dohnanyi left a list with me. Both he and his niece Greta Mayer are familiar with your work and think very highly of it. He said he would contact each one to find out if they were willing to talk to you and to give them your name if they were."

"Swell. Do you have his address? Or a telephone number?"

"Yes as to he former, no to the latter. He believes the Gestapo may be tapping his telephone and we know, from our mutual friend," Churchill said, referring to Kurt von Sturm whom he had recruited as a confidential source two years ago, "that wiretapping is widespread in the new Germany. I told him you always stay at the *Adlon* in Berlin. I wasn't sure when you would be able to go to Berlin, so I suggested he begin calling you there from a public telephone exchange starting tomorrow. When you do hear from him, you can arrange for a time and place to meet with him."

"Okay," Mattie replied, "that will work. What about the Americans who researched and prepared the Memorandum? I would love to find out who they are and interview them. How can I do that?"

"That will be difficult. Dohnanyi told me the Minister of Justice, Franz Gurtner, is not a Nazi, but he is not about to tangle with the Chairman of the Commission, a rabid Nazi, about the names of the Americans who did the research for that memorandum. He said it would have to be someone who had more clout with Hitler, someone like the *Reichstag* President Hermann Göring."

Just then, there was a knock on the door.

"Yes?" Churchill growled.

The door opened and one of Churchill's secretaries, Mrs. Pearman, otherwise known as 'Mrs. P', stuck her head into the room. "Excuse me, Sir, you have a long-distance, person-to-person telephone call from a *Herr* Strasser in Zurich. Are you in for this gentleman?"

"By all means, Mrs. P. Ask the operator to redirect the call to the unlisted number of the private line in my study," Churchill said and turned to Mattie with a smile.

"Not only has Special Branch of Scotland Yard put a listening device in my desk lamp as I told you—which I've disabled for today—but they also have a wiretap on Chartwell's main telephone line. Once Robbie discovered that earlier this year," he said to referring to Scotland Yard Detective Sergeant Robert Rankin, his occasional bodyguard, "I arranged for a separate telephone here in my study with an unlisted number that Robbie kindly checks for me once a week to make sure the line is clean. We leave the main line alone in the event there is misinformation I wish Stanley and Neville to have," Stanley Baldwin being the Prime Minister and Neville Chamberlain the Chancellor of the Exchequer, both Churchill's political enemies.

The telephone rang on Churchill's desk and he picked up the receiver. "*Herr* von Strasser, how good to hear from you. To what do I owe the honor of this call?"

Kurt? Mattie thought and then remembered that his family name was Strasser and Sturm was only a *nom de guerre*.

Churchill was uncharacteristically silent, muttering only an occasional "I see" or "Interesting, please go on". After fifteen minutes, however, Churchill actually interrupted. "*Herr* von Strasser, stop for a moment. This is a remarkable coincidence because I have already received a copy of the Prussian Memorandum from a member of the Commission and I have already shown it to my goddaughter Mattie who is here with me now. Let us pause so you can relate to her what you have told me."

Churchill placed the receiver down on his desk and turned to Mattie. "Briefly, *Herr* von Sturm has photographed Joseph Goebbels' copy of the Prussian Memorandum along with five letters between Himmler and Goebbels that relate to the memorandum. He showed them to *Reichstag* President Göring and, as a consequence, he appointed *Herr* von Sturm as the official liaison between the *Reichstag* and the German Commission on Criminal Reform."

Mattie was elated at the news. "Winston, that's fantastic! Let me talk to Kurt," she said and walked over to Churchill's desk where he handed her the receiver.

"Hello Kurt, it's Mattie. I'm investigating a story about this Prussian Memorandum and I could use your help. I'm flying tomorrow to Berlin where I'm going to try to interview several of the more moderate members of the Commission off-the-record."

"Off-the-record?" Sturm replied. "What does that mean?"

"It means I will keep their names in confidence and not use them in any articles I write," Mattie said. "Apparently, the memorandum was the major topic of discussion at the 5 June meeting of the Commission this year. Our sources don't have access to the transcript of that meeting, but they believe they can reconstruct them from notes taken by stenographers at the meeting. That will take a while to do. As the *Reichstag* liaison, would you be able to acquire a copy of the transcript of the June meeting?"

"It's interesting you should ask about the June meeting."

"Why's that?"

"I was at the Ministry of Justice Friday reviewing Commission correspondence and transcripts of meetings. Several items were missing such as the June 1933 Himmler-Goebbels correspondence and the transcript of the 5 June 1934 Commission meeting. I went to see State Secretary Roland Freisler who is the Chairman of the Commission. I asked the pompous little Nazi about the missing June 1934 transcript and he told me the meeting that month had been cancelled. Your sources say there was such a meeting?"

"Absolutely. One of our sources was there and says it was a long meeting. The Prussian Memorandum was the prime subject of discussion."

"I wonder why Freisler would lie to me?" Sturm asked.

"It beats me," Mattie said, "but it sure sounds suspicious. Say, are you aware that American lawyers were the ones who researched and wrote the Memorandum?"

"Yes. I saw it in one of the letters between Goebbels and Himmler. The SS arranged with the American Military Intelligence Division to have the work done."

"Really? MID? It wouldn't be the first time they've been in bed with the SS. So, in your position as the official liaison between the *Reichstag* and the German Commission on Criminal Reform, would you be able to find out the names of the American lawyers who researched and wrote the Memorandum? And, more importantly, would you give me their names?"

"I don't know. Why would the *Reichstag* need their names? Being Göring's liaison, I likely wouldn't have to give a reason, but I'd need one if *Unser* Hermann asks me why I wanted it."

Mattie laughed. "Well, not all lawyers are created equal. I'm not a lawyer, but I've read the Memorandum and it seems to accurately sum up the laws in those 30 American states. But, keep in mind that in the United States, as in Germany, the percentage of Jewish lawyers is out of proportion to the percentage of Jews in the country. You should not only want the names of the American lawyers involved but their personal, academic, professional and *racial* backgrounds as well. Why? To make sure the German Commission on Criminal Reform is not basing their recommendations to the *Reichstag* on sloppy legal work done by *Jew* lawyers. Don't you think that would be embarrassing?"

"Yes, it would," Sturm said with a laugh. "You are a seriously clever woman, Mattie McGary. Has anyone ever told you that?"

"People say that to me all the time and you're just finding that out now? Are all Germans as thick as you? 'Never forget Mattie is clever'. You might want to write that down." Mattie smiled as Kurt laughed again. "So, you'll do it? You'll try to find out who these American lawyers are?"

"Of course. First thing tomorrow. I didn't like Freisler when I met for the first time on Friday. I'd welcome the chance to take him down a peg or two. As for telling you what I find, let me think about that."

"What's there to think about?" Mattie asked.

"Well, based on what Göring told me, I think a story like you're planning to write would tie in with what Göring wants, which is to stick it to Goebbels, Himmler and the radical Nazis on the Commission The question I want to ponder is do I ask *Unser* Hermann's *permission* to give the names to you or do I just give you the names and ask his *forgiveness* if it turns out he would not have given his permission? I'm naturally inclined towards the 'forgiveness' option, but, for Mr. Churchill's sake, I have to weigh that against losing the confidence of the *Reichspresident*. What time does your flight tomorrow arrive in Berlin?"

"Sometime in the late afternoon."

"Good. You'll be staying at the *Adlon*?

"Yes."

"I'll leave a message for you there. Perhaps we could have dinner together? I'll tell you what happened with Freisler and how I've decided to proceed."

"Sure, dinner would be lovely. Thank you. Would you like to talk to Winston again?"

"No, I've told him what I know and I've mailed the package to him that has both the Memorandum and the Himmler-Goebbels letters. I'll have a set of the letters for you at dinner, with or without Göring's permission."

After she replaced the telephone receiver, Mattie recounted to Churchill what Sturm would be doing the next day for her and that they would be having dinner tomorrow night.

That evening, after dinner, Mattie called Hearst at his castle in Wales to tell him she would be going to Berlin tomorrow where she would begin interviews of moderate Commission members as well as the news that Sturm was the *Reichstag* liaison to the Commission and she was meeting him tomorrow to see what help he might be able to provide. Next, she called Joe Willicomb at his home in Scarsdale and told him the same thing. Finally, she called Cockran at the Cedars, but there was no answer. She called their Fifth Avenue townhouse with the same result. Bourke might be between homes on his way back to Manhattan, she thought, or he and Patrick might well have gone for an afternoon horseback ride.

Mattie looked at her watch. It was 10:00 p.m. and she wanted to get a good night's sleep before her flight tomorrow morning. She decided the best solution was to call Cockran's secretary at her Greenwich Village apartment above an old speakeasy and leave the message with her.

The transatlantic call went through surprisingly quickly. "Hello, Alexis? It's Mattie. Yes, I'm fine, how about you? Good. Listen, I'm in England with Winston and I'm flying to Germany tomorrow morning. I've not been able to reach Bourke at either The Cedars or the townhouse. Please tell him tomorrow that I've gone to Berlin for that story I told him about earlier in the week. I'll be at the *Adlon*. I'm going to do interviews for maybe a week and then I'm going to join Winston in Amsterdam where we have a meeting scheduled with one of our sources. When I know the exact date and where we'll be staying in Amsterdam, I'll let him know. One more thing. Tell him Göring has appointed Kurt as the *Reichstag* liaison to the Commission on Criminal Law Reform and I'm having dinner tomorrow night with him to find out what help he can give me on the story. Got all that? Great, thanks very much. What? Bourke is going to Pittsburgh tomorrow morning? Okay. William Penn. Then Cleveland on Thursday at the Alcazar and Chicago on Sunday at the Drake? OK, got it. You're the best, Alexis. Thanks again."

19

My Husband Did *Not* Commit Suicide

991 Fifth Avenue
New York City
Monday, 10 September 1934

"ALEXIS DID *what* last night?" Bobby Sullivan asked after Cockran had hailed a taxi in front of his townhouse and the two hopped in for the short ride down to Grand Central Station.

"Mattie called her from England when she couldn't find me at either the Cedars or the townhouse. Patrick, his grandmother and I were probably en route back to Manhattan. She took a message from Mattie about her travel plans to Germany and gave her my travel plans. Then, since she knew I wouldn't be in the office this morning as you and I were going straight to the train, she typed the message and rode her motorcycle up here from the Village and put it in the mail slot. When Mattie's on assignment, especially out-of-the-country, Alexis knows how important it is for each of us to know where the other is."

"Little blonde Alexis has a motorcycle?" Sullivan asked, his tone of voice expressing his skepticism.

"Sure, a Harley-Davidson RL 45."

Sullivan shook his head. "And she did this despite the fact that Saturday and Sunday are her days off?"

"Of course."

"And you pay her overtime for something like that?"

"Uh, well…I'm not sure what the firm's policy is on things above and beyond like that."

"It's not fair."

"What's not fair?"

"'T'is not enough that you have Mattie, but you also get Alexis? They're each more than your sorry…"

Cockran laughed. "Than my sorry Irish arse deserves? I know, I know. I think I must have been something of a Saint in a previous life. Mattie and Alexis are both my reward now for being so good then."

Sullivan just shook his head. "You could have been St. Francis of Assisi and it's still not fair."

"Life is unfair, Bobby. How many times do I have to tell you?"

They walked across the concourse until they found the track for the Pennsylvania Railroad's early morning express to Pittsburgh with a stop in Harrisburg. Once they found the Pullman compartment Alexis had reserved for them and ordered a pot of coffee from the porter, Cockran took out O'Hanlon's folder on Joseph Carmody that included his military record.

"Carmody left MID approximately five years ago. According to Tim, promotion was not in the cards and, unlike Tim, there was no family business to support him or a young family. He got a position as the only litigator for Miller and Brown, a small ten-lawyer business law firm in downtown Pittsburgh. He handled all the litigation for their business clients and they paid him 25% of the fees generated from those clients. It was okay money—a lot better than MID according to Tim—but Carmody got to keep 75% of the fees generated by his own clients. He called Tim after he received the MID assignment and thanked him for the referral, explaining why it was so good financially for him."

"What's his military record?" Sullivan asked.

"Not bad. West Point followed by law school at Yale, but no commission until after the war. No heroics. Went right into MID as a CI agent chasing imaginary Bolsheviks in the early twenties, with several foreign postings after that in Cairo, Rome and finally London where he met his wife, Alice Livingstone, in '28 and married her a year later. When his London tour was over, he resigned his commission and hitched on with Miller and Brown. Carmody grew up in Mount Lebanon, a suburb of Pittsburgh, and he and Michael Miller went to high school together."

40 Marlin Drive West
Mount Lebanon, Pennsylvania
Monday, 10 September 1934

ALICE LIVINGSTONE CARMODY was what was usually described, Cockran thought, as a classic English beauty. She was tall, 5'7', in her early 30s with light brown hair, clear blue eyes and an erect posture that bordered on regal. A posh, Mayfair accent completed the picture.

It was a beautiful, late summer day in Pittsburgh, just shy of five p.m., and the Carmody home was a yellow brick, two-story bungalow with a long, covered front porch. Cockran rang the doorbell and a woman opened the front door moments later. He introduced himself.

"Pleased to meet you, Mr. Cockran," she said as she extended her hand, "I'm Alice Carmody. I've heard so much about you from Tim, including the fact that you married a Scottish girl last year. My congratulations."

"Thanks. Just lucky, I guess," Cockran replied as he took her hand.

"You can say that again," Sullivan grumbled under his breath.

"And this is my colleague, Robert Sullivan, who came to America about the same time as you. Unfortunately, we're still trying to housetrain him."

Alice smiled as Sullivan shook her hand and smiled back, but Cockran could see from her wary expression that she hadn't recognized it as a smile.

"We're both sorry for your loss, Mrs. Carmody, and that we have to meet under such circumstances," Cockran said.

"Thank you. Please call me 'Alice'. Won't you join me for tea?"

"Yes, certainly. I'm 'Bourke' and he is 'Bobby'.

They followed her into the living room where a full English tea, complete with crustless cucumber sandwiches and assorted *petit fours*, was on a butler's table between a chintz-covered sofa on one side and two similarly covered chairs on the other side. To Cockran's surprise, a young tow-headed boy in short pants, knee length socks, shirt and tie was sitting on the sofa.

Alice motioned Cockran and Sullivan into the two armchairs. "This is my son, Joseph, Jr. This is Mr. Cockran and Mr. Sullivan. Say hello to them."

Alice's son stood up and gave short bow. "How do you do, Sirs, pleased to meet you," he said and sat back down.

Cockran raised his eyebrows at her son's presence and Alice understood his unspoken question. "Joseph will be six in a few months. He is the man of the house now and he deserves to listen to any discussion about his father. This is especially true since Tim told me you are investigating the circumstances of his death and the MID project he had worked on prior to that. Correct?"

"Yes, that's correct."

"Well, my husband did *not* commit suicide and I don't give a damn what the coroner found. It was not like Joe and I want our son to know it. So, ask me your questions. What do you want to know," she said with a smile, "besides milk, sugar or lemon with your tea?"

"Milk, no sugar," Cockran said.

"Milk and sugar, please," Sullivan replied.

Alice played Mother and, when all four had their tea, Cockran began. "Why don't you think it was suicide?"

"Two reasons. First, Joe was an upbeat, optimistic person for whom the glass was always half full. That suicide note where he supposedly claimed he was despondent over the last case he lost? It's a fake. No one wins all their trials although Joe won well over half the cases he tried. Losing is part of the job. While he never shared it with clients, Joe had a saying about trials: 'Sometimes you win; sometimes the client loses'."

Cockran smiled. He had heard the same thing from his father. "What was the case?"

"A lousy contract dispute! His client could have settled for ten grand. The jury awarded the plaintiff fifty grand. Joe thought his client was an idiot for not settling. He didn't like losing, but he wasn't upset. Joe would never kill himself over a client he thought was an idiot. Damn it! He had a family he loved! He would never leave us like that."

"You said there were two reasons?"

Alice dabbed at her eyes with a handkerchief. "Yes and it's actual proof, but the coroner was so bloody stubborn that he wouldn't reconsider his initial finding. Once Joe's effects were released to me which included the so-called 'suicide note', I didn't recognize the typeface. I had it examined by an expert Joe used in the past in some of his cases and he said the note was typed on an Underwood!"

Cockran nodded. "And that's significant because?"

"Because all of the typewriters at Joe's law firm are Smith Coronas! And so is the typewriter in Joe's study here at home. Joe didn't have access to an Underwood."

Cockran nodded again. Alice was upset, angry, but in complete control of her emotions. It might have been her English accent, but he didn't think so. If all the lawyers who lost court cases—and half of them by definition did—committed suicide, there would soon be a shortage of lawyers. He believed her. Her husband didn't commit suicide. Someone killed him. Based on Bobby's dealings with Owney Madden, he thought he knew who. Now, they needed to know why.

Cockran turned to address Joseph, Jr. "Young man, your mother is absolutely right. I'm a lawyer myself. Your father didn't kill himself. Someone else did and I'm going to do my best to find out who did it and make them pay."

"Aye, lad," Sullivan chimed in. "We'll make them pay."

"Alice, did your husband ever tell you the nature of the project he was working on for MID?" Cockran asked.

Alice shook her head. "No, never. Even before he resigned his Army commission, Joe never talked about his work for MID. On this last project, all he said was he didn't particularly like what he was doing, but the client was paying good money and he wasn't in a position to turn legitimate business away."

"I understand," Cockran said. "Can you give us the names of Joe's colleagues at his law firm or any friends in whom he may have confided about his work for MID?"

"Yes. Tim told me you would want information like that so I prepared a list of his friends both at the law firm and the Pittsburgh Athletic Club along with their business and home addresses and phone numbers. Here, let me get it for you."

With that, Alice rose, walked over to a small period writing desk and picked up two sheets of paper that she handed to Cockran. He looked at them and saw in neat, cursive handwriting the names of four men along with addresses and phone numbers.

"This is great, Alice," Cockran said. "Thanks very much. Mr. Sullivan and I will talk with these gentlemen tomorrow to see what they know. You've been a big help and we appreciate it."

"You'll let me know if you find anything that shows Joe didn't commit suicide?"

"Count on it," Cockran replied. "After we finish here, we're going to Cleveland to talk with Doris Sandler and see what we can learn from her. Tim is determined to get to the bottom of this and so are we."

Alice shook her head and sighed. "I feel so bad about Doris, having to witness her husband's murder. I wanted to go to the funeral, but I was still in a state of shock after Joe died. All four of us were in Tim and Cynthia's wedding party. It's all too much to bear, but I would be ever so grateful if you could clear Joe's name."

"We'll do our best M'am," Sullivan said as the two men stood up to leave. "We'll be in touch."

40 Marlin Drive West
Mount Lebanon, Pennsylvania
Monday, 10 September 1934

NICHOLAS CARSON watched Cockran and Sullivan descend the porch steps from the Carmody house as he sat in a gray Plymouth 1933 sedan parked on a side street that ended in a T-intersection at

Marlin Drive West, one house to the left of the Carmody's. They had been with Carmody's widow for about an hour. Carson had little hope that the house would be a serviceable spot for taking out Bobby Sullivan, but it was worth a try as he had never been to Carmody's house before. It was his last chance to do the job in Pittsburgh as his plan to do so earlier that afternoon when Sullivan and Cockran arrived at the William Penn Hotel had failed.

Upon receiving the assignment from Owney yesterday, Carson had taken the night train to Pittsburgh and checked in this morning at the Monongahela House, a five-story hotel beside the river of the same name. It was five blocks from the William Penn Hotel on Mellon Square. He had gone to the top of his hotel and saw it gave him a good line of sight to the front entrance of the William Penn. He then paced off the distance from his hotel to the William Penn and found it was a little over a half mile. The effective range of his Springfield M1903 sniper rifle was only 1000 yards, but his longest kill was 600 yards with the Springfield so he had thought the kill was doable. After he took down Sullivan, he figured he would have a good shot at Cockran if, as expected, he rushed to the side of his stricken comrade where he would be a stationary target, a sitting duck as the Americans say.

In the event, it hadn't worked. He knew from the train schedule that their train arrived from New York at 3:07. That meant they would arrive by taxi at the William Penn by no later than 3:30. The front of the hotel was crowded with taxis coming and going. That morning, however, the front of the hotel had not been that busy and the few taxis there were picking up passengers, not dropping them off. When he settled into position at 3 p.m., he saw the problem at once. Arriving taxis were facing away from him. The right rear door of the taxis opened toward the back of the motorcar, thus shielding the passenger as he exited the taxi so that only a headshot was possible. That didn't bother the Killer. What did bother him was that the hotel's uniformed doorman opened each taxi door and stood behind it as the passenger left the car. The doorman wore a tall, bearskin hat akin to those worn by the guards at Buckingham Palace that effectively blocked a headshot when the passenger left the taxi. The problem was that Carson had to shoot the target when he was stationary, which almost everyone was as they stepped from the taxi. Once they began to move, the game was over. Hitting a moving target from over a half mile was virtually impossible, strictly a matter of luck. He tried a few dry runs on other passengers as he waited for Cockran and Sullivan to arrive, but that damned bearskin hat blocked his shot every single time. He waited until their taxi arrived, but it was the same story.

Carson had left the roof right after their arrival and drove his Plymouth to the Pittsburgh suburb of Mount Lebanon where he quickly discovered that there was no sufficiently concealed spot to shoot both men as they stood motionless at the Carmody front door. Carson had not left after he came to that conclusion. He still waited here because he wanted a good look at Cockran and Sullivan as that had not been possible when they arrived. Only the backs of both men had been visible to him while they walked up the front steps to the Carmody front porch. Once he had a good look at the two men as they walked down the front steps and into a Chrysler Air Flow Coupe, he switched the ignition on in his Plymouth and put the motorcar into gear.

On the way back to the Monongahela House, Carson began to plan his next steps. He would leave for Cleveland first thing tomorrow morning. That would give him most of the day Tuesday to set up a hide in a tree in the woods across from the Sandler residence on North Park Boulevard in Cleveland Heights. Having been there last December when the trees were barren of leaves, he knew just where he was going to go to accomplish this. Then, as Cockran and Sullivan were not due in Cleveland until Thursday, that left him free Wednesday to renew relations, so to speak, with the beautiful blonde widow who was Doris Sandler. Carson smiled at the thought that the second time is always better than the first.

20

Give Her All the Help She Needs

Karinhalle
Friedrichwalde, Germany
Monday, 10 September 1934

IT SEEMED that Hermann Göring had as many different uniforms as he had official positions, Kurt von Sturm thought, as the man greeted him at the front door of *Karinhalle*, his country estate. It was a bright, sunny afternoon and he greeted Sturm at the front door of *Karinhalle* wearing a double-breasted brown tweed jacket, tweed plus-fours and light tan knee high socks topped off by a snap-brimmed hat with a colorful feather jutting up from the hatband, presumably what Göring thought made him look like a 'Country Squire'. Or, Sturm wondered, was this outfit his Reich's Chief Huntsman uniform, the *Reichsjagermeister?* He smiled. He supposed it didn't matter. Göring's almost childish delight in his uniforms was somehow humanizing because he otherwise was one of the most intelligent and ruthless men Sturm had ever known. He suspected that Göring had hired him as his principal adviser on airships last year less for his expertise in that field than for the fact he believed he and Sturm were alike in several key respects.

For one, they were both *bona fide* heroes, holder of Imperial Germany's highest military honor, the *Pour le Merite*, the coveted

'Blue Max'. For the other, Göring likely believed Sturm was every bit as ruthless as he was. In that, Sturm thought, he was probably right for Sturm had spent ten years as the Executive Director of the Geneva Institute for Scientific & Industrial Progress, informally known as the Geneva Group. It was a fancy title for someone who was essentially a professional assassin for an international group of arms dealers, manufacturers and financiers. Their business was blood and steel and business had been good.

What Sturm didn't know was whether Göring realized how vast the differences were between the two of them. The *Reichspresident* was a pragmatic, freebooting pirate whose attitude towards those he considered his enemies was "What's mine is mine and what's yours may soon be mine if you get in my way." In contrast, Sturm came from a line of aristocratic Imperial German officers who had served Prussian kings for generations. His father was Peter von Strasser who had been the head of the Imperial German Navy's Airship Division during the Great War and also a holder of the Blue Max. He had perished in a flaming zeppelin during the War's last days in the L-70, a remarkable airship that was capable of flying to New York on a bombing run and returning home to Germany. As an Imperial German Navy officer, his father had lived by a rigid code of honor that he had passed on to his son. These were values that Hermann Göring did not possess.

Göring walked with Sturm into the house through the foyer and into the Great Hall. They walked under massive wooden beams and three equally massive chandeliers to the open fireplace at the far end of the room. They sat in two leather club chairs on either side of the fireplace where a young, blond, white-coated servant waited to take their drink orders.

"Do you have 'The Singleton'?" Sturm asked. "It's a single malt Scotch whisky from a distillery near Inverness."

"Yes, Sir. We do."

"Two fingers, over ice, with just a splash of water."

"Of course, Sir," the servant said and turned to Göring. "And you, Herr *Reichspresident*?" he asked, using the diplomatically highest office held by his master.

"The same, Eric!" he boomed. "And be quick about it!"

"Yes, Sir. Very good, Sir."

After the drinks were served and Eric left, Göring took a sip. "This is excellent! Eric!" he bellowed.

"Yes, sir?" Eric said moments later.

"Bring the bottle, a bowl of ice and a pitcher of water."

"Yes, Sir."

Göring looked suspiciously at Sturm. "How did you know I would have this brand of Scotch? I don't recall ever having it before."

Sturm smiled. "When I was here last Thursday, I suggested to Eric that he find a bottle of The Singleton. I told him I thought you would like it."

"Hah! Well, my thanks. How did you come across it? I wasn't aware you were a Scotch connoisseur."

"I'm not, but a year ago last summer, I was in Inverness for the McGary-Cockran wedding and this is the only Scotch they served."

"Ah, yes, one of your wild Irish mercenaries who saved the Fuhrer's life at Berchtesgaden. Our invitations must have been lost in the mail, but Hitler and I both sent them wedding gifts. He sent some silly silver tray with his initials on it! Hah! What a colossal ego that man has! I sent them *two* gifts, one of them was a huge silver punch bowl that had both the Cockran and McGary crests on it. McGary even sent me a thank-you note, but for some reason she did not mention my other gift, the marble statue of a rearing centaur on its hind legs clutching a struggling, naked female. Well, you can't please everyone. So, enough of that. I understand you have a report on your new duties as my liaison to the German Commission on Criminal Reform and that cold-blooded lizard Roland Freisler. So, let's have it."

"I do, *Herr Reichspresident,* and I think you will find it most interesting. Freisler is playing games and lying to me and, coincidentally, Mattie McGary has given me information which, if true, proves it."

Göring made a 'tell me more' gesture and Sturm continued. "Let me begin with Freisler. As I told you last Friday, he cleansed the correspondence files of the Himmler-Goebbels letters and lied to me about using American race laws as a model when we know the Prussian

Memorandum does precisely that. I also thought he was lying to me about there being no meeting of the Commission on 5 June this year where the minutes of the May meeting indicated that making Jews 2nd class citizens would be the main topic of discussion at the next meeting."

Sturm paused and took a sip of whisky. "Last night, I learned for a fact that Freisler lied about there being no June meeting of the Commission. *Frau* McGary talked to me by telephone about a new story she is investigating. It seems she has acquired a copy of the Prussian Memorandum as well…"

"The devil you say!" Göring exclaimed. "I'm the Prime Minister of Prussia and I wouldn't even have a copy myself had you not been screwing Magda Goebbels! Where did McGary get a copy?"

"She didn't say," Sturm replied. "In America, *Herr Reichspresident*, the laws do not require journalists to disclose their sources."

"Not even to the Government?" Göring asked, his tone of voice incredulous.

"Especially not to the Government."

Göring shook his head. "The Americans never cease to amaze me. What kind of government worthy of the name can't compel journalists to do what they're told?"

"Anyway, I disclosed that you had recently appointed me as the official *Reichstag* liaison with the Commission. *Frau* McGary then told me she has at least two sources, one of whom was actually present at the meeting on 5 June. She is attempting to secure a transcript of the meeting and asked if I could help her obtain one. She also asked if I could ascertain the identities of the American lawyers who researched and prepared the Memorandum. I told her I would have to ask your permission to do that."

Göring narrowed his eyes, drained the rest of his Scotch and held up the bottle and wordlessly asked Sturm if he wanted a refill. Sturm nodded 'no' and Göring filled his short crystal glass halfway to the top and added two ice cubes. "How well do you know McGary?"

In one sense, Sturm thought, about as well as he knew Magda Goebbels in that he had slept with both women, twice with McGary three years ago at a time when she was temporarily estranged from her then-boyfriend Cockran and rather more frequently this year with Magda.

"I'm not sure what you mean, but both *Herr* Cockran and his wife are my friends."

"Where does she stand politically on what the Commission is studying, making marriage and sexual relations between Jews and Aryans illegal? Is she a Jew-lover like you?"

Sturm knew Göring was baiting him, but he also knew he was expected to rise to the bait. "*Herr Reichspresident,* it is not that I 'love' the Jews, but that I believe…"

Göring cut him off with a wave of his hand. "Yes, yes, I know. A man cannot help how he is born and should be judged as an individual, etcetera, etcetera. Look, what I want to know is will she portray Himmler and Goebbels as the idiots they are if we let her have copies of their letters? And will she keep confidential that you were her source for these letters?"

"Yes, Sir, she will as to both questions if I ask her."

"Okay. Here's what I want you to do. Tell her you decided, upon reflection, not to ask my permission, but rather to ask for my forgiveness after the fact. Then, after she promises to keep your name out of it, give her copies of the Himmler-Goebbels correspondence. Then try to locate a transcript of the 5 June meeting as well as the identity of the American lawyers involved and give that to her as well. If she wants anything more, do that also. Give her all the help she needs, but…" Göring said and held up index finger, "make sure she first agrees that it will be a two-way street. She keeps you informed of everything she learns about the Commission in exchange for your help. Then, you keep me informed as to everything you're doing and everything you learn from her. *Everything.* Understood?"

"Yes, *Herr Reichspresident.* I understand."

"Good," Göring said and drained his glass again. Without asking, he poured them each new drinks, smiled a wolfish grin and raised his glass in a toast. "And, of course, this conversation never took place."

""Of course *Herr Reichspresident,*" Sturm said as he accepted the glass from Göring, "but there's one more thing."

"Yes?"

"In order to ask him for the identity and background of the American lawyers, I believe it will be necessary to disclose to Freisler that we have a copy of the Prussian Memorandum. May I?"

"Of course. Don't disclose where you got it. Pretend you're an American journalist!" Göring said with a laugh. "Then tell him how displeased I was that I had not received a copy from him. After that, say that if he ever keeps a single thing from me again, like the minutes of the June 5 meeting, I'll have him arrested for obstruction of justice!"

Office of the Director
Federal Bureau of Investigation
The United States Justice Department
950 Pennsylvania Avenue, N.W.
Washington, D.C.
Monday, 10 September 1934

J. EDGAR HOOVER placed the five sheets of paper neatly in middle of a large mahogany desk covered by a clear sheet of glass. The desktop was otherwise immaculate. It was early morning and the sun shining through the wooden blinds cast stripes over its surface. He reached over and punched a button on his intercom device. "Find Clyde and send him in."

Moments later, Clyde Tolson, the Associate Director of the FBI, came into the room. He was a tall, good looking 34-year-old-man wearing a dark Brooks Brothers suit over an immaculate white shirt and tightly knotted maroon tie. He and Hoover, both bachelors, were close friends. They drove to work together, ate lunch together, travelled together, went to racetracks together and even took vacations together. There were those in Washington, including the President of the United States, who believed they were lovers.

"Yes, Edgar, you called for me?" Tolson asked.

"Take a look at this," Hoover said as he shoved the five pages across the broad expanse of his desk. "It's the transcript of a wiretapped telephone conversation last night between Joe Willicomb of the Hearst papers and their reporter Martha McGary who is working on the Prussian Memorandum story."

Tolson took the pages and began to read. Five minutes later, he looked up and whistled. "Boy, FDR is *not* going to like this. Not only is this McGary broad in Berlin interviewing members of the German Commission on Criminal Law Reform, but one of her sources is the *Reichstag* official liaison to the Commission and he's promised to find her the names of the American lawyers who prepared the memorandum. If she learns that, the shit is really going to hit the fan."

"In more ways than you can imagine, Clyde. I don't think Louie Howe knows this, but all six of the MID agents who worked on the memorandum are dead. I opened files on all six last year when we first learned of what MID had done and I had our field personnel keep track of them after that. All six died in various ways last November and December. So did the two field agents who conducted our own investigation. That really can't be a coincidence. We have no proof, of course, but I rather suspect that our General Marlborough over at MID is so scared of FDR that he has been covering his tracks as well as his ass."

"So what are you going to do?"

"Nothing. It's really not our problem, is it?" Hoover said and smiled. "All I'm going to do is what the White House—in the person of one Louis Howe—told me to do. Make two photocopies of the transcript, stamp 'Top Secret' in bright red ink on both and place them in sealed envelopes. Address one envelope to Howe at the White House and the other to that ex-ONI guy, Harold Canfield, at the D.C. headquarters of RVD International. Mark them both 'Personal & Confidential' and have Special Agents hand deliver them this afternoon."

Tolson rose to leave, but Hoover stopped him short of the door. "Clyde? One more thing."

Tolson turned and faced Hoover. "Yes, Chief?"

"Place the original in our FDR file we keep at home, you know, the one in the safe?"

Tolson grinned. "Yes, Sir."

21

Greta Mayer

MATTIE McGARY, uncharacteristically, woke up with a hangover. Scots were not known for that and she was embarrassed because she and Kurt von Sturm had dined the previous evening at Restaurant *Horcher*. It had been his choice, not hers. She usually avoided it as a matter of principle because *Horcher* was a prime watering hole for Nazi party bigwigs. Being Hitler's favorite foreign journalist was business. That didn't mean she had to see Nazis socially and there was too great a chance for that at *Horcher*. In fact, the last time she had dined at *Horcher* was also at Sturm's suggestion over a year ago and they had been seated at Hermann Göring's table just as they had last night.

"Everyone knows this is *Unser* Hermann's table and that no one is seated here except with his permission," Sturm had explained. "Once you begin interviewing members of the German Commission on Criminal Law Reform, however discreetly and confidentially, word is bound to leak out. The fact that you dined here with one of Göring's aides will serve as his *imprimatur* and afford you no small measure of protection from any *Gestapo* types who may question or disagree with what you're doing."

That was the extent of their conversation at dinner on what assistance Göring was willing to allow Sturm to give her on the Prussian Memorandum story. Details had to wait until they returned to her suite at the *Adlon*. There, seated in two green leather arm chairs on either side of a coal fireplace and over a bottle—well, actually nearly two bottles—of *Remy Martin*, Sturm had told her of Göring's order to 'Give her all the help she needs' and the fact that Sturm was not to tell her of this, but to give her the impression Sturm was doing this all on his own.

"This is *Unser* Hermann's way of covering his ass," Sturm had said.

Mattie had laughed. "That's a lot of ass to cover!"

Sturm joined in the laughter and explained that he would initially attempt to find out the identities of the American lawyers and their credentials rather than the transcript of the June meeting where the Prussian Memorandum had been the main item on the agenda. "The transcripts of the other meetings are there in the records I've reviewed, but not the June meeting that State Secretary Freisler has denied ever occurred. I don't see how I can ask for a transcript of a meeting he denies ever took place. You'll have better luck if your sources can produce a transcript and have the Commission members you interview corroborate its accuracy."

After that, and lubricated by more than one snifter of *Remy Martin,* they had reminisced over old times and the many adventures the two good friends had shared over the past three years. They had first briefly met in California when the *Graf Zeppelin* had stopped in Los Angeles completing the third leg of its historic around the world flight from Lakehurst, New Jersey to Friedrichshafen, Germany, Tokyo, Los Angeles and back to Lakehurst. They met again in 1931 when Mattie was on a quest in the Austrian Alps for an ancient Christian artifact that Sturm was seeking for the Kaiser and the SS were seeking for Hitler. Sturm fell in love with her and seduced a vulnerable Mattie on two occasions in the Alps at a time when she erroneously believed that Cockran had thrown her over for a new blonde client. Had it been true about Cockran, Mattie had to admit, she likely would have fallen in love with Sturm as well, so alike were the two men. But it hadn't been true and Mattie was now a happily married woman and Sturm was secretly engaged to Cockran's biggest client, the beautiful, blonde, anti-Nazi New York publisher Ingrid Johansson. The Austrian Alps, however, was the one adventure together that they both carefully avoided discussing. Their affair in the Alps, however brief, had been passionate and Mattie was not about to tempt fate by making even a passing reference to it while alone with him in a hotel room. She assumed Sturm felt the same way.

By midnight, they were well into the second bottle of *Remy Martin* and might well have finished it had there not been a knock on the door to her suite. Motioning for her to stay where she was, Sturm had pulled a Luger from his shoulder holster and walked to the door. Standing with his back to the wall to the left side the door, holding the pistol beside his head, Sturm spoke.

"Who is it?"

"The Bellhop, Wilhelm Hartmann, Sir. I have a message for *Frau* McGary."

Sturm had relaxed, as both he and Mattie knew Willy Hartmann. Still, Mattie hadn't been surprised at Sturm's reaction. Nazi Germany was a gangster state with many competing factions to whom the law didn't apply. Well over 200 of Hitler's political enemies, both inside and outside the Nazi Party, had found that out the hard way on 30 June of this year in the SS bloodbath now known as 'The Night of the Long Knives'.

Sturm opened the door and took the sealed envelope from Willy and handed him a single *Reichsmark*. "*Danke*, Willy."

"You're welcome *Herr* von Sturm and thank you!"

Sturm walked over, handed the envelope to Mattie, and resumed his seat. Mattie opened the envelope and began to read.

Dear Frau McGary,

My Uncle Georg is being watched by the Gestapo and does not believe it wise for you to meet him. I have made reservations for us tomorrow at the restaurant Zur

> letzten Instanz *for 1 p.m. The address is Waisenstrasse*
> *14-16. I will have information for you from my Uncle.*
> *Please make sure you are not followed and destroy this*
> *letter after reading.*
>
> *Sincerely,*
> *Greta Mayer*

Sturm had raised his eyebrows in a silent question.

"One of our sources," Mattie had replied. "She wants to meet tomorrow for lunch. Some place called *Zur letzten Instanz.* Have you heard of it?"

"'In the Last Instance'? Yes, it's the oldest restaurant in Berlin, dating back to the 17th century. You'll like it."

Sturm had left after that and, as requested, Mattie burned the note in the coal fireplace and went to bed.

Now, with a hangover, Mattie ordered a full English breakfast and a large pot of coffee rather than her usual Scottish Breakfast Tea. Lunch was several hours away and she needed all her wits about her.

Zur letzten Instanz
Waisenstrasse 14-16
Berlin,
Tuesday 11 September 1934

"*FRAULEIN* GRETA Mayer, please," Mattie said to the young, rosy-cheeked hostess. "I'm meeting her here." As requested, Mattie had taken care to insure she hadn't been followed. She had taken a taxi to the *Friedrichstrasse* railway station where, after going inside, she had promptly walked across the concourse and taken a second taxi to the restaurant.

"This way, please," the hostess said and led Mattie across a room with dark wood wainscoting below cream-colored walls with a series of black, cast iron sconces evenly spaced on both sides of the room. They walked between tables lining each side to a baroque circular iron staircase at the far end of the room. She followed the hostess up the staircase and over to a corner table overlooking the square below. A young, beautiful blonde girl sat behind the table, her back to the wall. She rose when she spotted Mattie. She was tall and lithe, Mattie thought, probably an inch or two taller than Mattie who was 5'7" and she didn't look a day over 21. The 34-year-old Mattie was suddenly feeling her age.

"*Fraulein* Mayer?" she said, extending her hand. "I'm Mattie McGary."

The girl smiled and took Mattie's hand in hers. "I'm so pleased to meet you. Thank you for coming. I'm a great admirer of your work."

"Really?" Mattie asked as she sat down in the chair the hostess had pulled out for her.

"Oh, yes! The Ministry of Justice subscribes to the *New York Examiner* and other American newspapers. Uncle Georg brings them to me when he's finished with them. I loved your interview with Hitler in July about all those horrid murders. You really pinned him down with your questions. What's he really like? Hitler, I mean. Is it true that you're his favorite foreign journalist?"

Actually, Mattie thought, she hadn't been able to pin Hitler down about the Night of the Long Knives. Hitler had a message he wanted to convey to an American audience and he had done just that, ignoring Mattie's questions when they didn't suit his purpose.

Mattie laughed. "I don't know about being his favorite foreign journalist, but I first interviewed him in 1923 before his failed *putsch* in Munich and I think today he is a far more effective and polished politician than he was then." Right, Mattie thought, he hides his anti-Semitism much more adroitly today than he did then when he made no pretense about it. But she wasn't about to tell any German girl she had just met what she really thought of the ruthless bastard who was leading her country. "So, what do you have for me from your Uncle Georg?"

Just then, their waitress arrived and took their orders. Greta ordered the pan-fried fish with carrots and new potatoes and a mineral water. Mattie ordered the grilled breast of guinea fowl and was tempted to order a glass of *Pinot Grigio,* but likewise opted for mineral water.

When the waitress left, Greta tapped the folded newspaper on the table. I will leave this behind. Take it with you. Inside is what Uncle Georg has prepared for you with much more detail than the list he gave Mr. Churchill —the names, addresses and telephone numbers of all the members of the Commission on Criminal Law Reform along with a brief description of their careers and what he believes to be their position—moderate or radical—on the definition of who is a Jew for purposes of the new law. Uncle Georg has talked to who he believes to be the moderate members and given them your name. He's asked them to talk with you confidentially as a way to expose what the radicals are attempting to do. All of them said they would think about it, but only two said 'yes'. He placed a red check beside their names. Those are the ones you should first ask for an interview."

"Good, thank your Uncle for me. Now, how are you coming along with re-creating a transcript of the June 5 meeting of the Commission?"

"Not as quickly as I had hoped. Our Track and Field coach established a new training schedule for autumn and it leaves me less time to work on the transcript. I have to do it at home as I can't do it at the Ministry. I've finished typing up the shorthand notes I took at the June meeting, but now I have to incorporate *Frau* Schmidt's official notes and it's not as easy as I thought."

Their meals came and they ate in silence for a few minutes.

"You mentioned track and field," Mattie said. "Are you an athlete?"

Greta smiled. "Yes, I'm a runner and I'm training for the Olympics in 1936."

"That's great. What events?"

"The 100 Meter and the 400 Meter relay."

Mattie nodded. The girl looked fit and she certainly had long legs. "So, if you have typed up your shorthand notes of the meeting, may I see what you have while you work on the official notes?"

"Oh, no, I couldn't do that. I'd be too embarrassed. My shorthand isn't that good, really, and there are just too many gaps where I just couldn't get down what was being said. Even with my new training schedule, I promise I'll have it done before Uncle Georg leaves for the conference in Amsterdam later this week."

"Are you sure? Even a partial transcript would give me a better idea of where the members are coming from on this subject."

"I'm sure, but I will show what I have done to Uncle Georg and let him decide. I think he will agree with me. If the wrong people saw my partial transcript, they would know it was me and, at a minimum, I'd lose my job and probably my chance at the Olympics."

Greta's excuse sounded lame to Mattie, but this was Nazi Germany, after all, and being paranoid didn't mean there weren't people out there trying to get you. Besides, she was just a kid and the Olympics were a big deal. She decided to drop it. But, as soon as she got back to the *Adlon,* she was going to call Bella Fromm and set up a meeting with her to see what Bella knew about the Commission members on Dohnanyi's list.

Back at the hotel, Mattie had ordered dinner from Room Service when the telephone rang. She picked up the receiver. "Mattie McGary."

"Mattie, it's Kurt. I saw Freisler today and gave him until the end of the day Thursday to come up with CVs for the American lawyers. He's to deliver them to the office of the *Reichspresident.* I reported this to *Unser* Hermann. He will have them sent over to you at the *Adlon.* I'm flying the *Graf Bismarck* to America this evening and I'll return late Saturday evening. If you don't receive anything by noon Friday, call Göring."

22

Walter Schellenberg

SD Foreign Intelligence Section
8 Prinz Albrechtstrasse
Berlin
Tuesday, 11 September 1934

WALTER SCHELLENBERG, the *SS-Sturmbannfuhrer* in charge of the SD's Foreign Intelligence Section, picked up the decoded cable from Wilhelm Krueger at the German embassy in Washington on his large mahogany desk. The cable was a decidedly unnecessary complication in his life. That damnable Prussian Memorandum was rearing its ugly head. He stood and, holding the cable, walked to the window that overlooked the courtyard at SS and *Gestapo* headquarters.

Schellenberg was a tall man in his mid-twenties, dark blond hair with a trim body and a boyish face handsome enough to have drawn the attention of more than one German *frau* looking for an illicit adventure. A lawyer by profession, he had joined the Nazi Party in 1932 right out of school because jobs were scarce and someone had told him that a party membership and service in the SA or SS would go a long way to securing a permanent position in the Ministry of Justice. Schellenberg had chosen the SS because it had a higher class of people among its ranks as compared to the rough louts, thugs and nancy boys who made up the SA. The fact that the black with silver trim uniforms of the SS were much more stylish than brown shirts and trousers worn by the SA was frosting on the cake of his decision.

Schellenberg had been with the Ministry of Justice for less than a year when the Nazis took power on 30 January and he had leaped at the chance for a permanent position with the SS. There, his rise in the ranks had been swift thanks to his mentor and immediate superior, *Obersturmbannfuhrer* Reinhard Heydrich, the #2 man in the SS who reported directly to *Reichsfuhrer-SS* Heinrich Himmler himself.

According to Krueger's cable, the MID contact person with the SS in America, someone named Harold Canfield, had discovered that Mattie McGary either had, or was soon to have, a copy of The Prussian Memorandum and was coming to Germany to investigate the story further. This Canfield wanted the story killed either by effecting McGary's demise or tossing her into a concentration camp. That idiot Krueger had helpfully suggested handing this assignment to the *Gestapo* now that it had passed from the control of Hermann Göring to Himmler. Schellenberg made a mental note to give the little blond shit a failing grade on his next annual fitness report.

The fault of course began with Heinrich Himmler. Someone had put a bug in his ear about the potential usefulness of state laws in America as a model for dealing with the Jews and he, in turn, had delegated the task of finding out just what was in those laws to Heydrich who had Schellenberg send it on to the SS man in the German Embassy in Washington—that idiot Krueger—with orders to contact American MID for their assistance. While Heydrich had told Schellenberg what he was doing, he hadn't asked Schellenberg for advice on how to do it despite the fact that he was a lawyer whereas Heydrich and Krueger were not. Heydrich was the most brilliant and ruthless man Schellenberg had ever met, but he didn't know everything. He understood why Heydrich had gone to the Americans because the SS and the MID had key common interests and values— anti-Communism and anti-Semitism being the principal ones.

Schellenberg wouldn't have done it that way. Instead, he would have approached a major German corporation like the Krupp Works, I.G. Farben or the Hamburg-Amerika Line and asked them what American law firm they used the most. Schellenberg knew this to be a

176 Michael McMenamin & Kathleen McMenamin

large New York law firm named Sullivan & Cromwell for all three companies. Then he would have asked one of them as a patriotic service to the Fatherland, to engage Sullivan & Cromwell to conduct the research on the relevant American state laws without ever disclosing the hand of the German government. American lawyers were required to keep the identity of their clients confidential and no one would have been the wiser.

Now, the American government was desperately trying to cover up their role in facilitating the legal research in question, a cover-up that called for the death of the journalist Mattie McGary. Schellenberg could not permit that to happen. For one thing, she was exceptionally beautiful and he had something of a crush on her, despite her being ten years his senior. More importantly, he had strict orders from his boss Heydrich to look out for her safety whenever she was in Germany. Heydrich had never told him why, other than that she was Hitler's favorite foreign journalist. He sensed, however, that for some reason, Heydrich feared McGary. This had been confirmed by McGary herself earlier in the summer when, acting on Heydrich's orders, he had saved her from some thugs working for Henry Ford who were intent upon doing her harm. She said something about a Highlands Blood Feud she had declared when Heydrich had someone close to her killed and threatened the lives of her relatives in Scotland. Far from being intimidated, McGary had responded in kind. She made the same threat on his relatives and had someone leave the severed head of one of his adjutants on Heydrich's doorstep to prove she meant business. But why did Heydrich threaten her in the first place? She had refused to say, despite Schellenberg employing all of what he thought to be his considerable charm.

The 'why' really didn't matter to Schellenberg. His orders were to protect McGary even if Heydrich didn't know that she had returned to Germany or that some MID-connected Americans wanted her dead. Speaking of things Heydrich did not know, Schellenberg looked at his watch. Yes, it was nearly 1 p.m. With Heydrich in Munich for the next two days, he had a standing engagement with his superior's lovely blonde wife Lena at his apartment overlooking the Brandenburg Gate. Given that her husband was a notorious philanderer with women as well as men, Lena Heydrich believed that what was sauce for the goose was sauce for the gander. Schellenberg was, for the moment, the happy beneficiary of her beliefs.

Schellenberg took both the coded and decoded versions of Krueger's cables into the ashtray on his desk; struck a match; lit the cables afire; and watched them burn and shrivel into ashes. The *Gestapo* had more important things on its plate than a Scottish journalist bent on exposing, if not embarrassing, the American government. So did Schellenberg—the lovely Lena, to be precise.

SCHELLENBERG GROANED when he returned to his office at 3 p.m. rested and refreshed from his tryst with *Frau* Heydrich. Sitting in his waiting room was a special FA courier holding on his lap a very large, locked heavy canvas pouch. He hated the sight of him because he knew that inside the pouch were red double thickness envelopes and inside the envelopes were the 'Brown Pages'. Reviewing the Brown Pages was easily the most boring, most time-consuming and, at the same time, most critical of Schellenberg's many duties as head of the SD's Foreign Intelligence Section.

Schellenberg was the authorized recipient of all intercepted cables from outside Germany as well as all recorded telephone conversations between people outside Germany and a long list of foreign embassies, foreign newspaper offices, foreign law firms and foreign security agencies like Pinkerton's that were located inside Germany. It typically took him at least a full half-day to review the Brown Pages that arrived twice a week. He sighed as he signed a receipt of the pouch from the SA courier who then unlocked the pouch and left the key with Schellenberg. Once he finished reviewing the contents, he would relock the pouch and his office would call the FA who would send the same courier to retrieve the pouch.

Schellenberg and Lena had enjoyed, among other things, a bottle of *Pol Roger* champagne both before and after their passionate coupling so that Schellenberg knew that a large pot of coffee was going to be required were he to stay awake during his review of the latest batch of Brown Pages.

"Hilda!" he shouted into the intercom on his desk. "Coffee! Lots of it. We're going to have a long night."

Three hours later, Schellenberg's eyes were bleary as he passed the halfway point in the red envelopes, having found nothing of value so far, when a name leaped out at him. Martha McGary! He quickly scanned back to the top of the first page of the document and saw that it was a German translation of a conversation in English. Schellenberg was fluent in English so he went back to the stack of pages and found the original pages in English. Then, he began to re-read it.

Monday, 10 September 1934

Transatlantic telephone call from New York City USA to RVD International offices, Berlin

Participants' identities not known

Unknown New York caller = UC
Unknown RVD receptionist employee = RVD
Unknown RVD Duty Officer = DO

RVD: RVD International. How may I direct your call?

UC: Duty Officer 'Rupert'.

RVD: Very good, Sir.

DO: Yes?

UC: Rupert, I want a two-man surveillance immediately placed on a British citizen staying at the Adlon. *Use our best men. Her name is Martha McGary and she works for the Hearst newspaper chain. Stay with her all day until one hour after she appears to retire for the night. Resume surveillance the next morning at 6 a.m. I want daily reports of where she goes and who she sees. Got that?*

DO: You bet, Chief. What's the broad done?

UC: Wait. I'm not finished. I'm told she's a real looker, a sexy little twist. If you can get her alone with no witnesses, rough her up a little. Nothing permanent, mind you, but put a scare into her. Tell her she needs to go home and find something else to work on. That's because she's working on a story that one of our clients doesn't want to see the light of day. It's a very important client who wants the story killed. The best way to do that is to neutralize the journalist.

DO: Roger that. So it's okay if we have a little fun with her while we're roughing her up?

UC: [laughter]. Sure, why not? A little fun, but no nookie. Listen, I've also got the Krauts working on it right now because, on behalf of our client, I've made it clear to them it's in their best interests to do so. I've also made clear the consequences to them if the story ever sees the light of day. One way for the Krauts to neutralize her is to toss her into one of their many concentration camps. The other way is more permanent. My wife and I are sailing on the Europa *in a few hours and we'll be in Bremerhaven on Friday and Berlin Saturday morning. If the Krauts haven't neutralized her by then, one way or another, we'll take over and the gloves will be off.*

DO: Roger that.

Schellenberg returned the document to the red envelope and sat back in his desk chair. Well, he thought, the 'Krauts' were not going to 'neutralize' McGary before Saturday because the *Gestapo*, thanks to him, had not been given the word. The fact that someone might 'rough her up' did not sit well with him. He pressed the intercom button. "Hilda, please see if we have a file on a Harold Canfield and a company called 'RVD International'."

To his surprise, the SS did indeed have such files, ones that Hilda produced less than fifteen minutes later. He leafed through one of them, noting that RVD's founder was General Ralph Van Deman, the original head of the American MID, and that it had large branch offices in London, Paris and Berlin as well as its headquarters in New York City. Aha! RVD's Executive Vice President, he saw, was the same Harold Canfield mentioned in Krueger's cable. He had joined the company in 1931, fresh from the Office of Naval Intelligence.

Schellenberg then read Canfield's file. Prior to leaving ONI, he had been the adjutant to the Director of ONI, Captain Roger Welles. That explained why, before he joined RVD, all the RVD operatives had been ex-MID agents. The Berlin office, opened only last year, employed only ex-ONI agents. He briefly wondered why Canfield was bringing his wife to Germany on what was otherwise obviously a business trip. Then he looked at their photographs in the file. Canfield was a good-enough looking guy, but his wife Camilla was stunningly beautiful, clearly in Mattie McGary's league and Marlene Dietrich's as well. Were she his wife, Schellenberg thought, he wouldn't leave her home alone either.

So, Schellenberg thought, Mattie was at risk of being 'roughed up' this week, but after Saturday, she would be in deadly peril. How to lessen those risks? He again pressed the intercom. "Hilda, send a directive to the *Zolgrenschutz* in Bremerhaven to put a hold on two U.S. Passport holders Harold and Camilla Canfield who are booked on the *Europa* which will dock there sometime this Friday. I want them detained by the Customs Border Guards until I or one of my men arrives there to interview him and place him under surveillance. Next, send a directive to all the major Berlin hotels to advise my office at once if Canfield checks in. When he does and he delivers their passports for the hotel to hold while he and his wife are guests there, I want them delivered to me. Finally, here is a list of employees at the Berlin office of this RVD International. Run a cross check on all of them with the *Reich* Gun Control Registry. Let me know if any of them are licensed to carry firearms. Finally, send a request over my signature to the *Forschungsamt* with a copy to Hermann Göring for all the Brown Pages on cables from the *Europa* from now until she docks on Friday."

"Very good, *Herr Sturmbannfuhrer*", Hilda replied.

"Now, find Eric Bulow and Franz Globke and send them to me."

Thirty minutes later, *SS-Obersturmfuhrers* Bulow and Globke appeared in the doorway to Schellenberg's office. "Heil Hitler!" they shouted as they clicked their heels and shot out their right arms.

Schellenberg sighed and waved them into his office and gestured for them to sit in the two wooden armchairs in front of his desk. Bulow and Globke were both tall, blond Aryan poster boys for the SS.

"I have pleasant assignments for you. There are two Americans I want you to tail for the rest of the week. They will be following a red-haired version of Marlene Dietrich. Her name is Mattie McGary. She is a Brit journalist upon whom the *Fuhrer* looks with favor. She is staying at the *Adlon*. You will allow no harm to come to her. If necessary, deadly force is authorized. Otherwise, do not interfere with their attempt to follow her. Then, Bulow, I may want you in Bremerhaven on Friday to meet the *Europa* when it docks. I'll let you know. Globke, you stay with the red-haired version of Marlene. Here are the details…"

Schellenberg finished ten minutes later. "Is that all clear, Gentlemen?"

"*Jawohl! Herr Sturmbannfuhrer!*" they both said in unison.

"Good. Here at two *Gestapo* medallions for you to use if you need to confront these Americans. Don't let them go to your head. I want them back when this assignment is over. If the Americans try any rough stuff with McGary and you don't have to kill them, turn them over to the *Kripo* and swear out a complaint. Now, get to work," Schellenberg said with a wave of his hand.

Both men shot to their feet with another "Heil Hitler" and extended right arms. After a crisp about-face, they left the room.

Schellenberg just shook his head.

23

Dead End

The Hotel William Penn
Mellon Square
Pittsburgh, Pennsylvania
Tuesday, 11 September 1934

"FACE IT Bobby, we're at a dead end," Bourke Cockran said, "when it comes to finding out anything more about Joe Carmody's death."

"Aye, you're right," Sullivan replied.

"We know he didn't commit suicide. But we don't know why he was killed even if you think you know who killed him."

"Aye, the Killer, Nick Carson. But why? Aye, we don't know."

The two were having a late dinner at the Terrace Room, the main dining room of the hotel. Brass sconces lined the wood-paneled walls and several elaborate brass chandeliers hung from the coffered ceiling. Their cocktails had just arrived, a martini for Cockran and Jameson on the rocks for Sullivan. Then, they ordered dinner, French Onion Soup and New York Strip Steaks for both along with a bottle of St. Emilion.

They had interviewed four people that day. Two were attorneys in Carmody's law firm. They were interviewed separately and both claimed no knowledge of what Carmody had been doing or who his own clients were. The law firm's Managing Partner, however, refused to allow them access to Carmody's own client files, citing attorney-client privilege. The other two persons interviewed were squash partners of Carmody at the Pittsburgh Athletic Club. They told him Carmody, after a few beers, was more than willing to talk about his court cases that were a matter of public record. But never did he disclose a client confidence. It was always only what had been in the public record in a trial.

"We need to go to Cleveland tomorrow," Cockran said, "and hope that Sandler's widow can see us a day early."

"Should we call her now?" Sullivan asked as their steaks arrived.

Cockran looked at his watch. "9:45. Pretty late. She may be asleep. Let's do it first thing in thing in the morning."

Cleveland Heights, Ohio
North Park Boulevard
Tuesday, 11 September 1934

IT WAS, Nick the Killer thought, a perfect hide. Perched maybe ten feet up in the crook of an Oak tree in the woods across from the Sandler home, Carson had a clear, unobstructed field of fire over a distance of approximately 150 yards to the front door of the Sandler's. That was where he expected Bobby Sullivan to be standing when he and Cockran arrived on Thursday. Carson had chosen the site during the early afternoon after the widow Sandler had left the house for, presumably, her daily luncheon with her female friends somewhere downtown. Even with the tragedy of her husband's death, it was comforting to know she still maintained her daily routines.

Now, Carson had returned after sundown to his shooting hide in the tree. He told himself this was primarily to see ahead of time whether the darkness made any difference in his shot. It didn't. Truth to tell, however, what Carson really wanted to know was whether the delicious Doris had retained another daily routine, the one that had inspired the scenario for her husband's murder. He was disappointed. Where she once walked nakedly about in her bedroom, secure in the belief no one in the woods across from her house would be watching her through windows with the drapes open, now the drapes were fully closed. Oh well, Carson thought, he was a patient man. Come the morrow would be soon enough to take in the sight of the unclothed body of Doris Sandler that once again would be his.

24

There Were No Jews

Reich Ministry of Justice
Berlin
Tuesday, 11 September 1934

STATE SECRETARY Roland Freisler was not a happy man. There was a frown on his narrow face as he looked up at Sturm. His secretary had told Sturm that he was in conference and could not be disturbed. Sturm had ordered her to interrupt whatever Freisler was doing and tell him that if he did not see Sturm immediately, he would have to explain why to *Reichspresident* Göring who, Sturm assured her, was in a particularly foul mood today. Sturm was promptly ushered in.

"Yes, *Fregattenkapitän* von Sturm? What can I do for you today?"

Sturm had decided that what this occasion needed was a touch of good, old-fashioned Prussian arrogance, something he believed he did quite well. "For starters, you little shit, you can stop lying to me—and, by extension *Reichspresident* Göring as well."

Freisler almost visibly recoiled and gulped, his Adam's apple standing out. "I'm sure I don't know what you mean."

"Really? Didn't you tell me Friday that the Commission wasn't relying or using American laws as a model for laws the Commission was considering for German Jews?"

"Well…yes. American laws consider Jews to be Whites."

"Then how do you explain *this*!" Sturm shouted as he slammed down on Freisler's desk a copy of the Prussian Memorandum.

Freisler picked up the Memorandum and visibly blanched. "Where did you get this? How did you get this? This is a 'Top Secret' document."

Sturm laughed. "Of course it is. It's stamped on every page. As to where and how the *Reichspresident* received a copy is not something you have a need to know. What you do have a need to know is that the *Reichspresident* is furious that he did not receive a copy from *you*. He told me to advise you that if you ever withhold any other documents or lie to me again, he will have you arrested for obstruction of justice. It is a crime, *Herr* Freisler, to keep information from the President of the *Reichstag*. Now, I want to review the resumes of all the lawyers who worked on this document."

"Resumes?" Freisler asked, "I'm not sure I understand…"

"CVs, *curriculum vitae* you fool! Where are they?"

"Why would you want to see…" Freisler began, but Sturm cut him off.

"Why the *Reichspresident* wants to see anything is *none… of… your… business*! In America as well as Germany, a disproportionate number of lawyers are Jews."

"This all happened last year and I'm not certain where these documents are stored now, but I can assure you that there were no Jews among the American lawyers who worked on the Prussian Memorandum."

"Freisler, let me be clear. The *Reichspresident* would not accept your assurances that the sun will rise tomorrow. I want those CVs and I want them now!"

"As I said, I'm not sure where they are, but I will put my secretary to work immediately to locate them."

"You have until close of business Thursday. I fly the *Graf Bismarck* to America today. The ship will arrive in America late Thursday afternoon. If those documents have not been delivered to the Office of the *Reichspresident* by the time I reach America, I will inform the *Reichspresident* that you are once again withholding documents from us. He will not be happy to hear that. And when *Reichspresident*

Göring is unhappy…" Sturm said and then stopped, leaving Freisler's imagination to complete the sentence.

SS Reich Security Office
Prinz-Albrecht Strasse 8
Berlin
Wednesday, 12 September 1934

ROLAND FREISLER walked down the main hall of SS Headquarters in Berlin toward the offices of *Reichsfuhrer*–SS Heinrich Himmler. A former art museum, the building had high, arched ceilings, marble floors and blood red and black Nazi banners hanging down the walls between the windows through which the rays of the early morning sun streamed in. Freisler entered the anteroom to Himmler's office where he was greeted coldly by Himmler's adjutant Karl Wolff.

"Freisler is here," Wolff said into the telephone in a bored tone. He looked up with a bland expression on his face. "You may go in now."

Inside Himmler's large windowless office, Freisler was impressed and not a little intimidated. It had high ceilings with a large tapestry on the wall to the left of his desk while the opposite had gilt-framed paintings Freisler did not recognize, but that doubtless were Hitler approved. Himmler, it was rumored, had an almost pathological fear of offending the man who had made him the head of not only the SS but, now, the *Gestapo* as well. On the wall behind Himmler's desk was an assorted collection of swords, shields and a coat of arms. The desk was easily twice as large as the one manned by Wolff. It had a faded red cushion on its front edge on top of which was a seven-foot-long, ancient leather case. Inside the case was an equally ancient battle spear that Himmler wanted visitors to believe was the fabled Spear of Destiny that a Roman soldier used to pierce the side of Christ while he was on the cross.

Freisler approached the desk and extended his right arm in a salute once associated with the Romans, but now indelibly appropriated by the Nazis. "*Heil* Hitler!"

Himmler, his elbow on the desk, weakly waved his right hand, but otherwise ignored him, continuing to write on the notepad in front of him. Five minutes passed before Himmler looked up and blinked at his visitor through thick, *pince-nez* glasses. His hair was shaved at the sides and back of his head, leaving a dark round island of hair on top, an imitation of Hitler's mustache under his nose.

"Yes, Roland, what can I do for you?"

"*Herr Reichsfuhrer,* I'm having a problem with von Sturm, the man Göring appointed as the liaison from the *Reichstag* to the Commission on Criminal Law Reform. I'm not certain he is trustworthy."

"Really? What sort of problem? And why don't you think he can be trusted?"

"Somehow, he acquired a copy of the Prussian Memorandum the Americans prepared and he has demanded to know the names of the lawyers who prepared it as well as their CVs."

"Do you have their CVs?"

"Of course, but I told him they were in storage and it would take several days to locate them. He told me that if I didn't deliver them to him by Thursday, Göring would have me arrested for obstruction of justice."

Himmler smiled and placed the tips of his fingers together "I don't see why that is a problem. Give him the CVs. Again, why don't you trust him?"

"I was dining at *Horcher* Monday evening and I saw von Sturm there with a foreign journalist sitting at Göring's regular table, the woman who interviewed the *Fuhrer* in July. I fear he will give her the Prussian Memorandum and the CVs of the American lawyers who prepared it. The work of the Commission must be kept confidential until we are ready to present our proposals to the *Reichstag.* As you know, there is considerable dissension among the members of the Commission as to how to define a Jew. You and *Herr Doktor* Goebbels have made it clear you want the broadest definition possible and that is why I asked you to commission the Prussian Memorandum. I fear that if the Memorandum is made public, it will be almost impossible for the Commission to reach a consensus for the expansive definition you and *Herr Doktor* Goebbels prefer."

Himmler pursed his lips and was silent for a moment. Finally, he spoke. "Well now, we can't have that, can we? What would you have me do?"

"If von Sturm does supply the woman with the Memorandum and the identity of the American lawyers who prepared it, we must find some way to keep her from publishing a story about it."

Himmler pressed the button on his intercom. "Karl, what is the name of the woman journalist who interviewed the *Fuhrer* in July about the *coup d'etat* by the SA that he prevented?"

"McGary, Martha McGary, *Herr Reichsfuhrer.*"

"Good. Bring your steno pad and come in here. I have an assignment for you."

"*Jawohl, Herr Reichsfuhrer!*"

Moments later, Wolff appeared with a steno pad in his left hand; came to attention; and shot out his right arm. "*Heil* Hitler!"

Freisler watched Himmler give Wolff the same dismissive wave of his right hand that he had given him earlier.

"Go see Heinrich Muller," Himmler said to Wolff, referring to the head of the *Gestapo*. "Tell him that, beginning this afternoon, I want round the clock surveillance until further notice on a foreign journalist named Martha McGary. Two men will do, but they must be good. 12 hour shifts for each. Also, have him find out the hotel she is in and place a recording device in her room. Retrieve and have it transcribed daily. Make two copies of the transcript, one to me and the other one to State Secretary Freisler at the Ministry of Justice."

Himmler looked at Freisler. "I'd love to have her phone tapped, but we'd need *Unser* Hermann's consent for that which I very much doubt he would give. And I would prefer that he not know of my interest in this. In any event, we should learn from the recording device how she is progressing on her story. At the appropriate time, based on your recommendation, we can arrange for the *Gestapo* to confiscate all her research and either place her in a concentration camp or eliminate her, whichever seems more expeditious."

Part III

United States, Germany, England & The Netherlands
12 September—17 September 1934

I never saw in Nazi Germany any indication of tension or fear of the future. People discussed Hitler and everything openly just as we talk of Roosevelt in the United States.

Roscoe Pound,
Dean, Harvard Law School
Paris *Herald*,
4 August 1934

There was no persecution in Nazi Germany of Jewish scholars or of Jews who had lived in Germany for any length of time.

Roscoe Pound,
Dean, Harvard Law School
New York *Herald Tribune*
16 August 1934

25

Doris Sandler

3386 North Park Boulevard
Cleveland Heights, Ohio
Wednesday, 12 September 1934

DORIS SANDLER was sitting in the breakfast nook off the kitchen when the telephone rang at 9:15 a.m. She picked up the receiver. "Hello?"

"Mrs. Sandler, please. Bourke Cockran calling."

"This is Doris Sandler."

"Mrs. Sandler, I apologize for calling so early, but I wonder if it would be convenient for me to meet with you later today, rather than tomorrow. I'm in Pittsburgh now and we've finished our work here sooner than we anticipated."

"Please, Mr. Cockran, call me Doris. What time did you have in mind?"

"Anytime this afternoon that's convenient for you is fine with me. And please, call me Bourke. We're leaving Pittsburgh as soon as my colleague, Mr. Sullivan, pays our hotel bill."

"Well, I'm having lunch with some girlfriends, but I'm usually back by 3:00 p.m. so why don't we say 3:30 at my home?"

"That would be swell, Doris. Thanks very much."

"Oh, Bourke, wait. There's something I was going to tell you when we met, but let me mention it now. When Tim O'Hanlon called to tell me he had hired you to investigate the deaths of Hank and the five other former MID agents, he asked me if I knew what kind of legal work Tim had been doing on behalf of MID. I told him I didn't. Hank rarely talked to me about his work, but I do know he didn't like what he was doing for MID. He told me that. He said it was dirty work, but someone had to do it. If it wasn't him, someone else would do it and given the Depression, he told me he couldn't afford to turn the work away. Anyway, what I think you should do when you're in Cleveland is look over Hank's old files to see if there is anything in them about what he was doing for MID. Tim rented space in the Leader Building from a law firm there, Walter & Haverfield, and that's where his files are. One of the name partners, Paul Walter, is a good friend and he agreed to keep the files for me at no charge."

"That's interesting. I met Paul last year when we were both working for Rabbi Silver on the anti-Nazi boycott. Perhaps we should look at those files before we see you. We'll be in Cleveland by 1:00 p.m. That would give us two hours to review the files there before we see you."

"I'll call Paul and set it up right after I hang up."

"Great. Thanks again. See you at 3:30."

Doris marked "Cockran: 3:30 today" on the note pad beside the phone and on the calendar hanging above it. Then she called Paul Walter who wasn't in. She left a message for him to return her call and went upstairs to shower and change clothes for her ladies lunch.

Doris was in the shower when the telephone rang in her bedroom. She stepped out of the shower, grabbed a towel and wrapped it around herself as she walked from the master bath to the telephone by her bedside. She picked up the receiver and stood in front of the window that looked out on the broad expanse of her lawn and beyond that the woods between North and South Park Boulevard.

"Hello?"

"Attorney Paul Walter returning your call."

"Oh, hi Paul. Thanks for calling back. I need a favor about some of Hank's old files…"

When she hung up ten minutes later, Walter had agreed to have all of her husband's old files brought up from the file room and placed in the firm's library for Cockran's review.

After dressing and putting on her makeup, Doris walked over to the side table beside her bed where there were three objects. One was an alarm clock. Another was a compact Browning FN1906 semi-automatic pocket pistol that fired .25-caliber ammunition, the 'Baby Browning'. A third was her late husband's Mark I trench knife, a double-edged dagger blade for both thrusting and slashing strokes with a finger guard handle that resembled 'brass knuckles'. She placed both weapons into her leather handbag, the knife going into a custom scabbard sewn into the top of the bag's interior.

Today, Doris Sandler was proficient with both weapons. On the day she was raped and her husband murdered, she was not. Prior to that, she had not given a moment's thought to her personal protection. That was her husband's job. With him gone, she had vowed she would never be that helpless again. She had called Tim O'Hanlon and asked for his advice. He had recommended the Browning and gave her the name of a former MID agent in Cleveland who would teach her to shoot. He also suggested she look for her husband's Mark I trench knife—which she thought looked lethal just sitting there with its brass knuckles handle—and have the same former agent teach her a few knife-fighting moves. She had done both and she no longer felt helpless. True, there had been no occasion to use her new skills since Hank had died, but they did wonders for her confidence and self-esteem. She was never going to be a victim again.

Doris was looking forward to lunch as she walked to the garage and started up her Auburn Speedster. Wednesdays were her day to pick the restaurant and she had picked Fred Harvey's English Oak Room in the Terminal Tower complex. She especially liked their Snapping Turtle Soup with a splash of Sherry.

3386 North Park Boulevard
Cleveland Heights, Ohio
Wednesday, 12 September 1934

NICHOLAS CARSON put down the field glasses that had been trained on the front of the Sandler residence as the Auburn Speedster rolled down the driveway. A little earlier, she had talked on the phone for nearly ten minutes while she paced back and forth in front of the large bedroom window. He was disappointed that she kept her towel on while she talked, but it did little to disguise her shapely curves. He was really looking forward to renewing his acquaintance with her this afternoon. With no husband coming home, they wouldn't be disturbed. Yes, he thought, they would have all the time they needed.

Carson once more picked up his Springfield M1903 sniper rifle and looked through the Warner & Swasey telescopic sights to the front door of the Sandler residence 150 yards away where tomorrow taking out Bobby Sullivan and Cockran would be like shooting fish in a barrel.

Leaving the rifle in its carrying case on top of the hide, Carson climbed down from the tree, crossed the road and walked to the back door of the house where he once more let himself in.

In the kitchen, Carson walked around and noticed a note pad by the telephone. "Cockran: 3:30 today." Damn! He looked at his wristwatch. 2:15. Double damn! If she wasn't home until 3:00 like she had been in December, he thought, there wouldn't be time for another tryst with her. He smiled when, at 2:30, he heard the Auburn in the driveway. Showtime, he thought, as he pulled a white bandana from his pocket and tied it over his face.

The second she opened the back door and stepped inside, Carson grabbed her wrist with his left hand and, as before, waved the Fairbairn-Sykes knife in her face with the other hand.

"Surprise!" Carson said, "I was in the neighborhood and I thought I'd just drop in and say hello. We had so much fun together the last time that I thought we'd give it another go. What do you say?"

"Screw you, you murdering bastard!"

Carson laughed. "My dear, I'm not the one who's going to be screwed this afternoon. Come on, you know the drill. Upstairs," he said with a wave of his knife.

The woman, still clutching her handbag, walked into the living room and began to go up the stairs. Carson followed, transfixed by the sight of that lovely bottom, still not sheathed in a girdle. Once in her bedroom, she stopped in the middle and stood there, her back to him.

"Come on," he said, "I don't have all day. "Off with your clothes."

The woman made no reply, but stepped out of her high heels.

"That's a girl. Now the rest."

The woman made no reply and simply stood there.

"If you don't, I'll just have to cut them off. Do you want that? I know I'd enjoy it," Carson said and walked up to her and placed a hand on her left shoulder. "Okay, Lady, you were warned."

Suddenly, the woman dropped her handbag, whirled around, her right arm extended with a large knife in her hand which, to his astonishment, she slashed across his right forearm and the middle of his stomach, cutting through his shirt and drawing blood.

Carson tightly grasped his right forearm to stop the bleeding whereupon she stepped in and stabbed him in the right shoulder.

Carson howled. "You stupid, stupid bitch! It's not like I never fucked you before. You sure sounded as if you were liking it then. Is avoiding another shag worth your life? Because now I'm going to gut you just like I did your husband," he said as he advanced toward her, his knife blade extended and pointed at her.

The woman was backing away now, but she had picked up the handbag she had dropped. Her hand dipped into the bag and she pulled out a small automatic pistol, which she fired twice. The first shot missed, but the second caught him in the thigh. He winced, but he kept on coming, albeit with a slight limp. Whatever her gun was, he thought, it had no real stopping power and he weighed over 200 pounds.

"That baby gun isn't going to stop me, Bitch," he said and continued to lurch forward as she retreated until her back was against the window. "I'm going to enjoy carving you up."

Law Offices of Walter & Haverfield
1215 Leader Building
Cleveland, Ohio
Wednesday, 12 September 1934

PAUL WALTER was a big bear of a man, nearly 6' tall, with broad shoulders and a massive chest. Easily 200 pounds, Cockran thought. He wore a vested pinstriped navy blue suit and looked to be in his early 30s with thinning dark brown hair and wire-rimmed spectacles.

"Bourke, how good to see you again," Walter said, grasping Cockran's hand in both of his.

"The feeling is mutual, Paul," Cockran replied. "And this is Robert Sullivan, my investigator on this case."

The two men shook hands. It was a few minutes past 1:00 p.m. and they were in the small reception room of the law firm with its dark paneled wainscoting. Above that, on cream-colored walls, were oil paintings of ships that reflected Cleveland's maritime heritage as one of the major ports on the Great Lakes.

"Come with me. As Doris requested," Walter said, "I've had all of Hank's files moved up from storage and put in our library."

Walter led them down a short corridor followed by a turn to the left that took them into a large room with desks for five secretaries, all of whom were busy typing. To the right was the law firm's library with floor to ceiling bookshelves. In the middle of the room was a long mahogany table around which were twelve matching wooden armchairs. There were six large cardboard boxes on top of the table.

"Those are all Hanks' client files," Walter said. "He just leased space here with access to a secretary, but my partner Rusk Haverfield is our Managing Partner and he insisted that Hank open all his files within our filing system. That means each client is given an identifying number and then files are opened for that client within the identifying number. So, if a client had the identifying number of, say, 450, then the first file would be 450-0, the second file 450-1, the third 450-2, etcetera. Got that?"

Cockran nodded and Walter continued. "So, all the files are maintained chronologically based on when the client first had a file opened for him. All other files for that client, even the most current, are kept in the box from the date of the client's first file. I don't know exactly what you're looking for, so I can't help you more than this."

"I appreciate all you've done, Paul," Cockran said. "Thanks very much. I can't disclose our client's name, but we're investigating the suspicious deaths of six men, including Hank, who were doing some kind of legal research, directly or indirectly, for the U.S. Army's MID."

"Interesting," Walter said. "It would have to be indirectly, because Rusk reviews the Case Information Sheets on all new files to check for conflicts. That would have included Hank's files as well. Our firm is only two years old and if a file with the U.S. Government as a client had been opened, Rusk would have told me."

After Walter left, Cockran divided up the file boxes. "Bobby, you start with the oldest client files and I'll review the newest. We'll meet in the middle."

It was slow going and by 2:15 p.m., Sullivan had made it through two boxes and Cockran only one. He thought they were going to have to come back tomorrow if they were going to keep their appointment with Doris Sandler this afternoon. Ten minutes into the second box, Cockran struck pay dirt.

"Look at this, Bobby," Cockran said. "A client file with RVD International. If memory serves, it's a big security outfit owned by General Ralph Van Deman who was head of MID when I was there. Marlborough and Van Deman, his immediate predecessor at MID, are close friends and I know from Tim O'Hanlon that MID farms out assignments to RVD from time to time. Since MID placed a Black Drape over the project to keep Tim in the dark, it stands to reason MID would want a cutout between it and the lawyers hired for this mysterious project."

Cockran opened the file and was disappointed to see it contained only the Case Information Sheet and a single letter. Cockran looked at the Case Information Sheet. It contained the address of RVD's New York office, phone number and cable address. The contact person at

RVD was Harold Hudson Canfield, III, a name Cockran did not recognize. He made a mental note to call Tim O'Hanlon tonight to see if he knew anything about Canfield. Cockran picked up the letter.

> *Roscoe Pound, Dean*
> *Harvard Law School*
> *Cambridge, Massachusetts*
>
> *Dear Dean Pound:*
>
> *As Harold Canfield of my client, RVD International, has directed, I enclose all of the confidential legal research I have performed on its behalf as well as all my notes and the Legal Memorandum I prepared based on that research. These are all of my original notes and I have made no copies. Likewise, no carbon copies of the Legal Memorandum were made. Finally, as requested, I enclose the typewriter ribbon used to prepare the Legal Memorandum.*
> *I have maintained a carbon copy of this letter to you, as it is required by the terms of my legal malpractice insurance policy.*
>
> *Yours Very Truly,*
> *Henry Sandler*

"This is it!" Cockran said. "This has got to be what we're looking for! Tim said that Sandler had called to sarcastically thank him for sending him legal business from some 'Ivy League fascist' whom Sandler otherwise refused to identify when Tim asked him who that was. After we see Doris this afternoon, I'll call Tim tonight and tell him what we've found. If I'm right and Tim agrees, we can cancel our Chicago appointment and I'll have Alexis make an appointment for us to see Dean Pound. Then, we can take an overnight train to Boston."

Cockran then looked at his watch. 2:45 p.m. "Come on," he said, shoving the RVD file into his briefcase, "We've just got enough time to make our 3:30 appointment with Doris Sandler."

26

Bella Fromm

MATTIE LIKED Bella Fromm. For one thing, she was a journalist like Mattie and female journalists were a small sorority. In her late 30s, she came from a wealthy Jewish family. Her parents were dead, but they had left her well off. Her inheritance, however, was wiped out in the German hyperinflation of 1923. After that, she became a diplomatic correspondent for the Ullstein newspapers, primarily the *Berliner Zeitung* and the *Vossiche Zeitung.* Mattie had met her right after Hitler's so-called 'Beer Hall *putsch*' in 1923 and they had been friends ever since.

Bella's contracts and sources were widespread despite her being Jewish. She knew everyone from the assassinated former chancellor Kurt von Schleicher, to Hitler's foreign press secretary Ernst Hanfstaengl, the German Foreign Minister Konstantin von Neurath, the filmmaker and Hitler confidant Leni Riefenstahl, as well as the *Reichsbank* President Hajalmar Schacht. Sadly, Bella was no longer using those contacts in any meaningful way. Propaganda Minister Goebbels had forbidden the Ullstein newspapers from carrying her byline and Bella was too proud to accept their offer to publish her articles under another journalist's name.

Mattie was early for their luncheon, a trait she did not share with her husband or her godfather Winston, both of whom were perpetually tardy. The interior of *Café Kranzler* was two stories high with a balcony running around three sides of the room where other tables and chairs were available if the main floor became too crowded. She had arranged for a small corner table and was sitting in a white wicker chair with her back to the wall so she could more easily watch the crowds go by on the *Unter den Linden* as well as spot Bella when she arrived.

Mattie smiled when she saw Bella arrive and make her way through the tables to Mattie, stopping by at least five other tables to exchange pleasantries with others. Bella really did know almost everybody who was anybody in Berlin. She was extremely attractive, possibly several inches over five feet, with curly dark hair, ample curves and an irreverent attitude, especially toward authority in general and Nazis in particular.

Mattie stood up so Bella could see her and the two exchanged an embrace. A waiter arrived and both women ordered very dry martinis.

"So, Mattie," Bella began once their drinks had arrived, "what brings you back to Berlin? Has our beloved *Fuhrer* deigned to grant you another exclusive interview like he did in July?"

This was, Mattie knew, a reference to Hitler summoning her to Berlin in the wake of the Night of the Long Knives on 30 June where the SS had ruthlessly assassinated over 200 of Hitler's political enemies, both inside and outside the Nazi Party. This included Hitler's immediate predecessor as Chancellor, Kurt von Schleicher, and his wife Elisabeth, both of whom were Bella's close friends. Hitler had claimed in his interview with Mattie and subsequently in a speech to the *Reichstag* that, rather than settling personal scores, he had been compelled to crush a *coup d'etat*. Few believed him.

Mattie laughed. "Hardly. I was only in Berlin for a day, you know. He actually had me flown in from London in his personal JU-52 and I returned that night. We had lunch at 'The Merry Chancellor's Restaurant' in the remodeled Chancellery and he served me chicken hash made from the 21 Club's own recipe. How about you? What have you been up to? Other than your three-week holiday with Bobby Sullivan in New York, of course. Still on Goebbels' 'banned journalists' list?"

"For German newspapers, certainly, but Ambassador Dodd," Bella said, referring to the American Ambassador Thomas Dodd, "helped me get a weekly column in the English newspaper published in Berlin."

"Good for him! Congratulations!"

"I'm not down for the count yet, but I fear the handwriting is on the wall. I'm in Berlin because, while I'm a Jew, I'm still a German. You're not. So if you aren't here to see 'the Merry Chancellor' why in the world are you back in this cesspit?"

"Have you ever heard of something called the "Prussian Memorandum'?"

"I don't think so. Why?"

"Let me explain," Mattie began and finished twenty minutes later.

Bella laughed. "Well, I'm screwed no matter what this Commission does. I've got four Jewish grandparents and probably eight Jewish great grandparents! And the name Bella doesn't exactly scream 'blonde-haired Nordic beauty' does it? I am surprised, though, that they're using American law as a model. I thought America was better than that. Anyway, how can I help?"

Mattie handed her the list of Commission members. "Do you know any of the people on this list who my source has tagged as a 'moderate' and can you tell me anything about them?"

Bella took the list and looked it over, then shook her head. "The only persons here I've met socially are Helmut Winter, Werner Kramer, and Hanna Raeder. I don't care what your source says about Winter. I can guarantee Winter's not one of the moderate members on the Commission. He doesn't think one drop of blood means you're Jewish like some of those southern states in America where one drop of blood means you're a Negro, but he's close to it.

"The two with the red check marks, Werner Kramer and Hanna Raeder, are decent people. Kramer works for Schacht at the *Reichsbank* and Hanna Raeder is the wife of Admiral Erich Raeder, Chief of the

Naval Command. I've been to Hanna's cocktail parties at their home in Potsdam. I consider her a good friend. She was once a helluva good criminal defense lawyer and she's no anti-Semite. We have lunch together from time to time."

"Those are the two who told my source they would give me an off-the-record interview."

"Would you like for me to call them later this afternoon and vouch for you?"

"Thanks very much, Bella, but if I'm going to promise them confidentiality, it's not wise to let them know I've talked to you about them."

"Good point. I agree. A word of warning," Bella said and then paused as their waiter served their meals, Dover Sole for both along with a bottle of Reisling. "I've heard bad things about the Commission Chairman, Roland Freisler."

"What have you heard?"

"He's a ruthless bastard. He once published a paper on the 'racial-biological task' involved in the reform of juvenile criminal law where he argued that racially foreign, degenerate, incurable or seriously defective juveniles should be removed from society and segregated from 'racially valuable' Germans. Segregated or executed, as he also proposed in the paper to impose the death penalty and prison terms for juveniles. That would be a first for Germany."

"Sounds like a real sweetie," Mattie said.

"He's trouble for you, Mattie. He's in tight with Goebbels and Himmler and that means he has access to the *Gestapo* whose control Göring passed to Himmler earlier this year. If you can persuade any of the other so-called moderate Commission members to talk to you, watch your back. Make sure you're not being followed. Ever since the 30 June massacre, more people have started to disappear. One minute, they're here; then they're gone and no one ever sees them again."

"Thanks Bella, but I got a German permit for my Walther PPK back in 1931 and I never leave home without it, " Mattie said, patting her purse where she was carrying her Walther today and then grinned. "Besides, I'm Hitler's favorite foreign journalist."

"If you disappear and your body is never found, how will our beloved *Fuhrer* even know you're dead? Just be careful is all I'm saying."

"I will, but what about you, Bella? Isn't it time for you to get out of Germany like your daughter did back in May? Goebbels can't be happy you're back in print, even if it's only an English language newspaper. Shouldn't you be watching your own back?"

"As I told Robert when I was in New York, Rolf has my back and he will let me know when it's time to leave," Bella replied, 'Rolf' being her otherwise unidentified friend high in the Nazi hierarchy who was also her most highly placed source and who kept her informed of most everything the Nazis were doing. "I knew from Rolf about the massacre this summer before it happened so I went to Paris for a holiday that weekend. Until Rolf tells me to go, I'm going to stay here and help my people any way I can. More than once, Rolf has gotten friends of mine out of concentration camps."

"Well, it's your call. I admire your courage, if not your good sense."

After lunch, Mattie returned to her *Adlon* suite where she found a message from Sturm:

Mattie,

I saw Freisler yesterday and gave him until the end of the day Thursday to produce CVs for the American lawyers. He's to deliver them to the office of the Reichspresident. *I reported this to* Göring. *I fly to America this evening and I'll return late Sunday evening.*

Kurt

Next, Mattie called Hanna Raeder and Werner Kramer. Hanna agreed to see her tomorrow afternoon at Mattie's suite in the *Adlon*. Kramer was still at his desk at the *Reichsbank* and he suggested she come to his apartment in the *Savigny Platz* neighborhood that evening.

SS-OBERSTURMFUHRER FRANZ GLOBKE appeared in the doorway to Schellenberg's office. "Heil Hitler!" he shouted as he clicked his heels and shot out his right arms.

Schellenberg sighed and raised his palm. "Don't just stand there, Globke. Get your ass in here and warm one of those chairs," he said, pointing to the two wooden armchairs in front of his desk. Globke did so

"So, how went your first day with the red-haired Marlene Dietrich?"

"Splendid, Sir. She is every bit as beautiful as you told us."

"And was she being followed?"

"Oh, yes, Sir. By two teams. In the first team, there were two men in suit coats who spoke English to each other, but they made no attempt to harass her. They were never closer than 20 feet to her. We were actually closer than that. She had lunch at the *Café Krenzler* with the Jewish journalist Bella Fromm so Bulow and I got the table next to them. We couldn't make out everything they were saying, but I'm fairly sure she's going to try and interview people named Werner Kramer and Hanna Raeder tomorrow. Right now, she's back at her suite in the *Adlon*. Bulow is sitting in the lobby in case she goes out tonight."

"And the second team?"

"*Gestapo,* Sir," Globke replied. "A two-man team that picked her up when she left the *Adlon* for lunch."

"How do you know they were *Gestapo*?"

Globke laughed. "They wore cheap, ill-fitting suits and the same long dark overcoats and fedoras that Erik and I do. That, plus they looked stupid. It was plainly obvious they were following the McGary woman and just as obvious that they never noticed the two Americans who were also following her."

Interesting, Schellenberg thought and wondered who had put the *Gestapo* tail on her and how to find out why. "Listen, Globke, if the Americans ever try anything with the woman and you stop them, I want you to give her a message from me. Ask the red-haired Marlene Dietrich to join me for lunch the next day at *Horcher's*. Got that?"

"Yes, Sir.

Schellenberg dismissed Globke, sat back in his desk chair and stared up at the ceiling.

He smiled as he envisaged the scene, three two-man teams all following a single woman. Heydrich received the same Brown Pages he did so it was remotely possible he had read them and assigned the *Gestapo* to look after her just as Schellenberg had assigned two SD men. It was unlikely, however, because Heydrich had given him the task of McGary's safety and that had not been rescinded. He made a note on his calendar to see Heydrich tomorrow. Perhaps he knew or could find out why the *Gestapo* was following McGary.

27

This is Your Lucky Day

3386 North Park Boulevard
Cleveland Heights, Ohio
Wednesday, 12 September 1934

"THAT BABY gun isn't going to stop me, Bitch!" Doris Sandler heard the masked man say, now only ten feet away. With the window at her back, she was beside the head of the bed and, with the man approaching the foot of the bed, she couldn't let herself be trapped in this corner of the room. The man was so big, easily six feet tall and well over 200 pounds, the bullet wound seemed to have no effect on him. Maybe her 'baby gun' wasn't going to stop him. Still, she didn't think he was going to be as agile or as fast as her. She leaped onto the bed in her stocking feet and quickly bounded to the other side. The bedroom door was now at her back and the bed was between her and the man. She knew she could escape and run down the stairs to call the police, but she also knew she would never have as good a shot at the man than right now.

Doris turned and aimed her automatic at him with two hands extended like a triangle in front of her. She knew the Baby Browning held seven shots. She had used two already and she did not have ready access to more ammunition. So, three more shots and she was out of there. That would leave her two shots if she needed them before calling the police.

Shooting at a moving target, however, was a lot different than shooting at a paper outline on the range. Still, she remembered what her instructor had taught her—aim for center mass. She focused on the man's belt buckle and snapped off three quick shots. Two of them hit him right below his belt and blood spurted as he dropped to his knees. A third missed. Doris turned and sprinted for the stairs. She was halfway down when her front door crashed open and she saw two armed men charge in.

3386 North Park Boulevard
Cleveland Heights, Ohio
Wednesday, 12 September 1934

COCKRAN AND SULLIVAN parked their rented Packard on the street and walked up to the front door of the Sandler residence. Cockran reached out to press the doorbell, but before he could, he heard the sharp crack of two gunshots followed quickly by three more shots.

The carved wooden front door looked substantial, but when he and Sullivan simultaneously hit it with their shoulders, wood splintered and the door flew open and the two men rushed in, both drawing their Colt .45 M1911 automatic pistols. Cockran immediately saw a blonde woman stop halfway down the front stairs with a weapon in her hand.

"Doris!" Cockran shouted, coming to halt, holding both hands up so that the Colt .45 was pointed at the ceiling. Beside him, Bobby Sullivan did the same. "It's Bourke Cockran! Are you alright?"

"No, I'm *not* alright," Doris said. "There's a man upstairs who tried to rape me. He's the same man who killed my husband. He has a mask on, but I'd recognize that voice anywhere. I shot him, but I think he's still alive. Now, place your guns on the floor; step away from them; and show some ID. I think I recognize your voice, Bourke, but as you can appreciate, a girl can't be too careful."

"Fair enough," Cockran said and placed his automatic on the floor. Sullivan did the same.

"Okay, now come up here and place your IDs on the first step of the stairs; then go over there to my right, at least ten feet away, and stay there." Doris said as she waved her gun to the right.

Again, the two men did as instructed, Cockran with his driver's license, Sullivan with his New York State Private Investigator's card. Doris walked down the stairs, keeping her gun trained on the two men, and picked up and looked at each man's ID.

Doris sighed audibly. "Thank God, Bourke! Please, would one of you go with me to check on the man upstairs? I can't bear to do it alone. I only have two bullets left in my pistol and all my spare cartridges are in my bedroom where I left him."

"I'll do it," Sullivan said and looked at Cockran. "You and Mrs. Sandler stay here. If it's really Nick Carson up there—and I'm betting it is—I can handle him better alone. Mrs. Sandler would just be in the way. There's no need to give him another shot at her."

"He's right, Doris," Cockran said. 'Let him go alone." In fact, what Cockran really thought was that Sullivan didn't want any witnesses when he confronted a former Black and Tan who had been high on Michael Collin's hit list for Bloody Sunday during the Anglo-Irish war in the early twenties.

"Shouldn't we call the police?" Doris asked.

"Eventually," Cockran replied, "but first, let's see what Mr. Sullivan finds."

BOBBY SULLIVAN walked over to the foyer, picked up the two Colt .45 automatics and handed one to Cockran."

"Mrs. Sandler, "Is your bedroom to the right or left at the top of the stairs?" Sullivan asked.

"The first door on the right," Doris replied.

"Was the man armed?"

"He had a knife, some sort of stiletto like the one he used to kill my husband. I don't know whether he had a pistol. He might have, but I didn't see it."

Sullivan nodded. Then, holding his gun in his hand, his arm outstretched and his back against the wall, Sullivan began to slowly walk up the steps. When he reached the top, he paused. Ten feet away on the right was an open door that he assumed was her bedroom. He stepped into the hallway and, with his back against the right wall, he advanced toward the open door. Once there, he moved his weapon up to his chest and, keeping his head against the wall, he peered into the room. He saw the foot of a bed. He then slowly moved in a semi-circle around the doorway, keeping at least three feet away, peering over the gun sight into the room. After completing the semi-circle, he was now standing against the wall on the left side of the doorway. He had seen nothing on this side of the bed.

Sullivan decided he would enter the room from the right hand side, as the distance from it to the opposite wall was shorter than on the left hand side where at the far end of the room he had seen a bathroom. He retraced his semi-circle back to the right hand side. He reached inside his jacket and pulled from a shoulder holster a second Colt .45 M1911 automatic pistol and quickly entered the room. Keeping his back to the wall behind the bed, he scanned the room with both automatics. Again, nothing. He moved slowly down the room to the left toward the bathroom, his face toward the bed, the far wall and a large window. When he reached the foot of the bed, he saw a leg sticking out from the far side of the bed. He moved swiftly past the bed and trained both automatics at the figure on the floor.

A man with a white bandana over his face was in a sitting position against the wall. His left leg was bleeding and there were bloodstains below the belt on his tan trousers. Beside him was a Sykes-Fairbairn fighting knife similar to the one Sullivan had strapped to his leg. He was conscious and Sullivan thought he saw a flicker of recognition in his eyes. Holstering one pistol, he walked over, kicked the man's knife out of reach and yanked the white bandana down.

"My, oh my, and isn't it Nick the Killer himself?" Sullivan said. "Aren't you a long way from Belfast, me Bucko?"

Carson coughed. "No more than the Angel of Death is from Donegal, you bastard! If that bitch hadn't been armed with a knife and a gun, I would have been set up in the woods across the street and picked off you and Cockran when you rang her doorbell. It would have been like shooting fish in a barrel."

"And why would you be wanting to do something as unfriendly as that?"

"Twenty large from Owney for you; 15 more for Cockran, you Irish prick."

"Now, why would Owney want to go and do something like that?"

"I don't know and I don't care."

At some point, Sullivan thought, Owney Madden was going to have to pay for taking a contract out on him, but that could wait. Owney wasn't going anywhere and Sullivan would have plenty of time to think of an appropriate punishment. He looked down at Carson. The Big Fella had wanted this bastard killed in the worst way. It was one of the few times Bobby Sullivan had disappointed Michael Collins.

"Well, the widow downstairs has identified you as the man who killed her husband last year. What I'm going to do is check out how serious your wounds are so we can get you to hospital and ready for the trial that will send you to the electric chair. I saw the itty-bitty gun she was using so I can't believe your wounds are life-threatening."

Sullivan holstered his other pistol and picked up the man's own knife. He sliced open the left trouser and inspected the bullet wound on his thigh. It wasn't serious and was barely bleeding. He unbuckled the man's belt, unbuttoned his fly and pulled his pants down. The two wounds there didn't seem that bad either. He chuckled. "You are one lucky man, Nick me boy. Had either of those two shots below the belt been an inch or two lower, you'd be singing soprano in the boys' choir and your John Thomas would be nothing but a fading memory. Here let me see that knife wound above your wrist."

Sullivan inspected the cut above Carson's right wrist. It was superficial going straight across the radial artery, but it clearly hadn't gone deep enough. In his experience, the slice needed to be at least a ¼ inch deep.

Sullivan looked at Carson and grinned. For the first time since 1922, he was glad he had missed killing Carson on Bloody Sunday. Then, it would have been a quick bullet in the back of the head on a crowded Dublin street. Now it would be up close and personal. "I tell you Nick me boyo, this *really* is your lucky day. Had that knife cut been any deeper, it would have severed your radial artery and you would have been no more than two minutes away from bleeding out and heading for the hell you so richly deserve. Here, let me show you," Sullivan said and took the man's own knife, placed it on the cut that Doris made, pressed down hard and pulled the knife blade across Carson's wrist, severing the radial artery.

Carson screamed as blood spurted from his wrist. He grabbed it with his left hand in a vain attempt to stop the bleeding, but Sullivan seized his left wrist in a firm grip and pulled it away. Carson was not strong enough to resist and the blood resumed its flow. "You bloody Mick bastard!" he croaked.

"As I was saying, you've maybe got another two minutes to live, you sodding butcher. Michael Collins sends his regards." Sullivan said and continued to hold Carson's wrist for another thirty seconds until he lost consciousness. Sullivan released the wrist and it flopped down to the floor. "Give my best wishes to the Devil," Sullivan said to ears that could no longer hear.

Back downstairs, Sullivan found Cockran and Doris Sandler sitting side by side on a green leather sofa, each with a crystal glass holding several fingers of a dark liquid. Cockran pointed to a matching green leather club chair and a side table where there was another crystal glass with two fingers of liquid. "Doris and I are drinking Laphroaig single malt, but there's Jameson there for you," Cockran said. "So how is the man upstairs?"

"Gone to meet his maker I fear. He was dead when I found him."

"I thought I heard a scream," Doris said.

"Ah, but wasn't that me?" Sullivan said. "I'm sensitive to the sight of blood."

"**WHO IS** this Roscoe Pound fella?" Bobby Sullivan asked as he and Cockran were having dinner before taking a night train to Boston.

Cockran had called Paul Walter after Sullivan told him Carson was dead and asked him to come to the Sandler residence before she called the police to report the break-in, attempted rape and her killing the intruder in self-defense. "It's pretty open and shut, Paul, but she needs a lawyer licensed in Ohio and I've got to be in Boston tomorrow."

Walter had arrived within half an hour and Cockran and Sullivan returned to their hotel where he called Tim O'Hanlon to report on the day's events. Tim had agreed with Cockran that it was best to cancel their appointment in Chicago and confront Roscoe Pound as soon as possible. Then, they had taken a taxi to the Terminal Tower where they purchased tickets for two Pullman compartments on the Pennsylvania Railroad's night train to Boston. With two hours until their train departed, they went to the English Oak Room for dinner and to plan the next day.

The English Oak Room, the crown jewel of the Fred Harvey chain of railroad terminal restaurants, was on the ticketing and waiting room level of the Terminal Tower complex. It was only five years old, yet it looked like it had been there for hundreds of years. It was a large square room supported by four large oak paneled pillars. It had a high ceiling, over 25 feet, and the walls were lined from floor to ceiling with dark oak panels said to have been imported from England's Sherwood Forest. A single massive Art Moderne chandelier hung in the middle of the room and twelve smaller versions of the main chandelier were hung from the ceiling three to a wall around their larger sibling.

Cockran had a martini and Sullivan a Jameson on the rocks as they waited for their entrees to arrive, lamb chops for Cockran and a porterhouse for Sullivan.

"Roscoe Pound has been the Dean of the Harvard Law School since 1916," Cockran said in reply to Sullivan's question. "He's not quite a Nazi, but he's definitely a Hitler-apologist. He speaks fluent German and spent his vacation there this summer, right after the Night of the Long Knives. It was an event that apparently didn't bother him because earlier this month, he accepted an honorary degree from the University of Berlin presented to him by Han Luther, the Nazis' Ambassador to the United States. Harvard put out the fatted calf on that occasion and almost the entire Harvard law faculty attended a luncheon hosted by the Nazis."

"You said 'almost all' the law school faculty," Sullivan noted. "Who were the exceptions?"

"Felix Frankfurter for one," Cockran replied. "He objected to Harvard hosting the event and conferring 'special distinction upon an official representative of enthroned lawlessness'."

"Enthroned lawlessness? That's as good a description of Germany you'll ever get these days. How is this Pound a Hitler-apologist?" Sullivan asked.

"I read his interviews in the Paris *Herald* and the New York *Herald Tribune.* He said that he never saw 'any indication of tension or fear of the future' in Germany."

Sullivan laughed and held up his glass as a signal to their waitress he wanted another. "I would be thinking he didn't visit any concentration camps."

"I doubt it or else he wouldn't have claimed free speech was alive and well in Nazi Germany. He said something to the effect that 'People discussed Hitler and everything else openly, just as we talk of Roosevelt in the United States'."

Sullivan shook his head. "There are none so blind as those who will not see."

Now, Cockran laughed. "Been reading the Bible, have you?"

"The sentiment is from either Matthew or Jeremiah, but Jonathon Swift used the phrase itself in *Polite Conversation.*"

"My, what a scholar you've become," Cockran said, "but back to Pound. When the bigoted bastard got back to the States from Germany this summer, he actually claimed that there was 'no persecution of Jewish scholars or of Jews who had lived in Germany for any length of time'. Tell that to Albert Einstein."

"So, what do we do tomorrow?"

"We tell him we've been engaged by someone in the government—whose identity we're not at liberty to disclose—to investigate the murders of six lawyers, all of them former MID agents, who all were doing legal research under Pound's supervision. What was the nature of that work? Then, we wait and see what he says."

"What do we do if he stonewalls us?" Sullivan asked. "Will you untie my hands?"

Cockran just shook his head. Violence was always Sullivan's first choice. He hadn't believed for a minute that it was Sullivan who screamed in the Sandler residence. What he did believe was that Bobby had killed the man himself, which was probably for the best because a good lawyer may have gotten Carson off for the murder of Sandler as Doris had never seen the man's face. "Let's wait and see. I'll think of something."

28

How About a Martini?

HANNA RAEDER was nervous as she knocked on the door to Mattie McGary's suite at the *Adlon*. It was partly her fear of giving an interview at all, but mostly it was having to depend on the word of a complete stranger to keep her identity confidential. Still, she had researched the woman's work and read her Pulitzer Prize articles as well as her interviews with Hitler both before and after the assassination attempt on him in early 1933 and her July 1934 interview with him where he attempted to justify the Night of the Long Knives. She clearly was no Nazi apologist. The facts alone in those articles were damning. The lawyer in Hanna admired the manner in which she questioned Hitler in those interviews, but she had to admit that Hitler was quite clever in the way he avoided giving her the answers she so obviously wanted.

Hanna was confident, however, that she could size Mattie up at the outset as a lawyer would a trial witness. She intended to cross-examine her quite closely on what she meant by 'off-the-record' and thought she could quickly conclude if the woman was to be trusted. What bothered her more was whether she could persuade the journalist that there was a bigger story here than the Prussian Memorandum and the drive to forbid marriage and sexual relations between Aryans and Jews and strip them of their German citizenship. Hanna knew these were horrific enough in and of themselves, but she believed an even bigger story affecting many more people was the systematic destruction of the rule of law and using it as a political weapon against the Nazis' opponents. Would a foreign journalist care as much about that as she would the Jews? Well, she thought, she was about to find out.

The door opened and a tall, very attractive woman with a warm smile and short, tousled red hair extended her hand. "*Frau* Hinderman, I'm Mattie McGary. Call me Mattie. Thank you so much for agreeing to talk to me. Please, come in."

"You're welcome. I'm Hanna," she replied as she entered a large sitting room with a green leather sofa and two matching club chairs around a low butler's table. She watched as Mattie walked over to a drinks trolley at the side of the room and looked over her shoulder at Hanna.

"It's 5:00 p.m. Hanna and the Americans call this the cocktail hour. How about a martini? I'm making one for myself. It's one of America's better inventions and I'm pretty good at, if I do say so myself."

Hanna smiled. She liked this woman who still had a trace of a Scottish accent. She had never tasted a martini, but she had heard of them. "Sure, why not? Thanks."

Hanna accepted the martini and took a small sip. To her surprise, it was quite good, cold and almost pure alcohol. She sat in the corner of the sofa and the journalist sat in the armchair directly across from her.

"Right. So let's begin. Why don't I tell you how I got started on this story; where I am today; and what I want to do next. Then, before we begin the actual interview, I'll answer any questions you may have. Okay?"

Hanna nodded her acquiescence.

"I first learned of the Prussian Memorandum from two different sources. One of them was my godfather Winston Churchill who, as you know, received it from your friend Georg von Dohnonyi. The second source is confidential, but the two copies I've seen are identical. I also know from confidential sources..."

When she finished, Hanna was surprised at how much *Frau* McGary—Mattie—had learned that she didn't know herself. She knew that American lawyers had done the legal research for the Memorandum, but not that the SS had engaged American Military Intelligence to do this or that Himmler and Goebbels had agreed to share the costs of doing it. She also knew more about that bastard Roland Freisler than the average German who likely never heard of him.

"Any questions so far?" Mattie asked.

"You mentioned 'confidential sources' and you told Georg my interview would be 'off-the-record'. What does that mean? How does it work?"

"It's simple, really. I won't mention your name or your gender in my notes or my articles. I won't disclose your identity to anyone, not even my editor, without your consent."

"Are you interviewing other Commission members?"

"I'm going to try, but I don't know if I'll be successful. You're the first, Hanna."

"Hitler seems to give you a lot of interviews. Why is that?"

"My bad luck?" Mattie said with a grin and drank the rest of her martini.

Hanna laughed. Yes, she definitely liked this woman. "Okay, Mattie, what would you like to know?"

"How and why did you get appointed to this Commission on Criminal Law Reform?"

"I once was a practicing criminal defense lawyer..." Hanna began and walked Mattie through her retirement, her coming out of retirement, the Nazis coming to power and requiring defense lawyers to help in determining their clients' guilt, her resignation as an active attorney, and Justice Minister Gurtner's subsequent plea for her to fill a vacancy on the Commission and act as an adversary to the radical ideas of the Commission Chairman Roland Freisler.

"What does your husband Admiral Raeder think of your service on the Commission?"

Hanna bristled and finished her martini before answering in a cold voice. "I'll not answer any questions about my husband. On or off-the-record."

"I'm sorry. I understand. I apologize. Let's move on now to the Prussian Memorandum. Before we do, how about a refill on our martinis?"

"Sure," Hanna replied, "but before we proceed to the Memorandum, I'd like to discuss something else that, as a German, I think equally important, even if your American readers might not. Have you heard of the new Peoples Court the Nazis created in April of this year?"

"I've heard of it, but I can't say I know much about it," Mattie said from the side of the room where she was mixing martinis.

"The judges on the Peoples Court are completely political and they now hear all treason and other capital cases like murder, ones that used to be heard by the Supreme Court. There is no appeal from any of their decisions. They can deprive defendants of their choice of lawyers if they don't like the lawyers. There are no objective standards."

Hanna paused as Mattie brought over their fresh martinis. She took a sip and continued. "If, for example, a party member or SA Brown Shirt kills someone in cold blood, it is a complete defense to say he thought the victim was a Jew or a Communist even if the victim was neither. Since his *intent* was to help the common good by ridding the community of a Jew or Communist, then he's not guilty of murder because he made an innocent mistake in his choice of victim."

"Seriously?" Mattie asked in an incredulous tone.

"Sadly, yes. I could give you many more examples, but I can save you time. I wrote two legal memorandums that were circulated to Commission members, one opposed to the Peoples Court before it was created in April and another in August where I give many examples of miscarriages of justice in the first four months of the existence of the Peoples Court. I can arrange to have copies delivered to you where you can see for yourself what I'm talking about."

"That would be great. Does your name appear as the author on these legal memorandums?"

"Yes, Hanna Hindermann. Why?"

"If there is any difficulty in your getting me copies, I think one of my confidential sources can obtain them from the Commission files," Mattie replied.

Really? Hanna thought. Your source has access to Commission files? That *was* impressive. "I have my own copies at home, but if there is any problem, I'll let you know."

Over the next thirty minutes, Hanna answered all of Mattie's questions about the Prussian Memorandum and how it was used during Commission deliberations on the proposed law to make second-class citizens of all German Jews. She told Mattie that, while she was opposed to any new laws that made Jews second-class citizens, it quickly became apparent to her that the Commission was going to recommend to the Reichstag a law that does just that and criminalizes both sexual relations and marriage between Aryans and Jews.

"I'll vote against that and so will at least three other members including, of course, Georg von Dohnonyi," Hanna said, "but we'll lose."

She paused for another sip of her martini and continued. "The real dispute on the Commission will be how to define a Jew. The radical Nazis want to go back multiple generations—at least four or five—to find a single Jewish grandparent. The moderates do not. We propose only going back two generations and requiring that all four grandparents must be Jews. I don't agree, but some moderates might even go for a person being declared a Jew if three grandparents were Jews so long as one of them was the maternal grandmother. I won't name names, but if you ever read a transcript of the June 5 meeting, you'll see who they are."

"How will I contact you once I have a copy of the June 5 Commission meeting transcript?" Mattie asked when the interview was over and Hanna was preparing to leave.

"Let's continue to use Greta Mayer. She told me she has a boyfriend who regularly checks her telephone to make sure there's no wiretap on it. We usually have lunch several times a month so your asking her to call me to set up a date to meet is nothing new. I don't intend to leave Berlin until Erich is back from his sea trials in three weeks, but if that changes, I'll make sure Greta knows how to reach me."

With that, the two women shook hands and Hanna took an elevator down to the hotel lobby and outside to a taxi.

29

The Tiergarten

The Tiergarten
Berlin
Thursday, 13 September 1934

IT WAS a pleasant late summer evening, dusk falling, as Mattie McGary walked back to the *Adlon* from her interview with Werner Kramer at his apartment in the Charlottenburg section of Berlin which was on the west end of the *Tiergarten,* formerly the hunting grounds of Prussian kings. It was so pleasant that Mattie left her Burberry trench coat open when she decided against a taxi in favor of an evening stroll through Europe's largest metropolitan park.

In the distance, Mattie could see the *Siegessaute,* the towering Victory column erected after the Franco-Prussian War in the late 19th century. Topped by a gilded statue of Victoria known to Berliners as *Gold-Else,* the column was at the open center of the *Tiergarten.* Light from the globes of street lamps illuminated the open space around the Victory column and the gravel paths through the park, but darkness was thick among the surrounding trees and foliage casting long shadows.

It had been a good day, she thought, with excellent interviews from both Hanna Raeder and Werner Kramer. They essentially confirmed everything that Georg von Dohnanyi had told Winston. Better still, they also confirmed what Greta Mayer had told her, namely that there was a long, contentious meeting of the Commission on 5 June of this year where the Prussian Memorandum was the principal topic of discussion and debate. Both Hanna and Kramer were legitimate 'moderates' on the Commission and had agreed to review for accuracy any transcript, but their views on Jews were decidedly different.

As Mattie soon discovered when she interviewed Werner Kramer, she didn't need to see the transcript to identify him as one of those moderates. Kramer had reminded her of a younger and even stuffier version of his boss, the *Reichsbank* President Hjalmar Schacht. He was in his early 40s, hair parted in the middle, wireless glasses, high winged collar, and a Hitler mustache. It soon became apparent to Mattie that he had no strongly held views of his own, but was merely parroting his master's voice. Jews had it coming to them, Kramer had told her, but the need for foreign reserves to finance German rearmament was more important. Hence, any new laws about the Jews had to take into account their effect on the worldwide boycott of German exports. That was why he and President Schacht opposed the radicals on the Commission.

Shortly after passing the *Siegessaute,* Mattie veered off from the main path through the center of the *Tiergarten* to a narrower gravel path where shrubs and brush, rather than grassy lawns, lined the sides. After crossing a small, arched wooden bridge with green-painted iron railings, she heard loud footsteps behind her on its wooden surface. She turned to see who was causing the racket. Two very large men in trench coats that resembled hers seized her, lifting her off her feet. A big hand clamped over her mouth, stifling her scream as they carried her into the overgrowth a good thirty yards into the trees beyond, effectively out of eyesight and earshot from passers-by on the path. Mattie was furious rather than frightened. She had no more expected to be attacked in Berlin's *Tiergarten* in the early evening on her way back to the *Adlon* than she would have in New York's Central Park returning from an evening stroll to her husband's Fifth Avenue townhouse.

The initially evident intent of her attackers became obvious when they reached a small, secluded, pine-needle-covered clearing and the two men mauled her to the ground, one in front and the other behind her. The one behind clasped her breasts through her blouse while the one in front tried to thrust his tongue into her mouth as his big hands reached around her, slid beneath her skirt and silk step-ins and embraced her bare backside. Just great, Mattie thought, the day she wears a skirt rather than trousers, she meets up with your average Berlin rapist and more easily accommodates his mauling her.

"Harry was right. She *is* a sexy twist!" the man groping her bottom said in English.

Bloody hell! Mattie thought. More Americans! Fortunately, she had held tightly onto her handbag when she was abducted and, now that they were relatively stationary, she reached into it and found her Walther PPK automatic. Unfortunately for the rapist embracing her bum, the relative position of the three meant her only real target was the man's groin grinding into her pelvis. She thumbed off the safety and, just as she was about to terminate his life or his ability to procreate—there were arteries or something like that down there, right?—two words she thought she would never be happy to hear caused her to slacken her pressure on the trigger.

"Halt! *Gestapo!*"

Instantly, the hands on her breasts and bottom backed off. Mattie looked up to see two men in dark overcoats and gray fedoras looming over them, oval *Gestapo* medallions in their left hands, Luger automatics in their right pointed directly at her two would-be rapists who held their hands up in the universal sign of surrender. Hey, she thought, it's fine with me if you shoot the bastards. To her startled surprise, that's just what they did, two silenced point-blank shots into each man's head.

Mattie emitted a small, involuntary scream and looked up again at her *Gestapo* saviors who doffed their fedoras, revealing two blond-haired specimens of Aryan manhood. They were very young, probably early twenties, and both very handsome. Then, they rolled the bodies over, relieved them of their holstered weapons that looked like Colt .45 automatics. They placed the weapons in the right hand of each body. One man lifted the right hand on one body and pulled the trigger of the automatic. Mattie winced at the loud discharge. After that, they pulled from each man's suit coat what looked like U.S. Passports. One of them pulled a sheet of paper from inside his suit coat and then compared it to each passport. The other nodded.

"Americans. Their names are not on the list," one of them said. "This means they have no permits to carry these pistols, which undoubtedly explains why they resisted arrest and fired a shot at us. We had no choice but to shoot them in self-defense. Once we finish here, Franz, take the weapons and these wallets to the *Kripo* and tell them what happened and where they can find the bodies. Tell them the woman these two attacked refused to give her name. I think a statement from you should suffice, but if they want one from me, tell them I will come around in the morning and answer any questions they may have."

The man then turned to Mattie. "*Sturmbannfuhrer* Walter Schellenberg sends you his personal regards. I am *SS-Obersturmfuhrer* Eric Bulow and this is *SS-Obersturmfuhrer* Franz Globke. '*Heil* Hitler!'" they shouted as they clicked their heels and shot out their right arms.

"Uh...*Heil*, I guess. Thank you," Mattie said weakly as she got to her feet and began to dust off her clothes. "So, tell me. How did you guys happen to be here just in the nick of time to save my somewhat tarnished virtue?"

"Two days ago, *Sturmbannfuhrer* Schellenberg directed us to look after you once he learned that two Americans would be following you with instructions to rough you up if they could get you alone with no witnesses," Bulow said. "Apparently there is a story you are working on that someone does not want published. We were told to allow no harm to come to you and that lethal force was permitted to accomplish this. That they had illegal, unregistered firearms on them left us no choice."

Really? Mattie thought. Both Americans had held up their hands in an obvious attempt to surrender. Still, Mattie wasn't about to complain, especially as she had been moments away from shooting one, if not both of them, herself with her Walter PPK, a weapon that was, thank you very much, duly registered with the proper German authorities. More importantly, who the hell knew she was investigating the Prussian Memorandum? "Well, again my thanks. Please convey my gratitude to *Herr* Schellenberg."

"I will, *Fraulein* McGary, but *Sturmbannfuhrer* Schellenberg also asked me to convey his invitation for the 'red-haired Marlene Dietrich' to join him for lunch tomorrow at *Horcher's*."

Mattie laughed. That was Walter Schellenberg, all right. "Thank you, but it's *Frau* McGary and tell him I accept. Why do you suppose he wishes to see me?"

"He did not say, but I imagine he wishes to warn you that, in addition to these two," Bulow said, gesturing at the two corpses over which they were having this conversation, "the *Gestapo* has two men following you as well."

"*Gestapo*? I thought you two were *Gestapo*. I saw your medallions."

"Oh no," Bulow said quickly. "Franz and I are SD, the Security Service for the SS. The *Gestapo* medallions are for show. We have to return them to *Sturmbannfuhrer* Schellenberg after this assignment. Besides, Franz and I don't meet the qualifications for the *Gestapo*," he said with a grin and paused for effect. "Both our parents are married."

Mattie laughed again. Schellenberg's men apparently shared their superior's irreverence as well as his ruthless nature. It had been Schellenberg himself who earlier this year had saved her from two other Americans. They had been working for Henry Ford's right-hand man, Ernst Liebold, who wanted her to stop investigating a story that would have ended Liebold's professional career. Though he had only wounded them, Schellenberg then had executed both men just as coldly as these two blond SS poster-boys had done. "While Franz goes to report this to the *Kripo*," Bulow said, extending his elbow for her to grasp, "I will escort you safely back to the *Adlon*."

30

Dean Roscoe Pound

Office of the Dean
Harvard Law School
Cambridge, Massachusetts
Friday, 14 September 1934

ROSCOE POUND was a large, chubby-faced, pink-cheeked man, close to six feet tall and over 200 pounds. Gray hair parted in the middle, wire-rimmed glasses and a full gray mustache completed the picture. He wore a three-piece navy-blue herringbone suit with a green eyeshade on his forehead and a cigar clutched in the corner of his mouth.

Pound's office befitted the Dean of the Harvard Law School. Its walls were lined with bookcases and his desk was covered with piles of law books, multiple paper bookmarks stuck in most of them. It was late afternoon and Cockran, Sullivan and Pound sat in three of four cracked red leather club chairs around a butler's table on which sat a silver tray with a crystal decanter containing a clear brown liquid—Scotch, perhaps? Cockran wondered—and four matching crystal tumblers. The Dean, however, did not offer them a drink.

Cockran knew Pound was a legal legend and some, if not most, of it was probably warranted. In 1903, he became the dean of the University of Nebraska College of Law at age 33. He began teaching at the Harvard Law School in 1911 and became its dean in 1916, the first who was not a Harvard Law graduate. Nonetheless, his pro-Nazi sympathies rubbed Cockran the wrong way. Having spent extensive time in Germany on behalf of clients on five occasions in the last four years, three of those occasions occurring after Hitler became Chancellor, he knew from first-hand experience that everything—and he meant *everything*—that Pound recently said about and in praise of Nazi Germany was false. Whether Pound knew it was false was entirely another question, but Cockran didn't care what the answer was. He needed something else from the man.

"Thank you, Dean Pound," Cockran began, "I appreciate your courtesy in seeing us on such short notice. As my secretary explained to your secretary, I'm a partner with the New York and Washington law firm, Donovan & Raichle and…"

"Is that Wild Bill Donovan's firm?" Pound interrupted.

"Yes, Sir, it is."

"Please give him my regards. He was an excellent head of the Antitrust Division of the Justice Department during the Coolidge years. I admired the work he did there."

"Yes, Sir, I will. Now, as I was saying…"

"Forgive another interruption," Pound said, "but are you by chance related to Bourke Cockran, the famous orator?"

"Yes, Sir, he was my father."

"Wonderful speaker, but what I admired most about him was his courage as a politician. I'm a Republican as you may know even though I said a few nice things about FDR last year. What your father did in 1896, supporting McKinley over Bryan, the Democratic candidate, was the most courageous political act I have ever witnessed. I was only 26 and practicing law in my home state of Nebraska and I heard him speak during the campaign at the University. My goodness, but it was one of the largest crowds ever for a speech in Nebraska, over 10,000 people.

Based on what I read in the New York newspapers, your father's speech in Lincoln was much like the one he gave at Madison Square Garden at the outset of the campaign. President Roosevelt, uh,

Theodore Roosevelt, told me your father was the finest orator he ever heard."

"Yes, Sir. Colonel Roosevelt and my father were good friends. Their estates on Long Island's North Coast were only minutes apart. I grew up there with the Roosevelt boys as my playmates. The Colonel even had my father review and edit the galley proofs of his autobiography."

"You don't say. Well, I'm an old man and I dwell too much in the past. So what can I do for you today, Mr. Cockran?"

Cockran breathed a sigh of relief. He hadn't wished to be rude because he wanted something from Pound, but he was pleased to be back on topic. He was also pleased that Pound seemed impressed with his bona fides. Pound had not been born to wealth, growing up in Nebraska, but he clearly aspired to it now that he was at Harvard teaching the sons of the rich elite. As an anti-Semite, he was among his own kind at Harvard, which enforced a strict quota on the admission of Jewish students. Given his father's and Bill Donovan's reputations, one a wealthy Democrat, the other a wealthy Republican, he hoped that it would be enough to persuade Pound that Cockran was one of them.

Regardless, though, he had a strategy worked out for the meeting. He was going to pretend he knew more than he really did. Pound had to be the 'Ivy League fascist' that Henry Sandler had complained about to Tim O'Hanlon. It also was clear to Cockran from Sandler's cover letter to him that Pound had been the one who either supervised or coordinated the legal research of the six lawyers who were former MID agents. In fact, it was quite likely that Pound had chosen the six lawyers from the list of twelve that O'Hanlon had given to Marlborough. What Cockran didn't know was the nature of the legal research, but he couldn't admit that to Pound. He had to pretend that he did and hope that Pound didn't catch on.

Cockran's advantage was that he was an experienced trial lawyer and Pound an academic. It was, of course, a cardinal rule of cross-examination that you never asked a question to which you didn't know the answer, but there were always exceptions to the rule and this was one of them.

"Dean Pound, our law firm has been retained by a high government official in Washington—whose name and position we are not at liberty to disclose—to investigate the deaths late last year of six former MID agents, all of them lawyers, who were performing legal research under your direction and supervision. Our firm was retained because I am a former MID agent myself and both Colonel Donovan and I retain the 'Top Secret' government clearances we had during the war when I was Colonel Donovan's Intelligence Officer with the Fighting 69th. Those clearances continued after the war when I was an agent with MID and the Colonel was with the Justice Department, initially as a U.S. District Attorney in Buffalo, then with the Antitrust Division, and finally as Acting Attorney General under President Coolidge."

Actually, Cockran thought, he had no idea what, if any, security clearances he and Donovan had ever had, let alone what they had now which was probably none. But Pound probably didn't know that and, unlike him, Bill Donovan was a genuine war hero who had the Congressional Medal of Honor and Cockran, while not especially a hero in his own eyes, had the Silver Star. Would war heroes lie?

"I assume, Dean Pound, that you have a comparable security clearance because you would not have been given this assignment by MID otherwise."

Pound nodded, but didn't reply. Cockran then tried his first, but not his last, bluff. "Here is a list of the twelve former MID agents who were lawyers that was submitted by MID to you from which you selected the six you believed best suited for the assignment," he said and handed the list to Pound.

The Dean studied the list and nodded his approval of its accuracy.

"Here is the list of the six you selected. Beside each name is the date and manner of their death," he said as he gave the sheet to Pound.

Cockran watched the elderly academic closely for any tell indicating prior knowledge of the deaths, but he detected none. Rather, he could see confusion and shock. The man was neither a trial lawyer nor, in all likelihood, a poker player, but he was definitely surprised.

"My God! This is incredible! All six of these men died within six weeks of each other? I knew them all! We met together once last fall here in my office. After that, we communicated by telephone or mail. But they all died in a different way. Could it possibly be a coincidence?" Pound asked.

Cockran shook his head. "No, Sir. Apart from the fact that MID agents—or even former MID agents like me—don't believe in coincidence, our investigation has already identified who we believe to be the killer."

"Really? Who?"

"The actual assassin was a professional killer named Nicholas O'Neill Carson who was engaged for the six kills by the New York Irish mob boss Owney Madden. What we don't know yet is who hired Madden and why. That's what we've been retained to find out."

"I don't understand. If these six men were killed because of the legal research they did under my supervision, why wasn't I killed also?"

Well, Cockran thought, that's a good question. So far, things were going well and Pound had confirmed almost all their suspicions. But they still didn't know the nature of the research MID engaged him to do. Time to move in for the kill before Pound figured out what Cockran was really trying to do.

"We don't know. We hoped that you, based on the legal research you supervised, might have some idea of who would want them killed and why."

"Well, Mr. Cockran, I didn't know of their deaths, but now that you've told me gangsters are involved in some way, I think I do know, at least generally, who would want them killed and why. I don't consider myself an expert on organized crime in America, but I do know a little about organized crime in Cleveland. You see, in 1922, my law school colleague, Felix Frankfurter and I undertook a detailed, quantitative study of crime in Cleveland. Have you ever heard of the Cleveland Syndicate?"

Cockran, who had taught for a year as a visiting professor at Western Reserve University's law school in 1929, had heard of the Cleveland Syndicate, a largely Jewish-run mob headed by Moe Dalish, but he thought it best at this point to feign ignorance. "No, Sir, I haven't."

"Most people haven't, including most people in Cleveland. It's why some people call it the 'Silent Syndicate' because all its leaders are Jews and they keep a very low profile. I can't tell you who in the Syndicate is responsible, but as Jews, any or all of them would have had the motive, means and opportunity to arrange for these deaths."

Cockran was confused. He understood means and opportunity. Any upper echelon gangster had that. But motive? Why would Jewish gangsters have motive? He had to be careful not to give away that he knew nothing about the legal research. If Pound sensed that he didn't, he would clam up.

"I'm not sure I understand. How would the legal research give a Jewish gangster motive?"

"Come on, isn't it obvious?" Pound said as he took the cigar from his mouth and laid it on a crystal ashtray.

"Not to me, Sir," Cockran replied. "Like Colonel Donovan, I went to Columbia Law School, not Harvard. I'm baffled at how legal research of any kind would furnish anyone, not just Jews, with a motive to kill."

Pound smiled at the implication Columbia lawyers were inferior to their Harvard brethren. "I don't have proof, of course, and I don't know how Jewish gangsters learned of our research. It seems to me, however, that when you perform legal research into the law in thirty American states that prohibit marriage and sexual relations between whites and a variety of non-whites like Negroes, Chinese, Filipino, Malays and the like, thus treating them as second class citizens, and you do that research at the behest of the German government for its use in drafting similar laws to render German Jews second class citizens, that might well offend Jewish gangsters and give them motive to kill the lawyers who made that possible. I can't give you more, but I hope that I have at least given you a place to begin a search for the actual culprits."

Cockran was at once elated at learning the nature of the legal research and terrified at its implications. Mattie's new story involved the same document over which six men had been killed. He and Sullivan had to get out of Pound's office quickly and warn her.

"Sir, that's brilliant!" Cockran said. "I just didn't know there were Jewish gangsters. I thought they were all either Italian or Irish. But I see it clearly now. Thanks very much. You've been a great help!"

The three men rose and shook hands. Once they were out of the Dean's office, Cockran grabbed Sullivan's arm. "We're going to Boston Airport and charter the fastest plane there. We've got to get back to New York as soon as possible and catch the next ocean liner to Germany."

Cockran explained to Sullivan on the taxi ride to the airport about the Prussian Memorandum and Mattie's investigation of it in Germany. "I'll call Alexis once we're at the airport and after we've chartered a plane. I'll get her started on securing our passage to Germany. Then, I'll call Mattie tomorrow morning in Berlin and tell her what we've found. This story of hers has just gotten a lot more dangerous. She needs to watch her back."

31

The Table of the Blond Beast

Restaurant Horcher
21 Lutherstrasse
Berlin
Friday, 14 September 1934

WALTER SCHELLENBERG wore the black, full dress, silver-trimmed uniform of a *SS-Sturmbannfuhrer,* complete with knee-high polished black leather boots. He rose when Mattie McGary entered the restaurant and motioned for her to join him.

Mattie was bemused because she had rarely seen the young SS officer in uniform rather than plain clothes. When she reached his table, he loudly clicked his heels, took her hand, palm down in his and kissed the back of her hand. "I am so pleased you were able to join me for lunch today, *Frau* McGary."

"I could hardly refuse after your men rescued me from an attack last night in the *Tiergarten.*"

They both ordered North Sea scallops along with a bottle of French Chablis and, when their waiter left, Mattie leaned into the table and said quietly, "I was surprised, *Herr* Schellenberg, that your men executed my attackers on the spot rather than arrest them."

Schellenberg gave her a boyish grin. "Might you at some point do me the honor of calling me by my Christian name? As for my men, I apologize. I gave them the authority to use deadly force if *necessary* to keep you safe. I fear they interpreted 'necessary' more broadly than I intended."

"Well, Walter, you have my thanks nonetheless. My friends call me 'Mattie'. Now, to what do I owe the pleasure of your invitation to lunch? And at *Horcher* no less? This is the second time this week I've dined here."

Schellenberg beamed at her use of his name. "Really? What was the occasion?"

"Kurt von Sturm is assisting me on a story I'm investigating. He thought some peril might be involved and that, by dining with him at *Unser* Hermann's table," Mattie said as she nodded to her right to an empty table reserved exclusively for Hermann Göring, "those who wished me ill would be warned that I was working under Göring's protection."

"Apparently, the Americans who attacked you last night were unaware of this."

Mattie laughed. "You might say that. So, why am I here?"

"For one thing, the same reason *Herr* von Sturm had you to lunch here. The difference is that, rather than *Unser* Hermann's table, you and I are sitting at the 'Table of the Blond Beast'," he said, referring to a common appellation for his immediate superior, *SS-Obersturmbannführer* Reinhard Tristan Heydrich, the #2 official in the SS, below only Heinrich Himmler. One of his other appellations was 'The Man With the Iron Heart', bestowed on him by none other than Adolf Hitler himself.

"Bloody hell!" Mattie said. "We're sitting at Heydrich's table?"

Schellenberg lowered his voice. "Yes, Mattie, you and I are playing a dangerous game in which there are many players. Now the gossip will be all over Berlin that both Heydrich and Göring are in your corner when it involves your investigation of the Prussian Memorandum.

"Double bloody hell!" Mattie said. "You know about that, too?"

They paused while the waiter brought the wine and opened it. Schellenberg fingered the cork while the waiter poured a small portion into his glass. He took a sip and nodded his approval.

"I do, from the day it was commissioned," Schellenberg said, after the waiter poured a full measure into both of their glasses. He then recounted to her Himmler's order to Heydrich in 1933 to commission legal research from the U.S. Army's Military Intelligence Division into the state laws on miscegenation in America; Heydrich passing on the assignment to Schellenberg who in turn tasked the SS liaison, Wilhelm Krueger, in the German Embassy in Washington to do so; the recent cable from Krueger indicating that his American liaison, Harold Canfield, III, wanted the *Gestapo* to have McGary killed or placed in a concentration camp in order to stop her story on the memorandum; and finally, the wiretapped conversation between Canfield and RVD International agents in Berlin giving them orders to tail her and 'rough her up' if they got the opportunity to do so.

"Clearly," he continued, "the Americans are embarrassed by this memorandum and don't want it publicized. That explains the attack on you last night by the RVD agents. Our intelligence says that RVD has more agents in Europe than the two we killed last night so the danger to you from that quarter is not over."

This was fantastic, Mattie thought, ignoring in the excitement of the moment that men were out to kill her. This was going to be one big story and she had just learned how it all began! She now knew it was Heinrich Himmler and Joseph Goebbels who were behind the Prussian Memorandum and had the SS engage the U.S. Army's MID who likely hired RVD International in some capacity. Cockran knew a lot more about RVD than she did, but she did recall that its founder was retired General Ralph Van Deman, the founder and first head of MID. Once Kurt secured the identities of the American lawyers and she received the transcript of the 5 June 1934 meeting of the Commission, all she had to do was have one or more members of the Commission verify its accuracy. Then she had her story and she could get out of Germany and back to America to interview the lawyers who had done the legal research. Damn! Sometimes it was better to be lucky than good. Still, the key was the 5 June transcript. She had to have it. She hoped Greta Mayer was hard at work producing a new one.

"Okay, but your men said last night that I was also being followed by the *Gestapo*. What's the story with that?" Mattie asked and then took a sip of wine.

Schellenberg did the same before he answered. "That is also a complicated story involving this Canfield fellow. I thought I had taken care of the *Gestapo*." He then explained that he had destroyed the cable from Krueger in Washington conveying Harold Canfield's request to have the *Gestapo* neutralize her. "I thought that was the end of it, but I was wrong. Freisler went straight to Himmler on Wednesday and complained about your friend von Sturm demanding background information on the American lawyers who had worked on the memorandum. Inasmuch as it was Himmler's idea to investigate American law as a possible model, he agreed to have the *Gestapo* follow you and report on where you went and whom you saw. I don't think, at this point, the *Gestapo* poses any real danger to you except for one thing…"

Schellenberg paused as their waiter arrived with their scallops and green salads and then refilled their wine glasses.

"Except for what one thing?" Mattie asked once the waiter was out of earshot.

"Himmler also ordered the *Gestapo* to place listening devices in your suite at the *Adlon*. If you wish, I can send someone over to locate them and teach you how to temporarily disable them. That would allow you to place telephone calls without being overheard as your telephone at the *Adlon* is not tapped."

Mattie smiled. "And just how do you know this?"

"Himmler knows Göring would never approve a wiretap on your telephone whereas he did approve a wiretap on Roland Freisler's office telephone that I requested last year after I arranged for the legal research into American laws. Everything I've told you today I learned from yesterday's 'Brown Pages' where Freisler was bragging on the telephone to one of his staff about his meeting with Himmler the day before and all that Himmler had agreed to do about you. Unlike this Canfield—who apparently wants you eliminated and plans to do so— Himmler has not yet given that order although he has kept that option open. Meanwhile, my men, Bulow and Globke, will continue to serve as your bodyguards and see to your safety."

Chartwell
Kent, England
Friday, 14 September 1934

"MR. CHURCHILL, you have a person-to-person telephone call from Prague," his secretary Mrs. P said. "The caller declined to give his name. Will you take the call?"

Churchill looked up from his stand-up writing desk where he had been correcting the page proofs of an article—'Ships *Could* Have Forced the Dardanelles'—a review of the naval memoirs of Admiral Sir Roger Keys for *The Daily Mail.* "Certainly, Mrs. P.," he replied as he took the Havana cigar from his mouth and placed it in a crystal ashtray. "Ask the operator to redirect the call to the unlisted number of the private line in my study."

Churchill walked over to the desk in his study where he carefully disabled the listening device in the base of his desk lamp that had been placed there by Scotland Yard's Special Branch at the behest of Neville Chamberlain, the Chancellor of the Exchequer. The telephone rang and he picked up the receiver.

"Churchill," he growled.

"Georg von Dohnanyi, Mr. Churchill. Thank you for taking my call. My niece Greta Mayer advised me yesterday that she has completed the transcript of the 5 June meeting of the Commission this year where the Prussian Memorandum was discussed at length. She gave me the original and a carbon copy. I have reviewed the transcript and it is exactly what you indicated your goddaughter would need to prove the Memorandum was not a forgery. I took a train to Prague this morning so that I could talk to you without fear my call was being wiretapped."

"Excellent news, Dr. von Dohnanyi!" Churchill said. "What arrangements do you propose for delivering the transcript to me and

Mattie this weekend in Amsterdam? We will be staying at the Grand Hotel *Krasnapolsky*."

"I fear I will not be able to deliver it to you personally as I originally had planned. The *Gestapo* have had me under constant surveillance ever since I returned from London and I anticipate that they will follow me to Amsterdam. Otto Lutze, a trusted colleague of mine at the Ministry of Justice who has no connection to the Commission on Criminal Law Reform, will be attending the same legal conference this weekend as I am. He and I will both be staying at the Victoria Hotel where the conference is being held. It is near the Amsterdam *Centraal* train station. It would not be prudent of me to have the transcript in my possession so Otto has agreed to take the carbon copy of the transcript to Amsterdam where he will lease a locker at the train station tonight and deposit it there. He will contact you at your hotel tomorrow and arrange a time and place where he can give you the key to the locker. Will that be satisfactory?"

"Yes, it will. Thank you. I look forward to hearing from your Mr. Lutze tomorrow."

Churchill rang again for Mrs. P, "Pray call my goddaughter again in Berlin at the *Adlon*."

The Hotel Adlon
Berlin
Friday, 14 September 1934

HAVING ACCEPTED Schellenberg's offer to locate the bugs in her suite, Mattie was feeling a little more secure when the telephone rang.

"Mattie McGary."

"Mattie, it's Winston."

"Winston! How good to hear from you, but you've called at a bad time. I've got a dinner engagement in a few minutes. Once I'm at the restaurant, I'll excuse myself and call you collect from the Ladies Powder Room. Are you at Chartwell?"

He was. After replacing the receiver and disconnecting the listening device, Mattie proceeded to call Churchill's private, unlisted number. "Winston? Sorry for the subterfuge, but we can talk now. Let me tell you what has happened."

"So, why did you call?" Mattie asked after she finished giving him a brief summary of the attack on her last night in the *Tiergarten* and what she learned at lunch from Schellenberg about the contract on her life by some American named Canfield who was working with both American MID and the *Gestapo*.

"I have heard from Dr. von Dohnanyi," Churchill replied. "His niece has finished the 5 June transcript. He is making arrangements for us to receive it in Amsterdam tomorrow. I have reserved adjoining suites for us at the Grand Hotel *Krasnapolsky* with a common rooftop terrace. My Imperial Airways flight will arrive at the *Schiphol* aerodrome in late morning. Will you be able to join me for lunch?"

"Sure. I'll have the *Adlon* concierge contact *Lufthansa* as soon as we finish our call."

After the concierge booked a ticket for her on the 9:00 a.m. Lufthansa flight to Amsterdam,

Mattie placed a call to Joe Willicomb in New York to bring him up to date on this latest development. Then, she called her husband's secretary, Alexis, in New York to advise her where she could be reached over the weekend. To her surprise, her husband was not in Cleveland as she thought, but was back in New York at his law firm and Alexis transferred the call to his office.

"Hey, Babe," Cockran said, "Good to hear your voice. I don't have much time as Bobby and I have a zeppelin to catch from Lakehurst in a few hours so let me tell you what we've found because it directly impacts your story. The main thing is you need to watch your back..."

Mattie listened with growing amazement to the fact that all six former MID agents who conducted the legal research for the Prussian Memorandum had been assassinated last year by a hit man hired through Owney Madden! She shook her head. Horrible, she knew, but it meant her story just kept getting better.

"So, I'd feel a lot more comfortable," Cockran said when he finished briefing her on what he had found, "if you could call

Winston; tell him what I've discovered; and ask him to try and arrange for Robbie Rankin of Scotland Yard to accompany him to Amsterdam. Bobby and I will be in Germany on Sunday. We'll call you in Amsterdam from Berlin when we arrive."

"Good," Mattie said, "Winston has booked us adjoining suites at the *Grand Hotel Krasnapolsky*. I'll register both of us as Mr. & Mrs. Cockran so you won't have a problem getting a key to a woman's suite whose name is different than yours." Mattie briefly thought about telling her husband the details of the attack on her last night in the *Tiergarten* by American agents of RVD International, but decided against it. It would just cause him needless worry about her safety when he couldn't do anything about it. Besides, she still had Schellenberg's two blond SS poster boys looking after her in Berlin and his suggestion to enlist Robbie Rankin as a bodyguard in Amsterdam was a good idea. She walked to the telephone and placed a call to England. Ten minutes later, it went through.

"Winston, I've just talked to Bourke about Amsterdam and he's had an excellent idea."

Mattie listened to Churchill with growing disappointment. The Home Secretary, Sir John Gilmour, under pressure from Neville Chamberlain, had forbidden Scotland Yard from providing bodyguard service to 'back bench' Members of Parliament, i.e., those who held no government office. Gilmour had apologized to Winston and explained that Chamberlain pressured him to do this because Churchill had embarrassed him the year before in the Commons over the anti-Nazi boycott Churchill supported and Chamberlain opposed. The policy applied to all backbench MPs generally, but its specific target had been Churchill.

"I told Sir John I understood and that I appreciated his explanation," Churchill said, "but I've really had no need for a bodyguard these past few years. Besides, Robbie still comes around on his own time to check for any new wiretaps or listening devices Special Branch may have installed either here at Chartwell or our London flat. As for our safety in Amsterdam, don't worry. I'll have my 7.65 mm Webley & Scott pistol and you will have your Walther PPK. All will be well."

32

Papers Please!

On Board the Europa
Near Bremerhaven, Germany
Friday, 14 September 1934

HAROLD CANFIELD stood at one of the two large portholes in his first class cabin and looked once again at the cable he had received two hours ago as the *Europa* neared its destination at the Port of Bremerhaven on the North Sea. It was in code, of course, as were all RVD cables and telegrams that necessarily passed through the hands of third parties. He had personally decoded the cable. It was not the one he had expected—a report on the successful assassination of that lawyer Cockran and his investigator Sullivan—and it was not good news.

> TO: CANFIELD ON EUROPA. STOP. ADAMS & MILLER KILLED LAST NIGHT IN TIERGARTEN ON MC GARY ASSIGNMENT. STOP. ACCORDING TO KRIPO, THEY WERE SHOT 'RESISTING ARREST' BY SS FOR POSSESSION OF UNREGISTERED FIREARMS. STOP. FROM WILLICOMB WIRETAP: MC

GARY IN AMSTERDAM ON SATURDAY &
SUNDAY WITH CHURCHILL TO RECEIVE
TRANSCRIPT OF 5 JUNE 1934 MEETING OF
CRIMINAL LAW REFORM COMMISSION
THAT DISCUSSED PRUSSIAN MEMORAN-
DUM. END. RUTLEDGE.

"What is it Harry?" Canfield's wife Camilla asked. "You seem concerned."

Canfield turned to look at his wife, a beautiful brunette in her late twenties, a good ten years younger than him and a figure to turn more than one young man's eye. She had persuaded him to bring her along on this trip as a sort of 'second honeymoon' to celebrate their fifth wedding anniversary.

"No, just business," he said. "I've got to get off a cable to our Berlin office before we dock."

"I'll leave you to it, then. I'm off on my morning constitutional. A girl has got to keep her figure fit for her husband."

After his wife left, Canfield sat down at the built-in desk in their spacious cabin that contained twin beds, two club chairs, a matching two-person settee and an adjoining bathroom and shower. The cable back to Rutledge in Berlin wouldn't take long to compose or, once finished, to encode. He picked up a sheet of heavy bond stationery with the heading *SS Europa,* screwed off the top of his *Mont Blanc* fountain pen and began to write.

TO: RUTLEDGE RVD BERLIN. STOP. TERMINATE
MC GARY AMSTERDAM SOONEST. END. CANFIELD.

Canfield unbuckled the straps on his black leather briefcase and reached inside for his copy of the ONI codebook. Five minutes later, he had encoded the cable in the U.S. Navy's most unbreakable code. Picking up the cabin's telephone, he called for a steward and gave him the cable for delivery to the ship's radio room.

Zolgrenschutz
Bremerhaven, Germany
Friday, 14 September 1934

"PAPERS PLEASE!" the young Customs Border Guard ordered when Harold and Camilla Canfield reached the head of the line. Canfield handed him both their passports. The Border Guard inspected both very carefully, looking at their photos, then at each of them several times before he placed the passports down. He picked up a sheet of paper, looked at it and then picked up the telephone and spoke so softly into it that Canfield could not make out what he was saying. This was, in his experience, unusual.

Three minutes later, two men in some sort of gray military uniform and peaked caps similar to the one worn by the Border Guard trotted up on the double, each with a *Schmeisser* submachine pistol slung over his shoulder with a leather strap. They stopped, came to attention and shot out their right arms. "*Heil* Hitler!" the two shouted in unison.

The Border Guard returned the salute. "Take these two into custody. Have them both stripped and thoroughly searched for weapons and contraband. If there's a matron available, have her search the woman; otherwise, feel free to search her yourself."

The two grinned as they looked at Canfield's wife giving Canfield the distinct impression that a matron would be unavailable. "*Jawohl! Herr Zollinspektor!*" they both shouted and gestured with their submachine pistols for the couple to head toward a whitewashed one story building some twenty-five yards away.

Canfield protested. "Wait! I don't understand. What have we done? Why are you doing this?" he asked the Border Guard.

The Border Guard held up the sheet he had looked at before summoning the two uniformed men. "Orders from Berlin. The SD says you are an employee of RVD International. Yesterday in Berlin, two RVD employees attempted to rape a woman in the *Tiergarten* and were shot resisting arrest by two SD officers. Someone from the SD is on his way here from Berlin to interrogate you. We have orders to detain you in the interim."

SD? The *Sicherheitsdienst?* The security branch of the SS? This was not good, Canfield thought. "I demand to see the American Consul in Bremerhaven," he said.

The Border Guard shook his head. "The orders from Berlin are quite clear. You are to have no visitors."

"This is outrageous! You can't do this."

"I am only following orders," the Border Guard said. "I suggest you move along quickly. We have only one matron on duty per shift so, if you don't want your wife strip-searched by these men here, you should make haste lest our matron be otherwise engaged when you arrive at the detention center."

With that and a prod from a pistol barrel in the back, both Harold and Camilla Canfield were marched off to the *Zolgrenschutz* Detention Center and placed in adjoining holding cells.

In the event, however, Canfield was pleasantly surprised at their treatment once in the Detention Center. While they were expertly patted down for weapons, there was no strip search and a matron had done his wife's pat down. Nevertheless, they were kept in their holding cells for nearly five hours before the arrival of *SS-Sturmbannfuhrer* Walter Schellenberg.

The uniformed guards arrived at 4 p.m. and took Canfield to an interrogation room. A good thirty minutes passed before the door opened and a boyish-faced, black-uniformed SS officer in knee-high polished leather boots and black leather holster with a Luger automatic pistol in it entered the room. Canfield rose.

"Sit, sit, Mr. Canfield," the man said as he took off his high peaked cap and placed it on the table. Then he carefully took off his black leather gloves, put them on top of his cap and sat down opposite Canfield. "I am *SS-Sturmbannfuhrer* Walter Schellenberg and you are Harold Hudson Canfield, III, and, until two years ago, you were the adjutant to the Director of ONI, Captain Roger Welles. You left the Navy then to become the #2 to retired General Ralph Van Deman— the so-called 'father of American military intelligence'—in his private intelligence-gathering company, RVD International, where you serve as Executive Vice-President."

Interesting, Canfield thought, that the young SS officer was reciting all this from memory, as he did not have a file from which he was reading. Well, that SS guy in Washington, Wilhelm Krueger, had said his immediate superior—Schellenberg—was 'a brilliant man' so maybe he was right.

"You and your first cousin, the late Theodore Stanhope Hudson, IV, were U.S. intelligence agents during and after the war, Hudson in Military Intelligence—MID—and you in Naval Intelligence—ONI. You and Hudson grew up together at your boyhood home, Canfield House on Long Island Sound, a 100-acre estate adjacent to Stanhope Hall, the estate where Hudson was raised. You and Hudson are what Americans call 'trust fund babies' whose net worth is well into eight figures."

Interesting, Canfield thought, that the SS knew about his trust funds, but apparently not the U.S. companies in which the trust funds held a controlling interest or that the trustees of those trust funds were appointed by him or that those U.S. companies Canfield effectively controlled through the trust funds were supplying Germany with the aircraft engines needed for the secret rearmament of the *Luftwaffe* forbidden to Germany by the Treaty of Versailles. Well, inasmuch as the SS was not involved in that venture, this self-important SS officer had no need to know. Canfield would hold that card in reserve and play it only as a last resort. After all, even in America, it was not widely known how powerful he and his trust funds really were.

Schellenberg paused, lit a cigarette and continued. "Both you and Hudson specialized during the war in counter-espionage against Imperial German agents operating in North America. And, from time to time, you were both assassins, eliminating those Americans who opposed the war too vigorously. Equally important, you and Hudson were close friends with Sebastian Stanford Slade, III, who also grew up on Long Island in his own family's respective mansion. You dubbed yourselves 'The Three Musketeers' and you all went to the same prep school—Choate—and then on to Harvard."

Schellenberg grinned. "Have I missed anything so far?"

"My wife's maiden name and place of birth?"

Without missing a beat, the SS officer promptly replied "Camilla Van Aken, born 11 June 1906 at McDonald House of University Hospitals in Cleveland to parents Joshua and Elizabeth Van Aken who resided in Bratenahl, Ohio."

Okay, Canfield thought, he was impressed. The arrogant young man and the SS didn't know everything about him, but they knew a lot more about him than he and MID knew about Schellenberg. And Canfield only knew anything about him because Wilhelm Krueger had told him Schellenberg was in charge of the SD's Foreign Intelligence Section. "So why were my wife and I detained all day?"

"It's over 400 kilometers from Berlin to Bremerhaven," Schellenberg replied with a smile, "and this is as soon as I was able to be here. Now, may I continue?"

Canfield didn't reply.

"So, back to the 'The Three Musketeers' of whom you are the last man standing, so to speak. Other than being childhood chums, do you know what else you three had in common?"

Again, Canfield didn't reply, but he was beginning to suspect where this was going.

"All three of you have attempted, in one way or another, to cause harm to the Hearst photojournalist Mattie McGary. Hudson did so on at least two occasions in 1932 and 1933. Slade did the same twice in 1933. Hudson was killed by persons unknown on 3 March 1933, the same day his attempt to kill the *Fuhrer* failed."

Schellenberg stubbed out the remains of his cigarette and lit another. It wasn't persons unknown who killed Hudson, Canfield thought. According to Slade, it was that bitch McGary who killed his cousin Ted.

"Sebastian Slade was killed on 29 June of this year after he kidnapped *Frau* McGary and killed one of my men. I personally shot him in the forehead at point blank range. Are you beginning to see what happens to men who try to harm this woman?"

Once more, Canfield didn't reply.

"So, knowing how positively unhealthy it is, why did you have two of your RVD employees attempt to rape her last night in the *Tiergarten*?"

"I don't know what you're talking about," Canfield said.

"Oh, I think you do," Schellenberg said and reached into his briefcase. He pulled out two United States passports and two glossy black and white photographs. He handed them to Canfield.

Canfield looked at the passports and then the photographs of two naked corpses, face-up, on steel trays with a single bullet hole in the middle of their foreheads. They were easily identifiable as former MID agents and RVD operatives Adams and Miller. But rape? What idiots! Canfield had given them orders to rough her up, nothing more.

"It's simply too much of a coincidence that two employees of the third and sole surviving 'musketeer' would attack McGary and, as an intelligence officer, I don't believe in coincidence. There's one thing that puzzles me. Would you like to know what is it is?"

Canfield, for the fourth time, didn't reply.

Schelllenberg picked up the two photographs and held them up. "Look at what tiny *schwanzes* they both have," he said with a grin. "I doubt the woman would have noticed even if they succeeded in their rape attempt. Tell me, is a miniscule *schwanz* a job requirement for MID agents?"

When Canfield made no reply, Schellenberg continued. "What you need to remember, *Herr* Canfield, is that, while in Germany, *Frau* McGary enjoys the personal protection of the *Reichstag* President and Prussian Premier Hermann Göring as well as *SS Obersturmbannfuhrer* Reinhard Heydrich…and me. Moreover, while she is no supporter of either the Nazi Party or the new German government and Joseph Goebbels would like her banned from Germany, she is held in high esteem by Adolf Hitler himself who gave her an exclusive interview in July to explain his role in what American newspapers are calling 'The Night of the Long Knives'. Now, what do you suppose this all means for you?"

Although Canfield said nothing, he knew what came next.

Schellenberg lit another cigarette. "What it means is that if any harm from any source comes to *Frau* McGary while you are still in Germany, the odds for you leaving Germany in anything other than a casket are not good. Am I clear?"

Again, Canfield did not reply.

Schellenberg stood up. He took his gloves from on top of his cap and put them on the table. He carefully placed his cap on his head and picked up his gloves and held them in his right hand. Almost casually, he swung his arm in a powerful forehand and hit Canfield in the face with a loud smack, followed by an equally strong backhand and another loud smack. "I asked you a question," he said in a cold voice. "If I have to ask again, you and your wife will stay in detention cells until I have you placed on the next ship departing for America in about a week or so. And, unlike today, there really will be strip searches. Daily. So, what shall it be?" he said, raising his eyebrows questioningly.

"Yes, you have been most clear," Canfield said with narrowed eyes through gritted teeth.

Schellenberg smiled and patted Canfield on the shoulder as he walked past him to the door. "Good, I'm pleased we understand each other. I know you missed your train this morning, but I've booked you a first class compartment on the early evening train to Berlin. One of the Border Guards will see that your luggage is put on the train."

Later, on the train, after explaining to his wife that their detention was a bureaucratic mix-up due to his former status as an ONI agent, Canfield pondered the implications of Schellenberg's threats. On one hand, he could give a flying fuck if FDR were politically embarrassed by public disclosure of MID's role in creating the Prussian Memorandum. It would serve the crippled bastard right. On the other hand, if it were exposed, FDR might sacrifice Marlborough as a scapegoat and replace him at MID. This would not be good for RVD International who received quite a few lucrative assignments from MID through Marlborough. His successor might not be as generous.

On balance, Canfield still came down on the side of silencing McGary. MID's business was important to RVD. Still, Schellenberg's threats had to be taken into account even though McGary would be in Amsterdam and outside Germany when she was killed. Someone in the SS had commissioned the Prussian Memorandum, yet here was someone else in the SS threatening him if he stopped McGary from publishing a story about it. He knew Nazi Germany was a virtual snake pit with many factions vying for Hitler's attention and favor, but he was surprised to find this kind of dissension within the SS itself. When he got to Berlin, he needed to find out who in the SS had commissioned the Memorandum and where he stood in the SS hierarchy compared to Heydrich and Schellenberg.

Meanwhile, he had to telephone Rutledge. Once he and his boys eliminated McGary in Amsterdam, he needed to know soonest. With her dead, Canfield would be on the first air flight out of Germany using a forged Canadian passport before Schellenberg's men either arrested or killed him. That meant leaving his wife, Camilla, behind as a potential hostage, but sometimes, you had no choice. Sacrifices had to be made.

33

Cruising Speed!

On board the Graf Bismarck
U.S. Naval Air Station
Lakehurst, New Jersey
Friday, 14 September 1934

KURT VON STURM always personally conducted the pre-flight inspection of his ship, the *Graf Bismarck*, the largest passenger dirigible in the world. It was attached to its mooring mast outside the massive airship hangar at the Lakehurst Naval Air Station. To the west, the sun was setting, casting a golden glow over the airship's silvery exterior. Already, he had inspected each of the giant circular gas cells that filled the interior of the ship, held in place by wire bracing. The wire bracing was an addition German engineers made when converting the airship from its British R-100 iteration to its new life as the *Graf Bismarck*. They thought it far superior to the elaborate leather bridles the British had used to keep the gas cells from surging fore and aft.

Sturm was outside inspecting the three engine cars slung beneath the ship and the six Rolls-Royce gasoline engines—two to a car—that powered the huge propellers at the rear of each car. These engines were the most dangerous aspect of rigid airships like the *Graf Bismarck* that used flammable hydrogen as its lifting agent rather than the inert helium used by the U.S. Navy on its giant rigid airships. In fact,

German engineers had wanted to replace the gasoline engines with diesel ones because gasoline was more flammable. They soon discovered, however, why the British had used gasoline engines. They were much lighter than diesel engines and gave the airship more lift and greater speed. The engineers reluctantly agreed and left the Rolls-Royce engines in place, rationalizing that any sparks generated would be within the engine cars that, like on all airships, were located outside the huge ship, away from the flammable hydrogen that filled its huge gas cells.

Satisfied with his inspection, Sturm reflected on his telephone call to the office of the President of the *Reichstag* two hours earlier. Yesterday, to his surprise, Roland Freisler delivered the CVs for all six American lawyers who conducted the legal research for the Prussian Memorandum. He called Mattie in Berlin to give her the news, but there was no answer in her suite at the *Adlon*. He did not leave a message as that would undoubtedly be read by others. The *Graf Bismarck* would arrive in Berlin on Sunday evening and he made a mental note to call her then.

Back in the airship's control cabin, Sturm received word that all passengers were safely aboard. He noted that, as usual, 40 men were standing below the airship, 20 on each side. He ordered the thick rope landing lines released and, behind him at the telephone switchboard in the mid-section of the control cabin, the telephone operator conveyed the order to the airship crewmembers at their posts in the interior of the vessel.

When Sturm saw that the men below had grasped the lines, he gave another order. "Release ship!" He felt the airship move slightly as it was unlocked from the mooring mast.

"Walk ship!" he said next in a voice that easily carried to the 40 men below. Slowly, the men holding the ropes began to walk the airship away from the mooring mast. When he judged that they were far enough from the mooring mast so that the ship could safely begin its ascent, he gave the order that always gave him a thrill.

"Up ship!"

Immediately, 600 tons of water were dumped from tanks stored inside the *Graf Bismarck* drenching those below who did not move quickly away from the ship. Standing motionless, with his hands clasped behind his back, as the ship rose silently in the air without so much as a shiver, Sturm waited until ship reached an altitude of 500 feet.

"Cruising speed!" he ordered and, to his right, the engine room telegraph operator conveyed the order over a wire to the three engine cars slung below the ship because the noise of the two Rolls-Royce engines in each car was so great that verbal commands by telephone could not be heard. After the *Graf Bismarck* reached its cruising speed of seventy miles per hour, Sturm turned the helm over to his second in command and returned to his own cabin where he summoned a steward.

"Please locate two passengers, Bourke Cockran and Robert Sullivan, and ask them to join me in my cabin."

Sturm's cabin was large and spacious. A round table covered by a crisp white linen tablecloth set for three was in the middle of the room around which were three wicker armchairs. Off to the right within easy reach against the wall was a table with a cold buffet and a small, well-stocked bar. To the left was a couch that turned into a bed at night. Above it, the top of a bunk bed had been folded into the wall. Beyond the table was a small desk and wicker armchair below a wide Plexiglas window and a stunning display of the setting sun aglow against fleecy white cumulous clouds.

Ten minutes later, Sturm heard a discreet knock on the door. "Enter!" he said.

A white-coated steward opened the door. "*Herr* Cockran and *Herr* Sullivan, *Fregattenkapitan*," the steward said.

Cockran and Sullivan entered and Sturm warmly shook the hand of each. "Won't you join me in a light supper," he said gesturing in the direction of the table that held the bar as well as an assortment of sandwiches, sausages, cheese and fruit. "Bobby, help yourself to the Jameson. Bourke, I would offer to mix a martini for you, but I fear it would not be up to the standards set by you and Mattie."

After the three men had served themselves, they sat in the wicker chairs at the round table. "So tell me, to what do I owe the pleasure of your company on this voyage?" Sturm asked.

"It's not to 'what' but to 'whom'," Cockran began, "and that would be Mattie."

Cockran then recounted the events of the past ten days culminating in their discovery that the six murders they had been investigating involved the same Prussian Memorandum that Mattie was investigating.

"So, the way we figure it, if someone went to the trouble of having all six lawyers killed, Mattie is quite likely in danger herself and in need of our protection. That's why Bobby and I are on our way to Berlin with you because your ship is twice as fast as an ocean liner and you were conveniently leaving today." Cockran paused to take a sip of coffee and continued. "Once we're in Berlin, we'll catch the next *Lufthansa* flight to Amsterdam where Mattie and Churchill will receive the transcript of the Commission meeting where this Prussian Memorandum was extensively discussed."

"Very interesting. This is what *Herr* Churchill once called 'a remarkable coincidence' because I independently located a copy of the Prussian Memorandum and was appointed by 'His Holiness' himself," Sturm said, referring to Sullivan's irreverent nickname for Hermann Göring, "as the *Reichstag* liaison to the Commission on Criminal Law Reform where I have been directed by *Unser* Hermann to give Mattie whatever assistance I can in investigating her story." With that, Sturm explained what he had done, beginning with his discovery of Goebbels' copy of the Prussian Memorandum and the Goebbels-Himmler correspondence and concluding with Freisler's delivery of the CVs of the six American lawyers to Göring's office yesterday.

Sturm had noticed Cockran's smile when he mentioned spending the night with Magda Goebbels. "So, are there any questions other than how long I've been sleeping with Magda?"

Both Cockran and Sullivan shook their heads 'no'.

"Good. I believe I can help you get to Amsterdam much sooner than you plan," Sturm said as he reached out to refill his coffee cup. "The Dutch have built an airship mooring mast to Zeppelin specifications at the *Schiphol* Aerodrome. They wish to persuade us to use Amsterdam as our last stop in Europe for our voyages to North America rather than Seville. In fact, I have a short training cruise from

Friedrichshafen to Amsterdam scheduled later this month to test the Dutch facilities at *Schiphol*. If I can secure Hugo Eckener's consent," Sturm said, referring to the Zeppelin Company's legendary leader, "to achieve landfall in Amsterdam on this voyage, rather than Seville, you can disembark there fully six hours before we reach Berlin. Would that meet with your approval?"

"Absolutely, Kurt!" Cockran replied. "That would be great!"

"Excellent," Sturm said. "I will send a wireless message to Hugo immediately. We have no passengers debarking in Seville so I don't anticipate he will have any objection to changing our initial landfall. Join me at the Captain's table for breakfast tomorrow. I should have heard from him by then."

34

A Confidential Report

Office of the Reichsfuhrer-SS
8 Prinz-Albrecht Strasse
Berlin
Friday, 14 September 1934

"THANK YOU for seeing me on such short notice *Herr Reichsfuhrer-SS*," Roland Freisler said. "Yesterday, I delivered the CVs of the six American lawyers to the *Reichspresident's* office as you had requested. Today, less than an hour ago, I received a confidential report about the McGary woman's investigation into the Prussian Memorandum."

Heinrich Himmler removed his *pince-nez* and rubbed the bridge of his nose and made an impatient gesture with his hand for the man to continue. He really didn't like Freisler. For one thing, he was a lawyer, and he didn't like lawyers unless they were men of action like Heydrich's man Schellenberg. For another thing, his baldhead was distracting and actually reflected the overhead light. Worst of all, he had been taken a prisoner of war by the Russians in 1915, thereby sitting out the war safely while learning to speak Russian. The Bolsheviks had even named him a 'Commissar' when they took over his prisoner of war camp and placed him in charge of the camp's food supplies. In fact, the only good thing about the thin-lipped Saxon was his rabid anti-Semitism, which Himmler shared. His writings strongly advocated the creation of criminal laws to punish *Rassenschande* or 'race defilement', meaning sexual relations between 'Aryans' and 'inferior races' like Jews, Gypsies, Asians and Negroes. That was why Himmler had 'encouraged' Justice Minister Gurtner to make him Chairman of the German Commission on Criminal Law Reform. He wondered now if he had made a mistake because the man's obsession with keeping the Prussian Memorandum a secret seemed overdone.

"Well," Freisler began, "our source says that the reporter McGary met with Hanna Raeder and Werner Kramer. Both are members of the Commission who firmly oppose our use of the Prussian Memorandum as a model to apply to German Jews. A carbon copy of the transcript of the 5 June meeting—I have the original transcript locked in my office safe—where the Prussian Memorandum was extensively discussed will be delivered to McGary and the English politician Churchill tomorrow in Amsterdam. As I thought, Gregor von Dohnanyi is the traitor behind it. He arranged for a Justice Ministry colleague of his, Otto Lutze, to take the transcript to Amsterdam today. Lutze will place it in a locker at the *Centraal* Station and deliver the key to McGary and Churchill sometime tomorrow. Our source doesn't know where Lutze is staying, but it's likely the Victoria Hotel where Lutze and Dohnanyi are attending a legal conference. We do know that Churchill and McGary will be at the Grand Hotel *Krasnapolsky*."

"What would you have me do, Roland?" Himmler asked.

"We need to stop them getting the 5 June Commission transcript. Since Sturm likely has already given McGary a copy of the Prussian Memorandum and doubtless she has made copies, we need to stop her from publishing a story about it. If we can't keep her from getting the transcript, we need to keep Kramer and Raeder's wife from validating it."

What I will do about it, dear Roland, is above your pay grade, Himmler thought. "Thank you for bringing this to my attention. I know your source has been reliable in the past, but I will handle it from here on."

"But...but...what will you do?" Freisler sputtered.

Himmler smiled. "I thought I just told you. I will handle it." With a small sweeping gesture of his hand, as if to say 'now, shoo!' he dismissed the bald lawyer. He pressed the intercom button. "Gertrude, be so kind as to connect me to *Herr Doktor* Goebbels at the Propaganda Ministry."

Himmler also disliked Goebbels. For one thing, he was a cripple with a foot deformity from birth that evolved into a clubfoot. For another, he was a sexual degenerate who took to his bed every actress up for a leading role in a UFA film, UFA being Germany's largest motion picture studio and under the thumb of Goebbels' Propaganda Ministry. In fact, one of Himmler's fondest hopes was that the definition of a 'defective' proposed by the Commission on Criminal Law Reform would include persons with Goebbels' congenital condition so that it would become a crime for the crippled clubfoot to defile any more Aryan women. The principal reason Himmler disliked Goebbels, however, was that, along with Hermann Göring, he was Himmler's primary rival for access to the ear of Adolf Hitler.

The telephone on his desk rang and he picked up the receiver. "Himmler, here."

"Goebbels here. To what do I owe the honor, Heinrich?"

"We have a problem, Joseph, and I seek your counsel," Himmler said and proceeded to tell Goebbels everything Freisler had learned about McGary's investigation into the Prussian Memorandum, the re-creation of the 5 June Commission meeting transcript, and the plan to transfer it to McGary in Amsterdam tomorrow. "So what next? Passing new laws to rein in the Jews is dear to Hitler's heart. Do we tell the *Fuhrer*?

"Oh my, no," Goebbels quickly said. "The *Fuhrer* is too busy to be bothered with something like this. Ordinarily, I'd say just recover the 5 June transcript and then kill the bitch, but that might prove to be counterproductive."

"Why?"

"For some reason, Hitler holds her in high regard. Out of all the foreign correspondents, he chose to give her an exclusive interview in July to explain his purge of Rohm and the SA. We can't have anything happen to McGary that could possibly be traced back to us. Not unless we want to turn over the keys to the kingdom to *Unser* Hermann and I for one have no intention of doing that."

Nor do I, Himmler thought. "What do you suggest?"

"Have the *Gestapo* put a tail on this Lutze in Amsterdam. Once he passes the locker key to McGary, arrest him, take him to a safe house and persuade him to tell us the locker number. Once we have the number, kill Lutze and toss his body into one of Amsterdam's canals. Then place a 24-hour surveillance on the locker and seize the transcript from whoever shows up to retrieve it."

"And if we don't retrieve it? Can we afford to let moderate members of the Commission like Kramer or the Raeder woman validate the accuracy of the new transcript?"

"Of course not. Take no chances. Kill Kramer now and scare the woman into silence with a threat on her life. She may be the wife of an admiral, but remind her what happened to General von Schleicher's wife during the Night of the Long Knives."

Himmler smiled. It was exactly what he had intended to do, but now, if anything went wrong, it was Goebbels' plan and Goebbels' fault. That left the question of what to do about the McGary woman. "And the British journalist of whom Hitler is so fond? What about her?"

"Talk to the leader of the *Gestapo* team you'll be sending to Amsterdam. Swear him to secrecy, even to the other members of his team. Tell him to kidnap McGary and bring her back to Germany. Then, lock her up under an assumed name at the *Oranienburg* concentration camp for political prisoners near Berlin. Once there, she can either rot or be shot attempting to escape. Meanwhile, have the leader of the *Gestapo* Amsterdam team killed."

Himmler was impressed. He and Goebbels were on the same page, but only Goebbels' fingerprints were on that page. He didn't expect any of this would ever become known, but if it did, Himmler could say he had been *extremely* reluctant to go along, but Goebbels had been *most* insistent.

"Why?"

Goebbels chuckled. "He's the only one who can tie us to McGary's fate. With him gone, we can blame it all on him if someone ever finds out she is there."

"Excellent advice, Joseph. Thanks very much. But what about Freisler?"

"What about him?" Goebbels replied.

"We're doing all this at Freisler's behest to protect the Prussian Memorandum from premature publicity or, in fact, any publicity. Wouldn't he, and not the leader of the Gestapo's Amsterdam team, be the appropriate scapegoat if things go wrong with McGary? If so, how do you suggest we go about it?"

"Hmmm. Good point. You may be right. Let's see. How about you direct the *Gestapo* Amsterdam team to report and take orders from Freisler? That way, we can have Freisler arrested and, if necessary, executed also while you and I swear he had no authority either to commission the Prussian Memorandum or to seize McGary."

"Again, Joseph, excellent advice. I appreciate your thoughts on this. Thank you."

"You're most welcome, Heinrich. Nice talking to you. Please keep me posted."

Himmler pressed the button on the intercom. "Gertrude, please locate Heinrich Muller and send him to me."

Fifteen minutes later, Heinrich Muller, second in command of the *Gestapo,* stood at attention in front of Himmler's desk and shot out his arm in the Nazi salute "*Heil* Hitler!"

Himmler casually returned the salute by lifting his right hand in the air while his elbow remained on the desk. He actually liked Muller who was a short, stocky Bavarian with the square head of a peasant and a dry expressionless face. Himmler admired his professional competence, blind obedience and his willingness to execute what Himmler thought of as 'delicate missions' and Amsterdam was certainly going to be 'delicate'.

"Muller, I have two assignments for you. First, I want you to arrange for Werner Kramer to be killed tonight during the course of a burglary of his residence. After that, I want this envelope dropped in the mailbox of this residence as soon as the occupant leaves tomorrow morning," Himmler said and handed the envelope to Muller.

"And the second assignment *Herr Reichsfuhrer-SS*?" Muller asked as he took the envelope and stuck it inside his suit coat.

"I want you to send me your most ruthless man. I have some assignments from Propaganda Minister Goebbels for him and the men he selects. One of the assignments is foreign. They will be working under the direct supervision of Roland Freisler, the State Secretary of the *Reich* Ministry of Justice. I need to see this man today and the less you know about it, the better. Who would you recommend?"

"Ruthless, eh? Well, that would be me," Muller replied with a smile.

"I know, but you're too highly placed," Himmler replied. "I can't have the *de facto* head of the *Gestapo* arrested in a foreign country for murder and kidnapping. So, who else?"

"That's easy. Josef Kleist. Even with a university degree, he's a cold-blooded bastard."

"I've heard of him. Send me his file and then have him here in my office in thirty minutes," Himmler replied.

Five minutes later, Josef Kleist's file was on Himmler's desk. As he leafed through Kleist's various assignments, he liked what he saw. Muller was right. Kleist was a downright sadistic bastard who enjoyed both humiliating and hurting people. A man after his own heart. Good. From all he knew, that British journalist could use a little humiliation by Kleist after he dispatched the traitor Lutze.

Twenty-five minutes later, Kleist was announced by Himmler's secretary. He looked up to see a tall, dark-haired man in his early thirties with sharp features and a dueling scar on his left cheek, his arm extended in the familiar Nazi salute. Himmler gave a weak wave in return and pointed to a seat.

"Sit dowh, Kleist. Select two good men you trust and take the next *Lufthansa* flight to Amsterdam. Once there, here's what I want you to do…"

When he finished, Himmler was pleased to see that Kleist was still smiling, a smile that began once he had mentioned killing Lutze and kidnapping the British journalist.

SCHELLENBERG CHUCKLED when, half-way through the stack of Brown Pages from yesterday's wiretaps, he came across the telephone conversation between Heinrich Himmler and Joseph Goebbels picked up from the *Forschungsamt* wiretap on Goebbels' telephone. How stupid was Himmler? Did he really believe Göring would never dare to have wiretaps on his or Goebbels' phones? Schellenberg didn't have access to the Brown Pages on either Himmler's office or home telephone lines so he couldn't be sure Göring had tapped those telephones the way he had tapped Goebbels' telephones. The odds were he had. After all, when Schellenberg had requested taps on Goebbels' telephones on the grounds that he frequently had conversations with foreigners in Hollywood and Europe, Göring granted it the next day and he had been reading transcripts of Goebbels' calls ever since.

Schellenberg had been disappointed to learn in the cables to and from Canfield that McGary was in Amsterdam this weekend without the escort of his two SD operatives Bulow and Globke. He had not anticipated her leaving the country so they had no instructions to follow her. Instead, they had returned to SD headquarters to report where she had gone. Having read the Canfield cables, Schellenberg already knew that, but he was not worried. Canfield's cable to this Rutledge to eliminate McGary—easily decoded by SD cryptanalysts—had been sent from the *Europa* before it docked and before Schellenberg had threatened Canfield should any harm come to McGary. His ego told him Canfield had been suitably intimidated.

Schellenberg's concern for McGary's safety changed the minute he read the transcript of the Himmler-Goebbels conversation about sending a *Gestapo* team to Amsterdam headed by Kleist to kidnap McGary. He had immediately asked his secretary to locate Bulow and Globke. He looked at his watch. Damn it! That had been four minutes ago! Where the hell were they? He looked at his watch again just as there was a knock on his door.

"Enter!"

A breathless Bulow and Globke walked in and came to attention. They shot out their right arms in a Nazi salute. "*Heil* Hitler!"

Schellenberg did not return the salute and slapped both hands down on his desk. "Where the hell have you two been? I had you summoned five minutes ago!"

"Sorry, Sir," Bulow said. "We were in the canteen for breakfast and we came as soon as we heard."

"Yes, Sir," Globke said, "and we ran all the way here."

"You're both back on the Marlene Dietrich detail. Get your sorry asses out to *Templehof* immediately! Go to Hangar 6. By the time you get there, Heydrich's personal *Fokker* FVII trimotor will have been fueled and a flight plan filed for Amsterdam. Once you land, go at once to the Grand Hotel *Krasnapolsky* and find McGary. Stick with her like glue. Keep her safe. Be *conspicuous*. There's a *Gestapo* team in Amsterdam out to kidnap her and she also might be in danger from more Americans like the ones you killed in the *Tiergarten* Thursday. If anything happens to her, your next assignments will be pulling guard duty on the night shift at *Sachsenhausen* Concentration Camp. Is that clear?"

"Yes, Sir!" both men said in unison and gave Schellenberg the Nazi salute with a "*Heil* Hitler!" Then, they did an abrupt about-face and hurried from his office.

35

The Transfer

CHURCHILL'S SUITE at the five-story *Grand Hotel Krasnapolsky*, known locally as 'the Kras', was on the top floor with a winding staircase inside its sitting room. Mattie walked up the staircase that led to a rooftop terrace where Churchill sat at a table set for luncheon for two.

Mattie wore a white silk blouse, tailored tan trousers and a matching Donegal tweed hacking jacket. The sun was shining and there was not a cloud in the sky on a beautiful late summer day. The terrace had a fine view of what she thought was Dam Square to the south and, to the north, Mattie could see the peaked roofs of houses that lined the canals and, in the distance, she could barely make out what she was pretty sure were the tops of the twin spires of the *Centraal* Station. And always the slight smell of the sea in the air from the canals that spoke to the city's seafaring heritage. The hotel's room service staff had placed a hamper on a serving cart along with two chilled bottles of Pol Roget champagne in a silver bucket. Mattie smiled as she sat down recalling what Churchill's close friend F.E. Smith once said. "Mr. Churchill is easily satisfied with the best."

Churchill poured them both a glass of champagne before he opened the hamper. "I asked the hotel kitchen to prepare a cold picnic lunch for us. Let's see what we have. Ah, excellent. Poached eggs and ham in aspic jelly; cold slices of beef; half a chicken; potato salad, bread and butter; strawberry tarts and Stilton cheese. A veritable feast. Dig in, my Dear."

As they ate, Mattie brought Churchill up to date in detail on all she had learned from Sturm, Schellenberg and Cockran as well as her interviews with the two moderate Commission members. "What this all means is my investigation is virtually complete. I know everything right from the beginning on the German side—Himmler, Goebbels and Freisler were responsible for engaging American intelligence to conduct legal research into American state miscegenation laws. Thanks to Bourke and Tim O'Hanlon, I know much the same on the American side—MID Director Leonard Marlborough and his immediate predecessor Ralph Van Deman engaged Harvard's Roscoe Pound to supervise the legal research of six American lawyers, all former MID agents who were killed by a professional hit man hired through the offices of the Irish-American gangster Owney Madden after completing their research. The only thing I don't know is who engaged Madden. Obviously, it was someone from MID."

Churchill took a sip of champagne and refilled their glasses. "You appear to have everything nailed down, but you seem to be relying on a number of sources to whom you have promised confidentiality. Since you can't identify them, won't that adversely affect the credibility of your story?"

Mattie grinned as she put down her fork beside a strawberry tart. "Nope. I've got documents that effectively corroborate what my confidential sources have told me—the Himmler-Goebbels letters, the Prussian Memorandum and, hopefully today, the transcript of the 5 June meeting this year of the German Commission on Criminal Law Reform. After that, all I need to do is have the two Commission members I interviewed earlier confirm the accuracy of the transcript."

"I see your point," Churchill replied. "Will you attempt to interview any of the principal actors like Himmler, Goebbels, and

Freisler in Germany and Generals Marlborough, Van Deman and Dean Pound in America?"

"I haven't decided. I'm not sure I want to poke the Nazi hornet nest like that when I already have the Goebbels letters to Himmler that spells everything out. I'll leave that decision up to the Chief and Willicomb. I really would like to interview Marlborough, though, just to sandbag him with the Goebbels letters. I'm not sure about Pound. If he tells me the same thing he told Bourke, that he thinks Jewish gangsters could be responsible for killing those six former MID agents, there are lots of people out there who might believe him."

When their picnic lunch was over, Churchill and Mattie made their way back down the spiral staircase. Mattie was about to take her leave and return to her own suite when the telephone in the sitting room rang.

"I'll take the call from the telephone in the bedroom. It may be this Lutze fellow. Once it stops ringing, pick up the receiver here and listen in," Churchill said.

Churchill walked from the sitting room to the bedroom while Mattie sat in an armchair beside the telephone and waited for it to stop ringing. Once it did, she lifted the receiver.

"Yes?" Churchill growled.

"Mr. Churchill?"

"Speaking."

"This is Otto Lutze from the Reich Ministry of Justice. I am a friend of Georg von Dohnanyi and I have left a package for you in locker # 225 at the Amsterdam *Centraal* Station."

"Thank you, Mr. Lutze, and how do you propose to deliver me the key to that locker?"

"Well, Sir, Georg asked me to do this because he was concerned he was being followed by the *Gestapo*. While I don't know the contents of the package, I am still reluctant to pass you the key in public or leave it in an envelope at the front desk. I propose I leave it for you to pick up at a museum, the *Ons Lieve Heer op Solder* or, 'Our Lord in the Attic'. Do you know it?"

"No."

"It's located on the *Oude Zijde Voorburgwall* canal right across from the Red Light District. It's a canal house built in the 17th century after Amsterdam officially became Protestant. The upper stories contain a secret Catholic church. The museum closes each day at 6 p.m. What I will do is tape an envelope with the key to the underside of the second chair from the right in the fourth row of chairs in the church. I will leave the key there at 4 p.m. I would ask that you not retrieve it before 4:30 p.m. so that we will not be in the building at the same time. Will that be satisfactory?"

"Yes, that will be fine. Thank you for your courage in doing this."

Lutze did not reply, but simply hung up the telephone.

Our Lord in the Attic Museum
Amsterdam
Saturday, 15 September 1934

OTTO LUTZE knew immediately who had seized him as he left Our Lord in the Attic Museum late in the afternoon. Two men in slouch hats and long gray overcoats shoved him into the back of a dark blue 260 D Mercedes sedan, a motorcar that screamed '*Gestapo!*' to anyone from Berlin. Now, he sat between the two men, one of them hawk-faced with a dueling scar on his cheek. That surprised Lutze because the scar identified him as someone from the upper classes, certainly a university graduate. That was unusual for the *Gestapo*, to say the least. The man on the other side was no surprise. With gray hair, a gray, slab-sided face and huge hands, he was the stereotype of a *Gestapo* thug.

Hawkface spoke first. "All we want, Lutze, is the number of the locker in *Centraal* Station where you left the transcript and the name of the person who gave you the package."

Ah, Lutze thought, so it was a transcript he had left there at Dohnanyi's request. He hadn't known that. But a transcript of what? He had no idea. "What transcript? I don't know anything about a transcript."

Hawkface nodded at the thug who hit Lutze with a backhanded fist that shot pain through his head and left him reeling.

"Be reasonable, *Herr* Lutze," Hawkface said, "it would not surprise me if you knew nothing of the contents of the package you stored in the locker, but you do know the number of the locker where you stored it and the name of the person who gave it to you. All I want is the locker number and a name."

Hawkface again nodded at the thug who took the index finger of Lutze's right hand and bent it back until a loud crack followed by unbearable pain told Lutze his finger had been broken. Lutze cried out, but said nothing. Hawkface nodded once more and the thug took the index finger of Lutze's left hand and broke it in the same manner.

"225," Lutze croaked through the pain. "Locker # 225. Dohnanyi, Georg von Dohnanyi gave me the package."

Hawkface nodded a fourth time and Lutze saw the thug pull an eight-inch long stiletto from his coat pocket and handed it to Hawkface who, in one fluid, powerful motion, thrust it up under Lutze's chin through his soft palate, impaling his tongue on its way to his brain. Lutze felt a single sharp, unendurable moment of pain and then felt nothing.

"HANS, STOP halfway down the block," Josef Kleist said to the motorcar's driver, after he pulled the dagger free from Lutze's throat with some effort and wiped it clean on the corpse's suit coat. Then, he turned to the large, gray-haired man. "Bruno, take his wallet out and dump him over the canal side." Once the Mercedes came to a stop, Bruno opened the door and shoved the body of Otto Lutze out of the motorcar and down into the canal.

"Take me to our hotel and then the two of you go to the train station and discreetly keep a watch on Locker #225. Follow anyone who opens the locker and report their destination back to me."

Once in his room at the Victoria Hotel, Kleist placed a telephone call to Berlin. All in all, he thought, it was a good night's work well begun. The British journalist was next. Judging by the photographs Himmler had shown him, she was a beautiful woman. He was looking forward to finding her.

"Freisler, here."

"It's Kleist, *Herr* Freisler," he said. "Lutze is dead and we have the locker number—225. My men have it under observation now."

MATTIE WAS surprised when she met Churchill in the lobby at 4:30 p.m. and he took her arm and guided her away from the hotel's main entrance on Dam Square. "Aren't we taking a taxi? That's where you get one," she said, pointing to the front of the lobby.

Churchill grinned. "We won't need a taxi as I've arranged for *private* transportation. It's waiting for us outside."

They walked to the rear of the hotel and exited onto a narrow street fronting on a narrow canal where a small classic saloon boat was docked. The smell of salt and brine was strong and she marveled at what a strange city Amsterdam was with streets filled with water coexisting side by side with streets paved with stones. It was her first visit and she was in awe. To lend credence to their role as tourists, she took out her Leica and snapped several photos of the boat. It was striking, typical of Winston once more being satisfied with the best. It looked to be approximately 25 feet long and 6 feet wide with a gleaming white body and highly polished teakwood trim. It had a white and teak canopy that covered the entire cockpit of the boat from the stern, where a captain sat at the boat's wheel, to the bow where there were teak benches for passengers. It was otherwise open to the air.

Mattie laughed. "So this is the private transportation you've arranged?"

Churchill just grinned.

When he saw Churchill, the captain rose, stepped up out of the boat and onto the street. He wore a crisp white jacket with navy blue and gold epaulettes on the shoulder. He was of medium build with close-cropped salt and pepper hair and a full black beard. "Mr. Churchill, I presume? I am Captain Miloe Spronk. Welcome to my boat *Farahilde* where you will receive the finest tour available on Amsterdam's legendary canals."

Introductions were made and Mattie and Churchill stepped down into the boat. The interior was all glossy teakwood. Halfway down the interior, two small tables, one to port, the other to the starboard side, extended from the sides of the boat, leaving a two foot wide aisle between them. To Mattie's surprise and amusement, a silver bucket filled with ice and two bottles of Pol Roger champagne was on one table while the other table contained a pot of black caviar, also set in ice, accompanied by toast points and two crystal flutes.

"Really, Winston? Champagne *and* caviar?"

Churchill smiled and spoke in a low voice. "I have hired Captain Spronk's fine vessel for 3½ hours. Our first stop will be at 'Our Lord in the Attic'. After that, our itinerary is up to the captain. The only other stop will be *Centraal* Station immediately before we return to the Hotel *Kras* at 8 p.m. Given the attack on you Thursday in Berlin, I did not think it wise to secure the locker key and proceed directly to the lockers at *Centraal* Station. Now, if anyone is following us, they will simply see two harmless tourists enjoying a sightseeing tour of the city followed by a delightful dinner. I've made reservations for 9 p.m. at the hotel's restaurant, The White Room. I'm told it's the oldest restaurant in Amsterdam."

Churchill now spoke in a louder voice toward the stern of the boat. "We are ready to proceed when you are, Captain."

"Yes, Mr. Churchill," he said. "The first stop will be in ten minutes at 'Our Lord in the Attic'."

Churchill opened one bottle of champagne and filled their flutes. "One reason I selected the *Farahilde* is that its width is sufficiently narrow to take us through the most narrow canals while its height will allow it to pass beneath bridges with the lowest clearances."

The boat pulled up ten minutes later in front of a typical canal house, five stories high, built of gray stone and white-trimmed windows.

"This is one of Amsterdam's oldest museums," Captain Spronk said. "It was built in 1663 and was converted into a museum in 1888. During that time, the top two stories were a secret Catholic church of which there were many built in the city."

"You go ahead, my dear," Churchill said. "I am unfamiliar with the interiors of most churches, secret or otherwise, and I propose to keep it that way. I offer my support to churches only as a flying buttress from the outside. I'll rest here with my cigar and champagne," he said as he lit a cigar, blew smoke up in the air and took a sip of champagne.

Mattie walked up the steps to the entrance to the house and into an antechamber where she bought a ticket. She made her way, as directed, to a winding staircase with well-worn wooden steps that carried her up two flights to the Attic Church. It was, she thought, a perfect little chapel with electric replicas of 19th century gaslights and rush matting on the floor. There were narrow balconies on either side of the room and, at the front, over the altar and between two marble pillars, was a painting *The Baptism of Christ* by Jacob de Wit.

Mattie walked down the nave of the church until she found the 4th pew from the front. To her relief, the room was otherwise empty. Out of an excess of caution, however, she genuflected, made the Sign of the Cross, and slipped into the pew, kneeling in front of the second chair from the right where she bowed her head as if in prayer. She knelt there for a full 60 seconds before she crossed herself again and, as she was rising, she felt with her right hand beneath the chair, elated to find an envelope taped to the underside. She peeled the envelope off and tucked it into the breast pocket of her hacking jacket.

Mattie made her way back down to the boat. Once on board, with her back to Captain Spronk, she gave Churchill a thumbs-up signal, nodded her head, and patted the breast pocket of her jacket. Mattie sat on a bench across from Churchill and beside the caviar. He refilled her flute and she spooned caviar onto a toast point. The sun was lower now and it promised to be a beautiful evening. She had been to Venice but never Amsterdam and the canals made them easy to compare because, except for the canals, the two cities were entirely different. Venice was much smaller and there were no motorcars or lorries whereas such vehicles were all over Amsterdam. And the bicycles! She had never seen so many bicycles in one place in her life as she had here.

Captain Spronk was an excellent guide and Mattie, the wide-eyed tourist, ran through three rolls of film taking photographs. Not only did he take them past all the historic sights of Amsterdam, from the Neo-Gothic twin towers of the *Rijksmuseum* through the canals in the notorious Red Light District where barely-clad women advertised their, uh, availability, but he also gave them the history of Amsterdam that went with the sights. Prostitution was not only legal in Amsterdam, but had been for over 280 years.

Mattie was disappointed when, at last, the twin towers of Amsterdam *Centraal* Station came into view. Its architectural style, Captain Spronk told them, was Gothic Renaissance Revival and she was not surprised to learn the same architect, Pierre Cuypers, had designed both it and the *Rijksmuseum*. Further, he told them, the cast iron and glass roof over the station's platform spanned over 40 meters.

When the boat docked in front of the station, both Mattie and Churchill stepped out. They had agreed that, unlike Our Lord in the Attic Museum, which had been near closing time and almost deserted, both of them were needed to retrieve the 5 June transcript. Once inside the station, Mattie was impressed by the soaring iron and glass roof of the Victorian era building. Following signs, they found an escalator that took them down to the left luggage room and the lockers. She quickly saw that there were only two sizes of locker, small and large. #225 was small, maybe a foot by foot and a half. She took the envelope from her jacket, fished out the key and inserted it into the lock. She swung the door open and spotted a manila envelope inside. She pulled it out and promptly shoved it into her canvas camera bag. She looked at Churchill.

"Let's go back to your suite and have cocktails before dinner while we look at the transcript."

Churchill agreed and fifteen minutes later the boat had turned onto a smaller canal that led to the even smaller canal that backed onto their hotel. Up ahead, Mattie recognized the low ceiling bridge over a wide two-way street they had encountered on their way out. The roadway was sufficiently wide that the boat had been plunged into darkness for nearly ten seconds until they emerged into daylight on the other side. It was dusk now, however, and the streetlights had just come on.

Mattie sat in the bow of the boat, taking photographs of a cascading wave of white, pink and red petunias on the railing of the approaching bridge when she saw in her viewfinder the silhouette of a man's head and upper body emerge from behind the flowers with his arm extended. The man held a gun with the long snout of a sound suppressor attached to its barrel.

"Winston! Gun! Get down!" Mattie shouted as she let go of the Leica so it hung by a strap around her neck. She drew her Walther PPK from the waistband in the back of her trousers and dropped to her knees on the deck. She braced her pistol on the side of the boat and heard the impact of silenced bullets hit wood as she got off two very loud shots of her own. She heard a man cry out just as the boat glided beneath the bridge, affording them momentary safety from the gunmen on the bridge. Above them, the boat's canopy was barely a foot below the bottom of the bridge.

"Captain! Stop the boat!" Mattie shouted. "Get down on the deck and stay there! Winston! Cover the stern! I'll take the bow!"

The boat slowed and came to a complete halt as Mattie held her pistol in both hands as she swung it from right to left and back again waiting for one of the shooters to appear.

Given that they were both armed, she and Winston weren't quite the proverbial fish in a barrel, helplessly waiting to be shot, but they weren't much better off.

"Ken! Look out! Behind you!" Mattie heard a voice shout from above. Bloody hell! she thought, that was an American accent! Americans were trying to kill them!

36

Werner Kramer is Dead

Americain Bar und Grill
Eden Hotel
Nurnberger Strasse
Berlin
Saturday 15 September 1934

HANNA RAEDER wore a dark gray jacket and matching skirt as she tried to spot Georg von Dohnanyi who had invited her to lunch. While she had dined from time to time at the Eden Hotel's *Pavillon* and *Café* and danced with her husband at the hotel's *Dachgarten*, this was her first visit to the *Americain Bar und Grill*. Unlike the *Pavillon* and *Café* that were grand two-story rooms with tall, airy windows and crystal chandeliers, the Grill was an informal one-story room with exposed wooden beams, a long bar at the end of the room, and a single brass chandelier hanging from the center of the room. She saw movement in the corner of the room where Georg had stood up from a small table for two and discreetly waved his right hand in a signal. She walked over and they exchanged cheek-to-cheek kisses before they both sat down.

A waiter arrived and Hanna ordered a dry martini. She'd had her first martini during her interview with Mattie McGary and was pleasantly surprised to find that she liked it very much. She had less time these days to make it to the target range and martinis were beginning to be a good substitute for her usual anger management therapy. *Frau* McGary had told her the martini was an American invention so Hanna assumed an *Americain Bar* would know how to mix a proper one. It came and she was not disappointed.

"So, Georg, to what do I owe the pleasure of your company this afternoon?" Hanna asked. "Erich is still at sea on fleet exercises and our two boys are away at school so I'm somewhat at sixes and sevens waiting to hear when you will supply *Frau* McGary with a transcript of the 5 June Commission meeting."

"That's one of the reasons I asked you to meet me. Greta has finished the transcript and it's on its way to Amsterdam and *Frau* McGary. As before, Greta will be a go-between so we can arrange for you to read it."

Hanna took a sip of her martini. "You said 'one of the reasons' you wanted to meet. What are the other ones?"

Dohnonyi's face darkened. "Only one other one. It wasn't in the morning newspapers, but a good friend in the *Kripo* told me that Werner Kramer was killed last night at his apartment in an apparent burglary. He was the only other Commission member to give an interview to *Frau* McGary. It may be only a coincidence, but with your husband away, you ought to be careful."

Hanna's stomach dropped. She was so used to the duplicitous political maneuvering inherent in her new position that she was caught off guard by the palpable sensation of physical fear. She was pleased that she had experienced the calming effect of a martini before Georg had given her the news. It meant, however, that if Kramer *was* killed for being interviewed by McGary, she was going to have to spend more time in target practice and less time with her new favorite cocktail.

Haus Raeder
Spitzweggasse 3
Potsdam-Neubabelsberg, Germany
Saturday, 15 September 1934

AFTER LUNCH, Hanna took a taxi back to their home. She was still shaken by the news of Werner Kramer's murder, but as was her custom, she stopped at the front door to check the post-letter box. She picked up the mail, unlocked the door and walked into the house. She placed the mail on a small table in the foyer and briefly looked at each envelope to see if any were addressed to her and not her husband. As she did, she noticed a blank envelope among all the others. Something about its nakedness alarmed her because it meant a stranger had placed it in the post-letter box. She held her breath for a second as fear sent pricks of heat through her arms and hands. It could just be a note from a neighbor, but she knew it wasn't. She steeled herself and opened the envelope. Inside was a single sheet of paper and four newspaper clippings.

The sheet was folded in thirds so its contents were not immediately visible, but the newspaper clippings caught her eye. They were from four different London newspapers from early July 1934. All had headlines about Hitler killing his political opponents on 30 June, the Night of the Long Knives. Each clipping had circled with a red grease pencil the name of Elisabeth von Schleicher who had been shot to death along with her husband, Kurt von Schleicher, Hitler's immediate predecessor as Chancellor. She placed the clippings down and opened the sheet of paper. She gasped at its contents:

> *Werner Kramer is dead. He gave an interview to a foreign journalist. Don't think your husband's high office will keep you safe if you ever talk to a foreign journalist again.*

Well, she thought, Kramer's murder was definitely not a coincidence. Had he received a similar threatening letter? It didn't matter. Her fear quickly gave way to anger. How dare they threaten the life of the wife of the head of the German Navy in her own home! She certainly intended to talk to McGary again and validate the transcript of the 5 June meeting of the Commission. She walked up to the master bedroom and over to her bedside table. She opened the drawer, took out her Walther PPK and checked to see that there was a full magazine. Then she placed the weapon inside the waistband of her skirt at the small of her back.

The weapon took care of her immediate safety, Hanna thought, but she needed to plan for the long term as well. Specifically, she needed to lay low for the next three weeks until her husband was back from his sea trials. She opened a closet door and took a suitcase down from the top shelf and began packing, grateful for being able to take action while she decided where to go. She closed her suitcase and made her decision. She knew exactly where she was going. It was a remote location where, now that the holiday season was over, she would have no trouble finding accommodations, possibly even the same place where she and her husband had stayed on their honeymoon. Better still, no one else except her husband knew where that was.

Hanna called a taxi and began to map out her journey. Obviously, someone—likely *Gestapo*—had followed her to the *Adlon* for her interview with McGary. She would have to make sure that didn't happen again. She didn't know if her house was under surveillance, but she decided she would change taxis at least twice at other train stations on her way to her eventual destination, the *Anhalter Bahnhof.*

37

At Your Service...Again

Off Canal Oudezijds Voorburgwal
Amsterdam
Saturday, 15 September 1934

"KEN! LOOK OUT! Behind you!"

No sooner had Mattie heard those shouted words and recognized them as an American voice than she saw a man with blood streaming from his throat drop into the canal with a loud splash. The man floated face down, motionless and Mattie assumed he was dead. Ten seconds later, there was another splash, this one behind her. She turned at the noise.

"Winston, what was that?"

"Another body, my Dear, and I fear he is quite dead. Someone cut his throat."

Mattie heard a voice above her. "*Frau* McGary, it's Eric Bulow. It's all clear. You may come out from beneath the bridge,"

Mattie gave a sigh of relief as she recognized the voice of *SS-Obersturmführer* Eric Bulow from her rescue in the *Tiergarten* on Thursday. She turned and addressed Captain Spronk.

"It's safe to move out. I know the man who spoke."

The boat nosed its way out and then stopped at Mattie's request. She looked up and saw Eric Bulow and his partner *SS-Obersturmfuhrer* Franz Globke. Both were in civilian clothes, trenchcoats, not their black SS uniforms, and both were hatless, their blond hair visible in the glow of the streetlight they stood beneath.

"Well, *Frau* McGary, at your service...again," Bulow said with a grin on his face. "I suggest you promptly be on your way back to your hotel unless you wish to spend the rest of your evening giving statements to the Dutch police."

Mattie could hear police sirens in the distance. "Good advice, *Herr* Bulow," she said and turned to the captain. "That's enough excitement, Captain Spronk. Please take us to our hotel."

The Grand Hotel Krasnapolsky
Amsterdam
Saturday, 15 September 1934

BACK IN Churchill's suite, Mattie mixed a martini for herself and poured a brandy for Churchill who was lighting a long Havana cigar. The suite had a view overlooking Dam Square and the two sat in large dark green leather club chairs with a small table between them. Mattie took out the transcript of the 5 June meeting and began to read, passing the first page over to Churchill once she had finished.

"Winston, I know we have 9 p.m. reservations at The White Room, but I'd much rather stay here and read the transcript. How about we order room service and bring The White Room to us?"

Churchill agreed and placed their order while Mattie read—Quail with *Foie Gras* followed by Sea Bass with Beetroot for her and King Crab followed by Venison with Jerusalem Artichoke for him. Dessert would be a cheese plate of five Dutch cheeses. Without a wine list in front of him, Churchill left the choice of a red and a white wine to the *Sommelier*.

As Mattie read, it was at once apparent to her that, from its very opening moments, the 5 June meeting involved repeated and detailed discussions of the example offered by the laws of American states and that American law was being championed principally by the Nazi radicals on the Commission. It was exactly what her story needed. Mattie paused occasionally, before passing the latest page to Churchill, to read aloud some of the more egregious excerpts.

"Winston, You won't believe what these people want to make a crime. Listen: '*Causing harm to the honor of the race must be made criminally punishable. It scandalously flouts the sentiments of the* Volk *when, for example, German women shamelessly consort with Jews, Negroes and other colored men. Protection of racial honor of this kind is already practiced by other* Volker. *It is well known, for example, that the southern states of North America maintain the most stringent separation between the white population and coloreds in both public and personal interactions*'."

Churchill shook his head in disbelief as Mattie passed the page over to him. She kept reading, pausing occasionally to take a sip of her martini. "Oh my, listen to this. It's the Minister of Justice Gurtner who I don't believe is a Nazi. I'm not sure what he means. '*I possess here a thoroughly comprehensible synoptic presentation of North American race legislation and I can tell you right away that the material was rather difficult to find. The material gives an answer to the question of what form race legislation in the American states takes. The material is as variegated as the American map. Almost all American states have race legislation, but the races that must be defended against are characterized in different ways. Nevertheless a fundamental idea can be very easily extracted. The laws list Negroes or mulattoes or Chinese or Mongols in motley variation. There are a few sections which make positive reference to the Caucasian race. This is not uninteresting; since I believe there is jurisprudence on the question of whether Jews belong to the Caucasian race*'."

"What the hell does he mean by saying 'there is jurisprudence on the question of whether Jews belong to the Caucasian race'?" Mattie asked. "All the American laws in the Prussian Memorandum make it clear that Jews are white."

"I don't know," Churchill said, shaking his head.

"Well, whatever it means, the radical Nazis want to make it a crime for Aryans and Jews to marry or have sex. This is Karl Klee who Dohnanyi told me is a radical Nazi lawyer. '*It is interesting to see what legal consequences are attached by the American laws to sexual union. That too is variable. All sorts of expressions appear: 'illegal' and 'void', 'absolutely void', 'utterly null and void' and 'prohibited'. From these shifting and not very sharply juristically defined words, it can be seen that civil consequences attach in all cases and criminal consequences in a great number of cases'."*

Room service arrived with their meals, but Mattie barely noticed. Later, except for having red wine with Quail and white with Sea Bass, she had no memory of her meal as she continued to read. "Klee is outrageous! He's using American laws to justify treating Jews as being an *inferior* race. Listen: '*Like popular attitudes in Germany, American race legislation certainly does not base itself on the idea of mere racial difference, but—to the extent this legislation is aimed against Negroes and others—absolutely certainly on the idea of the inferiority of the other race in the face of which the American race must be protected'.*"

Mattie held up her fork and pointed it at Winston. "This is just how you English treated the Scots—as an inferior race!" Then she laughed. "You're lucky your English ancestors didn't criminalize marriage between English and Scots like the bloody Germans are trying to do with Jews. Where would you be if it had been a crime for you and Clemmie to marry?"

"In Canada. If not there, then I would have been a much less happy man. But if such laws had been passed," Churchill said with a smile as he put down his cigar and took a sip of brandy, "I'm sure they would only have been applied to those uncivilized savage clans in the Highlands like the Campbells. That was the McGary's clan, right? The Campbells of the infamous 'Glencoe Massacre'?" Churchill asked referring to the 1692 massacre in the Scottish Highlands of the MacDonald clan—man, woman and child—by the guests at their castle, the Campbells.

Mattie laughed. "And don't you forget it. I'm sure the MacDonalds haven't," she said "Well, those few who are left anyway."

A few minutes later, she looked up again. "I think I've figured out the approach the moderates on the Commission are taking to counter the radicals. The Germans are a very precise people and a fundamental principle of German law, as I understand it, is that criminal law must be based on clear and unambiguous concepts. Listen to this lawyer Losener who is one of the moderates. His point is that there is simply no accepted scientific means of determining who is 'Jewish': *'An effective means of determining whether a given human being has an element of Jewishness on the basis of his behavior or outward appearance or blood or the like does not exist, or at least at present has not yet been found',"* Mattie said and paused to finish the last of her Sea Bass. "Losener goes on to say it's 'intolerable' to allow individual judges to make decisions on the basis of 'vague sentiments of Jew hatred' and that the presumption of innocence meant that the indispensable prerequisite for proper criminalization was a clearly delineated and scientifically acceptable definition of who counted as a racial Jew."

Churchill just shook his head. "So, even the moderate Germans agree to treat German Jews as second class citizens, an 'inferior race', so long as due process is followed in 'scientifically' determining who is a Jew. It is frightening how far and how fast a noble nation like Germany has fallen under this odious new regime."

"Tell me about it," Mattie replied. "I've spent more time in that country in the last three years than I care to admit. More than once, I've regretted learning to speak German in the 20s. All it's done is get me more assignments in Germany."

Mattie was quiet as she read for the next fifteen minutes, silently passing pages over to Churchill after she read them, when suddenly she exploded. "Bloody hell! Bloody Goddamned Hell!"

"Pray tell me, my dear, what caused such a profane outburst," Churchill calmly replied.

"See for yourself. The Chairman of the Commission, Roland Freisler, just explained how the radical Nazis are going to counter the moderates' position about a clearly delineated and scientifically acceptable definition of who counted as a racial Jew. And the radical bastards are using American law to do it! Here's what Freisler said. *'Now as far as the delineation of the race concept goes, it is interesting to take a look at this list of American states. I have not seen that any state speaks of foreign race, but instead they name the races in some more primitive way. It seems to me doubtful that there would be any need for Germany to expressly mention the Jews alongside the coloreds. I believe that every German judge would reckon the Jews among the coloreds, even though they look outwardly white, just as they do the Tatars who are not yellow. Therefore I am of the opinion that we can proceed with the same primitivity that is used by these American states. Such a procedure would be crude, but it would suffice'."*

Mattie stood as she handed the page to Churchill. "Read it yourself. Then, I'm going to tuck it in. This is disgusting. I'll finish reading it tomorrow morning when I'm in a better mood. Then I'll photograph all the pages and ship the film off to Joe Willicomb in New York. You go back to England. I'm going back to Germany. Originally, I only intended to show the 5 June transcript to the two moderate members I interviewed and have them attest to its accuracy. I'm still going to do that, but I'm also going to use Sturm and all his influence with Göring to secure an interview with that slimy bastard Freisler."

"Good," Churchill said. "I'll have the concierge arrange in the morning for my return flight to England. What about lunch tomorrow? Would 1:30 in The White Room be convenient?"

"Yes, that would be lovely. I'll see you then," Mattie said as she placed the transcript back into the envelope and left the room.

Two minutes later, Mattie was at the entrance to her suite beside Churchill's penthouse suite. She unlocked the door, stepped inside and turned on the light switch to her left. She froze. Twenty feet away, a man sat in one of the suite's leather club chairs, a crystal tumbler filled with an amber liquid in one hand, a silenced Luger in the other. He had a prominent sharp nose and a dueling scar stood out on his cheek.

"Ah, *Frau* McGary at last. I'm pleased you could join us. My men were getting bored waiting for your return. My name is Josef Kleist. Unlike the two SS officers sent by Schellenberg who rescued you from the Americans earlier tonight, I really am *Gestapo*. And you have something I want."

Rough hands seized her from behind and a big hand clamped over her mouth. Kleist drained the rest of the glass, got up from the chair and walked over to her. With his left hand, he snatched the envelope with the transcript. With his right, he rammed his fist deep into her stomach, doubling her over, but the hand over her mouth stifled her cry of pain. The hand briefly left her mouth, only to be swiftly replaced by a cloth before she could utter a sound or cry out. She barely had time to recognize the chloroform soaked into it before she lost consciousness.

On Board the Reussi
Eastern Docklands
Amsterdam
Sunday 16 September 1934

JOSEF KLEIST waited while the operator placed a telephone call to Berlin.

"Freisler here."

"*Herr* Freisler, it's Kleist. We have the woman and the transcript. We're at the safehouse, the *Reussi* houseboat, which we will use tomorrow morning to rendezvous with the *M.S. Krueger,* a Rhine River freighter which sails with the tide. I've decided to use that method to extract her from the Netherlands. Motorcars, trains and aeroplanes are too risky."

"Why?" Freisler asked.

"An unconscious woman or one in handcuffs will simply raise too many questions with the Dutch border guards and customs officials. It's safer to transfer the woman and my team to the freighter whose manifest will already have been approved by Dutch customs officials. Passports for passengers and crews are never checked. Once we are safely in Germany, we will debark in Dusseldorf and take her on the *autobahn* to Berlin and from there to *Oranienburg* Camp where we will place her as a 'Jane Doe'."

"Good. How long can we keep her there undetected?" Freisler asked.

"As long as we need. Oranienburg is scheduled to be closed next year so no new prisoners are being sent there. That is well known so no one should suspect she was sent there. If, as you believe, the new laws will be announced in September at the annual Party rally in Nuremberg, we can keep her there until the new laws are passed."

"Excellent, Kleist! Good work," Freisler said. "After the new laws are passed, who cares if she publishes a story on the laws of American states we used as a model."

38

The *Gestapo* Have Mattie?

The Grand Hotel Krasnapolsky
Amsterdam
Sunday, 16 September 1934

BOURKE COCKRAN unlocked the door to his wife's suite and walked in. "Hello? Mattie, it's me. Anyone home?"

Cockran looked at his wristwatch. It was 1:15 p.m. She might be at lunch, he thought. She hadn't known the *Graf Bismarck* would stop in Amsterdam, so she wouldn't be expecting him until this evening, flying to Amsterdam from Berlin after the zeppelin arrived there. Remembering Mattie said that Churchill reserved adjoining suites, he walked to what he assumed was the door to the next suite and opened it to face another door.

"Winston, it's Bourke, are you there?" he said knocking on the inner door.

Moments later, the connecting door in Churchill's suite opened and there was Winston in a navy blue, three-piece pinstriped suit, a cigar in the corner of his mouth.

"Bourke, my boy! How good to see you. Come in, come in. When did you arrive?"

"Bobby and I arrived an hour or so ago. I originally thought we'd have to go all the way to Berlin and take a plane back here but her commander, Sturm, did us a favor and landed in Amsterdam first. Mattie's not in. Do you know where she is?"

Churchill frowned. "No, I don't. We arranged last night for luncheon at 1:30 in the hotel's restaurant, The White Room. I was on the verge of calling her room to see if she was ready to go down when you knocked."

Cockran walked back to their suite and began an inspection. Her suitcase was still there and her clothes were hung neatly in the closet. The desk in the suite was clear of everything except a portable typewriter. What he didn't find was her canvas camera bag where she kept all her notes, exposed film cartridges and anything else to do with the story she was investigating. The fact that it wasn't there might mean she was out seeing a source. The fact that she had a prearranged luncheon date with Winston, however, made it strange that he didn't know where she was and that she hadn't contacted him to advise him of a change in her plans. He walked back into Churchill's suite.

"Winston, none of Mattie's notes are there and neither is her camera bag and camera. She may well be with a source so I'll leave a note for her to join us at the restaurant. Meanwhile, you can fill me in on everything that's happened since I talked to her on Friday before we boarded the airship."

The White Room lived up to its name. It was a large light-filled room. White tapestry walls with gold trim, three large crystal chandeliers, and gilt framed paintings of Amsterdam's canals greeted them. The white cloth-covered tables were set sufficiently apart from one another that privacy was assured.

Cockran and Sullivan both ordered trout and Winston ordered venison along with two bottles of *Pol Roger* champagne, but Cockran barely noticed the food or the drink as Churchill recounted what Mattie had told him about her attack Thursday night by RVD agents in the *Tiergarten*, an attack she had failed to mention during their telephone conversation Friday morning before he boarded the zeppelin. He knew why she hadn't told him. What could he have done about it except helplessly worry about her safety? He was already doing that. Still, it was comforting to know that Schellenberg, whom

Cockran grudgingly respected, was continuing to look after Mattie's safety.

Any comfort Cockran took in that, however, abruptly vanished when Churchill told him of the attack on them last night in the canals by two more Americans—likely RVD agents also—who were killed by the same two Schellenberg SD officers who had saved Mattie Thursday night. Two attacks in three days put an entirely new light on Mattie's absence today. She had the transcript of the 5 June meeting she had come to Amsterdam to acquire, but it was nowhere in her room. That meant she and the transcript both were missing and there wasn't a damned thing he could do about it. He had never felt so helpless.

Cockran was about to ask Sullivan if he had any ideas when the *maître d'* approached the table holding a black telephone with a long cord draped over his arm,

"Mr. Cockran?"

"Yes."

"I have a long distance telephone call for you from Berlin. I'm told it's urgent. Would you like to take it here or in your room, Sir?"

"I'll take it here. Thanks very much," Cockran said.

The *maître d'* knelt down, plugged a jack into the floor and handed the telephone to Cockran who lifted the receiver just as the *maître d'* turned to Churchill and asked "Are you Mr. Churchill?"

Churchill replied that he was and was given a folded slip of paper. "You had an urgent telephone call also. The caller asked that you return his call at the earliest possible time."

Churchill opened the slip of paper and read it. He took a last sip of champagne and stood up. "Mr. Sullivan, please come with me. Bourke, we'll be in my suite." Sullivan rose also.

Cockran nodded as the two men left and then spoke into the receiver, "Cockran here."

"*Herr* Cockran, it's Walter Schellenberg. I'm so pleased you accompanied your wife to Amsterdam. My men were concerned yesterday when they couldn't find her registered at the hotel. I suggested they describe her and ask if she were registered under her married name. That's when I learned you were both registered."

"I didn't accompany her; I joined her. I only arrived today," Cockran replied impatiently. "What do you want that's so urgent, Schellenberg?"

"Your wife was kidnapped last night by the *Gestapo*. I am flying to Amsterdam today to plan details for her rescue with the two men I had watching her."

Cockran was stunned. He wanted to shout, but he kept his voice low, but firm. "*Gestapo*! The *Gestapo* have Mattie?"

"Yes, I fear they do. They took her last night and somehow evaded the notice of my two men. They took her to a houseboat in the Eastern Docklands. My men have found the houseboat and have it under surveillance. The *Gestapo* plan to take the houseboat to a rendezvous tomorrow morning with the M.S. *Krueger*, a Rhine River freighter which sails with the tide, and transfer her there to take her back to Germany."

"How do you know this?"

"Wiretap transcript. A conversation between Roland Freisler, a Justice Ministry official and the Chairman of the German Commission on Criminal Law Reform whose telephones I've had tapped and Josef Kleist, the head of the *Gestapo* team who kidnapped your wife."

"Why are they moving her to a freighter?"

"Kleist told Freisler it was easier to avoid the Dutch authorities that way than if they tried to cross the border in an automobile. The same for trains and planes."

"What are they going to do with her if they get her to Germany?"

"They're going to put her under an assumed name in a concentration camp for political prisoners near Berlin to keep her from publishing a story about the Prussian Memorandum."

"And how do you know that?"

"The same wiretap, but read between the lines. Kleist may report to Freisler, but his orders come straight from Himmler. Freisler and some American agents would like nothing better than to see your wife dead as the best means for stopping her story. Himmler won't let the *Gestapo* do that."

"Why?"

Schellenberg sighed. "It's a long story. The short version is Himmler wants to stay in Hitler's favor.

"And your beloved *Fuhrer* has a soft spot for my wife?"

"Exactly. Don't get me wrong. Himmler would likely prefer to eliminate her as the most certain means of stopping her story, but he can't afford to have the *Gestapo* implicated in the murder of 'Hitler's favorite foreign journalist'. Trust me, I am positive your wife's life is not in danger from her *Gestapo* captors. I can't say the same, however, for the Americans who work for RVD International."

Van Deman! That bastard! Cockran thought. "What do you know about RVD and Mattie?"

"Well, this I *am* at liberty to disclose. I have wiretaps on RVD's Berlin offices and I know that the Executive Vice-President of RVD, Harold Hudson Canfield, ordered your wife 'roughed up' last Thursday and on Friday he ordered that she be killed in Amsterdam. I personally went up to Bremerhaven to warn him off, but I was apparently unsuccessful if last night's attack on her and *Herr* Churchill is any indication. That is not good for my reputation and I've had the SD enlist the services of the *Kripo* to locate him for us. My boss Heydrich approves of what I have done. I don't sense that he has any special fondness for your wife, but given his support, I daresay the odds of Canfield leaving Germany alive are slim. Trust me, the SD has Canfield under surveillance. Our immediate concern is the *Gestapo* and rescuing your wife from their grasp."

"I agree," Cockran said, "so what's your plan?"

"My plan is to fly to Amsterdam and work out the details with you. We were rather successful in doing that earlier this year," Schellenberg said, referring to their rescue of Mattie that summer in Berlin from agents of the foreign intelligence operation of Henry Ford run by his top aide Ernst Liebold. "I think I'd prefer, however, to wait until the *Gestapo* take her into Germany before we made our move."

"Why?"

"Well, as you will recall from this summer, it may get, ah, a tad messy," Schellenberg said, referring to the body count of Ford agents left behind at a Berlin safe house where Mattie had been held. "I don't have the kind of relationship with the Dutch authorities to enable us to cover up something like that quite as easily."

"I take your point," Cockran replied, "but my preference is to get Mattie out of the clutches of the *Gestapo* sooner rather than later."

"I understand. That is why I suggest we discuss this face to face before we make a decision. I'm leaving for *Templehof* as soon as we finish our conversation. *Obersturmbannfuhrer* Heydrich has once more kindly offered us the services of his private *Fokker* Tri-Motor to facilitate my travel to Amsterdam. I should see you within three hours from now."

Cockran laughed. "You mean you'll tell him later," he said, referring to Schellenberg commandeering Heydrich's *Fokker* on 30 June, the Night of the Long Knives, and flying Mattie, Sullivan and him to safety in Prague, one-step ahead of SS assassins bent on doing all three of them in.

Schellenberg chuckled. "Something like that. I *am* under his orders to keep your wife safe and we Germans *always* follow orders."

Cockran hurried up to their suite, elated that Mattie was safe and that plans to take her from the clutches of the *Gestapo* would soon be afoot. Once there, he opened the door between their suite and Churchill's suite. "Winston! Bobby! I know where Mattie is! The *Gestapo* have her captive on a houseboat in Amsterdam."

Churchill was sitting at a desk in his suite's drawing room and looked up with a startled expression on his face as he placed the telephone receiver in his hand back into its cradle. "Of course they have, dear boy. The question is what are we going to do about it."

39

The Brown Pages

STURM NEVER went straight to one of his several offices when he returned from a trans-Atlantic flight on the *Graf Bismarck*. Once he left the airship, his adrenaline levels dropped dramatically and all he wanted to do was sleep. Post-war passenger zeppelins had a perfect safety record and all zeppelin commanders were under enormous pressure to keep it that way. The pressure was mental, but the effect on the body was physical. The sky over the North Atlantic was a dangerous adversary even in the best of weather.

Sturm made an exception today because of what Cockran had told him on the flight about the danger posed to Mattie by her investigation of the Prussian Memorandum. Hence, he decided to go to his small office at *Forschungsamt* headquarters to review all the Brown Pages from the Roland Freisler wiretaps since the *Graf Bismarck* left Germany last Wednesday.

Sturm's taxi left him off on *Schillerstrasse* in Berlin's *Charlottenburg* district. His destination was a collection of four magnificent, three-story, turn-of-the-century apartment buildings set back from the street. The granite-faced structures, however, were no longer apartment buildings. Rather, they housed the most significant of all the many agencies under Hermann Göring's control, the *Forschungsamt* or FA.

Once inside, Sturm took a small elevator to the building's top floor and unlocked the door to his office. It was small and bare of ornamentation. A desk, a single chair and a window overlooked a small lake. A pouch was on his desk and he opened it with his pouch key. Inside were two thick red envelopes. One had the date of Thursday, 13 September at 7:39 p.m. and the other was today, Sunday, 16 September at 1:16 a.m. He opened the earlier envelope and began to read what Freisler had told a Justice Ministry colleague about his meeting that day with Heinrich Himmler.

It was interesting, Sturm thought, placing the transcript back in its red envelope, that Himmler put a listening device inside Mattie's suite at the *Adlon* but didn't do a wiretap. He opened the second envelope and found it strange, as he began to read, that Freisler had received such an early morning call from Amsterdam. Once he finished the transcript, it was no longer strange. That bastard Freisler had the *Gestapo* kidnap Mattie! And they were going to put her anonymously into a concentration camp for political prisoners!

Sturm returned the Brown Pages to the red envelope, placed both envelopes back in the pouch and locked it. He signed the receipt form in triplicate and placed it and the pouch in the 'out' basket on his desk. He left his office, locked it, and went out to *Schillerstrasse* to hail a taxi. On the way back to his rooms at the *Kaiserhof,* Sturm pondered his dilemma. He would call Cockran, of course, but should he alert Göring as well?

Once in his room, he called *Lufthansa* to book a flight to Amsterdam and found their last flight at 5:30 p.m. was sold out. Damn, he thought, but at least his dilemma was solved. He would call Göring after he alerted Cockran and see if he could borrow *Unser* Hermann's personal JU-52 and his pilot to fly him to Amsterdam today.

To his dismay, Cockran did not answer the telephone in his room at the Grand Hotel *Krasnapolsky.* "Would you like to leave a message, Sir?"

"Not yet. Please ring Mr. Churchill's room. If he's not in, I'll leave one message for both of them."

Churchill didn't answer his phone either so he left a single message addressed to both.

Then he waited. He didn't want to call Göring just yet for fear that it might interfere with Cockran or Churchill returning his call. Time enough for Göring later.

Ten minutes after leaving the message, Sturm's telephone rang.

"*Herr* von Sturm, it's Winston Churchill returning your call. What do you have for me that's so urgent?"

The Grand Hotel Krasnapolsky
Amsterdam
Sunday, 16 September 1934

ONCE CHURCHILL finished giving him the details of Sturm's call, Cockran turned to head back to his room and then paused. "Winston, call Kurt back. Tell him to hold off calling Göring for his aircraft. I may have an easier way for him to go. Keep him on the line until I finish my next call."

Back in his room, Cockran had the hotel switchboard place a call to Hangar 6 at *Templehof* Aerodrome in Berlin, which surprisingly took only two minutes to complete.

"I'm calling for Walter Schellenberg. He's flying today to Amsterdam in *Obersturmbannfuhrer* Heydrich's *Fokker* Tri-motor. Has he arrived? Great! Put him on."

"Yes?"

"Schellenberg? Cockran here. How would you like to meet one of your boyhood heroes and fly him to Amsterdam with you?" Cockran said, referring to the fact that Schellenberg once had confessed to Mattie that Sturm was a hero to young German boys for having destroyed the Imperial German Navy's zeppelins rather than turn them over to the Allies as the Versailles Treaty required.

"Who would that be?"

"Kurt von Sturm or, as you would have known him in 1919, Kurt von Strasser," Cockran replied.

"Really?" Schellenberg replied in an enthusiastic voice. "That would be such an honor. How soon can he be here?"

"He's at the *Kaiserhof* in Berlin. I expect he can be there within an hour."

"Excellent! Tell him how much I look forward to meeting him."

Cockran hung up and walked back into Churchill's suite. "Is Kurt still on the line?"

Churchill nodded 'yes' and gave the receiver to Cockran.

"Kurt? It's Bourke. I've got a ride for you to Amsterdam. Walter Schellenberg, head of the SD's Foreign Section. He's a charter member of your fan club for those naval zeppelins you torched back in '19. Go to Hangar 6 at *Templehof.* He's expecting you. And Kurt? One more thing."

"Yes?"

"Don't forget to give him your autograph."

40

Why Did the *Gestapo* Kidnap Me?

On Board the Reussi
Eastern Docklands
Amsterdam
Sunday 16 September 1934

MATTIE McGARY woke with a splitting headache and took stock of her surroundings. She was on a high bed, her hands tied in front of her, her feet unbound. She could tell she was on some kind of boat because there was a porthole beside her and above was a skylight from which she could see a single mast with ship's rigging. She sat up and noticed her head was only a foot from the ceiling. She carefully got off the bed, walked to the door and tried to open it. It was locked.

Mattie banged on the door with her fists. "Hey! Open the door! I need to use the head on this bloody boat!"

Moments later, the door was opened by Josef Kleist, he of the dueling scar and sharp nose. He was tall, lean and held a Luger with a sound suppressor extending from its barrel. Beyond him was a sitting area with club chairs and a sofa. Two men in shirtsleeves were seated at an oval table, coffee cups in hand, a younger one with brown hair, the other fairly large with gray hair. Kleist motioned with the pistol. "The head is down that corridor, first door on the left."

Mattie held out her hands. "Come on. Untie me. I'm obviously not going anywhere and you're the one with a gun."

"Hans, cut her bonds," Kleist said to one of the two men at the table.

The brown-haired man rose, reached down to his ankle, brought out an eight-inch stiletto and walked over to Mattie who held out her hands while he severed the rope.

"Thank you," she said to Kleist. Her hands now free, she went to the head. While there, she pondered her dilemma. She remembered last night before she blacked out that Kleist had said she had something he wanted. What was it? She finished in the head, combed her hair with her fingers and walked back to the sitting room and over to the club chair where Kleist sat drinking a cup of coffee, his Luger within easy reach on a small table beside the chair.

"How about some coffee?" Mattie asked as she began to work on an escape plan.

Kleist frowned. "Well, *Frau* McGary, I would prefer you not have a hot liquid in your hands that you might propel at my face. So, be a good little girl and go sit in that armchair at the far end of the room. Put one hand beneath you and leave the other free for the coffee that I will have Hans bring you," he said and then nodded at Hans.

Mattie stifled a sigh. As soon as she re-entered the sitting room, she had looked for an exit. It appeared to be there, less than ten feet from Kleist's chair and throwing coffee in his face and sprinting for the exit was exactly what she had intended to do. So, she did as she was told and accepted the cup of coffee from Hans. "So, why did the Gestapo kidnap me and what exactly do you want?"

"I wouldn't call it kidnapping. It's more of an extra-territorial arrest and extradition to Germany of a traitor to the *Reich*. As for what I want, it's this," Kleist said and held up the bound transcript of the June 5 meeting. "This is a highly classified, top-secret German government document which you are not authorized to have. I personally executed Otto Lutze, the man who left it for you in that museum's little chapel. The man who arranged to have the document recreated has been arrested by the *Gestapo* and will, in due course, be imprisoned while a decision will be made as to his fate."

"Who is that?"

"Georg von Dohnanyi."

"I've never met anyone by that name," Mattie replied.

Kleist smiled. "We know you haven't, but you soon will."

"Why? Where are you taking me?"

"I told you. You're being extradicted to Germany. That's all you really need to know, but I see no harm in telling you where you will be spending what little time remains of your life as a guest of the Third *Reich*. It's not as if you're going to be in a position to tell anyone where you'll be. Early tomorrow morning, this houseboat will take us to the port of Amsterdam where we will transfer to a river freighter that will take us to Dusseldorf where we will proceed by motorcar to *Konzentrationslager Orianenburg*. Your co-conspirator Dohnanyi will be transferred there as well along with the person we identify as the one who produced that transcript. As German citizens, they will be tried for treason. You will be tried for espionage. The penalty for both crimes is death," he said and then paused, grinned and struck his left palm with the side of his right hand, "by beheading."

Well, Mattie thought as she shivered, at least they didn't know Greta Mayer had prepared the transcript. Would her uncle give her up? The odds were he eventually would, but the rumors were that *Oranienburg* was not that bad. For a concentration camp, that is. In fact Bella Fromm had once told her that she knew several men and women who had been detained there and subsequently released after their political 're-education' had been deemed successful. While they had been required to work at various jobs such as sewing, woodworking, repairing shoes and even building a sailplane, they were well fed and not abused. In fact, some of them had even come out of the camp weighing more than when they went in. Those reports, however, were from a time when the SA had administered the camp. The 'Night of the Long Knives' gutted the top SA leadership this year on 30 June and the SA was replaced at the camp by the SS. Would the SS be as humane? The SA weren't exactly boy scouts, but after the Night of the Long Knives, it was clear the SS were far more ruthless.

"So, *Frau* McGary, be so kind as to return to your room," Kleist said. "Your meals will be served there. If you have need of the, ah, facilities again, simply knock on the door and either Hans or Bruno will escort you there."

Back in the houseboat's bedroom, Mattie pondered her situation. Clearly, her best chance to escape would come during the transfer from the houseboat to the freighter. So, the only thing to do now was rest and wait for tomorrow morning.

41

Whatever It Takes

The Grand Hotel Krasnapolsky
Amsterdam
Sunday, 16 September 1934

STURM AND SCHELLENBERG arrived at Churchill's suite shortly after 7 p.m. Both wore civilian suits rather than the uniforms of their respective employers, *Deutsch Zeppelin Reederi* and the SS. After Cockran introduced Churchill to Schellenberg as "Mr. Spencer", the SS man gave a brief report on the surveillance of the houseboat *Reussi* where Mattie was being held. Cockran could see no indication that he recognized who Churchill was.

"*Fregattenkapitan* Sturm and I visited the East Docklands on our way here from the aerodrome. My men have the boat under surveillance and they have seen nothing of *Frau* McGary today. They believe there are only three men in the boat as occasionally, one of them will come up on deck. Three different men have done so. It's possible, but unlikely, that there are four or more men inside. I gave my men the telephone number of this hotel and the room number for *Herr* Spencer's suite. There is a public telephone fifty yards from the houseboat so my men will promptly advise us of any activity at the boat."

"How are they armed?" Cockran asked in a crisp voice as the five men sat down around the table in the suite's dining room. Concerned as he was about Mattie's safety, Cockran knew he could not let that concern show in his speech or body language.

"I presume they all have Luger pistols, standard issue to the *Gestapo*," Schellenberg replied. "I confess, however, I did not ask my men about that."

"We must know that. Mr. Sullivan and I had just about agreed with your suggestion that we wait until Mattie is in Germany before we attempt a rescue. Your answer clinches it. Our primary reason is that we don't have permits for our Colt automatic pistols in the Netherlands whereas we do in Germany. And your point about not having official standing here compared to what you have in Germany is well taken. Finally, the fact that we have no active intelligence as to the weapons we will be facing if we try something in Amsterdam is conclusive. That's why, when we're finished here, I want you to go back to your men and tell them to locate the freighter. Once the houseboat sails tomorrow to its rendezvous with the freighter, your men must drive to the freighter's dock to observe the transfer closely to see if the *Gestapo* have any visible weapons like submachine pistols. If they see none, then we will proceed on your presumption that all we have to face are three Luger pistols."

Schellenberg nodded his understanding and reached down to open his briefcase. He brought out a large manila envelope from which he extracted what looked like a folded blue print. He began to unfold it on the table. "These are the schematics for the *M.S. Kreuger* that I obtained from the Ministry of Maritime Shipping."

"Hold up a second," Cockran said. "Let's make sure we all understand our strategic goal: extract Mattie from the Gestapo as soon as the freighter reaches its first port of call in Germany by any means necessary. Whatever it takes. Are we agreed?" he aksed and looked each man in the eye. In any military operation, there could be only one leader in the field and, since it was his wife in danger, that was him. Her life depended on it.

Affirmative nods came from all four men.

"Good. Now, let's discuss timing. What is the first port of call for the *Kreuger* in Germany and when will it arrive?"

Schellenberg reached again into his briefcase and pulled out a manila folder. "My office called the residence of the President of the shipping line that owns the *Kreuger*. He was quite upset to be disturbed at home on a Sunday until he learned it was the SD calling," he said with a smile. "After that, he couldn't have been more cooperative. The first port is Kinderdijk in the Netherlands. The first German port is Duisburg. The *Kreuger* will sail tomorrow morning at 8:15 a.m. It will have a two-hour stop in Kinderdijk and will arrive in Duisburg at approximately 8:45 p.m. It will spend the night in Duisburg, depart Duisburg at 8:00 a.m. and arrive in Dusseldorf at 11:10 a.m."

"Good work," Cockran said. "Do you possibly have a map or diagram of the port and the location where the *Kreuger* will be docked?"

"Of course," Schellenberg replied. "Ever since the former Minister of Maritime Shipping, Erich Klausener, was killed by the SS during the Night of the Long Knives, his successor says 'how high?' every time we ask him to jump."

Once more, Schellenberg reached into his briefcase and pulled out a document that he unfolded and placed over the interior diagram of the *Kreuger*. "I've circled with a red grease pencil Dock #8 where the *Kreuger* will lay up for the night. It will be parallel to the riverbank, underneath a large crane. Since it will have arrived after 6 p.m., it won't be unloaded until Tuesday morning. The crew will have been given shore leave so I expect there will only be a night watch officer on board along with the three *Gestapo* and *Frau* McGary."

"Good. Does this mean we'll be able to approach the river side of the freighter in a small boat?" Cockran asked.

"Certainly," Schellenberg said.

"Now, let's look at that diagram of the freighter's interior," Cockran said.

Schellenberg refolded the map of the port and pointed to the diagram of the ship's interior. "This is a typical layout for most river freighters. The elevated bridge is at the stern of the freighter and the crew's quarters, mess room and galley are located beneath the bridge. The cabin for passengers, or the owner's cabin, is located far forward in the bow of the boat. *Frau* McGary and the *Gestapo* have to be there. As you can see, there are three small bedrooms and a head off of the common area. There are no separate galley or dining facilities so either food will be brought to them or they will eat in the crew's mess."

"Okay, here's how I propose we proceed," Cockran said. "It's a variation of what Schellenberg, Bobby and I used last June in Berlin when Mattie was being held in a safe house by other guys trying to stop her from publishing a story." He then talked for the next ten minutes, each man nodding as he explained what their roles would be. He was pleasantly surprised when even 'Mr. Spencer' agreed with his assignment, albeit it was true that Cockran's original plan had not included Churchill. No one had questions.

"Well, I suggest we all get some sleep and leave here for the aerodrome at first light," Cockran said and then turned to Sturm.

"Kurt, have you reported Mattie's kidnapping to Göring yet?"

"No, I will try and reach him tonight from my room and tomorrow morning if I don't speak to him tonight."

"When you do, see if you can persuade him to have five silenced Schmeisser submachine pistols and three Prussian State Police badges delivered to us at the Duisburg air field. Schellenberg and his men won't need them, but I'd like the three of us to be acting under the color of law should things not go as well as we hope."

42

Let This Be a Lesson

On Board the M.S. Kreuger
Amsterdam
Monday 17 September 1934

AS SHE walked up the gangplank between the houseboat *Reussi* and the river freighter *M.S. Kreuger* that lay parallel to the riverbank, Mattie decided the only way for her to escape was to get wet. The first question had been whether to attempt an escape. She had mulled that over last night. It meant she would have to leave behind her *Leica* camera and notes for the story, but she could buy a new camera and her memory was good enough to recreate the notes. Moreover, leaving the notes behind would not burn any of her sources as she put nothing in her notes that could identify them, leaving that to her memory as well. Finally, she would lose the transcript of the critical June 5 meeting, but if Greta Mayer created it once, she could do it again. The fact that she was still alive meant the *Gestapo* had no orders to kill her so it was potentially possible, but highly unlikely, that she would be 'shot trying to escape'.

That decision made, the only other question was when to make the attempt. As they had kept her locked in her room on the houseboat until it pulled alongside the freighter, she knew this would be her only chance. Once she hit the deck of the new boat, she had to bolt. She still wore the white silk blouse, tan wool trousers and Donegal tweed jacket that she was wearing yesterday. Unfortunately, she was also wearing her trademark highly polished Red Wing boots that she always wore in the field, even if the 'field' was a major city like Amsterdam. Growing up near Loch Ness, Mattie was a strong swimmer, but she knew those boots would be a hindrance in the water. Still, she hoped she wouldn't be in the water that long and fleeing in her bare feet once on land did not seem advisable. Besides, she was betting the *Gestapo* thugs would not be eager to go swimming with her.

When Mattie emerged from the interior of the houseboat to the deck, her spirits lifted. They would board the freighter at the stern of the ship, right in front of the wheelhouse. That meant when she bolted, it would only be a short dash down the gangway beside the wheelhouse to the stern of the ship where a racing dive would take her into the Rhine and, she hoped, to freedom. One *Gestapo* thug—Hans, the one with a brown crewcut and thick neck—was ahead of her while Kleist and his other thug—Bruno, the large, bald one with a fringe of gray hair—were close behind her. Crewcut reached the deck of the freighter and turned to face her, holding out his hand in a gentlemanly gesture to help her down the last step.

Idiot! Mattie thought. *"Danke,"* was what she said as she took his extended hand, gripped it tightly and pulled him toward her. She grasped his elbow with her left hand, pulled him toward her with both hands and jammed her right knee hard into his groin.

The thug cried out, released her hand and doubled over, groaning. Mattie promptly turned to her right, dashed down the gangway to the stern of the ship where she stepped quickly onto the low railing and executed a perfect racing dive into the Rhine. She surfaced ten yards from the ship and heard Kleist shout "100 *Reichsmarks* to whoever brings her back to the ship!"

Mattie briefly switched from the Australian crawl to a back stroke to see who was pursuing her and was dismayed to see two burly sailors, not *Gestapo* thugs, standing at the stern, tugging at their shoes. Moments later, they plunged into the river and began to swim after her. She gave them a good run for their money, but in less than ten minutes, they overtook her. Her boots had done her in and she was exhausted, offering no resistance when one sailor clamped a beefy arm under her breasts and began a sidestroke back to the ship.

Once there, Kleist was as good as his word, slipping each sailor a 100 *Reichsmark* note.

"Take the bitch to our cabin!" Kleist ordered and the two thugs grabbed her on either side and frog marched her to the bow of the ship where they entered a low cabin. It was similar, Mattie noted, to the houseboat's interior, a sitting area with a table for dining, a sofa and several arm chairs.

Kleist came in behind them, closed the door and looked at the thugs. "Get her out of those wet clothes."

"I am perfectly capable of doing that myself, thank you very much," Mattie said.

"I'm sure you can," Kleist replied and hit her with a backhand slap on her face, followed quickly by an open hand slap, "but let this be a lesson to you. You've caused us a lot of trouble this morning by your foolish attempt to escape and now you have to pay the piper. Besides, it makes it more fun for the boys. Right, Hans?" Kleist said with a nod toward the crewcut.

Crewcut—he of the wounded groin—just leered at Mattie. "You bet, Boss," the thug Hans said as he and his colleague Bruno approached Mattie. They pushed her down onto the couch and none too gently—Crewcut especially—began to take off her clothes. Mattie, tried her best to kick and flail, but still exhausted from her swim, they quickly had her boots, blouse and trousers off. When they went for her bra and briefs, she got another kick into Crewcut's already damaged groin, but Bruno was sufficiently strong enough to hold her down while Crewcut removed her bra and briefs.

"Okay, boys, that's enough. Stand her up," Kleist ordered, calling a halt to their 'fun'.

The two pulled her up off the sofa, each holding her by one arm as she stood in front of Kleist who slowly ran his eyes up and down her body. "As a deterrent to any future attempt on your part to escape before we reach Dusseldorf tomorrow," Kleist said, "you will remain naked in your cabin for the rest of our voyage. I'm sure you will find a blanket there to keep you warm. Your clothes will be returned to you when we reach Dusseldorf. Should you nevertheless attempt to escape again before then, I will let the boys resume their 'fun' and," he paused for effect, "I will not tell them to stop. Is that clear?"

Yes, it's clear, you bloody wanker, Mattie thought, but she did not reply. Kleist stepped close to her and grasped her chin with his left hand. "I said, Bitch, is that clear?" he hissed and hit her with a solid right fist into her belly as he had the night before, once more doubling her over.

"Yes, you bastard, it's clear," Mattie said as she straightened up, shrugged free of the two men holding her, walked into the nearest cabin and closed the door. She was still chilled from her swim so she pulled the blanket off the bed, wrapped it around her and went over to the room's sole porthole and stared out. She felt the ship's engines engage and watched the riverbank grow smaller as the ship moved into the middle of the wide river. After a few minutes, she sat in the room's only chair and began to plan her next escape attempt. The porthole was actually rectangular and, if she could get it open, it was large enough for her to squeeze through. The question was when and where to do so.

43

You Are Smuggling a Jew!

Port of Duisberg
Duisberg, Germany
Monday, 17 September 1934

THE SPRAY from the Rhine subsided as Winston Churchill, aka 'Mr. Spencer', cut back the throttle of the handmade Hacker-Craft mahogany two-cockpit runabout at 9:30 p.m., 200 yards away from the *M.S. Koblenz*. As a result, the start of their approach to the freighter moored parallel to the dock was almost silent. The runabout was 30' long and capable of doing 60 mph. Cockran had hired the boat earlier in the day precisely because of its speed. In the event they had to make a hasty getaway after rescuing Mattie, he wanted to make sure any pursuit of them would be futile. He had been more than a little amused at the irony when the proprietor of the boats-for-hire company had advised him the previous owner of the boat had been 'the American Industrialist' Ernst Liebold who had been murdered at his boathouse in Berlin earlier that year. *That* sonofabitch had kidnapped Mattie to keep her from publishing a story about his role in the Great War facilitating a treasonous exchange of war materials between Great Britain and Imperial Germany. Cockran and Sullivan had rescued Mattie and, in the process, killed Sebastian Slade, Liebold's chief lieutenant, who had his own homicidal plans for

Mattie. He didn't know who had killed Liebold, but whoever it was, Cockran thought, had done humanity a genuine service.

Fifty yards from the freighter, Churchill cut the throttle entirely so that the boat's glide to the bow of the freighter was completely silent. Churchill at the helm of the boat in a night raid to free Mattie had not been Cockran's idea, but Churchill had insisted before Sturm and Schellenberg's arrival that he be involved in Mattie's rescue because the story on which his goddaughter was working had been at his instigation. Clever Churchillian cross-examination of Sullivan and Cockran had established that, while Sturm and Cockran had considerable sailing experience—the North Sea for Sturm and Long Island Sound for Cockran—their experience with small powered watercraft was limited and Sullivan's was nonexistent. In contrast, Churchill reminded them, his tenure as First Lord of the Admiralty from 1911 to 1915 had not only given him the opportunity to learn to fly, but to pilot small powered watercraft as well.

Cockran sat in the front cockpit beside Churchill who wore a jaunty blue sailor's cap with a black visor while Cockran was in khakis and a dark brown leather-flying jacket. In the second, roomier cockpit that could easily accommodate four passengers, Sturm and Sullivan were hunched low and from shore would not be noticed. Both were dressed all in black from their trousers to their wool sweaters and watch caps. Each held across his chest a Schmeisser sub-machine pistol, five of which had arrived earlier that day on Hermann Göring's personal JU-52. Both men had handguns in shoulder holsters, Sullivan with two Colt .45 1911 automatics while Sturm had a single Luger. Cockran had a Schmeisser on the deck beside him as well as a Colt .45 in a shoulder holster. All weapons had sound suppressors.

Churchill deftly attached a rope to one of the two anchors at the portside of the freighter's bow while Cockran looked at his wristwatch—9:43. He looked at Sturm and Sullivan and held up two fingers. Both nodded. At 9:44, he held up one finger. Sturm and Sullivan stood up, each holding a grappling hook clad in rubber. At 9:45, Cockran closed his fist and pumped his hand. The hooks went skyward right after a shot rang out.

"You are smuggling a Jew!" Cockran heard Walter Schellenberg shout from the rear of the boat. "You'll tell me all you know or, by God, the next bullet won't miss."

On board M.S. Koblenz
Port of Duisberg
Duisberg, Germany
Monday, 17 September 1934

WALTER SCHELLENBERG cut an imposing figure as he strode up the gangplank of the *M.S. Koblenz* in a full dress, black SS uniform with silver trim, knee-high polished black leather boots, a stiff-brimmed high peaked cap and a Luger automatic inside a black leather holster that matched his boots. He was followed by *SS-Obersturmfuhrers* Franz Globke and Eric Bulow, each holding at port arms a Schmeisser MP 36 submachine pistol identical to those carried by Cockran, Sturm and Sullivan.

A tall, middle-aged figure with a trim brown beard and clad in a navy uniform with gold braid and wearing a white hat with a black bill stood at the top of the gangplank. Schellenberg knew the man was one of the ships' officers, possibly the captain himself. He also knew it was customary, when boarding a ship, to ask permission to come aboard. He was not about to do that.

"I am *SS-Sturmbannfuhrer* Walter Schellenberg," he said without giving the officer an opportunity to identify himself. "We are reliably informed that you have one or more Jews on board who are attempting to illegally enter into Switzerland with more assets than German law permits. Please take me to the captain of this ship and produce the passenger manifest."

"I am Wilhelm Preuss," he said with a stiff formality, "the Captain of the *M.S. Koblenz*. I am not aware we have any Jews on board, but you are welcome to see our passenger manifest. There are three *Gestapo* officers and their prisoner in our passenger cabins. Come with me."

Schellenberg followed the captain down the side of the ship to the stern where he opened a door and invited them inside.

"Wait here," Schellenberg said to Globke and Bulow," as he followed Captain Preuss into his cabin. It was small, but well organized with a single bunk against one wall and a compact white desk and matching file cabinet beside it. The captain pulled out a ring of keys, opened the top drawer of the cabinet and pulled out a file folder. He took a sheet of paper from within the folder and handed it to Schellenberg.

"This is the passenger manifest for this voyage, *Sturmbannfuhrer*. Three *Gestapo* agents. I didn't ask if any of them were Jews," Preuss said.

Schellenberg took the sheet and looked at it. He recognized Kleist's name for he was rumored to be a Himmler favorite, but the other two names meant nothing to him. "There are only three names here. You mentioned they had a prisoner, but I don't see his name here."

"They didn't give me *her* name and I didn't ask. Once on board, she attempted to escape by leaping into the river and making for shore. Two of my sailors retrieved her, but I must say she gave them a good run for their money. For quite some time, however, I have made it a practice never to question the *Gestapo*," Preuss said and paused for a moment before adding "or, for that matter, the SS."

Schellenberg flashed him a smile. "Probably prudent on your part, but I have no such qualms when I am looking for Jews or Jew smugglers who pose as *Gestapo* agents. Let me see their passports."

"I don't have them."

"What? You don't have them? You crossed the German border with passengers whose passports you have not seen?" Schellenberg asked with a tone of incredulity.

Captain Preuss shifted uncomfortably. "Well...uh, they showed me their *Gestapo* discs and I thought that would be sufficient."

"Really? How accommodating of you. Who appeared to be the leader of this group of supposed *Gestapo* agents?"

"*Herr* Kleist identified himself as the senior *Gestapo* agent."

"Do you have a communication line between your cabin and the passenger cabin?"

Preuss nodded yes and pointed to a telephone on his desk.

"Excellent. Ring up this Kleist and give me the receiver."

Preuss did so. "*Herr* Kleist, this is the Captain and there is someone here who wishes…"

At that point, Schellenberg grabbed the receiver. "Kleist!" He shouted. "This is *SS-Sturmbannfuhrer* Walter Schellenberg. I am head of the Foreign Section of the SD. Captain Preuss advises me you have smuggled a foreign national—likely a Jew or a spy—into Germany aboard his ship without showing him a passport as you are required by law to do. Report immediately to the Captain's cabin and bring with you all your passports including the one for the Jew!"

"But…but…" Kleist sputtered, "we are *Gestapo*. We don't have to…"

"Kleist, I am SD! You will do what I tell you. If you don't have your sorry ass back here in two minutes with those passports, my men will drag you back here by the scruff of your neck. If you or any of your men offer the least resistance, they will be shot! And bring with you those alleged *Gestapo* warrant discs and any *Gestapo* ID to prove you are who you say you are. Is that clear?"

Kleist, in fact, arrived within two minutes, red-faced, out of breath, and sandwiched between Globke and Bulow who were holding his arms. Schellenberg immediately noted his dueling scar and decided that he was dealing with a university graduate and therefore a cut above your average *Gestapo* thug. He held out his hand. "Your warrant discs and ID, please."

Kleist handed them over and Shellenberg made a pretense of carefully examining each one. He did not return them to Kleist, however, but casually tossed them on to the captain's desk. "Now, the passports," he said.

Kleist reached into his pocket and hand him four passports, three German and one British. Schellenberg examined each, McGary's British passport last, and then tossed them onto the desk as well. "I commend you *Herr* Kleist. These are all excellent forgeries, but they are still forgeries," Schellenberg said and picked up the British passport and waved it in Kleist's face. "This one gives the game away. You are smuggling a Jew with money out of Germany to Switzerland. If it's really a woman, I'll bet she's a dusky Jewess with a big nose."

"No, no. We really did arrest her," Kleist protested. "She is our prisoner and tried to escape by going overboard. Once we got her back to our cabin, we stripped off her wet clothes. I saw her naked. She is quite fair-skinned with freckles and the red hair on her head is the same shade as between her legs," he said and motioned with his hands as if outlining a female body. "She is a most attractive woman."

"That proves nothing you fool! Jews come in all shapes and sizes as well as hair and skin color. Where did you arrest her and why?"

"In Amsterdam for espionage, theft of state secrets."

"Hah! Let me see your arrest warrant."

"*Arrest* warrant? The *Gestapo* need no arrest warrant..."

Schellenberg looked at his watch. 9:44. The boarding party should be alongside by now, he thought so he pulled his Luger and fired a shot through the open cabin door within inches of Kleist's head. "You are smuggling a Jew! You'll tell me all you know or, by God, the next bullet won't miss. I won't need an *arrest* warrant either to execute you on the spot."

Kleist flinched, his face white as the bullet few past him. "Please, I swear we are *Gestapo* agents returning from a mission in Amsterdam."

"Liar! I am head of the Foreign Section of the SD and I was not told of nor did I approve any such mission. Who is your immediate superior?"

"On this mission, it is Roland Freisler of the Ministry of Justice. He is the Chairman of the German Commission on Criminal Law Reform"

"What was your mission?"

"To recover a Top Secret transcript of a meeting of the German Commission on Criminal Law Reform; to arrest the British journalist who had the transcript; and to bring her to the *Oranienburg* concentration camp in Germany."

"Who gave you this so-called *mission*?"

"Heinrich Himmler."

"Really? You expect me to believe *Reichsfuhrer-SS* Heinrich Himmler gave you a mission in a foreign country and just *forgot* to tell the head of the SD's Foreign Section that he had done so? How big a fool do you think I am?"

Kleist did not reply and Schellenberg looked at his watch again. Twelve minutes had elapsed since his first shot and twelve minutes was all the time the boarding party had allocated to extract Mattie. Okay, time for the final act. "Alright, Jew smuggler, let's go see if you're telling the truth about this," Schellenberg said and mimicked Kleist's hands outlining the curves of a woman's body, "and see this attractive British journalist whom you claim you saw naked."

"I very much did," Kleist said, "and now you will too."

44

Mattie's Not In The Cabin!

On board M.S. Koblenz
Port of Duisberg
Duisberg, Germany
Monday, 17 September 1934

STURM AND SULLIVAN quickly scaled the eight feet up the side of the freighter, after the two grappling hooks took hold, their *Schmeissers* slung over their backs. The instant Sturm hit the deck, he brought the *Schmeisser* around to a firing position just as a man with a brown-haired crewcut and clad in a dark gray suit came out of the passenger cabin with a *Luger* in his right hand. The man looked in the direction of the stern from where the sound of the pistol shot had come.

"Josef? *Was ist los?*"

Sturm smiled to himself. Turn around, my friend, he thought, and you will find for yourself what is going on. Hearing no reply to his question, the man turned toward the bow of the boat, his eyes wide in surprise at two figures in black holding submachine pistols aimed at him. His surprise was short-lived, however, as, before he could raise his pistol to fire, he was hit in the chest by four rounds, two from Sturm and two more from Sullivan, each firing his weapon in semi-automatic mode.

The man cried out and slumped to the deck, the pistol dropping from his lifeless fingers. While the silenced weapons had made little sound, another gray-suited man, this one large and bald, appeared in the door with a *Luger* in his right hand, the same question on his lips.

"*Was ist los?*"

The same result obtained as four more rounds hit the man in his chest, knocking him off his feet and back into the room. Sturm looked at Sullivan just as Cockran scaled the side of the ship and joined them. "I'll check the cabin for Mattie. You two lower the bodies into the runabout."

The two men nodded their agreement and picked up the nearest body and carried it to the side of the ship and began to lower it head first to Churchill. Sturm stepped over the body in the doorway to the passenger cabin.

"Mattie, are you here? It's Kurt," Sturm asked as his eyes took a quick inventory of the cabin. There were three closed doors off the common area. He opened each in turn, asking the same question. The first two were empty.

"Mattie, are you here?" Sturm asked again as he looked into the third room. Empty!

Had their intelligence been faulty? Where was Mattie?

Sturm left the cabin to look for Cockran and Sullivan who had just finished lowering the second body into the runabout.

"Mattie's not in the cabin!" he told the other two. "There's no one else in there."

MATTIE HEARD the telephone ring in the common area. She put her ear to the door to see if she could hear what was said.

There was silence for a good thirty seconds before she heard Kleist's voice say "But...but... we are *Gestapo*. We don't have to..." followed quickly by "Yes... yes, Sir."

"I've been summoned to the bridge to show the Captain our passports," she heard Kleist say. "I'll be right back."

What was that all about, Mattie wondered as she walked back to the bed to continue her efforts to open the window above the bed. Five minutes later, through sheer effort, she pulled it back on its side hinges and lifted it up. Right then, she heard the sharp crack of a pistol shot. What the bloody hell was that, she thought. Whatever it was, it might be sufficiently distracting to warrant another attempt to escape.

Mattie pulled back the blanket from her bed. Earlier, she had ripped the sheet below into two pieces, one twice as large as the other. She took the smaller piece and folded it lengthwise twice, giving it four layers of cotton. She wrapped it around her breasts and tied it in back, a homemade bandeau top. She took the larger piece and folded it once before wrapping it around her waist twice before tying it at her hip, a homemade sarong with the same four layers of cotton. Not the most modest outfit, she thought, but it was better than going out starkers. She stepped up on the bed and wriggled through the window onto the deck beside the cabin. Her room had looked out on the starboard side of the boat, which was up against the pier. To escape now that she was on the deck, she had to move around the bow to the portside and try once again to use the river as her route to freedom. She had heard the crew leave noisily after they docked so, this time at least, there would be no brawny sailors around to bring her back to the boat. If the *Gestapo* wanted her that badly, they'd just have to get wet right along with her. Mattie liked her odds. She was a strong swimmer and she wouldn't have her work boots to slow her down.

After Mattie hit the deck, she paused, motionless, when she heard the voice of one of her *Gestapo* captors cry out from the portside of the passenger cabin "*Was ist los*?" She next heard the faint 'pffft' of a sound-suppressed weapon followed by the sound of a body falling to the deck. Then, more 'pffft' sounds and another body falling. What in bloody hell was going on?

"I'll check the cabin for Mattie. You two lower the bodies into the runabout."

Kurt von Sturm! Mattie was elated when she heard her former lover's voice. *That's* what was going on. She was being rescued! She heard his voice again through the open cabin window,

"Mattie, are you here? It's Kurt," but she resisted the urge to call out in reply. Instead, keeping low, she carefully inched her way along the deck to the front corner of the passenger cabin and peered around it. Damn! Two men with their backs to her were at the rail leaning over. Then, having completed whatever they were doing, they turned and she recognized them. Her husband and Bobby Sullivan! Sturm soon joined them. "Mattie's not in the cabin," he said. "There's no one else in there."

Mattie stood up and walked around the front of the passenger cabin to face them. "Of course not, you idiots! I'm out here about to attempt an escape for the second time."

All three men stared at her for a moment until Cockran broke the silence. "Interesting costume. Thinking of auditioning for the sequel to *Flying Down to Rio*?" he asked, referring to a 1933 motion picture musical set in South America.

"I am *not* in a good mood, Cockran, and I suggest you save the humor for later. I tried to escape once in Amsterdam by diving into the Rhine and, to deter me from trying to do so again, they stripped me of all my clothes. This is the best I could do on short notice. Let's find my clothes and camera bag and get the hell out of here."

Cockran looked at his watch. "We have five minutes to get clear of the ship. I'll help Mattie. You two keep a lookout for the other *Gestapo* guy back in the wheelhouse."

Three minutes later, a newly clothed Mattie lowered herself on the rope into the runabout and, to her surprise, the arms of her godfather. "Winston! What are you doing here?"

"Later, my Dear. For now, let's just say they needed a master mariner to pilot this craft."

Moments later, the other three were on board, Cockran beside Mattie in the front cockpit and Sturm and Sullivan in the rear cockpit along with the two bodies. Churchill, having detached the runabout from the commercial ship's anchor, quietly eased the boat away, keeping the throttle low.

"Thirty seconds to go," Cockran said, "head toward the far shore and then down river."

A hundred yards from the freighter, Churchill opened the throttle and the runabout leaped forward. Mattie looked at the speedometer and saw the arrow quickly move past 30 miles per hour. She turned to look into the rear cockpit and saw Cockran, Sturm and Sullivan tying metal weights to the ankles of the bodies of her two *Gestapo* guards.

Good riddance, Mattie thought, briefly recalling the pleasure they had taken yesterday in stripping her of her wet clothes. Five minutes later, they had left the lights of Duisberg behind and the riverbanks on both sides were in total darkness, the light of the moon covered by clouds.

"Winston, slow down," Cockran said, "so that we can dump the bodies."

Churchill throttled back and the runabout came to a halt in the middle of the river where Mattie watched Sturm and Sullivan lift both bodies over the side and into the water where, helped by the weights, they quickly disappeared.

"The Rhine is only 14 feet deep in the middle," Cockran said, "but we tied 150 pounds of weights to each man and stripped them of all ID. Eventually, they may rise to the surface and float downstream to the ocean, but we should all be long gone by then."

"How did you learn I had been kidnapped by the *Gestapo* and be on board that freighter tonight?" Mattie asked.

Cockran grinned. "Two members of the Nazi Party's official Mattie McGary Admiration and Appreciation Society."

"Watch it, Cockran. I'm still in a bad mood. I have my notes and the transcript of the commission's June 5 hearing, but I couldn't find my passport."

"Inconvenient, but you can always go to the British Embassy in Amsterdam and get a temporary one issued. As for how we found where you were, I'm serious. Göring has wiretaps on someone named Freisler and Sturm and Schellenberg are both on the recipient list for the Freisler wiretap transcripts. The ones from early Sunday morning contained a phone call to him from some *Gestapo* guy named Kleist who told him you had been nabbed. He also told Freisler where you were being held and how they were going to bring you back into Germany without going through Customs or Border guards. Schellenberg told me and Sturm told Winston. *Herr* Schellenberg flew us all to Duisberg from Amsterdam this morning in Heydrich's *Fokker* where we had all day to plan your rescue. Once we drop this hired boat off, we'll meet Schellenberg at the Duisberg aerodrome where he'll fly us all back to Amsterdam. Once there, we can regroup and decide what you want to do next on this story."

"Oh, I know what I'm doing next. I'll tell you all about it once we're on our way to Amsterdam.

WALTER SCHELLENBERG smiled as, holding four passports in his hand, he followed Kleist and Captain Preuss up the deck to the bow of the ship and the passenger cabin whose door was open. *SS-Obersturmfuhrers* Franz Globke and Eric Bulow were right behind him. In the distance, he heard the faint sound of a motor growing ever more faint. All three men entered the cabin, but no one was there. Kleist seemed genuinely confused as he opened the doors to the three bedrooms and the WC. "I...I don't understand. I left her here with my two men. I can't imagine where they all went."

'Well, I can, you incompetent moron! Your men obviously helped a Jewess escape! They're probably on their way to Switzerland as we speak! I'll notify the Border police to be on the lookout for two incompetent *Gestapo* thugs and a red-haired Jewess. Meanwhile, I'm confiscating all your passports," Schellemberg said, making an elaborate show of stuffing them into his pocket. "If you're really a *Gestapo* agent and want your passport back, you can come to SD headquarters in Berlin with a letter from this Freisler or even Himmler himself to back up your story."

Schellenberg turned to leave and then stopped, looking over his shoulder directly at Kleist. "You know, I'm starting to believe you did have a mission from Himmler to recover a transcript of a meeting from a British journalist who you were to arrest and bring to the *Oranienburg* concentration camp."

Kleist looked relieved. "Thank you, *Sturmbannfuhrer.*"

"Do you know why?"

"Uh, well...that is, uh, I'm not exactly certain..."

"It's because only knuckle-dragging *Gestapo* goons like you would be so incompetent as to successfully secure the transcript and the British journalist only to lose them both once you were back in Germany. We have a saying in the SD every time the *Gestapo* makes mistakes. 'MAFI', we say, 'simply more MAFI'. Know what that means?"

Kleist shook his head to signal 'no'.

"*Machen arbeit fur idioten*—Make work for Morons."

Captain Preuss gave a short barking laugh. Globke and Bulow did the same.

Not bad, Schellenberg thought. Actually the SD didn't have that saying, but once he returned to Berlin, he would make sure they did.

45.

Tempting Fate?

En route to Amsterdam
Tuesday 18 September 1934

THE SUN HAD just risen when Reinhard Heydrich's *Fokker* Trimotor FV II took off from the Duisberg airfield on its way to the *Schiphol* aerodrome in Amsterdam. The passenger cabin of the *Fokker* contained six wicker armchairs in two seating groups, three in the front of the cabin, three in the rear corner. Two of the chairs in each grouping faced a single chair for ease of conversation. Cockran and Sturm sat in the two chairs in the front grouping with Mattie facing them in the single chair. Sullivan sat in one of the two chairs in the rear grouping within easy earshot of the others. Schellenberg's two men were in the remaining two seats. Schellenberg himself was flying the plane from the left hand seat in the pilot's cabin and Churchill sat in the right co-pilot's seat.

"Once we're back in our hotel suite in Amsterdam," Mattie said in English so that the two SD men behind them would be privy only to what she wanted them to know, "I'll take two photographs of each page of the transcript. Winston will take the film back to England to be developed. He'll send one set of photos to Joe Willicomb in New York and save the second set for me. It won't take more than a few hours to accomplish that and then we'll fly to Berlin with Schellenberg and his men."

"Is that wise?" Cockran asked, "I mean going back to Germany. Will you be safe there?"

"Reasonably so," Mattie replied. "What do you think, Kurt?"

"I agree. These two," Sturm said, nodding at the two SD men behind him, "seem to have done a competent job so far at looking out for your welfare. Still, I wouldn't press your luck. How long do you plan to stay in Germany?"

"Not long. I need to have Hanna Raeder and Werner Kramer validate the accuracy of the transcript. That plus one more interview if you can arrange it. Then, I'll go back to Ireland and write the story."

"What interview?" Cockran asked.

"I'd like Kurt, in his capacity as the *Reichstag* liaison to the German Commission on Criminal Law Reform, to arrange an interview with the its Chairman, Roland Freisler."

"What the hell!" Cockran exclaimed. "You want to interview the guy who had you kidnapped in Amsterdam and wants to put you in a concentration camp? Are you daft, woman?"

"I agree with your husband," Sturm said. "The SD may be able to look after your safety in Berlin, but don't you think an interview with Freisler is tempting fate?"

Mattie just smiled. Tempting fate was second nature to her. Not to mention ignoring warnings from the overly concerned men in her life. After reading the transcript of the June 5 meeting, she knew that Freisler was going to be the villain of her story. So, like she had done with Ernst Liebold—the villain of her story about the optics for rubber deal between Imperial German and Great Britain during the Great War—she wanted to hear Freisler's side of the story

"C'mon guys," Mattie said with a grin, "I'll take Schellenberg's two SD bodyguards with me to the interview. I'll be fine. The real question," she said to Sturm, "is whether *Unser* Hermann will be willing to strong arm Freisler into agreeing to do the interview. Do you think he will?"

"Yes, I do."

"Excellent," Mattie said.

46

Accidents Can Happen

RVD International Office
Shell-Haus
Berlin
Tuesday 18 September 1934

HAROLD CANFIELD was furious as he sat across from Rupert Rutledge in the RVD offices in Berlin. The RVD suite was on the tenth floor of the new German offices of Shell Oil in a modernistic building of undulating curves completed in 1932. The building was in the *Tiergarten* District and Canfield could see the green expanse of the park, the morning sun shining bright in the window behind Rutledge's desk.

"What kind of amateur hour are you running here in Berlin?" Canfield asked. "You had two operatives killed in Berlin last week and two more killed in Amsterdam over the weekend."

"The two guys who bought the farm in Berlin deserved it," Rutledge replied. He was a tall man with slicked-back black hair and a pencil thin mustache that he probably thought made him look like the actor Ronald Coleman. Ex-ONI, Canfield had personally selected him to head the Berlin RVD office. "Typical ex-MID agents Van Deman hired before you came on board. They thought raping the McGary woman was the same as roughing her up. We don't need guys that dumb."

"I agree. What happened with our guys in Amsterdam?"

Rutledge threw up his hands. "I have no idea. Your guess is as good as mine. They were both ex-ONI. I gave them your assignment to take the woman out at their earliest opportunity. The next thing I know, I receive a call from the police in Amsterdam that two of our men were found floating face down in a canal with their throats cut. I already borrowed two agents from our Paris office after those two ex-Army idiots were killed. Once I heard about Amsterdam, I arranged for two men from our Prague office to be assigned here. They should arrive later today. I do have further information, however, about what happened to McGary in Amsterdam."

Canfield made an impatient 'out with it' gesture with his hands and Rutledge continued.

"As you know, I have a confidential source, code name 'Otto', in the *Gestapo*. He told me this morning the rumors there are that McGary is under the protection of Heydrich's SD, but no one in the *Gestapo* knows why. What he does know is that Himmler put Josef Kleist of the *Gestapo* under the control of this Roland Freisler, the Chairman of the German Commission on Criminal Law Reform, but it was Himmler himself who ordered Kleist to kidnap McGary and bring her back to one of the concentration camps in Germany. Kleist told Otto that he successfully kidnapped McGary in Amsterdam late Saturday night or early Sunday morning. He and two other *Gestapo* agents were taking her to Germany on a Rhine River freighter. At its first port of call in Germany, according to Kleist, she somehow escaped and the other two *Gestapo* agents are missing."

This was helpful, Canfield thought. Apparently, he and Himmler had a common interest when it came to McGary. "Did Kleist tell Otto why Himmler wanted her kidnapped?"

"No, but he told me something else that was curious," Rutledge said. "Himmler apparently told Kleist that McGary was not to be harmed in any way, only brought to a camp."

"Did he say why?"

"Yeah, Himmler said that Hitler likes her. *Der Fuhrer* told Himmler she's the only foreign journalist who ever asks him intelligent questions. Himmler thinks Hitler would be quite upset if something happened to her. He figures he can explain her detention in a concentration camp as a bureaucratic mix-up which he promptly corrected once he learned of it."

"I need to see this Himmler guy," Canfield said. "We need to pool our resources. Call your secretary in. Tell her to bring her steno pad."

An attractive blonde woman in her mid 20s gave a quick nod after entering the room and sat down.

Canfield began to speak in fluent German. "Take a letter on plain paper to *Reichsfuhrer-SS* Heinrich Himmler at *8 Prinz Albrechtstrasse*: '*Herr Reichsfuhrer,* I am an American intelligence officer who delivered the Prussian Memorandum to *SS Obersturmfuhrer* Wilhelm Krueger at the German Embassy in the United States in September 1933. I believe our countries share a common interest in seeing that no newspaper articles are published on this subject. May I have twenty minutes of your time this afternoon to discuss how, by working together, this can best be accomplished? I can be reached at the telephone number below. Thank you.' Got all that?" Canfield asked the secretary.

"*Ja,*" she replied.

"Good. Then close with 'With My Deepest Respect' along with my full name 'Harold Hudson Canfield, III' and the unlisted number for *Herr* Rutledge's private telephone. Address a plain envelope to Himmler and, in large capital letters, 'PERSONAL & CONFIDENTIAL'."

Ten minutes later, the secretary returned with the letter and envelope. Both were perfect. Taking a solid Mont Blanc fountain pen from inside his suit coat, Canfield signed the letter with a flourish. "Have this delivered immediately by messenger."

"Have you given your private number to anyone in Germany?" Canfield asked after the secretary had left.

Rutledge shook his head. "No."

"Okay then," Canfield said, "now we wait. Have some coffee and sweet rolls sent up."

With that, he put his feet up on the front of Rutledge's desk, picked up that day's edition of the *Paris Herald Tribune* and began to read. Two hours later, the phone on Rutledge's desk rang.

"I'll get it," Canfield said as he rose and picked up the receiver. "Yes?"

"Mr. Canfield?"

"Speaking."

"The *Reichsfuhrer-SS* will see you at precisely 4:40 this afternoon for the twenty minutes you requested."

Before Canfield could say a word, the other party hung up.

Office of the Reichsfuhrer-SS
8 Prinz-Albrecht Strasse
Berlin
Tuesday, 18 September 1934

HEINRICH HIMMLER did not impress Canfield even though the sheer size of his large office and its massive desk were designed to awe visitors. The little man behind the desk with a receding chin and *pince-nez* glasses looked like a country schoolmaster, albeit with the eyes of a stone-cold killer. Canfield was pleased, therefore, that he had worked out beforehand precisely how he was going to treat Himmler—like the ruthless gangster he no doubt was. Anyone at the top of an organization like the SS who could have his hit squads eliminate over 200 of Hitler's enemies in one night was a man deserving of respect. Canfield doubted whether Owney Madden or even Al Capone in his heyday could have pulled off something like that. Hell, Capone only got seven in the St. Valentine's Day Massacre.

Harry wasn't going to beat around the bush. "Thank you for seeing me on such short notice, *Herr Reichsfuhrer*. You are a busy man so I will get right to the point. I am a former naval intelligence officer and I'm now employed by a private intelligence agency owned by retired General Ralph Van Deman who founded the U.S. Army's Military Intelligence Division in 1918. We have been engaged by MID at the direction of the highest levels in the American government to see that

MID's role in creating the Prussian Memorandum is never made public. I have been given a free hand to accomplish this. To that end, I arranged for the deaths of the six American lawyers, all former MID agents, who conducted the legal research that went into the Prussian Memorandum. A Hearst journalist named McGary somehow acquired a copy of the Memorandum and is working on a story about it. I sent a team to Amsterdam over the weekend to kill her, but they failed. I seek the assistance of your organization in helping us to accomplish this."

Himmler's cold dark eyes stared at him for a long beat and Harry was chillingly reminded of the 200 dead men. "Why does your government want to keep MID's assistance in this matter confidential?" Himmler asked.

Canfield hesitated. Himmler's stare was disconcerting. Should he reveal the real reason? What the hell, he thought, he had to answer the question if he wanted Himmler to help and, frankly, he didn't have a persuasive lie to tell him. "We have elections for our national legislature in November and we have a presidential election in 1936. Both the Negro vote and the Jewish vote are very important to the Democratic Party that controls both Houses of Congress as well as the Presidency. That control might be jeopardized if the Negroes and Jews don't support the Party and the President as strongly as they did in 1932."

"What would you have me do? And why should I do it?" Himmler asked.

"Let me answer your second question first as I already told this to your man Krueger in Washington. The fact is the leak of the memorandum came from some big mouth on that Commission on Criminal Law Reform. I told Krueger that if this story about MID involvement with the memorandum ever appears in the press, the Roosevelt Administration is not only going to deny it, they will announce their support for the Jewish boycott of German exports."

"Really? This is the first I've heard of this." Himmler said.

"That's strange. Krueger told me he would pass the message to his immediate superior, some guy named Schellenberg." Canfield said, the same bastard who roughed him up and warned him off McGary in Bremerhaven. He wondered briefly if he should mention this to

Himmler and decided against it. If Himmler didn't know this, it had to be because Schellenberg didn't pass it on. A complete report would have referenced the need to kill McGary, and Krueger wasn't high enough up the food chain to do that himself. Canfield didn't know anything about the internal politics of the SS, however, so he saw no upside in telling this to Himmler.

Himmler didn't blink an eye and said nothing. Canfield said nothing either. Finally, Himmler broke the silence. "What would you have me do?"

"Well, as I told Krueger, first, find out where the damn leak came from and plug it. Permanently. Second, and more important, kill the story by killing the journalist. As Stalin once said 'Death solves all problems. No man, no problem'. Or, in this case, no woman, no problem."

"Just so," Himmler replied, "it's true that we have a common interest in keeping the Prussian Memorandum confidential. At least for now, but the SS can have no hand in or appear to have any hand in the death of this woman."

"Why?"

"It's complicated. Our plan is to take her and keep her anonymously in one of our camps until she no longer poses a threat. We thought we had done so successfully in Amsterdam, but somehow she escaped. As for killing her? No. *Der Fuhrer* would not be pleased to learn the SS was involved in any way with her death."

"Why, exactly?"

"Hitler has a weakness. He is easily charmed by beautiful women. He likes to flirt with them and they with him. The McGary woman is different. He enjoys sparring with her precisely because she doesn't flirt back with him. She challenges him and he likes being challenged. He knows she opposes the Nazis, but all her stories about him and us are factual and do not contain anti-Nazi speculation or innuendo. It's why he gave her an exclusive interview on our suppression of the second revolution by Rohm and the SA on 30 June."

"What if her death appeared to be an accident?"

Himmler paused, his dead eyes flickering for just a moment before answering. "Well, I suppose accidents can happen."

HEINRICH HIMMLER smiled inwardly as he watched the American carefully. This was almost too good to be true. If the Americans killed her and they were caught doing so, the SS would be in the clear with Hitler. If the Americans tried to kill her and failed, the *Gestapo* would still have a chance to put her in a camp.

Himmler pulled open a drawer in his desk and took out a sheet of heavy bond stationery. He reached over to a pen in an inkwell on the desk and began to write.

Kleist,

You and Freisler are to assist this man. We have overlapping, if not common, interests.

H.

Himmler folded the sheet of paper in half and slid it across his desk to Canfield who picked it up, opened it and began to read.

"See this man," Himmler said once Canfield looked up from the note. "His office is two floors down, Room 304. Give him this note. McGary escaped from our custody last night and has returned to Berlin. She's at the *Adlon*. We have her under surveillance and we have activated a recording device we placed earlier in her suite. Kleist will supply you with anything we learn about her. The rest is up to you."

After Canfield left, Himmler pressed the intercom button. "Gertrude, be so kind as to connect me again to *Herr Doktor* Goebbels at the Propaganda Ministry." The telephone on his desk rang and he picked up the receiver. "Himmler, here."

"Goebbels here. Two calls in a week. I am honored again. What can I do for you today?"

You can give me cover and be a scapegoat with the *Fuhrer,* Himmler thought, in the event something went wrong with the American's attempt to kill McGary. "I have just met with an American intelligence officer who has the same interest we do in suppressing any report about the Prussian Memorandum. I would welcome your advice on how to proceed with him," Himmler said and then told Goebbels everything he had learned from Canfield, everything except the fact that he already had ordered Kleist to assist the American.

Fifteen minutes later, Goebbels had advised him to have Kleist get together with the American and assist him in effecting the 'accident' resulting in McGary's death.

"Thank you Joseph. As always, your advice is original and creative, far beyond what a poor policeman like me could conceive," Himmler said and placed the receiver back in its cradle.

Himmler wondered if he should have sacked Kleist after he inexplicably lost not only the McGary woman, but also two fine Gestapo agents. Well, this was Kleist's last chance. If he botched this, he would lose more than a job. His freedom? Certainly. His life? Quite possibly.

Part IV

Germany
18 September—21 September 1934

The racially pure and still unmixed German has risen to become master of the American continent and he will remain master as long as he does not fall victim to racial pollution.

Adolf Hitler, *Mein Kampf*

The United States of the new world have come to understand the monstrous danger of the 'great melting pot of races' over the course of the last decade, and put a check on bastardization through draconian immigration law. To these circles of tribally related Americans, we reach out our hand in friendship.

National Socialist Monthly
November 1933

47

You Bald Little Worm!

Official Residence of the President of the Reichstag
Berlin
Tuesday, 18 September 1934

STURM PAUSED in his recounting of last night's events to Hermann Göring and took a sip of The Singleton 12-year-old single malt Scotch whisky in a crystal tumbler on the small table between the two maroon leather club chairs where and he and the *Reichspresident* sat in the book-lined library of the Official Residence. Göring's own crystal glass of Scotch, a bowl of ice and the bottle of whisky were also on the table.

By this point in Sturm's story, he and Sullivan were about to board the ship armed with the Schmeiser submachine pistols that Göring had so helpfully supplied the day before. He knew this would be the part that the *Reichspresident* would enjoy the most for, at heart, he was a romantic and ruthless pirate himself. Sturm had spared no detail up to this point other than the presence of Churchill at the helm of their runabout, allowing Göring to assume, as he had, that the helmsman was another of Sullivan's 'Irish mercenaries'.

"Grappling hooks? You used grappling hooks?" Göring asked, drained his glass and poured himself two more fingers of whisky.

"We did."

"Go on, go on. Just like pirates! Don't keep me in suspense. What next?"

"Once Sullivan and I hit the deck, we were confronted by two of the *Gestapo* agents who had kidnapped McGary. They each held Lugers so we shot them both. With our *Schmeissers* set on semi-automatic, Sullivan and I put four rounds into each agent's chest. Cockran and Sullivan then took the bodies and dumped them into our runabout while I went to look for McGary."

Sturm smiled inwardly at the old fighter pilot's reaction to his description of Mattie's *dishabille* when he found her.

"What? Only wearing a torn sheet? Those *Gestapo* bastards stripped her naked?"

"Yes, as a punishment. When they were transferring her from the houseboat to the freighter, she attempted to escape by diving into the Rhine. When some sailors from the freighter captured her, Kleist had her stripped of her wet clothes and locked in a cabin with nothing but a blanket for warmth. She was wearing the torn sheet because, once she heard Schellenberg's warning shot, she was going to make another attempt to escape and didn't want to be completely naked."

Göring shook his head in admiration. "That McGary is one hell of a brave woman. You know I commandeered her Mercedes convertible during the Munich *Putsch* in '23. I mounted a machine gun on it and the gutsy broad insisted on staying with it so she could take photographs of our march. The *verdammt* state police shot out her motorcar's windscreen and riddled the coachwork with bullets but she got several photographs right when the shooting began. Incredible that she wasn't hit."

Actually, Sturm did know that. Mattie herself had told him about it during their time together in the Austrian Alps in 1931. "So, after that," Sturm continued, "we located her clothes and left in the runabout. All told, we were on the freighter for less than ten minutes. We tied weights to the feet of the two *Gestapo* bodies, stripped them of all identification and dumped them into the Rhine. It will be many weeks at least, if at all, before the bodies are discovered. At dawn, Schellenberg flew us back to Amsterdam so McGary could take photos of the June 5 transcript and mail the film to her editor in New York.

Then Schellenberg flew us all back to Berlin in Heydrich's private plane and assigned two of his SD men to serve as her bodyguards to deter any more kidnappings."

"Good for Schellenberg. Nice to know he's not a complete toady to Himmler and Heydrich. So, will McGary be doing a story about what that idiot Freisler is trying to do with the Commission about the Jews?"

"Oh yes, but in that regard, she has a favor that she asked me to put to you."

Göring made an 'out with it' gesture with his hands and Sturm continued. "She would like you to pressure Freisler into giving her an interview."

Göring roared with laughter, downed his drink and poured each of them another. "By God, that woman has the courage of a lion! That bastard Freisler has her kidnaped; his agents strip her naked; and she wants to interview him!" Göring said and shook his head again in admiration. "No wonder Hitler likes her. She's just like that pilot Hanna Reitsch, the filmmaker Leni Riefenstahl or the architect Gerdy Troost. They're all bold, beautiful risk-taking women. I've watched them all stand up to Hitler in ways that he would never tolerate from a man."

"So, you'll talk to Freisler about an interview?" Sturm asked.

"Of course! When would she like to do it?"

"If possible, she would prefer to do it tomorrow."

"Done! Wilhelm, attend to me!" Göring bellowed.

Moments later, a harried blond young man in his twenties wearing a dark suit and tie rushed into the library. "Yes, *Reichspresident?*"

"Get that bald-headed worm Freisler at the Ministry of Justice on the telephone for me."

"At once *Reichspresident*," Wilhelm said and scurried out.

Ten minutes later, Wilhelm returned. He picked up a telephone receiver with five buttons, one of them flashing, from a side table. The telephone cord attached to the receiver was exceptionally long and easily reached to Göring's chair as Wilhelm walked it over and placed it on the table between the two chairs.

"Herr Freisler is on line two, *Reichspresident.*"

Göring picked up the receiver in a large hand and stabbed the button flashing light with a thick finger. "Freisler? Göring here. The Hearst reporter McGary will be at your office at 1:30 tomorrow afternoon. You will give her an interview."

Göring was silent for a moment as he listened to Freisler's reply, but Sturm couldn't make out what was being said.

It didn't matter because Göring soon loudly cut him off. "I don't give a flying fuck how busy your schedule is in the afternoon. Change it! After your *Gestapo* goons kidnapped her in Amsterdam, it's the least you can do. And don't try any more funny business with her. She'll have her own bodyguards."

Again, Göring went silent as he listened to Freisler. Once more, he exploded. "Listen to me, you bald little worm! I don't give a rat's ass for what you think. You will do as you are told! You will not enjoy the consequences otherwise. Don't think for a moment that your patron Himmler will be able to save you."

With that, Göring slammed the receiver into the cradle of the telephone and looked over at Sturm with a grin. "I thought that went rather well, don't you?"

Sturm grinned back. "Yes, it did, Sir. I will advise *Frau* McGary."

"Tell me, Sturm," Goring said with a twinkle in his eye, "I know you slept with her three years ago, how was she in bed? A real tigress, I'd bet."

Damn! Sturm thought. How did *Unser* Hermann learn about *that*? He knew a report of their brief affair in the Austrian Alps in 1931 was contained in her SS file because Mattie told him about it last year. That blond beast Heydrich had showed her a copy of her SS file when he had been attempting to blackmail her into poisoning Hitler. Did Göring have access to SS files?

Sturm smiled. "As a fellow officer and gentleman, you know answering a question like that about any woman would not be honorable." It would be especially dishonorable, Sturm thought— notwithstanding he loved another woman to whom he was unofficially engaged—if he still loved Mattie McGary. Which he very much did.

Göring laughed. "Well said, but that's the difference between us fighter pilots and you zeppelin flyers. Our code of honor doesn't extend to nookie unless it's another fighter pilot's wife," he replied and then paused with a grin. "And I'd still bet she was."

Well, *Unser* Hermann, Sturm thought as he took his leave, you would have won your bet.

> *The Hotel Adlon*
> *Berlin*
> *Tuesday 18 September 1934*

WHEN MATTIE and Cockran stopped at the front desk to pick up the key to their suite, she was surprised to find she had mail, an envelope postmarked 'Berlin' addressed in feminine handwriting to '*Frau* Martha McGary, Hotel Adlon, Berlin'. There was no return address.

Once in their suite that overlooked the Brandenburg Gate and *Unter den Linden*, Cockran ordered a bucket of ice and, after it arrived, began to make martinis while Mattie read the letter.

Dear Frau McGary,

A fellow member of the German Commission on Criminal Law Reform, Werner Kramer, has been murdered and a threat was made on my life for allowing you to interview me. I have gone into hiding until my husband, who is presently at sea, returns. He will know where I am, but I have told no one else. Notwithstanding the threat, I remain willing to review the transcript of the 5 June 1934 meeting of the Commission once you have it.

Please call Greta Mayer when you are ready for me to review the transcript. I call her periodically and she will pass on to you my instructions on the time and location for our meeting.

Sincerely,
Hanna Hindermann Raeder

"Look at this," Mattie said as Cockran handed her a martini and she passed the letter up to him. "One of my two sources was killed. The other received a death threat and went into hiding."

Cockran took the letter, read it and shook his head. "Well, now there are two more reasons why you're crazy to interview Freisler."

"Don't start, Cockran, not if you want to get lucky tonight. If Kurt can arrange the interview, I'm going to do it. After that, I'll call Greta and arrange to see Hanna again. Then we leave town and go back to Ireland where I can begin writing my story. And, speaking of Ireland, now that my story is wrapping up and you don't have pressing business back in America, why don't we revert to our original plan and bring Paddy back to Ireland? He's only missed the first few weeks of the fall semester. He's a bright boy; I'm sure he could catch up on his studies in no time."

"It's a good idea," Cockran replied, "but I'm not sure I'm comfortable with him travelling alone on a ocean liner. He's only 14-years-old."

"Come on, Cockran! The boy is almost as tall as you. Besides, Sturm will be flying the *Graf Bismarck* to America later this month. If Paddy takes that, he won't be alone. Or you could always ask his grandmother to accompany him, but he'd really love to fly here.

"Okay, the zeppelin makes sense, but you need to wrap things up here in Germany first before I book a ticket or let Patrick know. And now, I believe you mentioned something about my 'getting lucky' tonight?"

Mattie laughed. "Let's finish our martinis first, Sailor. Then we'll see."

48

Hiddensee Island

Hiddensee Island, Germany
Wednesday 19 September 1934

HANNA RAEDER looked out at the overcast sky from her small cottage on the Baltic Sea and wished that she wasn't alone. The weather had been this way ever since she had arrived on the island by the last ferry from the mainland on Sunday. It suited her mood. It was hard being in this special cottage alone because she and Erich had spent their honeymoon here in 1920. He was still at sea and she hoped he would join her here when he returned. She had sent a letter to him on Saturday before she left, in an envelope addressed in her own hand and labeled "Personal & Confidential" so that none of his adjutants would dare to open it. Even so, she was cryptic in the message and didn't have to name her location. As a consequence, no one but her husband knew where she was hiding out from what she assumed was the *Gestapo*. And, as he was at sea for another three weeks, he wouldn't know until he returned and read her letter.

Hiddensee Island was almost the perfect refuge. By mid-September, all the summer people had left and there had been no problem leasing their honeymoon cottage for a few weeks using her maiden name. A barrier island on the Baltic Sea, it was approximately ten miles long and two miles wide at its broadest point and only 270 yards at its most narrow. Accessible only by ferry, no automobiles were permitted on the island. Transportation was limited to a few public buses

Hanna thought she would be safe from the *Gestapo* when Erich returned. She would tell him everything. Except for wanting a narrow definition of who was a Jew, she did not think that he would otherwise care what the radical Nazis planned to do to the Jews. He had never expressed in her presence any dislike for Jews, but he had always said that the military should not involve themselves in domestic matters. Still, he respected her past as a criminal defense lawyer and agreed the changes the Nazis had already made to the German criminal law code were terrifying. Worse, there was more to come. That idiot Freisler's creation of a so-called 'People's Court' was nothing more than a Star Chamber where even an accused's choice of counsel could be vetoed by the President of the court for any reason.

Hanna looked at her watch. Almost nine a.m. Time to catch the bus and then the ferry to the mainland where she would place a call to Greta. She had been doing this for the past two days, calling Greta from different telephone exchanges to see if the journalist McGary was ready to have her verify the June 5 transcript.

Central Telephone Exchange
Stralsund, Germany
Wednesday 19 September 1934

"GRETA? IT'S Hanna. Any word from *Frau* McGary?"

"Yes! She called me last night!" Greta Mayer said. "If you can believe it, she has an interview today with Roland Freisler! She said she could meet you anywhere tomorrow or any day after that which is convenient for you. So, where are you staying so I can give her directions?"

"We've been through this before Greta. No one except my husband knows where I am and it's going to stay that way until he's back from his sea trials. I assume the *Gestapo* learned that I gave an interview to *Frau* McGary by having me followed to her hotel. It's probable that they will follow her and I don't want her to lead them to my refuge."

"But I won't tell anyone except *Frau* McGary. You can trust me," Greta protested.

"I do trust you, but no one can know where I am, neither you nor *Frau* McGary."

"Okay...I guess. So what do I tell her?"

"Say that I will meet her tomorrow at 1:30 p.m. at the New Market Square in Rostok. Tell her to take extra precautions not to be followed. This is important. She is to buy a small flowering plant at one of the market stalls and place it at her table under one of the several restaurants' umbrellas, yellow flowers if she's positive she hasn't been followed, red if she believes she might have been followed. If it's yellow and I don't think she's been followed, I will join her at her table within 30 minutes. If it's red or I don't join her within 30 minutes, she should check into the nearby Hotel *Am Hopfenmarkt* after 2 p.m. I will have left her instructions for a new meeting place and a new time for Friday. Do you have all that?"

"Yes, I do."

"Good, now repeat it back to me."

Greta did and Hanna breathed a sigh of relief when she got it all right. "Thanks, Greta, I appreciate all you're doing."

Hiddensee Island, Germany
Wednesday 19 September 1934

ONCE OFF the ferry and back on the island, Hanna decided to walk back to her cottage rather than take the bus. She needed time to clear her head and review her reasons for risking her life by cooperating with Mattie McGary. She had agreed initially with Georg von Dohnanyi's request that she give the journalist an off-the-record interview because she wanted the Commission exposed and that was never going to happen in German newspapers. It was too bad that Dohnanyi used the Prussian Memorandum to attract the interest of McGary, but she understood why Nazi ill treatment of the Jews would be of great interest outside Germany.

Unfortunately, the fate of the Jews was already sealed. Only she, Werner Kramer, Franz Gurtner and Dohnonyi had opposed stripping Jews of their citizenship and banning marriage and sexual relations between the so-called 'Aryans' and Jews. And Kramer was dead. If the Nazi radicals had their way—one Jewish great grandparent out of eight was enough to make a person a Jew—then, rather than 500,000 German Jews, there could be millions who had otherwise been assimilated or converted to Christianity!

It was important to Hanna to spare as many people from this fate as possible. Still she hoped that McGary also included in her story all the other atrocious changes in German criminal law that the Commission had recommended or was planning to recommend. This hope was the reason she agreed to verify the June 5 transcript because McGary had made it clear that she could only use the transcript and quote from it if a member of the Commission who had been there for the entire session verified it.

Would her husband approve? She honestly didn't know. He was an 'Old School' officer of the Imperial German Navy whose rigid code of honor governed his conduct. True, he had approved the purge of the SA Brownshirts on the Night of the Long Knives, but the murders of former Chancellor von Schleicher, his wife and Gregor Strasser had appalled him and he hadn't been quiet about saying so. Where would protecting his wife's life fit within that code of honor?

49

Roland Freisler

Reich Ministry of Justice
Berlin
Wednesday, 19 September 1934

MATTIE McGARY sat opposite Roland Freisler, silently appraising the little man who had ordered her kidnapping in Amsterdam. He had a ferret-like face with a bald dome and he was not happy to see her. Too bloody bad, she thought. Actually, what he was even more unhappy to see were her bodyguards, *SS-Obersturmfuhrers* Eric Bulow and Franz Globke in all their blond-haired Aryan glory in jet black, silver trimmed uniforms, knee high polished black leather boots with matching black leather holsters for their Luger automatic pistols. They stood at parade rest, flanking the door inside Freisler's office.

"Thank you *Herr Doktor* Freisler," Mattie said with a smile, "for agreeing to see me on such short notice. I realize you have a very busy schedule." As if you had any choice, you bigoted little weasel, she added silently.

"I must protest, *Frau* McGary, at the presence of these...these..."

"Oh, you mean Eric and Franz," she said and turned her head to smile at both men. "*Reichspresident* Göring thought I needed bodyguards and I specifically requested Eric and Franz. They're tall and handsome and ever so brave. And I assure you that they are quite skilled at killing people who attempt to harm me, aren't you boys?"

Both Bulow and Globke beamed at the praise and each stood a little taller. "*Jawohl, Frau* McGary."

"So, *Herr Doktor* Freisler, they stay. Now, let's get down to business. Why did you have the SS approach the American Military Intelligence Division to conduct the legal research that resulted in the Prussian Memorandum?"

"I don't know what you're talking about," Freisler replied.

"Of course you do. SS *Obersturmfuhrer* Krueger at the German Embassy in America approached General Leonard Marlborough of American MID to conduct the research into the miscegenation laws of the various American states. MID provided six American lawyers, all ex-MID agents, to do the research under the supervision of Roscoe Pound, the dean of Harvard Law School. That research was then delivered at Pound's behest to *Obersturmfuhrer* Krueger who in turn forwarded it to you in Berlin where it became the Prussian Memorandum. I have a copy. Would you like to see it?"

Freisler made no reply but his eyes narrowed into hard little coals.

"No? Well then, answer my question. Why?"

"To see how Americans approached forbidding marriage and sex between whites and non-whites to see if it provided a model we could follow regarding Jews, Gyspies and others."

"And did it?"

"No. All the American laws treat Jews as whites. In Germany, we know better."

"Do you deny telling the Commission that 'American jurisprudence would suit us perfectly, with a single exception. Over there, they have in mind, practically speaking, only coloreds and half-coloreds, which includes mestizos and mulattoes; but the Jews, who are also of interest to us, are not reckoned among the coloreds'."

"That's my point. Jews aren't considered to be colored in the United States."

"Yes, but didn't you say to the Commission that it didn't matter?" Mattie asked.

"No."

"Really?" Mattie said and she reached into her camera bag and pulled out notes she had made from her copy of the transcript of the June 5 meeting of the Commission.

"Didn't you say at the June 5 meeting of the Commission that 'It seems to me doubtful that there would be any need for Germany to expressly mention the Jews alongside the coloreds. I believe that every judge would reckon the Jews among the coloreds, even though they look outwardly white, just as they do the Tatars who are not yellow. Therefore I am of the opinion that we can proceed with the same primitivity that is used by these American states. Such a procedure would be crude, but it would suffice'? "

"There was no June 5 meeting of the Commission," Freisler replied.

"Ignore *when* you said it. I'll come back to that. Answer my question. Is that your opinion?"

"Well...yes, I suppose it is."

"And that every German judge would consider Jews to be colored?"

"Every true German would. Of that I'm certain."

"How would you define who is a Jew?"

"Anyone with at least one great grandparent who was a Jew."

"Really? You'd go back four generations? One great grandparent out of eight?"

"Of course."

"It's my understanding that the Commission will recommend that all German Jews be stripped of their citizenship. Is that correct?"

"Yes."

"And the only real dispute among Commission members is how to define who is a Jew?"

"There is no consensus today, but I expect my views will eventually prevail."

"Are you aware that all six American lawyers who conducted the legal research for the Prussian Memorandum are dead? That they all died under questionable circumstances during a six-week period last November and December?"

"Uh...well, no I didn't know that," a clearly surprised Freisler replied.

Mattie believed him. In over a decade as a journalist, she had developed a keen sense of when sources were lying. The expression on his face gave him away. This was something he really hadn't known. That's almost all she needed, she thought, but it still puzzled her as to why the Germans wanted to do this to the Jews when, in less than two years, Jews already had been excluded or marginalized from almost all aspects of private and public life in Germany. All sorts of bigotry, including anti-Semitism, she put down to ignorance; to judge anyone as a member of one group or another rather than as an individual. So, the Nazis were bigots, yes, but why pile on now with laws like the Commission was considering? What the hell, she thought. Why not ask?

"One thing puzzles me, *Herr Doktor* Freisler, and I expect it puzzles a lot of people outside Germany. Since the Nazis took power at the end of January 1933, the Jews have been systematically excluded from all positions of influence or power in Germany they once held—from medicine and law to politics, banking and teaching. They're already *de facto* second-class citizens. Why pass laws that make them *de jure* second class citizens?"

"German blood and German honor. We want to make it illegal for Jews to pollute our Aryan blood by marriage or sexual relations. Today, it's perfectly legal for Jews to do this even though they are, as you say, '*de facto* second class citizens'. Tomorrow, it won't be. Tomorrow belongs to us, not the Jews. You Americans do the same thing to your coloreds."

Mattie just shook her head in disbelief. "I'm a Scot, not an American. We don't do that. Our civilization is more advanced. Up until the Nazis took over, I thought the Germans were also. My mistake. One last thing. Let's briefly go back to your denial that there was a meeting of the Commission on 5 June 1934. Was there really no meeting? Or rather there *was* a June 5 meeting where the Prussian Memorandum was the subject of a heated discussion, but there is no longer a transcript of that meeting because you destroyed it?"

"That's preposterous! Where did you hear that?"

"In Amsterdam, actually, from the *Gestapo* agents who said they kidnapped me at your direction and were going to take me to a concentration camp in Germany."

"That's an outrageous accusation for you to make. There are laws in Germany on defamation."

Mattie grinned and stood up. "It's not my accusation. I'm just repeating what two of the *Gestapo* agents told me. I didn't get their names, but the third agent, their leader, was named Josef Kleist. You can check with them," Mattie said, knowing full well that dead men like those two Gestapo agents would be telling no tales.

"Thank you again *Herr Doktor* Freisler for being so generous with your time today. I'll be sure to give a good report to *Reichspresident* Göring," Mattie said with a smile.

Just then, the telephone on Freisler's desk rang and he picked up the receiver. "Hello? Really? Excellent news. Tell me more," he said as he returned Mattie's smile.

The Hotel Adlon
Berlin
Wednesday, 19 September 1934

MATTIE RETURNED the telephone receiver to its cradle and, after picking up her martini, turned to face her husband. "That was Greta Mayer. I'm to meet Hanna Raeder tomorrow afternoon in the New Market Square in Rostok. I went through it earlier this year on my way to visit the Baron von Kuhlmans on Rugen Island. Hanna is nervous and she wants to be certain I wasn't followed before she'll meet with me."

Mattie then explained the elaborate precautions Hanna was having her take once she reached Rostok. "Those are good for when I arrive, but I have some ideas on what we can do before then. Rostok is approximately 145 miles from Berlin so it should take less than three hours to make it there. I think you and I should take my Mercedes and drive south for a good 30 minutes to see if we have anyone tailing us other than my two SD bodyguards. Once we're sure we have no tails, we'll head north to Rostok."

Mattie paused for a sip of her martini and continued. "Meanwhile, Bobby should head north to Rostok after we leave. He should wait for us in Wittstock, which is roughly 40% of the way to Rostok. It's where we switch from Route 24 to Route 19. I drove it earlier this year on my way to Rugen Island. After we pass him by, I'll cut our speed by maybe ten miles per hour. Bobby should wait another five minutes to see if any suspicious motorcar is following us. If no one is, he should catch up with us. If there is a motorcar following us, he should discourage it from doing so. I'll leave it up to Bobby as to how to best accomplish that. A Prussian state police badge from *Unser* Hermann possibly?"

"What about Sturm?" Cockran asked. Can he help?"

"No," Mattie replied. "He told Bobby he has to fly to Friedrichshafen tomorrow to supervise the *Graf Bismarck* being fitted out for its next voyage."

"Okay. When do we begin tomorrow? I'll need to let Bobby and Schellenberg know."

"Well, you can tell them eight a.m., but you," Mattie said, as she put down her martini glass, walked over to Cockran, sat on his lap, and put her arms around him, "can begin right now."

50

Your Source Is Reliable?

8 Prinz-Albrecht Strasse
Berlin
Wednesday 19 September 1934

CANFIELD RESENTED the expense of leasing a top of the line *Maybach Zeppelin* limousine for the day, but he could not think of a more secure place to meet—and impress—Kleist and Freisler with the importance of his staging an 'accident' that would end the life of Mattie McGary. And the *Mayback Zeppelin* was unquestionably an impressive motorcar. From its aerodynamic styling to its plush and spacious dark blue leather interior with a foldout burled walnut bar, it was exactly what Canfield needed to convey to these mid-level German functionaries that he was a man of substance. Of course, the note from Heinrich Himmler telling these two to assist him and, implicitly, do whatever he wanted conveyed much the same thing.

Canfield admitted to himself that he was paranoid about the widespread wiretapping going on in Nazi Germany, but just because he was paranoid didn't mean there weren't enemies out there trying to get him, Walter Schellenberg specifically. That meant meeting Kleist or Freisler in their government offices that potentially were bugged or wiretapped was out of the question. So was a meeting in Canfield's hotel room. Not only might it be bugged or wiretapped, but he would have had to send his wife Camila away. While she was a stunningly attractive woman with an incredibly beautiful body, she was far too indiscreet and inquisitive for her own good. He made a mental note. No more Camila on missions.

As the *Maybach* pulled up in front of *8 Prinz-Albrecht Strasse* to pick up Kleist before proceeding to the Ministry of Justice to pick up Freisler, he reflected that Himmler's note Tuesday had been most effective. Canfield had gone directly to Kleist's small office; showed him Himmler's note; and drew him from his office into the hallway away from any bugs. Then he explained the two pieces of information he needed Kleist to find for him. Once they had secured the information, Kleist was to call and leave a short message— 'We have it.' After that, Canfield would pick each of them up in a *Maybach Zeppelin* limousine in front of their respective government buildings in 30 and 35 minutes.

Canfield's driver, an ex-ONI agent, got out of the motorcar and opened the rear door for Kleist who entered and sat on the leather fold down bench seat across from Canfield who extended a hand to Kleist and they shook.

"Welcome, *Herr* Kleist. May I offer you a drink? Scotch, brandy, champagne?"

Kleist ordered brandy. After Canfield gave him a half-full crystal snifter, he spoke to his driver. "The Ministry of Justice, next, William. After that, you may raise the partition."

Five minutes later, the *Maybach* arrived at the Ministry of Justice where Freisler was waiting. William opened the rear door for him and Freisler entered and sat on the leather bench beside Kleist who introduced the men to each other. Freisler opted for Scotch as did Canfield whereupon the big motorcar smoothly pulled away into the Berlin traffic. Such was the soundproofing in the *Maybach,* however, that the interior was perfectly silent.

Canfield broke the silence. "When and where will McGary meet the Raeder woman?"

"Tomorrow at 1:30 p.m. in the New Market Square in Rostok," Freisler replied. "I reluctantly gave an interview to that odious bitch this morning upon orders from the President of the *Reichstag*. Our source telephoned me with the information just as McGary was leaving."

"Where is Rostok?" Canfield asked.

"Due north of Berlin on the Baltic Sea, approximately 150 miles or so."

"What routes?"

"Route 24 out of Berlin to Route 19 into Rostok."

"Okay, good work *Herr Doktor* Freisler. Your source is reliable?"

"Very much so."

"Excellent! *Herr* Kleist, what do you have for me?"

"I have talked with the people at *Sixt*, the major German automobile rental company, and they advise me that *Frau* McGary has hired a Mercedes 500K Cabriolet with a cream-colored body and caramel-colored fenders front and rear."

"What is its license number and where is it located?"

Kleist gave its number and the location as the *Adlon* Hotel's garage for its customers' motorcars.

"William!" Canfield said into the speaking tube at his right hand. "Return to central Berlin and take our guests to where we picked them up."

Canfield raised his crystal tumbler of Scotch. "Gentleman, to the success of our mission to eliminate the threat to both of our nations from the Scottish journalist Martha McGary!"

All three men touched their glasses together and downed their contents.

Canfield smiled. "Now, Gentlemen, I trust you have in place what we Americans call a 'Plan B' in the event that my plan does not succeed?"

"Oh, yes, *Mein Herr,*" Freisler responded enthusiastically. "If *Frau* McGary should somehow make it to Rostok, she will only leave in the custody of the *Gestapo* from which, Kleist assures me, she will not escape. Once we have her in *Konzentrationslager Oranienburg*, I intend to have her tried for espionage before The People's Court over which I will personally preside. Once the bitch is convicted, she will receive the death penalty."

354   *Michael McMenamin & Kathleen McMenamin*

Yeah, right, Fritz, Canfield thought. Why should it be any different from when your *Gestapo* screwed up the last time in Amsterdam? As for trying her for espionage and executing her? Well, apparently Freisler didn't receive the memo from Himmler that Hitler's favorite foreign journalist was untouchable. That was Freisler's problem, not his. Besides, he believed the chances for his 'Plan A' were pretty good because he intended to see to it personally.

After returning both men to their office buildings, Canfield lowered the partition between his driver and the passenger cabin. "William, find Route 24 North out of Berlin. I need to locate just the right spot. If I don't find it by the time we reach Route 19 North, take that. When we're back in Berlin, drop me off at the *Adlon*. I've got some business to attend to there. You take the *Maybach* back to *Sixt* and swap it for the Mercedes SSK I've hired for tomorrow."

With that, Canfield settled back into the soft leather of the *Maybach,* poured two more fingers of Scotch into his crystal tumbler, and took a sip. Not bad, he thought, and picked up the bottle. 'The Singleton". Hmm. He had never heard of it. No matter, it was damn good. So long as he found the right spot on Routes 24 or 19, the *Gestapo's* 'Plan B' would be stillborn. Damn, but that was really good Scotch, he thought, and picked up the bottle again to study it. Aged 16 years. That was worth remembering.

51

Sabotage

"YOU'RE RIGHT," Bourke Cockran said as his wife downshifted from 4th gear to 3rd and passed a slower moving *Horch* sedan, making it the 5th motorcar in the past half hour that had been going too slow for Mattie's taste. In his experience as a passenger in a vehicle driven by his wife, a motorcar passing her was a rare experience. "This is a beautiful convertible and it handles well. Would you like one for your birthday?" Cockran asked, referring to the Mercedes-Benz 500K Cabriolet that Mattie had hired upon her arrival in Germany.

"I can afford to buy my own motorcars, thank you very much," Mattie replied with a laugh. "With all Hearst pays me and how much he keeps me busy on my stories, I barely have a chance to spend money on anything."

It was a splendid, late summer day with a bright sun shining through puffy cumulus clouds dotting a vivid blue sky. Mattie wore a navy blue cotton turtleneck over tan trousers while Cockran was in his leather flying jacket and white buttondown shirt and khaki pants. The top was down on the Mercedes and they had been on the road for a little over an hour. Driving south with Mattie at the wheel, they had been satisfied after thirty minutes that no one was following them except Schellenberg's two men so they changed direction, returned to Berlin and picked up National Highway 24 North. They were now a few miles from Wittstock where they would switch to National Highway 19 North.

As they approached Wittstock, Cockran kept an eye out for Sullivan's dark blue Auto Union coupe. Soon, they passed an Esso filling station and Cockran saw Sullivan's motorcar at one of the pumps. A sleek, black 1932 'Black Prince' model Mercedes-Benz SSK roadster was at another pump, virtually an identical twin to Cockran's own 'Black Prince' model SSK that he had raced earlier in the year at one of the 'Collier Cup' automobile races on the Collier Estate in Westchester County. The SSK had teardrop shaped fenders on the front and rear wheels and a boat tail. With its slanted windscreen, snug-fitting black canvas top, and no running boards, the SSK looked fast standing still.

"We just passed Bobby," Cockran said. "He was at that Esso station along with a *doppelganger* for my own Black Beauty SSK."

"Really?" Mattie replied as she cut her speed from 75 to 65 miles-per-hour. "Maybe if he's going our way, we'll see if the SSK is as good as you say. My 500K is no slouch."

Ten minutes later and now on National Route 19, Cockran saw from his side view mirror that Sullivan's coupe had caught up with the Mercedes 190 sedan of Schellenberg's men. "Bobby's caught up with us. You can open her up again. Mattie did and the Mercedes 500K was soon cruising at 75 mph.

Five minutes after that, Cockran heard the unmistable roar of an SSK's supercharged single overhead camshaft 7-litre straight-6 engine. He turned in his seat and, in a flash, the black SSK went past them as if they were standing still. Since Mattie was doing 75 mph, the SSK must have been doing 95 or even 100 mph. Inasmuch as this was the first motorcar today to pass Mattie, he was not surprised when his wife floored the accelerator and took off in pursuit of the black SSK.

"Mattie, you're not going to catch him. It's the fastest motorcar in the world," Cockran said. "On the Collier's track, I red-lined mine at 120 mph. I don't think your 500K can match that." He looked over and saw that Mattie was approaching 100 mph as well as the red-line for RPMs. She was an excellent, albeit an extremely competitive, driver and Cockran was not about to point out what she by now already knew—100 mph was the 500K's limit.

The road had gentle curves with a series of lakes off to the right, down grassy slopes that dropped some 50 feet below the surface of the road to the water below. To the left was a forest that initially blocked the view of the road going into a left hand curve until you were already in it. Up ahead, Cockran saw a white triangle with a bright red border and a large black 'Z' inside that signaled a significant bend in the road ahead rather than a gentle curve. Calling Mattie's attention to an obvious road sign would be akin to questioning her competence as a driver and he wasn't about to go there. Indeed, Mattie had seen the road sign for she had let up on the accelerator and their speed had dropped to just under 90 mph as they entered the sharp curve, but he was surprised she hadn't yet touched the brakes.

"Bloody hell, Bourke! The brakes are gone!" Mattie shouted and Cockran could hear the deceleration as Mattie down-shifted from 4th gear to 3rd and 2nd to slow the motorcar. Then, he chilled as they rounded the sharp curve to see the black SSK sideways on the road, completely blocking their path.

Cockran braced for the impact as Mattie, almost simultaneously, pulled the handbrake below the gearshift, turned the steering wheel sharply to the right and downshifted into 1st gear. The 500K skidded sideways heading towards the right berm and the lake 50 feet below, coming to a halt barely two yards away from the black SSK.

In a cold fury, Cockran opened the door and stepped out to confront the idiot driver of the SSK who had almost got them killed. He made it within two feet of the black motorcar, but he only got a glimpse of the face of a man with dark blonde hair who put the SSK in gear and sped away. It was a face he would remember. He made a note of the SSK's license plate as he walked back to the 500K where Mattie still sat, her hands clutching the steering wheel.

"Are you okay, Babe?" Cockran asked. Mattie looked white as a sheet. "That was one hell of a piece of driving! You saved our ass!"

"I'm fine. I just need a moment to catch my breath. I've never had my brakes fail like that. It's a good thing Papa taught me how to slow a motorcar with the gearshift."

"A very good thing. Scoot over while I get us out of the middle of the road and onto the berm so the next motorcar doesn't t-bone us."

Mattie slid over to the passenger side and Cockran got behind the wheel, started the ignition and maneuvered the 500K off to the side of the road just as the two SD men and Sullivan rounded the curve in their respective motorcars and pulled in behind them.

Sullivan was the first to reach them. "What the hell happened?"

"I can't be sure until I check under the hood and the chassis," Cockran replied, "but my best guess is failed brake lines. Check the boot and see if there's an electric torch there."

Sullivan did and came back with an electric torch and the two SD men were right behind him. "There wasn't one in this car but my Auto Union had one."

Cockran opened the bonnet of the 500K and soon found the master brake cylinder. He unscrewed the cap on the top and directed the torchlight into it. It was bone dry. Next, he crawled underneath the chassis and looked at the rear brake lines on each tire that were fed by the master cylinder. The left rear metal line had been cut! The right seemed intact. He checked the brake lines on the front tires, and saw that the right front line had been cut, but not the left.

Cockran got up, dusted himself off and walked over to the passenger side door. "Mattie, the master brake cylinder is empty of brake fluid and the front right and left rear brake lines have been cut. I'm no mechanic, but I'd say someone intended to disable the brakes after you'd driven a fair piece. With those two lines cut, you'd still have braking power on two of the four wheels for a while, but eventually, the two cut lines would drain the master brake cylinder. We've been driving for an hour and a half and that, apparently, was enough braking by you in that period to drain the master cylinder. As I said, I'm no mechanic so I may be all wet, but it sure looks like sabotage to me. If so, someone may know you are going to Rostok."

Mattie looked at her watch. "Maybe so, but maybe not. Hanna has us meeting in a very public place so I think we'll be safe from the

Gestapo. After all, she is the wife of the Grand Admiral of the *Reichsmarine.* It's 11:30, so we still have plenty of time to make it to Rostok for my meeting with her. Bourke, you and I will go with Bobby. Once we reach Rostok, Eric or Franz can call *Sixte* and tell them what happened and where they can find their motorcar."

With that, Mattie grabbed her camera bag, walked over to the Auto Union sedan and settled into the front passenger seat while Cockran got into the back. "You drive, Bobby. I've had enough for one day."

52

New Market Square

New Market Square
Rostok, Germany
Thursday, 20 September 1934

MATTIE McGARY stepped from the Auto Union sedan onto *Steinstrasse* at the southern edge of New Market Square and Cockran did the same. Presently, Eric Bulow joined them while Bobby Sullivan and Franz Globke took their vehicles in search of a car park. Mattie then left them and walked into the square.

The square was a large pedestrian-only marketplace with colorful umbrellas over tables in front of the many restaurants and cafes on the west side of the square. Off to the right were stands selling fruit, vegetables, meats, breads and flowers. It was alive with people pushing trams, shopping or sipping coffees under the umbrellas. To the north was a large gothic style church and two blocks beyond that was the waterfront of a busy major port on the Baltic Sea. It was a very crowded public space and Mattie could see why Hanna Raeder had chosen the locale—safety in numbers.

Cockran had suggested—and Mattie agreed—that he, Sullivan, Bulow and Globke would take up stations on each side of the square, all with a line of sight to whatever table she eventually chose after buying flowers. Cockran was on the west or left side of the square as more restaurants were there and it would put him closest to Mattie. He told her he planned to have his coffee two restaurants away from the one Mattie selected.

Mattie never looked back to see if Bobby and Franz had joined Cockran and Eric. She trusted them to be in position. She walked over to the stalls, passed one selling vegetables and another selling fruit until she came to a flower vendor. She looked around and finally spotted a small square pot of marigolds. After her purchase, she walked over to the west side of the square and began to look for an empty table. It was not an easy task as most of them were taken.

Finally, she found a small, open table under a bright red umbrella in front of a small café on the corner where *Kropeliner* Strasse ended at the square. She sat down and put her marigolds in the middle of the table.

A waiter in a white coat and black trousers took Mattie's order for a coffee and she looked at her watch—1:25 p.m., five minutes early. By 1:45, there was still no sign of Hanna. Mattie ordered another coffee and resisted the temptation to look around to see if she could spot Hanna. Suddenly, she had a sinking feeling. She knew no *Gestapo* had followed her here, but there were four men at different locations in the square who *were* watching her. What if Hanna thought Cockran, Sullivan or the two SD men were *Gestapo*? She quickly dismissed the thought of Cockran or Sullivan being mistaken for *Gestapo*. Cockran looked and dressed like the American he was. Sullivan with his dark hair, bright blue eyes, Irish tweed jacket and matching cap would not be mistaken for a German. That left Bulow and Globke, the tall, blond SS poster boys. Mattie's contact with the *Gestapo* was limited, but she could not recall ever meeting any tall, blond *Gestapo* agents.

In the event, Mattie's worries were for naught as ten minutes later, at 1:55, Hanna Raeder was at her table. She sat down, hailed a waiter and ordered a coffee. Still blonde and beautiful at 38, she wore a navy blue skirt and matching jacket over a crisp white blouse with a red and yellow silk scarf at her throat. Her hair was cut in a fashionable bob, her make-up light if at all.

"Hello, *Frau* McGary, Mattie, I'm pleased to see you again," Hanna said as she extended her hand and shook Mattie's. "You have the transcript?"

"Thank you, *Frau* Raeder, Hanna, I too am pleased to see you. Yes, I have the transcript," Mattie said and reached for her camera bag. She pulled out the transcript and pushed it across the table to Hanna.

Hanna took the transcript, left it flat on the table, turned the first page and looked at Mattie. "I don't propose to read the entire transcript. I will read my comments as well as Chairman Freisler's comments as we both did a lot of talking that day. I am frequently Roland's chief adversary and I certainly was on 5 June. If the stenographer correctly captured what he said and what I said, I will have no doubts about the rest of the transcript. Will that be satisfactory?"

Mattie said that it was and, with that, Hanna began to read while Mattie watched in silence. Thirty minutes later, she turned the last page of the transcript and slid it back to Mattie.

"Yes," Hanna said. "The transcript accurately reflects what Roland and I said about the Prussian Memorandum during the 5 June Commission meeting."

"That's great!" Mattie said. "Thanks so much for coming to see me like this, especially with the threats you received. You're a brave woman and I admire your courage."

The two women stood, shook hands and turned to go in opposite directions, Mattie south to *Steinstrasse* and Hanna north to the harbor when Mattie heard the roar of the engines of several motorcars and the screech of brakes. From all four corners of the square, four men from each corner—16 in all—exited black Mercedes sedans and advanced toward the two women.

All the men wore long, dark overcoats and fedoras. They held high in their left hand a bronze oval medallion that Mattie recognized as a *Gestapo* disc and all held a Luger automatic pistol in the right hands while chanting "Make way! Make way! *Gestapo*! *Gestapo*! Make way! Make way!"

Mattie's pulse quickened and her blood pressure spiked when she and Hanna were surrounded by 16 men with Lugers pointed right at them. Then, a hawk-nosed man with a dueling scar stepped forward. Josef Kleist! The bloody kidnapper who stripped her naked!

"Ah, *Frau* McGary, we meet again. You are a most elusive woman, but I'm pleased you found your clothes," Kleist said with a leer and a short bow. "And your lovely companion must be *Frau* Raeder," followed by another bow. "You two ladies are under arrest."

"On what charge?" the journalist and the lawyer said almost simultaneously.

Kleist laughed. "Oh, we'll think of something. There'll be plenty of time for that later after you two are safely tucked away in *Oranienburg*," referring to Nazi Germany's first concentration camp for political prisoners and dissidents. "I tend to favor treason for *Frau* Raeder and espionage for *Frau* McGary, but it will be up to *Herr Doktor* Freisler to decide that. He's a lawyer and I'm just a simple policeman."

"You won't get away with this, you bastard!" Mattie said. "Hanna is the wife of Grand Admiral Raeder, the head of the *Reichsmarine*! You're the one who's going to end up spending a lot of time in *Oranienburg*."

Kleist smiled. "I think not. I'm arresting a lawyer on the commission named Hanna Hinderman. I will be shocked—shocked—when it is discovered a year or so from now that *Fraulein* Hinderman was married to a distinguished admiral who was so many years older than her. A regrettable mistake, but I'm sure *Reichsfuhrer-SS* Himmler will make appropriate groveling apologies to Admiral Raeder and suggest he might wish, in the future, to, ah, keep his young wife on a shorter leash and closer to home." With that and a nod of the head, two men grabbed each of the women by their arms and frog-marched them to *Steinstrasse* and into the Mercedes sedan waiting there.

COCKRAN WATCHED helplessly less than ten yards away as the *Gestapo* put his wife and Hanna Raeder into a motorcar and sped away. He quickly looked around and spotted Bobby Sullivan and signaled for him to come over.

"Where's our car?" he asked when Sullivan arrived.

"A block away."

"Get it and pick me up here. I'll try and spot where they're going."

A minute later, Sullivan pulled up with the Auto Union sedan and Cockran hopped in. "They're two blocks away. They took a right at the light. It just turned green."

Sullivan floored it and hung a right at the light. Cockran could see the Mercedes several blocks ahead. They followed the *Gestapo* motorcar for several miles until they reached the Rostok Aerodrome where the Mercedes drove directly onto the tarmac and right up to a JU-52 Trimotor. The plane's nose was high in the air; sun glistened off its corrugated metal fuselage; and its three propellers were slowly rotating. He saw Mattie exit the Mercedes followed by Hanna Raeder as both women were taken at gunpoint to the foldout stairs in the middle of the aircraft. After the women and the four *Gestapo* thugs guarding them were inside, the stairs were pulled up; the aircraft door was closed; and the three large propellers began to spin more rapidly as the JU-52 turned and moved onto the runway.

As the big trimotor lifted off, Cockran turned to Sullivan. "We've got to get back to Berlin, but first, we need to call Sturm and tell him what's happened. When they had her in Amsterdam, they said they were taking her to a concentration camp outside Berlin called *Oranienburg*. There's a good chance that's where she'll be, but Sturm is in a better position than we are to find out for sure."

53

Betrayed

Rostok Aerodrome
Rostok, Germany
Thursday, 20 September 1934

HANNA RAEDER was furious as she walked up the stairs behind Mattie McGary into the passenger compartment of the *Junkers* Trimotor. She had known ever since the *Gestapo* showed up in full force in New Market Square to arrest them that McGary had not been followed to their rendezvous in Rostok. No, a raid with that many men had to be planned in advance which meant they had been betrayed and Hanna was all but certain she knew who it was.

There were eight rows of two single leather seats on either side of the aircraft's cabin with a middle aisle between the seats. Kleist directed Hanna and Mattie to walk up the aisle to the fifth row and take those two seats. Kleist and the three *Gestapo* agents took seats behind them.

The aircraft began to move, the sound of the three radial engines increasing in volume and moments later they were airborne. Hanna could see that there were two other passengers in the cabin sitting in the first row, a man and a woman, the former bald, the latter a blonde. She knew them both. The bald-headed snake was Roland Freisler. The blonde was that long-legged bitch who betrayed them—Greta Mayer.

Once the JU-52 reached cruising altitude, Freisler and Greta rose from their seats and made their way back to the seats occupied by Hanna and Mattie.

Hanna looked up at Greta, her face a mask, her voice flat and emotionless, "Why?"

Greta laughed. "It wasn't you we were after. It was nothing personal."

Hanna suppressed her irritation. She didn't give a damn whether it was personal or not. The Nazi bitch had betrayed her! "Why?" she asked again, more forcefully.

"We set a trap for my Uncle Gregor, the traitor, after he delivered a copy of the Prussian Memorandum to the Englishman Churchill. We couldn't try him for treason then without tangible evidence. All we would have had was my testimony, which *Herr Doktor* Freisler didn't want to use because it would reveal my role as a secret *Gestapo* agent on the Commission staff. So, I conceived the fiction of my creating a *new* transcript of the 5 June 1934 Commission meeting that I delivered to Uncle Gregor and he in turn arranged for it be delivered to Churchill and the British journalist. Now that we have the transcript back, we have all the evidence we need to prove my Uncle is a traitor."

"What did you mean by 'the fiction' of your creating a new transcript for the 5 June meeting?" Mattie asked in an aggressive tone of voice that matched Hanna's.

Good for her, Hanna thought. Don't back down. Don't show any fear.

"Just that. My stenographic skills are quite limited," Greta replied. "It's impossible to create a transcript from my stenographic notes taken at that meeting or any other meeting. Besides, I also can't decipher the official stenographic notes that well. I was given a carbon copy of the *official* minutes that *Herr Doktor* Freisler keeps in his office safe. On page 22 of the transcript, he placed a small checkmark that was barely visible. I delivered it to Uncle Gregor who, in turn, entrusted it to Otto Lutze from the Reich Ministry of Justice who left it in a dead drop in Amsterdam for Churchill and you."

"Exactly so," Freisler said, speaking for the first time. "I examined the transcript that Agent Kleist took from you and it has the p. 22

checkmark I placed on the carbon copy I gave to *Fraulein* Mayer. Prior to our taking off, I called *Gestapo* headquarters in Berlin and ordered von Dohnanyi's arrest. By now, he should be in the *Gestapo* segment of *Oranienburg* where he will be tried tomorrow morning before a Peoples Court. Tomorrow afternoon, the verdict of guilty by the Peoples Court will be carried out and his neck will be stretched out under a *fallbeil* which translates to 'falling ax' in English or what the French call a *guillotine.* Upon my command, his traitor's head will be severed from his traitor's body."

"Hardly a fair trial," Mattie said, "if you already know what the verdict is going to be."

"To the contrary, *Frau* McGary, it will be a fair *German* trial because I will be the Presiding Judge. *Heil* Hitler!" Freisler said with his right arm extended upward.

"*Heil* Hitler!" Greta Mayer echoed as her right arm shot up. Then Freisler turned, walked up the aisle followed by Greta and they resumed their seats.

It was too bad, Hanna thought, that they had confiscated both her pistol and Mattie's Walther PPK. A bullet in the back would have been just what Greta deserved.

54

Killers Always Know One of Their Own

Zeppelin Reederei Headquarters
Friedrichshafen, Germany
Thursday, 20 September 1934

STURM PLACED the telephone receiver back in its cradle on the desk in his office in the *Zeppelin Reederei* headquarters building. He was surprised, to say the least, to learn from Cockran that the *Gestapo* had tried again and once more succeeded in taking Mattie into their custody, this time when she was meeting with Admiral Raeder's wife in Rostok. The question was what to do about it. Cockran thought she likely would be taken to the *Oranienburg* concentration camp because the *Gestapo* team leader in Amsterdam had told her that was her eventual destination in Germany. Perhaps, but they would have to know with certainty where she was before deciding what to do about it.

This was going to be tricky. Doubtless, Freisler was behind it and he was sure the man would receive a report of it from someone on the telephone. That would eventually appear on the Brown Pages from the wiretaps on Freisler's home and office phones and he and Schellenberg would know by tomorrow where Mattie was being held. Was there a way to speed that process up so that he and Schellenberg would receive Freisler's Brown Pages from today sooner rather than later?

Neither Schellenberg nor he would have the individual influence with the *Forschungsamt* to accomplish this. No, only Hermann Göring himself would have the clout to do that. Or, Sturm thought, someone the *Forschungsamt* knew was close enough to Göring to speak on his behalf. Someone who was not afraid to speak first in the *Reichspresident*'s name and ask his forgiveness afterwards.

Sturm rose from his desk and walked down the hallway to the office of the *Zeppelin Reederei* Chairman of the Board and President, the legendary airship pioneer Hugo Eckener, who in 1929 had successfully flown the *Graf Zeppelin* around the world from the Naval Air Station in Lakehurst, New Jersey to Berlin, Tokyo, Los Angeles and back to Lakehurst. This historic voyage had demonstrated both the feasibility and safety of trans-oceanic airship voyages and ushered in the new era of passenger airships. He stopped in front of the desk of Eckener's long time secretary, Trudy Schmidt, a trim, middle-aged woman whose brown hair was beginning to show flecks of gray.

"Good afternoon, Trudy," Sturm said with a smile. "Is the big boss available?"

Trudy returned the smile. "Not today, Kurt. Hugo took his grandsons sailing on the *Bodensee*," she replied, using the German name for Lake Constance on whose shores Friedrichshafen was located.

"Ah…well, might I use Hugo's private line for a few telephone calls to Berlin that I don't wish to be overheard by anyone less than friendly to *Zeppelin Reederei*?"

"Of course, Kurt, I'm sure Hugo wouldn't mind, " Trudy replied. She knew 'anyone less than friendly to *Zeppelin Reederei*' meant Nazis because, while Eckener was not a political person, he had personally thrown out a Brownshirt who had threatened Eckener if he didn't put swastikas on the huge tail fins of his zeppelins. He was no more likely to do that, Sturm thought, than enroll his grandsons in the Hitler Youth. When Sturm had warned Eckener of the widespread wiretapping by the *Forschungsamt*, Hugo had a private, unlisted telephone line installed in his office that was checked daily to make sure his telephone calls weren't being monitored.

Eckener's office was large and spacious with a huge picture window that looked out on the two cavernous zeppelin sheds and beyond that the shores of Lake Constance. Sturm picked up the telephone receiver, reached an operator and placed a call to *Forschungsamt* headquarters in Berlin, which quickly went through.

"This is *Fregattenkapitan* Kurt von Sturm. I'm calling on behalf of *Reichspresident* Göring. Who is the Officer of the Day?"

"*Oberleutnant* Emil Haber."

"Good. Put him on the line."

"Haber here. How can I help you today *Fregattenkapitan* von Sturm?"

"You have wiretaps on the office and home telephone lines of a Roland Freisler of the Ministry of Justice. Walter Schellenberg of the SD and I are on the distribution list for the Freisler Brown Pages along with *Reichspresident* Göring. The *Reichspresident* wishes all telephone calls to and from Freisler today transcribed immediately, ahead of all other wiretaps. Once transcribed, the Brown Pages for those calls are to be promptly sent by messenger to Schellenberg at SD headquarters and *Reichspresident* Göring at his official residence. I am presently out of Berlin, but I will be flying back tonight. Have my copies of the Freisler Brown Pages delivered to me at my rooms in the *Kaiserhof* Hotel by 9:30 p.m. Will this be a problem?"

"No, of course not, *Fregattenkapitan* von Sturm, I will put our transcribers to work on the Freisler wiretaps immediately."

Sturm hung up; clicked the receiver and once more got the operator. "Place a call to Walter Schellenberg at SD headquarters in Berlin."

"Schellenberg."

"Schellenberg, it's Sturm. That idiot Freisler has done it again!" Sturm then proceeded to tell Schellenberg what he learned from Cockran about the *Gestapo* arrests of Mattie and *Frau* Raeder in Rosotk and what he had done with *Forschungsamt* headquarters to expedite preparation of the Freisler Brown Pages and their prompt delivery to Schellenberg, Göring and him.

"If you learn from the Freisler wiretaps where they have taken Mattie—and I'm certain you will—call me at this number and let me know," Sturm said and gave him Eckener's private number without disclosing whose it was. Trudy was under strict orders never to answer that phone and only two people other than Sturm even had the number. Hugo used it far more for making calls than receiving them.

"I'll be here until 6 p.m. when the *Zeppelin Reederei* JU-52 Berlin shuttle will be wheels-up," Sturm said, referring to the twice daily shuttle between Berlin and Friedrichshafen taken by *Zeppelin Reederei* employees.

With Trudy's permission, Sturm waited in Eckener's office for Schellenberg's call that came 1½ hours later at 5:00 p.m. "Sturm."

"Schellenberg. Kleist called Freisler at 3:39 p.m to report Mattie's arrival at *Oranienburg*. Like all camps formerly run by the SA, it's now run by the SS, but Kleist told Freisler that both *Frau* McGary and *Frau* Raeder have been placed in a special section of the camp apart from the other prisoners and administered by the *Gestapo* and not the SS. According to Kleist, the head of this little *Gestapo* camp, Franz Forster, reports only to Himmler, not to the camp commandant."

"Good work, Schellenberg. I'll get back to you, but I think we may need your help again. Are you up for it?" Sturm asked.

"Of course! Hey, should I bring Heydrich into the loop? I mean I'm acting under his general orders to keep *Frau* McGary safe. That's why we went with you to rescue her on the Rhine."

"No. The fewer people who know about this, the better. The only other person I'm telling besides Cockran is Göring whose help we're going to need. Besides, it's my understanding that Admiral Raeder personally kicked Heydrich out of the Navy so I don't think Heydrich has much love lost for him or, by extension, his wife. I don't even intend to alert Admiral Raeder until we have those women safely out of the camp. And perhaps not even then. I may just leave it to *Frau* Raeder's discretion as to how much she wishes to tell her husband."

After concluding his call from Schellenberg, Sturm looked at his watch. 5:15. He had time for one more call. He placed it. "*Herr Reichspresident?* We have a problem. I don't have time to explain now as I have a 6:00 p.m. plane to catch, but I had the Brown Pages on Roland Freisler for today expedited and delivered to you. Once you read them, you'll understand the problem. If you could possibly spare me some time tomorrow morning to discuss the problem and how you think would be the best way to resolve it, I'd be most grateful. If that's possible, please leave word at the *Kaiserhof* when it would be convenient to meet. I should be there by 9:30 tonight."

Sturm smiled as he stepped into the Mercedes touring car that was to take him to the Friedrichshafen Aerodrome. Asking Göring how he thought would be the best way to solve their 'problem' did the trick. Sturm already had several feasible plans in mind, but that question had caused Göring to ask Sturm to describe the 'problem' in ten words or less.

"The *Gestapo* took *Frau* McGary and *Frau* Raeder to *Oranienburg*," Sturm had replied.

"Tomorrow morning for breakfast at my official residence at 8:00 a.m.," Göring promptly said. "Bring her husband and that Irish mercenary who calls me 'Your Holiness' with you. I like him. Like me, he's a cold-blooded killer…and killers always know one of their own."

55

To Hell With Himmler!

Official Residence of the President of the Reichstag
Berlin
Friday, 21 September 1934

IT WAS early morning and Sturm was waiting for them when Bourke Cockran and Bobby Sullivan's taxi arrived at the entrance of the *Reichspresident*'s residence and pulled up beneath a two-story high portico flanked by two large marble pillars on either side. Cockran thought it was an imposing building, but its architectural style was difficult to describe, possibly a turn-of-the-century Second *Reich* eclectic variation of Gothic. The entrance was at the side of the building right next to a tall circular tower with a cast iron roof that resembled a lighthouse, with windows only at the top. To its left was a long terrace running along the front of the house directly across from the burned-out cupola of the *Reichstag* Building.

Once inside the residence, a black-coated butler led them down a long marble corridor lit by elaborate crystal chandeliers and lined with gilt-framed paintings of naked Rubenesque-figured women that seemed to be a favorite subject of Hermann Göring. They entered a large, dining room with a gilt-edged, coffered ceiling from which hung two large crystal chandeliers over a long damask-covered table.

Five places were set at the table, which easily seated 20. One large armchair at its head was obviously intended for the *Reichspresident*. Four other places were set, two to a side. At the far end of the room, Hermann Göring stood talking to Walter Schellenberg. Göring wore a pale blue *Luftwaffe* uniform with a wide dark blue vertical stripe down each side of his trousers that were tucked into polished black leather knee high boots. Schellenberg, unusual for him in Cockran's experience, was in his full-dress black SS officer uniform with silver trim and polished black leather knee high boots that matched those worn by Göring.

"*Fregattenkapitan* von Sturm, *Herr* Cockran and *Herr* Sullivan," the butler announced.

Göring broke off his conversation and approached the three newcomers with outstretched arms and a big smile. "Kurt; *Herr* Cockran, the lucky American bastard who captured the hand of the beautiful *Fraulein* McGary; and my favorite Irish mercenary! Welcome!" Göring boomed and grasped each man's hand in both of his.

Göring then led them to the table. "Kurt, you sit to my right; Sullivan on my left. We killers have to stick together, eh? You two lawyers," he said, gesturing imperiously towards Cockran and Schellenberg, "take what's left."

When they were all seated, Göring spoke again. "I summoned Schellenberg here against my better judgment because, as a rule, I can never stand more than one lawyer at a time in my presence. Shakespeare had a good point about lawyers, but Schellenberg is on the distribution list for the Freisler Brown Pages. So, once I read them after we talked last night, Kurt, I thought I should make an exception, especially since Schellenberg was instrumental in helping *Herr* Cockran's wife escape from the *Gestapo* a few days ago."

"*Danke, Herr Reichspresident*," Schellenberg replied with a modest bow of his head, and damned if it didn't persuade Cockran that it was genuine deference to *Unser* Hermann.

"You're welcome!" Göring bellowed, "But I'm starving so let's eat while we discuss how we begin to carry out Shakespeare's advice and eliminate that bald little lawyer Freisler and reunite *Herr* Cockran with his wife. William! Alert the kitchen! We're ready to eat!"

Göring turned back to his guests. "It's about time you Irish had a good German breakfast. I did the best I could last year when we flew you to Munich to save the life of our *Fuhrer* from those incompetent idiots Himmler and Goebbels. An aircraft's galley, however, is no substitute for my Berlin chef's kitchen so I hope you brought your appetites."

Now, Cockran knew that a 'good German breakfast' was not that much different from a typical 'American breakfast' of juice, coffee, bacon, eggs, toast and milk. Germans substituted smoked ham or salami for bacon and added cheese or perhaps rolls for toast, but that was it. On their flight in the personal JU-52 of Göring from Berlin to Munich where, in fact, they had gone on to save Hiter's life as a bi-product of saving Mattie, the breakfast was much more elaborate: two kinds of eggs, bacon, four kinds of sausage, Black Forest ham, broiled tomatoes, three different cheeses, venison from Göring's own estate, and both cherry and apricot strudel.

Cockran was expecting something similar this morning so he was surprised when four white-coated servants brought in a veritable cornucopia of provisions. In addition to the fare served on Göring's aircraft, there was caviar, grilled mushrooms, croissants, fried potatoes, pancakes, French toast, Belgium waffles, maple syrup, scones and, in deference to the 'Irish mercenary' Sullivan, soda bread and Irish breakfast tea.

"'Tis a bountiful feast your Holiness," Sullivan said, "but I hope you won't take it amiss if I spread your caviar on my croissants rather than soda bread?"

Göring laughed. "We killers can eat whatever we want, my Irish friend."

Last night, Cockran had worked out with Sturm how they wanted to proceed in rescuing Mattie and what assistance they needed from Göring. To his surprise—and probably Sturm's as well—Göring took over their meeting, speaking through mouthfuls of food as he sampled every single dish on the table except soda bread and Irish breakfast tea.

"I've read this nonsense in the Freisler Brown Pages," Göring said, "about some alleged 'special section' in *Oranienburg* run by the *Gestapo* and answerable only to Himmler and not the SS commandant of *Oranienburg*. Well, to hell with Himmler! I am Prime Minister of Prussia, not him! Here's what I'm going to do. After I find out the strength of the *Gestapo* guards in that 'special section', I'm going to send in a unit of my Prussian State Police that is four times the size of the *Gestapo* guards. If they refuse to release *Frau* McGary and *Frau* Raeder, my men are to open fire; kill all the *Gestapo* at *Oranienburg*; and liberate the two women."

Cockran winced at this. Freisler and MID clearly wanted to kill Mattie's story. That's why the *Gestapo* twice tried to kidnap her and keep her in *Oranienburg* indefinitely, but literally killing her would achieve the same result. What if the *Gestapo* had orders to kill their prisoners during an assault like Göring proposed and blame it on 'friendly fire' from the Prussian State Police? Cockran was about to point this out when Sturm spoke up.

"With all respect, *Reichspresident,* I think such a plan is premature unless we already know where in the camp the women are being held. Without that, they may be wounded or killed during the rescue attempt. Simply sign an order as Prussian Prime Minister directing that the two women be delivered into my custody. Schellenberg and I will serve your order later this morning and we'll see what happens. If they refuse to obey the order, we will demand access to the women to make sure they are safe and well treated. Then, we will alert them to 'Plan B" that we'll implement tonight."

"And what is this 'Plan B'? My Prussian State Police?" Göring asked.

"Not exactly," Cockran replied. "We will need, however, two autogiros at *Templehof* late this afternoon with swastikas prominently painted on their fuselages along with four Prussian State Police badges." He then proceeded to outline for Göring how they planned to liberate the prisoners.

"That is a bold plan," Göring began, "but I like it! I will limit the role of my Prussian State Police to what you propose. Are you sure only the four of you," he said, pointing with both hands to the four men sitting at the table with him, "and Schellenberg's two aides will be sufficient to bring this off?"

"Well, your Holiness," Sullivan replied, "we still have the Schmeisser sub-machine pistols with sound suppressors you so kindly supplied us for our little operation the other night in the Port of Duisberg. That, plus these," Sullivan said, opening his tweed sport coat to reveal twin leather shoulder holsters containing two Colt M1911 .45 automatics, "should do the trick."

"Hah! In the hands of two killers like you," Göring said, "I daresay any *Gestapo* who resist won't be seeing the next day's sunrise. William! Attend me!"

Moments later, the butler appeared. "Go to my study and bring me six Prussian State Police badges."

William did so and Göring passed out the badges, giving three to Schellenberg. "I hope your first plan works, but if not, good hunting. Remember, shoot first; ask questions later. If you leave any dead bodies behind, don't worry. I'll tell the officer in charge of the Prussian State Police squad to list any casualties as 'shot while resisting arrest'."

56

Guilty As Charged

The Peoples Court
Konzentrationslager Oranienburg
Oranienburg, Germany
Friday, 21 September 1934

HAROLD CANFIELD sat in the back of the makeshift 'courtroom' for the treason trial of Georg von Dohnanyi in the Peoples Court, a windowless conference room. The Presiding Judge, the bald-headed Roland Freisler, sat at a long table in the front of the room wearing a long, black red-trimmed robe. The defendant Dohnanyi sat at a smaller table below that. Behind the Presiding Judge, an immense floor to ceiling Nazi flag, red with a black swastika inside a white circle, dominated the room and drew your eyes to the small bust of Adolf Hitler mounted on a pedestal. It was 9:00 a.m. Canfield was not a lawyer, but it was one of the most unusual trials he had ever witnessed. Unusual, but damned efficient, he had to give the Nazis credit for that. There was neither a prosecutor nor a defense lawyer, only the Presiding Judge.

"*Herr* von Dohnanyi," Freilser said, "I hand you a carbon copy of the transcript of the 5 June 1934 meeting of the German Commission on Criminal Law Reform. Please turn to page 22."

Dohnanyi leafed through the pages and then looked up and nodded. "I am at page 22."

"Good. Now, half way down the page, do you see a small black checkmark?"

"I do."

"Excellent, let the record reflect that I personally placed that checkmark before I turned it over to the defendant's niece, Greta Mayer, who told me in my investigation that, at his direction, she gave the transcript to the defendant. Let the record also reflect that Otto Lutze, right before his unfortunate death Saturday last in Amsterdam, said that the defendant gave him the transcript to deliver in Amsterdam to certain British citizens, namely a Member of Parliament and a female journalist for an American newspaper chain. Let the record further reflect that this same transcript was recovered yesterday in the city of Rostok in the possession of that same British female journalist. Does the defendant deny any of this?"

Dohnanyi did not reply, but simply stared directly at Freisler.

Freisler was clearly annoyed at the defendant's silence. "Come on, man, speak up! What do you have to say for yourself?"

Dohnanyi said nothing for a good ten seconds. Then he spoke in a clear, even voice. "You are an evil man, a despicable stain on the honorable legacy of the German judiciary. You ought to be ashamed of yourself, but a bottom-dwelling slug like you has no shame!"

Freisler's face grew so red that Canfield thought he would have a stroke. "If you have nothing to say for yourself, then kindly keep your mouth shut!" Freisler said in a loud, squeaky voice.

"Bring the defendant to his feet," Freisler ordered and two burly *Gestapo* guards lifted Dohnanyi up from his chair.

"Georg von Dohnanyi, I find you guilty as charged of treason against the German *Reich* by delivering Top Secret material to foreign nationals. I hereby sentence you to death by beheading as soon as the *fallbeil* can be transported to the courtyard and the necessary witnesses assembled. Guards, take him away. Give him a last meal if he wants one."

Freisler then turned to his right. "Bailiff, please have the guards bring the two female prisoners to me."

WHEN BOTH prisoners stood before him, handcuffs around their wrists, Freisler ignored them and pretended to read the papers in front of him. He let two minute go by before he looked up. "Hanna Raeder, you are charged with treason against the German *Reich* for discussing Top Secret material with a foreign national. You will be tried tomorrow morning before The People's Court at 9:00 a.m. How do you plead? Guilty or Not Guilty?"

"I refuse to acknowledge your authority over me," Hanna replied.

Freisler ignored her. "Martha McGary, you, as a foreign national, are charged with espionage against the German *Reich* for receiving Top Secret material. You also will be tried tomorrow morning before The People's Court at 9:00 a.m. How do you plead? Guilty or Not Guilty?"

"What she said," Mattie replied, pointing her handcuffed hands at Hanna.

Freisler was disappointed. Both women stood there with their heads held high and not the least bit intimidated. It was time to shape both of these bitches up and put the fear of God in them. Give them a foretaste of what they would face tomorrow.

"Well, Ladies, for your information, Georg von Dohnanyi was tried and convicted earlier this morning for treason. I personally sentenced him to death by beheading."

Aha! *That* got their attention, Freisler thought, as the eyes of both women went wide at the announcement, but neither one said anything. "German law requires the presence of two official witnesses at any beheading. Inasmuch as the two of you may be facing the same fate if you are each convicted tomorrow, I thought you might like to see what German justice may be in store for you. Therefore, I appoint each of you to be the official witnesses to the execution of the traitor Georg von Dohnanyi. Do you have anything to say for yourselves?"

The two women still said nothing and Freisler was again disappointed. Both looked defiant and if looks could kill, he would be as dead as Dohnanyi once his severed head was rolling on the ground. "Guards, take them to the courtyard."

CANFIELD STOOD at an open window that overlooked the courtyard of the *Gestapo* section of the concentration camp. It was high noon without a cloud in the sky. He had never witnessed an execution before, let alone a beheading. He had to admit to himself he had a macabre curiosity in seeing a man's head cleaved from his body in one swift stroke. He was looking forward to it as much as he was looking forward to witnessing the interrogation techniques the *Gestapo* applied to the two women arrested yesterday in Rostok. Truth be told, he would have preferred to be in the courtyard and much closer to the execution, but Freisler had insisted that the two women be the official witnesses to the beheading. Canfield didn't care whether the German woman saw him, but he didn't want a journalist like Cockran's wife to know he was there. Hence, he was as close to the beheading as anonymity permitted. He consoled himself with the thought that he would be much closer to the *Gestapo* interrogation of the two women, as close as a one-way mirror permitted.

Canfied turned to Josef Kleist who stood beside him. "Are all executions in Germany carried out by beheading?"

"Oh yes, beheading has been the preferred form for capital punishment in Prussia for centuries," Kleist said. "But executioners as tradesmen are dying out. When Hitler came to power, there was only one *fallbeil*—falling ax—in Germany. To make up for the shortage of qualified executioners and in order to be more humane—lopping off heads with a sword is so medieval, don't you think—our *Fuhrer* ordered the immediate manufacture of 19 more *fallbeil*. Prior to coming to power, he promised many times that 'heads would roll' when he took over and now they do. Literally."

"Have you ever witnessed a beheading?" Canfield asked.

"Of course, many times. Is this your first?"

Canfield nodded 'yes'.

"Well, you're in for a treat. It varies from one man to another, but the blood spray from the neck can be spectacular. The first beheading I saw, the *fallbeil* had a metal container attached to its front to catch the severed head. I'm told that when the *Fuhrer* learned of this, he ordered all the containers removed so that the head would drop straight to the ground. I guess he wanted to make sure that the heads really would roll, eh?" Kleist said and laughed.

Canfield turned to look out the window again. The *fallbeil* was a rudimentary structure, primarily made of wood. Its front was roughly four feet wide and ten feet tall. A large blade with a 45-degree diagonal cutting edge was set on metal tracks within the 4'x 10' structure. A rope pulley drew the blade up to the top of the structure where it was locked into place. At the bottom were two pieces of wood set in tracks just behind the track for the blade. The piece on top had a semi-circle cut out of its bottom while the one beneath it had a semi-circle cut out of its top. When the top piece of wood was lowered, the head of the person to be executed extended through the resulting circle. The rear of the *fallbeil* was a 6' long, 3' wide and 3' tall wooden bench on which, Kleist explained, the person to be executed usually lay on his stomach. The top semi-circle piece of wood was lifted so the person could have his head placed under it until his neck was directly below the blade. The top piece of wood was then lowered and locked into place, thus immobilizing the person's head and neck.

Canfield watched as two uniformed *Gestapo* guards brought out Georg von Dohnanyi, hands tied behind his back, and placed him face up on the bench and slid him forward under the front of the *fallbeil* and locked his head and neck into place. "I thought you said the prisoners are placed face down on the bench. Why is he face up?" Canfield asked.

Kleist laughed. "It was my suggestion. Freisler really has it in for this guy so I told him he deserved to see what was going to happen to him once that big blade comes sliding down. Freisler agreed."

Canfield saw two guards march out with the two women, one guard holding each by the arm. They positioned the women directly in front of the *fallbeil*, no more than 20 feet away.

Kleist chuckled. "That Freisler is one sadistic bastard."

Canfield was confused, but then it *was* his first beheading. "Why do you say that?"

"For one thing, those two women are going to be tried tomorrow before The People's Court and then beheaded. That's cruel enough by itself to make them watch what their fate is going to be. What's worse is I've seen at least five beheadings and I've never seen official witnesses standing in front of the *fallbeil* like those two women are. Anyone present, including official wirnesses, stand off to the side."

"Why do they stand to the side?"

Kleist laughed. "Blood spray! That's why I said Freisler was a sadistic bastard. Those two women are official witnesses against their will. Given how close Freisler has them standing to the *fallbeil*, there's a definite possibility they'll be hit with Dohnanyi's blood. I've seen two other beheadings where blood spray went that far. Look at where the two guards are standing. They're *behind* the women and holding their arms. They know what's coming and I guarantee that when the blade begins to fall, they'll both duck down so that only the women are hit with blood spray."

Canfield nodded. Kleist was right; Freisler *was* a sadistic bastard. He watched a black-hooded executioner walk into the sunlight from the shadows. He was a big man with enormous biceps and forearms and Canfield wondered if he had been an executioner when a broadsword, not a *fallbeil*, had been the instrument of death.

MATTIE McGARY was no stranger to beheadings, but most were at the hands of a group of warrior monks in 1931 and the victims were SS for whom she had shed no tears. Last year, however, the Nazi government had executed someone close and dear to her and the memory was still fresh and painful. That had been with a broadsword while today would be the first time she had seen the use of a *fallbeil*. It was no more humane than a broadsword, she thought, but at least once the blade fell and did its grisly work, its presence would block the blood spray from the victim's neck. Given that she and Hanna were less than 20 feet ftom the *fallbeil*, that was no small consideration.

Freisler and a small group of approximately ten people, including Greta Mayer, stood off to the side. When the executioner reached the *fallbeil*, he raised his hand to the lever at the top of the structure that would release the razor-sharp blade. He paused and looked directly at Freisler, as if seeking the man's permission to proceed. Freisler gave a firm nod of his head; the executioner yanked the lever; the blade swiftly descended in less than a second; and Dohnanyi's severed head fell to the ground, rolling over twice.

Hanna screamed; Mattie looked away; and then, to her horror, the executioner raised the blade and blood spurted out from the mutilated stump of the man's neck. Mattie flinched as she felt the warm spray of blood hit her and Hanna screamed again and fell to her knees, retching, her eyes tightly closed.

The executioner walked in front of the *fallbeil* and picked up Dohnanyi's head by its hair. He took it over to Freisler and held it up for his inspection, blood still dripping from the severed neck, eyes wide open as if the head was still alive. Freisler looked at it with what appeared to Mattie as a satisfied smile. Then, he spit directly into Dohnanyi's face and, with a wave of his hand, directed the executioner to show the head to the two women, but both turned their heads away.

"Make them look!" Freisler ordered. "They are official witnesses."

The executioner grasped the hair on the top of the Hanna's head in his large hand and effortlessly pulled her to her feet. He turned her head forward and thrust the severed head into her face until its nose touched hers. She instinctively recoiled, involuntarily opening her eyes in the process, and closed them again at the sight.

The executioner smiled as he grabbed Mattie by the hair and stuck the head in her face. That was a mistake getting this close to me, Mattie thought, as she pivoted on her left foot and swung her right foot into his kneecap with her steel-toed Red Wing boot. The executioner bellowed in pain, dropped the severed head in the dirt and sank to one knee, clutching his wounded knee with both hands. Mattie's next kick caught him square on the underside of his jaw. The giant fell flat on his back, unconscious. My, but that felt good, Mattie thought, as strong hands grasped her arms from behind and pinned them to her side.

Freisler rushed over to where Mattie was standing. "Take both those traitors back to their cells!" he shouted in a high-pitched voice and then slapped her face hard, first with the back of his hand and then the palm.

Mattie's head rocked from the blows and her face stung, but she did not cry out. She tasted blood that trickled from a split lip as she and Hanna were marched back to the barracks where they were locked in and confined. It occurred to Mattie that, by calling them traitors, the Presiding Judge in their trials tomorrow morning sounded a wee bit biased. Should she point that out tomorrow morning and suggest that he recuse himself and have a new judge appointed in his place? Why not? Apart from her head, what did she have to lose?

"**THAT WAS** fascinating," Canfield said, turning to Kleist. "His head really did roll. What time tonight do you begin the interrogation of Hanna Raeder? I'm looking forward to seeing what techniques the *Gestapo* use."

"9:45 p.m. in Building #2, the same room where we held the trial. We find prisoners to be more vulnerable—and voluable—at night. The technique we'll be using is simulated drowning. We'll interrogate the British journalist after we finish with Raeder. Then, we'll put them on trial together in the morning."

Canfield had never heard of 'simulated drowning', but he didn't want to display his ignorance. He would find out soon enough. "Good. That gives me plenty of time to go back to Berlin and have a nice dinner with my wife at Restaurant *Horcher*. I'll meet you here at 9:30. I'd like you to explain beforehand your version of this technique and why you do it."

57

We'll Be Back

Konzentrationslager Oranienburg
Oranienburg, Germany
Friday, 21 September 1934

BOURKE COCKRAN looked down at the familiar triangle shape of a Nazi concentration camp from the cockpit of a PCA-2 Pitcairn-Cierva autogiro, one that had the large black swastikas he requested from Göring painted on both sides of the fuselage and vertical stabilizer. The autogiro's propeller was powered by a Wright Whirlwind 420 HP radial engine. Stubby wings on the fuselage and four huge rotary wings perched on top of a steel pylon between the pilot and passenger cockpits gave the autogiro lift as well as its distinctive appearance and the nickname 'the flying windmill'.

Bobby Sullivan was in the front passenger cockpit taking photographs of the *Oranienburg* camp as they overflew it. Schellenberg had produced architect's drawings of the camp, which were helpful, but Cockran thought a first-hand view was even better, especially as they would be landing after sundown if Sturm and Schellenberg were unsuccessful in liberating Mattie and Hanna Raeder on the strength of Göring's order to deliver them to his custody.

Cockran knew from both the architect's drawings as well as his own visit to another concentration camp earlier that summer that the entrance to the camp was in the middle of the base of the triangle along with the commandant's office on one side of the entrance hallway and administrative offices on the other side of the hallway. Schellenberg had told him that the *Gestapo*-run section of the camp was at the top of the triangle and began roughly ¾ of the way up from the base. The SS-run portion of the camp was far larger, fully ½ of the way up. In between was a courtyard where Cockran intended to land both autogiros tonight should such an operation prove necessary.

Cockran flew low and slow over the camp several times as he wanted the guards in the towers at each point of the triangle to see the swastikas on the aircraft so they would not be unfamiliar to them when they landed and were bathed in the floodlights of the courtyard. In both passes over the courtyard, he saw in its middle some sort of wooden structure in front of which was a dark narrow stain nearly 20 feet long that looked like blood.

"Bobby," Cockran said into the autogiro's speaking tube, "we'll want to land tonight on either side of that wooden structure. I'll go in first and land on the far side; you follow on my tail and land on the near side."

"Aye," Sullivan replied.

"Also, even though we shouldn't be a surprise after our fly-by today, I want to land as silently as possible. Tonight, I want to approach the camp at close to 1,000 feet altitude. In my experience, once we cut power to the engine, we'll go forward 4 feet for every foot we drop in altitude. I think when we're a little under a mile from the camp at 1,000 feet, we'll cut the engines and float in silently. I'm going to take several practice approaches to see what works. Keep your eye out for landmarks that we can use tonight as the point where we cut our engines."

"What exactly do you think you'll be seeing in the darkness?"

"There's a full moon, smart ass."

Sullivan chuckled and Cockran began to make his approaches. Sullivan agreed that the tall steeple of a church was exactly the point where they needed to cut their engines and let the four huge rotary wings slowly 'autorotate' without power to the ground.

"Let's pray we don't need to do this," Cockran said.

"Aye," Sullivan replied.

STURM AND SCHELLENBERG stepped out of the large, open Mercedes touring car that Schellenberg had commandeered from the SS motorpool. Both wore black SS dress uniforms, but only Schellenberg's was genuine. He was, in fact, an SS *Sturmbannfuhrer*. Though Sturm wore the uniform of an SS *Obersturmbannfuhrer*, it had been given to him by SS-*Reichsfuhrer* Heinrich Himmler himself in a misguided attempt to curry Sturm's favor because of the high regard in which Adolf Hitler held him.

Given the disparity in their ages and apparent SS ranks, *Sturmbannfuhrer* equivalent to a Major in the *Reichswehr* and *Obersturmbannfuhrer* equivalent to Lieutenant Colonel, the two had agreed that Schellenberg would take the lead as the arrogant aide of an equally arrogant *Obersturmbannfuhrer*.

The front of the camp—the base of the triangle—was a long, three story masonry building. A tall metal gate in the middle of the building was the entrance, guarded by two men whose rank was SS-*Sturmmann* or corporals. Both came to attention and shot out their arms accompanied by a 'Heil Hitler!'

Both Sturm and Schellenberg raised their right hands, palm out, in a weak gesture that resembled how Hitler himself responded to a Nazi salute. "We are here to see Commandant Brandt. Take us to him!" Schellenberg barked.

Moments later, they were ushered into the fairly Spartan office of Camp Commandant Emil Brandt that looked out over a semi-circle of 16 wooden buildings that Sturm assumed were barracks for prisoners. Brandt was in his late 40s, close-cropped brown hair and an ample belly that oozed out over his belt. He stood and thrust out his arm and gave them a "*Heil* Hitler!"

They returned the salute and Schellenburg spoke first. "I have an order signed by Hermann Göring in his capacity as Prime Minister of Prussia to release into our custody two female prisoners brought here yesterday—Martha McGary and Hanna Raeder. Kindly produce them!"

"Those names are not familiar to me," Brandt said as he sat down behind his desk. "The only women we took in yesterday were named Schmidt and Hinderman."

"Describe them."

"Well, Schmidt is tall, as tall as me, and she has red hair…" Brandt began, but Schellenberg cut him off.

"That's *Frau* McGary; the other is *Frau* Raeder. Bring them to us at once!"

"I can't. We processed them yesterday, but they were brought here by the *Gestapo* and were placed in the *Gestapo* section of the camp where Franz Forster is the commandant. You'll have to see him. Frankly, he's something of an asshole and I wouldn't mind seeing him taken down a peg or two."

Brandt stood, walked over to a window that looked out at the camp's courtyard, and pointed in the distance. "Out there, beyond the *fallbeil* is the *Gestapo* section of the camp. That building at the top of the triangle is where you will find Forster."

Gestapo Section
Konzentrationslager Oranienburg

"I'M SORRY," the young, blonde receptionist said, "but *Herr* Forster is busy and cannot be disturbed."

"Oh really?" Schellenberg said. "Do we look like men who would let a minor *Gestapo* bureaucrat keep the SS cooling their heels in his outer office?" Schellenberg said as he walked past the young woman, yanked open the door to Forster's office and walked in with Sturm right behind him.

A man in his early 30s with thinning brown hair and wire-rimmed glasses sat behind a desk with his feet propped up, reading a newspaper. Startled, he quickly stood up, gave the Nazi salute and a 'Heil Hitler'! Neither Sturm nor Schellenberg returned the greeting.

Forster was barely 5'7" and wore a brown uniform that was vaguely military in design. "What…what is the meaning of this?" he sputtered. "What do you want?"

"Are you Franz Forster?" Schellenberg asked.

"Yes, but what is this all about?"

"Two female prisoners were brought to your section yesterday. I have an order signed by Hermann Göring in his capacity as Prime Minister of Prussia to release them into our custody. Kindly produce them at once."

"I can't. I mean, *Reichsführer-SS* Himmler's office specifically ordered me to hold these women indefinitely until further notice. You're both SS. Surely you know I have to follow orders."

"Well, I daresay that the Prussian Prime Minister outranks the head of the SS. So does the President of the *Reichstag* and the *Reichsminister* of Aviation," Schellenberg said, "and, of course, *Unser* Hermann holds all three positions. So I think any order of his naturally supersedes an order from a lesser official. So, in terms of obeying orders, don't you wish to reconsider your decision to disobey *Unser* Hermann's order?"

Sturm could see that the little man was in a quandary. Being put in the middle of conflicting orders from two of the most ruthless men in the *Reich* was not a pleasant position to be in. It would come down, Sturm thought, to which person Forster feared the most—the humorless *Reichsführer-SS* or the jovial *Unser* Hermann.

Finally, Forster chose. "I regret, *Sturmbannführer,* that I cannot disobey *Reichsführer-SS* Himmler's order."

"Well, it's your funeral," Schellenberg said with a smile. "We'll be back and under less pleasant circumstances. *Unser* Hermann will be, ah, *disappointed.* He is not accustomed to his orders being disobeyed. He likely will conclude that you fear Himmler more than him. He will take that as an insult. But, as I said, it's your funeral. So, take us to see both women. We wish to make sure they are being well-treated,"Schellenberg said.

"I can't do that either. My orders specifically said they were to have no visitors."

Schellenberg drew his Luger from its holster and chambered a round. "Well then, it's going to be our little secret that you disobeyed that order. We won't tell if you don't. Otherwise, it would be tragic if my Luger accidentally discharged and sent a bullet into your brain. Accidents do happen you know. I would feel really bad about that while you…well, you'd be dead."

Moments later, a *Gestapo* guard led them from Forster's office to a small frame building with a padlock on the door. The guard used a key to open the lock. "The women are inside. I'll wait here until you're finished.

Sturm turned to Schellenberg. "I'll brief Mattie on the details of the rescue tonight and have her tell *Frau* Raeder. That way, both women will have the same story. Tell *Frau* Raeder that Mattie will let her know how it's going to go down."

Sturm walked in and saw a bare room with twenty cots, a communal shower room and WC, and two trestle tables and benches, presumably for eating. Mattie was sitting on a cot at the far end of the room with her arm around another woman, presumably Hanna Raeder. Mattie and the other woman turned around at that point to see who had entered the building.

"Kurt!" Mattie shouted, stood up, ran over and embraced him in a tight hug.

MATTIE'S JOY at Sturm's appearance was short-lived when she learned he was there to visit, not free her. He took her by the hand and walked into the shower room and turned on all six showers.

"I don't know if there are listening devices in this building," Sturm said in a low voice, "but the sound of these showers should defeat them. We have an order signed by *Unser* Hermann to release you and the Raeder woman into our custody, but the man in charge of the *Gestapo* section of the camp won't obey it. Schellenberg had to threaten to 'accidentally' shoot him just for us to see you as visitors. Apparently, you're forbidden to have visitors. We'll be back in force tonight to take the two of you out. Here's how we're going to do it."

Mattie listened to Sturm outline their rescue. It was obviously a Cockran-designed plan quite similar in many respects to her rescue from the river freighter, substituting autogiros for a speedboat. It was not without its flaws, few plans were, but it was being executed by four of the most ruthless men she knew. She liked their chances.

"Timing is critical," Sturm said when he had finished. "The first part of the operation will commence precisely at 9:45 p.m. The autogiros will land in the courtyard five minutes later at 9:50. We'll synchronize our watches using my chronograph. I have 4:17 p.m."

Mattie adjusted her wristwatch accordingly. After Sturm and Schellenberg had left, she left the showers running and beckoned Hanna to join her. After explaining the plan, Hanna reset her watch to match Mattie's.

"Do you think it will work?" Hanna asked.

"It did the last time," Mattie said and explained to Hanna the details of her rescue from the *Gestapo* on the river freighter in Duisberg.

58

Where Are the Women?

Konzentrationslager Oranienburg
Oranienburg, Germany
Friday, 21 September 1934

COCKRAN CHECKED the altimeter one last time—1,000 feet—and then his wristwatch—9:45 p.m. If everything was going to plan, a squad of twenty Prussian State Police led by a Colonel Musser were now at the front of the compound entering it with weapons drawn. They carried with them both a warrant signed by Prussian Prime Minister Hermann Göring and an order signed by Walter Schellenberg as Deputy Director of the SD ordering the SS Camp Commandant to take control of the *Gestapo* section of the camp and disarm the *Gestapo* camp guards. Deadly force was authorized. The purpose of the Prussian State Police raid was to keep the SS Camp Commandant and the SS guards occupied with disarming the *Gestapo* camp guards while Cockran and his team liberated Mattie and Hanna Raeder.

The full moon illuminated a church spire straight ahead, the landmark Cockran and Sullivan had chosen earlier today as being approximately a mile from the camp compound. As they passed over the steeple, Cockran cut power to the Wright-Whirlwind rotary engine leaving the autogiro fairly silent as it lost altitude on its approach to the camp. The propeller powered by the Wright-Whirlwind engine was still now, but the four large rotors overhead were not powered and continued to automatically rotate—hence 'autogiro'—providing lift to the aircraft as it gently floated to the ground.

Kurt von Sturm and *Sturmbannfuhrer* Schellenberg were in the front passenger cockpit of Cockran's autogiro, each in a full-dress SS uniform. Schellenberg wore his official uniform while Sturm was still in his *Obersturmbannfuhrer* uniform from earlier in the day. Cockran, like Sullivan, was in civilian clothes, a leather flying jacket and khakis. The plan was to have the two highest ranking SS officers be the first off Cockran's aircraft. Both were similarly armed with Schmeisser submachine pistols slung by a strap over their chests and Luger automatics in black leather holsters at their waists.

The autogiro touched down and Cockran watched the two men step down from the passenger cockpit and take up a position at either end of his aircraft, their Schmeissers held at port arms.

Cockran waited until he saw Sullivan's autogiro drift in and land 15 yards behind him. The wooden structure they had seen earlier was no longer there. Schellenberg's two men—*SS-Obersturmfuhrer* Eric Bulow and SS-*Obersturmfuhrer* Franz Globke— exited the passenger cockpit of Sullivan's autogiro armed with the same weapons as their leader. Cockran left the cockpit and watched as Sullivan and the two men approached his aircraft, both in their official SS uniforms.

"*Heil* Hitler!" Bulow and Globke said as they came to attention in front of of Schellenberg and shot out their right arms.

Cockran smiled as he watched Schellenberg shake his head and briefly close his eyes. "God damn it, Eric! I told you and Franz we're on a bloody operational mission, just like in Duisberg! We don't follow protocol in the field! Now pay attention. You and Franz stay here and guard the two aircraft with your lives. If either of them are damaged and rendered unable to fly, I'll bust your butts back to *Untersturmfuhrer*. The four of us should be back in ten minutes with the persons we came for. You are not to leave your posts under any circumstances even if you hear gunfire. No one is to come closer than 20 yards to the aircraft. If they do or if they point a weapon in the direction of the aircraft, kill them! Is that clear? If *Herr* Cockran or

Herr Sullivan returns to the aircraft before I do, follow their orders. Is that clear?"

"*Jawohl!*" they said simultaneously, barely managing to keep their arms at their side.

Sturm placed a hand on Cockran's arm and pointed to a lighted barracks 30 yards off to the right. Cockran noticed it was the only one of ten barracks buildings that had any lights on inside. "That's the building where I talked to Mattie. It may well be that she and *Frau* Raeder are the only prisoners in this section of the camp. There was a guard stationed outside the barracks today, but there isn't one now. I'm not sure what that means. Schellenberg and I will go to the Administration Building," Sturm said, pointing to a well-lit building 50 yards to the right, "where I can see a guard. If we're not back here by the time you have Mattie and *Frau* Raeder, take off without us. Schellenberg and I can take care of ourselves. Just tell Bulow and Globke to go over to the Administration Building to see if they can be of help once you take off."

Cockran nodded. "See you in ten," he said and turned to Sullivan. "Let's roll."

The two men walked toward the barracks building with the lights on while Sturm and Schellenberg headed to the Administration Building. Once at the barracks, they drew and held M-1911 Colt .45 automatic pistols with their right hands and Prussian State Police badges in their left. Cockran approached the door to the barracks. The padlock Sturm described was there, but it was unlocked. He turned the knob and pushed open the door. By prior arrangement because he spoke fluent German and Cockran did not, Sullivan entered first, followed by Cockran.

"Prussian State Police! Prussian State Police!" Sullivan shouted in German as he held the badge high. "We have warrants for *Frau* Raeder and *Frau* McGary! Are they here?"

Silence greeted his questions and he turned to Cockran with raised eyebrows, as if to say "What next?"

"We search the place," Cockran said. "If they're not here, we go find Sturm and Schellenberg."

The search didn't take long. It was a large room with twenty cots, a communal shower room and WC, two trestle tables and benches, and one separate room beside the shower that held a desk and a more comfortable bed rather than a cot. Presumably, it was for a camp guard.

Five minutes later, they stood at the front door, having found nothing."Damn it!" Cockran said. "They're not here! Mattie and Hanna are not here! Come on, let's go find Sturm."

Twenty yards from the Administration Building, Cockran heard the sharp crack of a pistol shot. He watched as the uniformed guard at the front of the building turned and entered the building with a drawn pistol. Then another shot rang out.

STURM SAW Cockran and Sullivan head towards the barracks. Then he and Schellenberg walked over to the Administration Building and approached the guard standing outside the entrance. "We're here to see Commandant Franz Forster. Be so good as to fetch him for us," Schellenberg said with a smile.

"Do you have an appointment?" the guard asked. "Commandant Forster does not see visitors without an appointment."

Schellenberg's smile vanished. "Do we look like people who need an appointment? Do you see our aircraft? We're SS. We don't make appointments! Do you think I had an appointment the night I killed Ernst Rohm? Find Forster at once and bring him here or the body count from the Night of the Long Knives is about to be increased by one!"

After the suitably cowed guard left, the two men walked inside until a corridor ended in a T. Sturm watched as Schellenberg took the Luger from its holster and chambered a round. Sturm then did the same.

Moments later, the guard returned accompanied by Franz Forster, still buttoning his uniform jacket. He stopped and gave the Nazi salute. Sturm ignored it and watched a smiling Schellenberg wave his hand. "I told you we'd be back. Do you have a deputy?"

Forster looked wary as if he thought it a trick question, but after a moment of hesitation, he answered. "Yes, I do. Hugo Lang is my deputy."

"Good. Have your guard bring him here as well," Schellenberg said.

They stood in silence for several minutes, Forster looking increasingly uncomfortable with two SS officers holding Lugers pressed against the side of their trousers.

Lang arrived, dressed in the same brown uniform as his boss. He looked to be in his mid-twenties and was several inches taller than Forster with a full head of brown hair. He stopped, gave the Nazi salute and a 'Heil Hitler!' which both Sturm and Schellenberg ignored.

The guard left to resume his post at the entrance and Schellenberg pointed his Luger at Lang. "So, Lang, is it fair to say," he began in a light, conversational tone and lowered the Luger to his side, "that you and Commandant Forster see eye to eye on the day-to-day operation of your section of this camp?"

"Yes, *Sturmbannfuhrer,*" Lang replied.

"Are you aware that earlier today, Forster refused to obey an order from Hermann Göring in his capacity as Prime Minister of Prussia to release two female prisoners into our custody?"

"Yes, *Sturmbannfuhrer.*"

"Did you advise Forster that you disagreed with his decision to disobey that order?"

"No, *Sturmbannfuhrer.*"

"So, you still agree with what he did?" Schellenberg said with a smile and without a trace of menace in his voice.

"Yes, *Sturmbannfuhrer.*"

"A pity, really," Schellenberg said as he raised his Luger and fired a single round into Lang's forehead. The man fell backwards, his head hitting the floor as blood streamed from the neat hole in his head.

Sturm was shocked. He had not expected this, but then again, Schellenberg had to deal with Nazi morons on a daily basis and he didn't. Besides, Sullivan and Mattie each had warned him not to be taken in by Schellenberg's boyish good looks. "That boy's as cold-blooded a killer as anyone," the Irish assassin had told him.

Sturm turned when he heard the door to the entrance slam open and he saw the guard rush toward them, a pistol in his hand. Sturm reacted instantly, instinctively knowing that Schellenberg had to keep his weapon trained on Forster. He turned, raised his Luger and fired a single shot into the guard's face, just below the nose. It wasn't as accurate as Schellenberg's shot, but then he had been shooting at a stationary rather than a moving target.

Sturm turned back to Schellenberg, but he reversed course when he heard pounding footsteps behind him and brought his Luger up into firing position. He lowered it when he saw Cockran and Sullivan rush through the door, Colt .45 automatics in their hands.

"They're not there!" Cockran said when he reached Sturm. "There's no one in those barracks!"

The three of them joined Schellenberg who had kept his Luger pointed at Forster. "If the women are not in the barracks, I think it's time to give *Herr* Forster the chance to correct the error of his ways. *Unser* Hermann was most disturbed to learn that anyone would choose to obey an order from Himmler rather than him. It's bad for his public image if he's seen to be less than the 2nd most ruthless person in the *Reich*, after our beloved *Fuhrer* of course. He told me that if anyone even offered the slightest resistance to obey his order, he was to be shot. Sadly, Lang was the first to do so," Schellenberg said with a smile and then shrugged. "I was just obeying orders."

Sturm was amused to note the look of terror in Forster's face and the dark stain of urine on the trousers of his brown uniform.

"So, *Herr* Forster," Schellenberg said. "Where are the women?"

"I …I'm not sure. They're in one of the interrogation rooms."

"How many rooms are there and where are they located?" Schellenberg asked.

"Four. There are two to the left at the end of the corridor and two more to the right, also at the end of the corridor."

"Kurt," Cockran said, "you and Schellenberg check out the two on the left. Bobby and I will do the same on the right."

Sturm usually deferred to Cockran in life or death situations involving Mattie, but he thought this time his order contained a flaw. "What about Commandant Forster? Who looks after him?"

"Don't worry," Schellenberg said, "I'll look after him." With that, he raised his pistol and shot Forster in the identical spot in his forehead where he had shot Lang. "There, no man, no problem. Wasn't it Stalin who said that? Or was it our *Fuhrer*? It's confusing. They both have mustaches."

59

It's Only Water

Konzentrationslager Oranienburg
Oranienburg, Germany
Friday, 21 September 1934

HIS MISSION was a success, Canfield thought, as he sat behind a one-way mirror that looked out into the interrogation room where Mattie McGary was handcuffed to an arm chair while two *Gestapo* guards were in the process of stripping Hanna Raeder. The Hearst journalist was on ice here under an assumed name for an indefinite period, certainly well beyond the Congressional mid-term elections in November. And while that timid cripple in the White House had also professed to be concerned about his own re-election prospects in 1936, two years in politics was a lifetime and the public's memory had a short lifespan.

With his work in Germany done, Canfield originally intended to go back to Berlin, collect his wife and take her on a promised tour of Germany's new *autobahns* in the beautiful black Mercedes SSK roadster he had sitting in the parking lot outside the camp. When Freisler told him that Kleist was going to interrogate both women with the simulated drowning technique, he changed his mind. His professional curiosity got the better of him and he asked if he could watch. He had heard about it from fellow naval officers in ONI who had served as naval attaches in Tokyo. The *Kempeitai*—Japan's secret police equivalent of the *Gestapo*—used it frequently and claimed it never failed to produce results in a shockingly short time, seconds rather than minutes. Canfield was skeptical of this. Hell, it's only water. But if it worked, it would be a valuable tool in the future to teach RVD International operatives.

Hanna Raeder was a remarkably attractive woman for 38, Canfield thought, as the *Gestapo* guards stripped her down to her undergarments—a lacy pale pink brassiere and matching silk step-ins. He was surprised and perhaps a little disappointed when the guards didn't strip her completely. In his experience, having your prisoners naked during interrogation was a better way to go. It contributed to a feeling of vulnerability and helplessness on their part. The guards placed her on her back on a plain wooden table with her head at its top. The table was elevated slightly at its foot by two bricks placed under two table legs. Padded restraints were on either side of the table and the guard secured her wrists inside them. Similar restraints were at the foot of the table and these were clamped over her ankles, effectively immobilizing all four of her limbs.

Their work done, the two guards left the room and were soon replaced by *Herr Doktor* Freisler, the *Gestapo* agent Kleist and that dishy blonde *Gestapo* agent.

"Ah, *Frau* Raeder, if only your husband, the Grand Admiral, could see you now," Freisler said as he looked down at the woman. "What do you suppose he will say when he discovers his wife is a traitor to the *Reich*?"

"Go to hell, Freisler! You and that blonde bitch are the only traitors in this room, traitors to every value true Germans hold dear."

"We'll just have to agree to disagree on that, now, won't we? What I want from you are the names of all the moderate members on the Commission who secretly share your views on Jews. The sooner you give me those names, the sooner they will be joining you here to keep you company. Once you give me those names, we'll strap *Frau* McGary to the table and use the same tecniques on her that we're about to do with you to verify the accuracy and completeness of your answers. Then, we'll make her identify all her sources on the Commission."

Freisler walked to the other side of the table so that he was addressing both women. "If you won't answer voluntarily, you will within a minute of your interrogation. So, will you give me names?"

Hanna didn't reply.

"Kleist, give her 15 seconds of water to begin."

Canfield watched as Kleist placed a small hand towel over the woman's face so that it covered her eyes, nose and mouth. Then, he took a water pitcher and began slowly pouring the water over the towel. The woman's immediate reaction was fascinating. She gasped, sucking the cloth partially into her mouth as her body began to convulse. While her limbs were secure, the rest of her body was not and she began wildly bucking her hips and arching her back. It only lasted 15 seconds, but it seemed to Canfield to be a lot longer and he imagined it was the same for the woman. Her pale undergarments were now soaked from the water and so transparent as to render her naked.

Kleist lifted the wet towel off her face and that bald idiot Freisler loomed over *Frau* Raeder, leering down at her. "Are you ready now to give me names?"

Again, Hanna didn't reply, but if looks could kill, Canfield thought...

"Give her 30 seconds this time," Freisler ordered.

"Sir, the protocol calls for another 15 seconds before we do 30 seconds," Kleist said. "It usually does the trick. I've never had to go to 30 seconds with a woman before. You do realize we are actually drowning her. She could suffer permanent damage if not drown to death during a full 30 seconds."

"Do I look like I give a damn?" Freisler replied. "Give the traitorous bitch the full 30 seconds. Now!"

Canfield watched as Kleist replaced the wet towel over the woman's face and once more began to pour water over it from the pitcher. And once more, the woman's virtually naked body began its hip-bucking, back-arching convulsions. Truth be told, Canfield found it painful to watch and, apparently, the McGary broad did as well for she had turned her face away.

Canfield had been checking the time on the second hand of his watch and was surprised when, as it reached 25 seconds, the woman's convulsions ceased and she lay still. My God, he thought, has Kleist killed her? He apparently had the same concern because he promptly snatched the towel from her face; released her wrist and ankle restraints and pulled her up to a sitting position. He pounded her hard on her back, forcing her head down. He heard the woman give a choking cough as water spewed from her mouth onto the floor. More coughs followed and then, when she began to shiver uncontrollably, Kleist wrapped a blanket around her shoulders.

When her shivering had subsided, Freisler walked over, grabbed her by her hair and yanked her head up. "Well, are you ready now to give me the names? Or would you like another dose? I can make it 45 seconds this time. You barely survived 30 seconds. I think 45 seconds would finish you off. So, what's it to be?"

I'll be damned, Canfield thought, that water on a board torture thing actually worked in less than a minute! In the next room, the woman began to recite names in a dull monotone and the sexy blonde *Gestapo* agent took them all down. Just then, he caught movement in the corner of his eye from the window behind him that looked out on the courtyard.

What the hell! Canfield thought as he watched one of those flying windmills with swastikas on its fuselage and tail land in the courtyard. He wondered what that was all about. A second autogiro landed just as two men stepped from the front cockpit of the first autogiro. Oh my God! Canfield thought when he recognized Walter Schellenberg! This was not good. Being found by that SS guy in the same concentration camp as Mattie McGary when he had specifically warned Canfield to stay away from her raised all sorts of possibilities, including being subject to the same water on a board torture interrogation as *Frau* Raeder.

Canfield couldn't let that happen. He knew too much. He was on a mission from the President of the United States and it was time to get out of Dodge. Canfield put on his trench coat and picked up his briefcase. Then, he saw that the pilots of those flying windmills were none other than Cockran and Sullivan! Why were they still alive? How in hell did they get here? Well, it didn't matter because he wasn't about to stick around to find out. He saw Cockran and Sullivan walk in the other direction while Schellenberg and some other SS guy headed toward the Administration Building. The straps of Schmeisser submachine pistols were slung over their shoulders, Luger automatic pistols in their right hands. Kleist had told him the two women were the only prisoners in the *Gestapo* section of the camp so it didn't take an Einstein to figure out why they were here.

Canfield left the room, turned right and opened the door of the windowless interrogation room. *Frau* Raeder's arm now was handcuffed to a chair, the blanket still over her shoulders. Two guards were standing by McGary whose handcuff had been released and who was, presumably, about to be stripped and placed on the board. "Hey, Freisler!" Canfield said. "Two aircraft just landed in the courtyard filled with armed men carrying machine guns. I think they're here for the two broads. If I were you, I'd think about getting them out of here and taking them somewhere else."

Canfield walked down the long corridor to the point of the triangle where an exit door led to a small parking lot reserved for the use of the camp's Gestapo section. He was halfway along the corridor when he heard the crack of a pistol shot. He increased his pace. Another shot. He was getting out in the nick of time. As he opened the door to the parking lot, he heard a third shot.

His black Mercedes SSK roadster and Freisler's large Mercedes touring car were the only automobiles in the parking lot. As he pulled onto the street, he began to think about next steps, the first of which was to leave Germany. If Schellenberg captured either Freisler or Kleist, there was no question in his mind that one or both would disclose his role whether or not they were subject to that water torture. That could easily happen within the hour. If it happened, Schellenberg might well put his name on a detain notice at airports, train stations and ports. That meant he would have to use one of several forged Canadian passports with false names.

The second step was *how* to get out of Germany as quickly as possible. He briefly considered driving to the nearest border, Poland, because he really loved driving the SSK, but it was 250 miles and at least three hours away. He also rejected taking a train to Poland because it was four hours away and, like the SSK, it could be stopped at the border. *Templehof* Aerodrome, however, was only 40 minutes away and once he was on a plane to any other country, it didn't stop at a border. So, he would go to *Templehof,* leave the SSK in a parking lot for the auto rental company, *Sixt,* to retrieve and then take the first late flight out of Germany.

The third—and least important—step was what to do about his wife, Camilla. He didn't have time to go to their hotel in Berlin and tell her his plans. Likewise, he couldn't call her because that bastard Schellenberg might have tapped the phones in their suite. Finally, he decided that he would send her a telegram either tonight or tomorrow morning from whatever country he landed in. As he drove, he began to compose the telegram.

> CAMILLA. STOP. BUSINESS REQUIRED ME TO LEAVE GERMANY ON SHORT NOTICE. STOP. DANGER TO ME NOT YOU. STOP. DEMAND TO SEE U.S. CONSUL IF DETAINED BY AUTHORITIES. STOP. LEAVE GERMANY AS SOON AS POSSSIBLE BY FIRST CLASS. STOP. GOOD LUCK. STOP. SEE YOU IN NYC. STOP. LOVE HARRY.

Yes, he thought, that should do it. She might be inconvenienced if the Germans picked her up, but wasn't that just what 'for better or for worse' in their marriage vows was all about?

60

An Enemy of the State

Konzentrationslager Oranienburg
Oranienburg, Germany
Friday, 21 September 1934

MATTIE McGARY looked at the clock on the wall. It was 9:50 p.m. and if what Kurt told her this afternoon was correct, two autogiros should have landed by now in the courtyard. She hoped they found her before she suffered Hanna's fate. Watching her endure that water torture had been even more horrific than seeing the beheading of Dohnanyi for his death was quick, if not painless. Hanna had not been that fortunate. Mercifully, however, her torture had ended and two *Gestapo* guards reentered the room, helped the woman down from what Mattie thought of as the torture rack, placed her in an armchair, and attached her wrist with a handcuff to an arm of the chair. Hanna held the blanket over her shoulders together with her free hand.

"Strip the other woman and secure her arms and legs to the plank," Freisler ordered.

The two guards came over and one of them unlocked the handcuff on Mattie's right wrist. Then, both men took her arms and pulled her to her feet with the same vicious grins on their faces as when they had been stripping Hanna. These were men, she thought, who enjoyed their work as she hit one of them in the head with her elbow as her husband had taught her. He yelled inpain and stepped back. Then, she jammed a knee into the groin of the second guard.

Before the guards could recover, Mattie heard a door open behind her and a voice spoke German with what she recognized as an American accent. "Hey, Freisler! Two aircraft just landed in the courtyard filled with armed men carrying machine guns. I think they're here for the two broads. If I were you, I'd think about getting them out of here and taking them somewhere else."

No sooner had the door closed than Mattie heard a shot fired. Ten seconds later, another shot. The two guards who had recovered from Mattie's attack were now holding her by her arms. They looked over at Freisler as if to ask what they should do, but he seemed to be in a trance and said nothing.

Kleist took charge. "Release the handcuffs on the woman. I don't know what's going on, but we'd better move them to a more secure location."

This seemed to snap Freisler out of his stupor for he reached into his pants pocket and pulled a set of keys from it and handed it to Greta Mayer. "My Mercedes is parked in the small lot outside the top of the triangle where the two corridors meet. Run to the emergency exit there. Start the engine and move the motorcar into place beside the exit. Kleist and I will meet you there with the two women."

Freisler turned to the two guards just as a third shot was heard. "Cover our departure. Don't let anyone past you. Shoot anyone who tries."

With that, Freisler drew a Luger tucked in the small of his back and grabbed Hanna by the arm while Kleist did the same with Mattie. They pulled both women from the room and turned right into the corridor while the two *Gestapo* guards turned left and drew their weapons.

Kleist pressed the muzzle of his pistol in her back as he urged her forward while Freisler did the same with Hanna, who was still clad only in her undergarments and a blanket. She didn't know what Kleist meant by 'a more secure location', but at least Sturm and Cockran knew about *this* location and she was heartened by the sound of gunfire. It meant their rescue might be at hand!

Mattie heard two short bursts of automatic weapons fire and turned her head as Kleist pushed her forward. "Bourke!" she shouted as she saw the figures of her husband and Bobby Sullivan standing over the bodies of the two *Gestapo* guards 25 yards away.

"Release the women!" Sullivan shouted in German as Mattie watched the two sling their automatic weapons over their shoulders and draw Colt .45 M1911 automatic pistols. Sullivan had two, one in each hand while Cockran had one in his right hand. He fired a shot into the ceiling.

"Last chance! The next shot goes into you!" Sullivan yelled as he and Cockran began running up the corridor until they were ten yards away.

At Cockran's shot, Freisler and Kleist turned around to look at their new adversaries. They apparently decided that exposing their backs was not a wise move because they promptly put their left arms around the women's chests and held them in front as human shields. Mattie felt the muzzle of the Luger pressed against her head. Freisler clumsily did the same with Hanna.

"Stop where you are!" Kleist said "and put your weapons on the ground or the women die."

Well, that was pretty stupid, Mattie thought. Killing their hostages would only guarantee their own swift deaths. Kleist began to walk backwards, pulling Mattie with him as Freisler did the same with Hanna on their right. Freisler was barely an inch or two taller than Hanna and hence was able to shield most of his body behind her. Kleist, on the other hand, was a good head taller than Mattie leaving his head exposed.

Mattie wasn't worried and didn't panic. It wasn't her first rodeo. She knew her husband, not a great marksman, wouldn't risk a shot, but she'd played this scene before with Bourke and Bobby Sullivan in a castle high in the Austrian Alps three years ago. Mattie caught Sullivan's eye and lowered her eyes, hoping he caught her signal. Sullivan gave her an almost imperceptible nod of his head. Cockran held his Colt .45 in his right hand, its barrel pointing up at the ceiling as he slowly began to kneel while, beside him, Sullivan held up both of his Colt .45 pistols with the barrel up as he too began to kneel.

Mattie waited for the moment when Cockran placed his weapon on the floor. When he did, she made her move. She simultaneously ducked her head and went limp. Kleist was caught by surprise, unprepared to support the weight of Mattie's 125 pounds and she fell to the floor just as Sullivan sent two rounds from the pistol in his right hand into Kleist's chest, blowing him off his feet. Less than a second later, Sullivan fired a single shot from the automatic in his left hand that hit Freisler squarely in the forehead.

A shower of blood and bone exploded from his shattered skull and Hanna screamed as Freisler's body pulled her back onto the floor. Mattie rushed over and lifted Hanna to her feet. Freisler's blood and bits of bone had completely covered her face and, before the shock of it had a chance to settle, Mattie quickly used the blanket to wipe away the worst of it.

"Bourke, Hanna's been tortured. One of you take her back to the room we were in and get her dressed and into one of the autogiros."

"Aye," Sullivan said, "I'll do that."

"Good. Bourke, you go to the Commandant's office and find my camera bag. Check to see that the June 5 transcript of the German Commission on Criminal Law Reform is there along with my *Leica*, five film cartridges and my Walther PPK. Meanwhile, lend me your .45 automatic. I've got one more thing to do and then I'll meet you at the autogiros."

"What are you going to do?" Cockran asked.

"Settle a score with the woman who betrayed us and had Hanna tortured."

Cockran hesitated and Mattie held out her hand. "Now, Cockran. We don't have much time. I can handle her."

Mattie took the pistol, checked to make sure a round was chambered and ran up the corridor to the top of the triangle. Electric wall sconces every ten yards lighted the way. She reached the top of the corridor, but saw no exits, so she rounded the top and headed down the left hand side of the triangle and immediately saw a door to her right. She opened it and walked out into a small gravel covered parking lot lit by several overhead lights. The only car in the lot was a long, black Mercedes touring car with a canvas top. Holding the .45

automatic in both hands, she carefully walked over to the motorcar in the lot and swept the interior, but no one was in it. In fact, she doubted that Greta ever got here because Freisler had told her to move the Mercedes to the exit door. Yet, here it was, still a good twenty yards from the door.

Mattie tucked the pistol into the waistband of her trousers, ran back to the door into the compound. She opened the door and Greta Mayer and a *Gestapo* guard were ten feet away, with *Lugers* in their hands pointed directly at her.

Greta held up a *Gestapo* medallion in her left hand. "*Frau* McGary, I am placing you under arrest as an enemy of the state for which the penalty is death. Raise your hands. Gunter, place her in handcuffs" she said with a nod in the direction of the guard who stood to her left, "and stand her up against the wall."

The guard holstered his weapon, grabbed Mattie's hands, roughly pulling them behind her and attaching handcuffs to her wrists. He pushed her up against the wall and then Greta held her *Luger* in front of her and pointed it at Mattie. "Much as I would like to see your head roll in the courtyard just like my uncle's, I think I'll carry out your penalty myself right now."

Mattie had no time to think how to avoid her execution by Greta's bullets when three shots rang out in rapid succession and Greta's chest erupted in blood, her eyes wide in surprise, blood flowing from her mouth as she sank to her knees and then pitched forward onto her face. With Greta on the floor, Mattie could now see her assailant holding a still-smoking *Luger* automatic with both hands, a look of fierce hatred on her face. Hanna Raeder!

At the sound of the gunshots, the guard had turned to face the new threat, attempting to draw his *Luger* from his holster. His hand was still on the butt of his weapon when Hanna shot him twice in the middle of his chest. The impact sent him onto his back in front of Mattie, still alive and groaning. Hanna stepped over him, placed the muzzle of the *Luger* on the back of the man's head and fired a *coup de grace.*

"That was one of the bastards who stripped me and put me on that board," Hanna said as she took the keys from the dead guard and unlocked Mattie's handcuffs.

"Thanks, you're a life-saver. Literally. But where the hell did you learn to shoot like that?"

"I'm a Navy wife. After I married Erich, he insisted I continue my weekly visits to the target range. Berlin, indeed all of Weimar Germany during the 1920s, was not an especially safe place."

"Why did you come back here? You seemed to be in pretty bad shape."

Hanna smiled. "I heard you say you were going to settle the score with the woman who betrayed us. Once I was dressed, I thought I'd see if you needed any help."

"I'm glad you did. Come on, let's get to the courtyard," Mattie said, "where our flying chariots await to get us out of this little piece of hell."

Halfway down the corridor, they met Cockran, Sullivan, Sturm and Schellenberg running towards them with guns drawn. "We heard gunshots, " Cockran said as he came to a halt. "Are you two okay?"

"We're fine," Mattie said. "There are two more bodies back there. Greta Mayer and a *Gestapo* guard. Greta was an undercover *Gestapo* agent and Hanna shot her just just before she was about to kill me. Then she shot the guard in self-defense although that *coup de grace* to his head might be difficult to explain. Who's looking after the autogiros?"

"Your guardian angels Eric Bulow and Franz Globke," Schellenberg replied with a smile.

"I'll check out the two bodies," Sturm said, "then I'll meet you in the courtyard."

Two minute later, they were all in the courtyard. Sturm introduced himself to Hanna as the liaison from the *Reichstag* to the Commission on Criminal Law Reform and then looked at Cockran.

"Bourke, I think it best if you and Bobby take Mattie and *Frau* Raeder out of here. I don't think it wise for their names to appear in any of the many police reports that will be filed about tonights's events. I will stay behind and help Schellenberg make sure the Prussian

State Police prepare the proper reports. By my count, we have nine bodies of people shot 'resisting arrest', but it might be difficult for the head of the Prussian State Police squad to swallow that for the two *Frau* Raeder shot and I may have to ask *Unser* Hermann to bring some pressure to bear. That won't be a problem for him as he's had no use for the *Gestapo* ever since he had to turn it over to Himmler. Still, it's better to err on the side of caution."

"Good idea," Cockran said and then turned to Mattie and Hanna. "Ask *Frau* Raeder where she would like us to take her," he said in English.

Mattie looked at Hanna and asked in German "Where would you like to go?"

"Back to Berlin is fine," Hanna replied. "With Freisler dead, I don't think I'm in danger anymore. I'll go to our home there and see if there's been any new word from Erich as to when he'll be back from his sea trials."

Thirty minutes later, the two autogiros landed at *Templehof* aerodrome where Sullivan volunteered to see *Frau* Raeder safely home.

"Let's go back to the *Adlon*," Mattie said to Cockran. "I am so looking forward to a nice long soak in the tub."

The Hotel Adlon
Berlin
Freday, 21 September 1934

"WATER TORTURE is positively horrific," Mattie McGary said after she took a sip from the crystal glass of scotch resting on the flat marble surface surrounding the bathtub where she had been luxuriating for the past half-hour while Cockran sat on a stool at the foot of the tub with his own drink. "I've never seen anything like it. Hanna told me it felt like she was drowning. She is one tough woman, though. I thought she was in shock afterwards, but she told me that half of all the names she gave Freisler were radical Nazis, not moderates. Then, after that torture, for her to grab a gun and go after Greta Mayer? She's my new hero."

"Chopped liver am I now?"

Maddie grinned, "Well, by my count, the score is Hanna and Bobby four dead bad guys and Cockran zero."

Cockran laughed. "Are you going to use it in your story?"

"I'm not sure. I'll sleep on it overnight and let you know when we're back in Ireland. I've got to be careful to protect Hanna's identity so I'm inclined not to use it. I'm certainly going to use my two kidnappings and Dohnanyi's beheading after a sham trial before a so-called 'Peoples Court'. Speaking of Ireland, what time is our flight to Dublin tomorrow?"

"9:00 a.m. with a layover in London. We'll be in Dublin late afternoon. I'll have the *Celtic Princess* gassed and ready to go wheels up thirty minutes after we land."

"Excellent," Mattie said as she stood up in the tub. "Hand me a towel."

Cockran did and she toweled off after she stepped out of the tub. "Well, you've been such a good boy, waiting on me hand and foot since we returned, you've earned your reward," she said as she handed him the towel and walked from the bathroom into the bedroom.

"And my reward would be what?"

"Use your imagination. You'll think of something."

Part V

England, Germany & America
28 September 1934—10 October 1934

Hitler Deprives Jews of Citizen Rights,
Bans Intermarriage
Threatens Other Steps
to Solve Race Problem
The Baltimore Sun, 16 September 1935

Reichstag Backs Hitler Anti-Jew Program in Full
Relegates Race to Same Status Occupied
During Dark Middle Ages
The Associated Press, 16 September 1935

Berlin Works Out Anti-Jewish Rules
No Date Has Been Set
for Promulgating Regulations
to Enforce Recent Laws
The New York Times, 1 October 1935

61

Was Göring Really a Hero?

Chartwell
Kent, England
Friday, 28 September 1934

WINSTON CHURCHILL, truth be told, was flattered when his goddaughter asked him to read and offer his comments on the articles she had written about the Prussian Memorandum and her adventures investigating the story. He was doing so now as he sat at his writing desk in the library on the ground floor of his country home in the late afternoon, the front of the desk flush against the wall. Sunlight streamed in through the two tall windows on either side of the desk and illuminated the floor to ceiling bookshelves.

Churchill had a weak whisky and water in front of him, an unlit Havana cigar clutched in his mouth, and half-moon spectacles perched on his nose. Mattie McGary and her husband, Bourke Cockran, sat in chairs on one side of the desk with rather more strong whisky and waters on a side table between them. Patrick, Cockran's red-haired 14-year-old son, and Mary, Churchill's pretty blonde 13-year-old daughter, sat on a settee on the other side of the desk in their riding clothes openly holding hands in front of their fathers. Patrick was an especial fan of his stepmother's journalism and Mattie had persuaded

Churchill to allow the two young people to be present for the occasion.

Churchill was amused. The two children had become good friends the summer before last at the Cockran-McGary wedding on Loch Ness near Inverness at the McGary country home where, on a horseback ride after the wedding reception, they had been kidnapped and held for ransom by Nazi agents. Mary had told her father more than once how brave young Patrick had been throughout their ordeal. Their friendship had been renewed this summer in July when Bourke, Mattie and Patrick had been weekend guests after another perilous adventure by Mattie in Germany that ended with Hitler's assassinations of his political enemies during the Night of the Long Knives. Cockran and Patrick had left for the United States in late August, but Patrick had returned a month later and it would appear, Churchill thought, that the children's budding romance—if indeed that's what it was—had not diminished in the interim. They were both too young, of course, but Churchill—half-American himself on his mother's side—thought his daughter could do worse when she was old enough than to become romantically involved with the grandson of Churchill's own American mentor.

"It's going to be a seven-part story," Mattie had said when they all sat down in the library. "The articles will run for seven days, Monday, 1 October through Sunday, 7 October on the front page above the fold in all the Hearst newspapers."

After Churchill finished the first article, he put it down, took a sip of his scotch and water and smiled as he motioned for Mary to come over and he passed the article on to her. She took it back to Patrick and the two began eagerly to read it together. "Excellent article," Churchill said and, speaking of confidentiality, I especially appreciate your not disclosing that Dohnonyi's copy of the Memorandum passed through me."

Mattie laughed. "Yeah, well Kurt gave me a copy also, but I didn't think those little details added anything to the story. So here's the second article," she said, handing him four typewritten sheets and continued. "Part II reveals the U.S. Army's Military Intelligence Division's involvement in the legal research that became the Prussian

Memorandum and that the SS reimbursed MID for the money it spent to hire the lawyers."

"How did you know that about the SS reimbursing MID?" Churchill asked after he finished reading the article and, as before, passed it on to Mary and Patrick.

"I never promised any confidentiality to my source for that, but I didn't think it wise to identify him. It was Walter Schellenberg, head of the SD's Foreign Section and my personal guardian angel in Germany. He's the one who passed on the research assignment to the SS guy at their Washington Embassy."

Mattie reached into her camera bag for the third article and handed it over. "I think Part III is the biggest bombshell, namely that the six former MID agents who conducted the legal research were killed during a six week period in late 1933; that all of them were likely killed by Nicholas Carson, a former Black & Tan assassin and an occasional hit man for the New York crime boss Owney Madden. While police in all six cities where the former MID agents were killed have no leads as to who hired Carson, Bourke and I suspect it was Canfield who had Owney hire Carson because he tried to have me killed. I can't say that in print because we have no proof."

"Yes, Bobby and I were Mattie's confidential sources on that story," Cockran said from his chair across the room. "We know that Carson killed all those ex-agents because Madden tried to hire Bobby to do the job first. He showed Bobby the six names, but Bobby turned him down. Madden virtually told him that he was next going to offer the job to Carson. Bobby agrees with us that Canfield was the guy who likely dealt with Madden because when he talked to Bobby about taking the assignment to kill those six former agents, he said it was a matter of national security and Canfield used to be with the Office of Naval Intelligence."

"Right," Mattie said, "you and Bobby are two more of my 'confidential' sources. For the rest of the series, I don't have to rely on confidential sources as it's mostly about what happened to me."

After passing on the third article, Churchill occasionally looked over at his daughter and Patrick, but they appeared oblivious to the adults' conversation as they kept reading the articles and whispering to one another.

Mattie once more reached into her bag, walked over to his desk and handed a new article to Churchill. "This is Part IV where I begin my own involvement in the story including the attack on me in Berlin by agents from RVD International, the unknown assasilants—likely RVD again, but we can't prove it—who tried to kill me as I travelled back to my hotel in a boat on one of the canals in Amsterdam. And, as you well know, Winston, those lovely *Gestapo* agents then kidnapped me from my hotel and took me on a Rhine River freighter into Germany after my first attempt to escape from the freighter failed."

"You tried to escape from your kidnappers?" a wide-eyed Patrick asked. "What did you do?"

"As I was being transferred from a houseboat to a river freighter, I kicked one of them in the groin and leaped into the river," Mattie replied. "I tried to swim to the riverbank. Unfortunately, I didn't have time to take off my boots and I was caught and brough back to the freighter."

Churchill finished the article and handed it to Mary. "Thanks again for leaving my role in this out of the article," he said to Mattie and then lit a new cigar. "I trust you did the same for my stint as a getaway pilot on that American-made runabout?"

Mattie laughed as she walked over to Churchill's desk and gave him another article. "That's right. In the fifth article, I cover both my second attempt to escape from the freighter and my daring rescue in Duisberg, Germany which I attribute only to a 'special unit of the Prussian State Police' acting under the direction of the Prussian Prime Minister and *Reichstag* President Herman Göring. You're not mentioned and neither are Bourke, Bobby or Kurt. Given that they all had Prussian State Police badges from *Unser* Hermann, it was sufficient to just lump them all under that label."

"Wait a minute, Papa," Mary said. "You were the one who operated the speed boat that rescued Mattie?"

Churchill put down the article he had started to read. "Yes I was. It seemed the least I could do since I was the one who persuaded her to go after this story," Churchill replied. "I also hired the saloon boat in

Amsterdam that we used to retrieve the transcript of the June 5 meeting."

"So you were in that boat in Amsterdam where bad guys were shooting at Mattie?" Patrick asked. "Did you shoot back?"

"No," Churchill said and smiled. "Although both Mattie and I were armed, we had no chance to shoot back. There's no mention of it in the article, but, in fact, two SS men who were charged with keeping Mattie safe killed both of the men who had shot at us."

Churchill then resumed reading the article. "Very good," he said after he finished reading the fifth article and passed it over to Mary. His goddaughter was a fine writer and he was quietly proud of the role he had played in inspiring her to become a journalist when she was a young girl. "What's next?"

Mattie again walked to his desk and handed him a new article. "Part VI is where I report the brakes on my motorcar were cut for my trip to Rostok to meet a confidential source. This is followed by my arrest by the *Gestapo* along with Hanna Raeder, followed by our incarceration in the *Oranienburg Konzentrationslager*. Then I digress and, at Hanna's request, I outline the history of the Nazis' creation of 'Peoples Courts' and how they are nothing more than kangaroo courts driven by politics, not the law. That's a prelude to the bogus show trial of Georg von Dohnanyi and his being sentenced to death."

Churchill read the article with great interest. He had never heard of these Peoples Courts before now. They were exactly what a dictator needed to keep his opponents in line while piously claiming to be acting under the rule of law. Of course, executing 200 of your political enemies without using Peoples Courts or any other courts also helped keep people in line.

"Excellent article," Churchill said and again handed it to Mary. "I had no idea their courts were being politicized as well as cowed. This is a remarkable series. How do you conclude?"

Mattie gave Churchill a copy of the last article. "Part VII—the last article—begins with the execution of Georg von Dohnanyi after his kangaroo court trial, the water torture of Hanna Raeder, followed by our rescue by the Prussian State Police unit again acting on orders from Prussian Prime Minister and *Reichstag* President Herman Göring.

Then I briefly mention that Freisler and Kleist were killed while resisting arrest."

Churchill put down the last article, handed it to Mary, removed his reading glasses, took a sip of Scotch and smiled. "Was Göring really a hero? Does he know you're going to give him the lion's share of the credit for your two rescues from the *Gestapo*? From all you, Bourke and *Herr* von Sturm have told me about him, he appears to be a ruthless man who also favors stripping German Jews of their citizenship and banning marriage with Aryans."

Before Mattie could answer, Patrick and Mary looked up from the last article with horrified expressions on their faces. "You actually saw a man beheaded?" they asked in unison.

"Yes, it was really gruesome," Mattie said, "but it wasn't my first time. You remember my article on the search in the Austrian Alps for the 'Spear of Destiny' three years ago Patrick? I didn't include any photographs, but I mentioned in it several beheadings I saw in Castle Lanz where I found the Spear."

Mattie then looked over at Winston. "Yes, to answer your question, Göring knows he's going to get the credit. Kurt made sure he had no objection. In fact, he said Göring was flattered that he was one of the heroes in the articles. Besides, it's mostly true. Not only did he give Prussian State Police badges to Bourke, Bobby and Kurt for the Duisberg rescue, he also signed the release order from the *Oranienberg* camp for Hanna Raeder and me; he made the autogiros available for Bourke and Bobby; and he had the Prussian State Police raid the camp as a diversion for our escape."

Mattie paused, took a sip of her Scotch, and continued. "Sure, he's an anti-Semite, but it's not like the anti-Semitism of Hitler, Goebbels, Himmler and most high ranking Nazis. The fact is Göring helped stop most of the random violence against the Jews last year. True, he didn't do it on principle. He did it to undercut the worldwide boycott of German exports. For the same reason, he also favors the most lenient definition of who is a Jew rather than the radical notions of Himmler and Goebbels. According to Hanna, the Commission will have no choice but to recommend these laws against the Jews even though she and a few others will oppose it. After that, she and other moderates on the Commission will try and limit the laws to as few people as possible. For that, Göring will be on their side."

Churchill nodded and took a puff on his cigar. "You also omit any reference to American military intelligence engaging this RVD International to arrange for the legal research. Why?"

"Lawyers. Hearst's libel lawyers say that even though we know RVD did it, we can't identify it for the legal research done by anyone except Henry Sandler because the other five law firms won't confirm RVD was even a client. They say they can't ethically do so. Without that, we have no proof that the other five lawyers were engaged by RVD. True, Harvard's Dean Pound supervised all six lawyers and had the legal research delivered to the Nazis, but he didn't finger RVD either. I don't mention Dean Pound at all because Bourke told me he thinks Jewish gangsters, the Cleveland Syndicate, were behind the six murders. We know that's not true, so I didn't want Pound to have the chance to publicly blame the Jews for that."

"I understand, but you know from German wiretaps that this Canfield fellow from RVD had you roughed up in Berlin and tried to have you killed in Amsterdam. Why not mention that?"

"Kurt asked him, but Göring won't let me use wiretap transcripts. Moreover, he also won't let me use the Himmler-Goebbels letters about engaging the American MID to do the legal research. Speaking of wiretaps, Göring also told Kurt that Himmler has thrown the dead corpses of Freisler and Kleist under the bus. Once Göring told Hitler about his rescue of Hanna and me from the concentration camp, Himmler was called on the carpet by Hitler to explain why the *Gestapo* did this in the first place. Göring has a wiretap of Himmler and Goebbels making up their cover story that Freisler and Kleist acted without authority. This pleases Göring because now he has blackmail material on both of them."

Mattie laughed. "It's funny you should mention this Canfield guy because we think he was the one who sabotaged the brake lines on my Mercedes. Bourke took down the license plate of the black Mercedes SSK that blocked the road and almost sent us off the road on our way to Rostok to interview Hanna. It was a rental from Sixt by RVD International. We told Schellenberg this and he thought that was enough to issue a warrant for Canfield's arrest, but unfortunately he made it out of the country before they could nab him. So Schellenberg arrested his wife as an accomplice the next day."

"Really? On what basis?" Cockran asked.

Mattie laughed again. "Schellenberg said they were still trying to decide that. He told me it might take quite a while to do so. He showed me a telegram her husband sent her the same day we were rescued warning her to get out of the country and wishing her 'good luck'. Imagine that, abandoning your wife to save your own skin and then wishing her 'good luck'? What a swell guy! A source of mine at the American Embassy said the Nazis refuse to admit they even have her in custody. I told Schellenberg and he laughed, showed me her passport and assured me she was being treated well at a first class Berlin hotel under 'house arrest'." I felt sorry for her. Judging by her passport photo, she is really quite beautiful."

"So, why do you suppose Schellenberg arrested her?" Cockran asked.

"Beats me," Mattie replied, "but, after seeing her photograph, if I had to guess, Schellenberg plans to put the moves on her. He certainly tried it with me earlier this year. He's only 24 and he has a thing for older women."

"Really?" Cockran said. "I don't recall you mentioning this before."

"Dearest, if I told you every time a man made a pass at me," Mattie said as she patted him on his cheek," I wouldn't have much time for anything else. You're still the only man I need. I'll let you know if that ever changes."

Churchill smiled. Patrick and Mary laughed. "Good one, Mattie," Patrick said, a big grin on his face. "She got you, Dad!"

62

I'll Resign If You Wish

Haus Raeder
Spitzweggasse 3
Potsdam-Neubabelsberg, Germany
Wednesday, 10 October 1934

HANNA RAEDER placed the last article in Mattie McGary's series on the Prussian Memorandum down on the table beside her and shuddered at the memory of the water torture Kleist and Freisler had put her through. It was the single most horrifying thing that had ever happened to her. It comforted her to know that all three people responsible for it were dead, one of them by her own hand. She sat in one of the bamboo chairs on the veranda of their home in the early evening, sipping a light scotch and water waiting for her husband to arrive. The sun was low on the horizon and it promised to be a beautiful sunset. She hoped Erich was home in time to see it. He had called her yesterday from Bremerhaven upon his return from sea trials, alarmed that her life had been threatened and that she had gone into hiding on Hiddensee Island. She assured him that the danger was over, but declined to say more. "It's definitely not something to talk about over the telephone. I'll explain everything tomorrow night."

What she hadn't told her husband was that, based on what Kurt von Sturm had told her, *Reichspresident* Göring undoubtedly had wiretaps on her husband's offices and home. This came about after the two became good friends. As the *Reichstag* liaison to the Criminal Law Reform Commission, Sturm had suggested to Justice Minister Gurtner that, with the death of Commission Chair Freisler, he informally appoint Hanna as the Commission's liaison to the *Reichstag*. Gurtner did so and, as a consequence, she and Sturm had met on many occasions during the past two weeks about Commission business. They became friends after she learned from Sturm that both he and Göring supported the most lenient definition of a Jew; that Sturm himself—like Hanna—firmly opposed any laws making Jews second-class citizens; that Sturm had arranged for his blind sister to attend college in America with her Jewish fiancé specifically to avoid her possible forced sterilization under the eugenics laws the Nazis had passed in emulation of similar, if not almost identical, laws of many American states; and that Sturm was good friends with Mattie McGary and her husband.

In fact, Sturm had delivered, at Mattie's request, a complete set of her seven articles to Hanna just as she had forwarded several copies of the clippings to Sturm so that he could pass them on to Göring who had been eager to see the articles that placed him in a favorable light in countries outside Germany. While Hanna intended to disclose the official nature of the relationship between her and Sturm to her husband, she thought their personal friendship should remain private. Erich was old school and, being 20 years older than her, she didn't think he would understand a platonic friendship with a handsome man her own age.

After Erich had read all of Mattie's articles and she confessed she was one of the anonymous Commission members mentioned in the articles, she was going to offer to resign from the Commission. Whatever happened, she hoped she would still be proud he was her husband.

Hanna heard a motorcar pull up in the circular gravel driveway in front of their house. Erich was home! She immediately walked over to a drinks trolley and poured two fingers of scotch into a short crystal glass and added ice. She smiled as her husband walked onto the veranda in his full dress uniform. Though only 5' 6" tall—fully an inch shorter than his wife—Erich Raeder cut an imposing figure as he smiled back, opened his arms and embraced Hanna.

"Home is the sailor, home from the sea," Hanna said as she looked at the trim figure of her darkly handsome husband. His navy blue double-breasted uniform sported four narrow gold bands and one larger gold band on each sleeve and a row of ribbons over his heart. His hair was still black and parted in the middle and he wore an old-fashioned high wing collar with a small black bow tie. His face was brown from the sun and three weeks at sea. His looks didn't rival Sturm, but Hanna loved him and always thought he looked good for his age.

Hanna and her husband took seats in adjoining wicker armchairs with a small wicker table between them on which they placed their drinks. "So, Hanna, how did you come to have your life threatened and by whom?" Raeder asked.

"The threat was anonymous, so I can't be sure, but I believe it was a *Gestapo* agent named Joesph Kleist. For me, I suppose how it all began was when I had lunch with the lawyer Georg von Dohnonyi, a fellow member of the German Commission on Criminal Law Reform. He wanted me to meet off-the-record with a journalist for American newspapers who was investigating a story about the Prussian Memorandum. You remember I once told you about it?"

Raeder nodded and Hanna continued. "I received the threat after my interview with the journalist. Her name is Mattie McGary. She's from Scotland, but she's married to an American and works for an American newspaper chain owned by a man named Hearst. Here is what I received in an unmarked envelope in our mailbox," she said and handed him the newspaper clippings of the murder of former Chancellor von Schleicher and his wife and the note that read 'Don't think your husband's high office will keep you safe if you ever talk to foreign journalists again'.

Raeder looked at what she gave him and nodded.

"I took the threat seriously because I had every intention of meeting again with *Frau* McGary to validate the accuracy of the transcript of an important meeting of the Commission. I knew you were at sea so I decided the best thing to do was go into hiding until you returned. I decided the best place was somewhere only you and I knew about from our honeymoon—Hiddensee Island. What happened to me next and why I'm no longer in danger is part of a larger story. *Frau* McGary delivered to me copies of her seven articles on the Prussian Memorandum. I'm mentioned, but not by name, in the first and last articles. Still, I think you should read all seven articles. After you've read them, especially the last article, I'll answer any questions you may have," she said and handed him a folder with the articles.

Hanna watched as her husband took the folder, opened it and began to read. Occasionally, he frowned, but otherwise said nothing. Finally, she held her breath as he picked up the last article. She honestly didn't know how he'd react. The *Reichsmarine* was his life and she was only his wife, and his second one at that. If he thought this in any way jeopardized the Navy, she knew which one he'd choose. He suddenly paused.

"You were the unnamed Commission member arrested by the *Gestapo* in Rostok?"

"Yes."

Raeder resumed reading and paused again. "And you really were taken to the *Oranienburg* concentration camp?"

"Yes."

"And you witnessed this so-called Peoples Court trial of Dohnanyi before Roland Freisler?"

"Yes."

"And then you were present when Dohnonyi was beheaded?"

"Yes."

Raeder's eyes returned to the article for only a moment until his head shot up, a look of unmistakable anger on his face. "Wait a minute. You were stripped to your undergarments and then tortured by these so called men?"

"Yes. Mattie offered to keep that out of the story even though she didn't identify me as a woman, but I insisted she keep that detail in. These people are evil and my only regret is I didn't get to kill Freisler and Kleist myself."

Raeder finished reading the article and then looked up. "It's a good thing the police killed Freisler and Kleist although I very much doubt they were killed 'resisting arrest'. It saves me the trouble of challenging each one to a duel. I wonder, though, how the *Gestapo* knew you were in Rostok. Did they simply follow the journalist there?"

Hanna's heart leaped at her husband's declaration he would have fought two duels over her torture. Was Erich really going to favor her over the Navy? "Perhaps, but Mattie doesn't think so. I set up the time and place for meeting *Frau* McGary through Dohnonyi's niece, Greta Mayer. It's not in the story, but, unknown to me, Greta Mayer, was an undercover *Gestapo* agent who was out to entrap her uncle into treason by having him turn over a transcript of an important Commission meeting to a foreigner."

"Interesting. What happened to her?"

"She's dead. I shot the Nazi bitch three times in the back right before she was about to execute McGary. I also killed the *Gestapo* guard with her who was about to shoot me. None of that is in the police report of events that night. I've seen a copy. Göring's man von Sturm—he's the *Reichstag* liaison to the Commission—took care of it, he and a young man named Schellenberg who is head of the Foreign Section of the SD."

"Wait a minute. You shot and killed not one, but two *Gestapo* agents? Seriously?"

"Dead serious, my Dear. She had her uncle beheaded and then made us watch. The bitch deserved it. The *Gestapo* guard was self-defense."

"Even so, that means Göring, Heydrich and possibly even Himmler know what you did if their subordinates reported any of this to them. That will not be good for the Navy."

"Possibly, and I'll resign, if you wish, from the Commission if you think what I did might put the *Reichsmarine* at a disadvantage. I'm almost positive, however, that none of those three men know that I killed the two *Gestapo* people."

"Why's that?"

"The *Reichstag* liaison to the Commission, Kurt von Sturm, told me that he and Schellenberg agreed that they would only show their superiors the official police reports of our rescue at *Oranienburg*."

"You believe him?"

"Oh, yes. His real name is not Sturm. It's Strasser, Kurt von Strasser, and I'm sure you knew his father, Peter von Strasser."

"Strasser? Of course. He was head of the Imperial Naval Airship Division. A real hero. He had the Blue Max. Died in the last days of the war in an air raid on England. I never met his son, but I know who he is. A good Navy man. He was awarded the Blue Max also, the only father and son to both have that honor. After the war, he personally saw to the destruction of all our naval zeppelins to keep them from being delivered to the Allies as reparations. I heard the Socialist government tried to have him arrested for that, but they couldn't find him."

That's because, Hanna thought, he changed his name and went to work for Fritz von Thyssen as his Executive Assistant. There was a lot she and Sturm had told each other about their lives and his openness with her was a welcome respite from having to watch her tongue in her conversations with other Commission members now that Kramer and Dohnonyi were dead.

"His work for Göring is mostly part-time," Hanna said, "like his liaison with the Commission. His primary job is with *Zeppelin Reederi*. He's the commander of the *Graf Bismarck* and flies round trips to the United States twice a month."

"Well, if you can't trust the word of a man with the Blue Max, who can you trust? I believe him, although I'm not so sure about Schellenberg."

"I had the same concern and mentioned it to Sturm. He told me not to worry. Schellenberg is very young, only 24, but Sturm is a hero to him for his exploits in destroying those zeppelins. I watched them interact the night we were rescued from *Oranienberg*. Sturm took charge of what to do in the aftermath and Schellenberg was like a little puppy agreeing with every suggestion Sturm made. And whenever Schellenberg made a suggestion that Sturm agreed with, you could see him swell up with pride."

"Good. It's not fatal, but I would prefer that men like Göring, Himmler and especially Heydrich did not know how deadly my wife is."

"Why Heydrich, especially?" Hanna asked.

"There's bad blood between us. I never mentioned it to you at the time, but I personally had him drummed out of the *Reichsmarine* in 1931 for impregnating the daughter of a major naval supplier and not doing the honorable thing by marrying her."

"So, I take it you don't wish me to resign from the Commission? That my work on it won't hurt the Navy?" Hanna asked.

"Resign? Oh my Lord, of course not! I've already refused to dismiss Jewish naval officers and a law like the one the Commission is considering could have serious consequences for the Navy depending on how a Jew is defined. Like you, I'd rather no law be passed making Jews second-class citizens. If one is passed, however, I want it to impact as few of my men as possible. You're doing good work on the Commission and I'm proud of you. Keep it up."

Hanna stood up, leaned over and kissed her husband on the cheek. "Thank you. Having your support means everything to me." Yes, she thought, she was still proud he was her husband.

63

We Are a Civilized Country

The Berghof
Berchtesgaden, Germany
Wednesday, 10 October 1934

REICHSMINISTER **HERMANN** Göring waited patiently while Adolf Hitler, hands clasped behind his back, stood deep in thought before the huge window that occupied an entire wall of the Great Room in his mountain villa in Bavaria. The window itself had been lowered into the floor so there was simply a vast open space looking out at the spectacular Bavarian Alps. Göring preferred to meet Hitler here because being in Berchtesgaden always put his leader in a better mood, more relaxed and more jovial.

Hitler's adjutant, Rudolf Hoettl, had announced Göring's arrival a few moments ago, but Hitler had given no sign that he had heard him. Göring knew from past experience that his leader was not being rude. You simply had to wait until he finished thinking about whatever he was thinking and was ready to talk.

To emphasize the points he wished to make about rearmament being more important than new laws against the Jews, Göring wore his pale blue *Luftwaffe* uniform with a wide dark blue vertical stripe down down trousers tucked into polished black leather knee high boots. The gold and enamel cross of the 'Blue Max', Imperial Germany's highest honor, hung in a ribbon around his neck, a subtle reminder that both he and Hitler were legitimate war heroes compared to Himmler and Goebbels with whom the *Fuhrer* had held separate conferences today prior to meeting with Göring. Indeed, not only had Himmler and Goebbels never served in the military, it was Göring and not them who had been wounded at Hitler's side during the 1923 Munich *putsch*.

"Hermann! Our conquering hero!" Hitler said as he turned from the window, walked over to where Göring stood and grasped the man's hand in both of his. "Rudy!" Hitler shouted.

Hitler's adjutant appeared seconds later. "Yes, *mein Fuhrer*?"

"A stein of lager for *Unser* Hermann and a mineral water for me." Then, after Rudy left, he turned to Göring. "I read all the translations of the American newspaper articles by *Frau* McGary you prepared for me," Hitler said after Rudy left. "Thank you. Imagine, you rescuing a damsel in distress, not once, but twice! Who was the other person in the second rescue? The one who was tortured? The name was not in the articles you gave me."

Göring hesitated. Did Hitler already know it was Admiral Raeder's wife? Had Raeder already complained to him? He decided it didn't matter. It was Himmler, not him, who had his tit in a wringer. Time to tighten the wringer on the SS leader's tit. "Her name is Hanna Hindermann, *mein Fuhrer*, a lawyer on the Commission on Criminal Law Reform. That is her maiden name. She is married to Admiral Erich Raeder."

Göring paused when Rudy returned with the beer, mineral water and cream-filled little cakes.

"A woman! Raeder's wife? The devil, you say! Does the Admiral know?" Hitler asked.

"I'm not sure. The one way he would know is if his wife has informed him. Otherwise, only my men know and they will keep their mouths shut. They immediately executed all the men responsible for her arrest and torture."

"Excellent! Hmmm... do you have wiretaps on Raeder's official and private telephones?" Hitler asked as he snatched a cake and ate it in two quick bites.

"No, *mein Fuhrer.*"

"Do so and promptly advise me if he ever tells anyone he knows about his wife's arrest and torture. Then, I'll call, apologize and tell him I've had all those responsible executed," Hitler said and licked traces of cake from his fingers

"At once, *mein Fuhrer*, as soon as I return to Berlin," Göring said and took a swallow of lager. "How did your meetings with *Herr Doktor* Goebbels and *Reichsfuhrer-SS* Himmler go today?"

Hitler laughed. "Hah! Just as you predicted. They both lied through their teeth about giving their approval to kidnapping McGary in Amsterdam and arresting the two in Rostok and putting them in *Oranienburg.* I didn't let on, of course, that I had read the Brown Pages of their telephone conversations. I like them, but if they're so stupid as to talk about such things on the telephone, why should I save them from themselves? Besides, I like to know what my people are doing behind my back. Keep up the good work."

"Thank you, *mein Fuhrer*," Göring replied. "Did you discuss the new laws against the Jews being considered by the Commission on Criminal Law Reform?"

"Yes, of course, but before I got to that, I asked each one what *dumkopf* had the bright idea to engage American military intelligence to do the legal research in America. Both blamed it on Freisler who, conveniently, is now dead. By the way, you never told me how you found copies of the correspondence between the two of them sharing the cost of the American legal research."

Göring hesitated. He didn't want to reveal Sturm's seduction of Magda Goebbels as he knew of Hitler's fondness for Magda and his disapproval of Goebbels' notorious womanizing with UFA starlets. He decided to proceed cautiously. "One of my men found and photographed the letters in the study of Goebbels' lakeside house on *Schwanenenwerder* Island."

"Really?" Hitler asked, raising an eyebrow. "And how did he gain access to this house? Wiretaps are one thing, but breaking and entering? We are a civilized country after all. I would never condone that."

Göring was taking a sip of his lager when Hitler said this and almost choked, but caught himself in time. What was a little breaking and entering, he thought, compared to the cold-blooded murders on 30 June this year of Ernst Rohm, the head of the SA and one of Hitler's closest friends, as well as his predecessor as Chancellor of Germany, General von Scheicher and his wife? "No, *mein Fuhrer*, there was no forced entry. My man was there by invitation."

"Come, come, Hermann. Don't make me pull teeth. Who was your man and who invited him?"

"Sturm, *mein Fuhrer*, Kurt von Sturm. Gobbels' wife, Magda, invited him."

"By God, did she?" Hitler said with a laugh and slapped his knee. "Is she fucking Sturm? Well, of course she's fucking him! It would serve Goebbels right! Until I can persuade him that it's not in his best interests to screw every UFA actress he hires, why shouldn't Magda have her fun as well? Good for her! I admire her taste. Sturm and Magda are the perfect models for the Aryan race."

Göring breathed a sigh of relief at having dodged that bullet. He drained his stein of beer. "And the new laws about the Jews?"

"Both have the same outlook, just as you predicted," Hitler said. "They each want to go back four or five generations to find a single Jewish ancestor. They prefer five generations, but will settle for four. For different reasons, of course. Himmler's position is completely race-based, the contamination of Aryan or Germanic blood. He even mentioned some archeological expedition the SS is financing into Tibet to find evidence of our early Aryan ancestry.

"Goebbels is more pragmatic. Once we banned SA violence against the Jews last year, he thinks we have to come up with a legal way of sticking it to the Jews or else SA violence against the Jews may flare up again. The Night of the Long Knives has put the fear of God into most of the SA, but the longer we go without new laws legally putting Jews in their place, Goebbels says, the less of a deterrent the memory becomes of that night. So, Hermann, this is all as you predicted. What do you think we should do?" Hitler asked as he picked up the last of the cream-filled cakes.

After eating the cake and taking a sip of water, Hitler called once more for his adjutant. "Rudy, more beer for *Unser* Hermann and mineral water for me."

This was the moment Göring had been waiting for. He knew how deeply held Hitler's anti-Semitism was even though he could mask it with an actor's consummate skill when he wanted to. It was equally as deep as Himmler's and Goebbels' anti-Semitism. Göring wasn't like them. Sure, he agreed that a large number of Jewish finaciers and their profiteering had helped bring about Germany's defeat in the Great War, but he did not have similar views about all Jews. His godfather, Ritter von Epstein was a Jew; so was Erhard Milch, his second in command in the Richthofen Squadron and now his Chief Deputy at the *Luftwaffe,* the principal architect of its rearmament.

As Göring was wont to privately tell his fiancée, the actress Emmy Sonneman, the Jews were just like any other people, some good, some bad, but—he would say to her with a grin—a bit smarter. It didn't matter to him what laws were passed about the Jews. If he liked someone who the law defined as a Jew, then they weren't a Jew! 'I shall decide who is and who is not a Jew' he had told Emmy more than once. Truth to tell, however, if some Jew had artwork that Göring coveted, then he was a Jew no matter how much he or Emmy liked him. *Unser* Hermann loved to buy art at bargain basement prices with what he called 'his Jewish discount'. Still, with Hitler, he would have to be especially careful *not* to say that. *Der Fuhrer* was something of a Puritan when it came to acquiring artwork on the cheap.

"*Mein Fuhrer,* you can take care of the Jews at any time, now or in the future," Göring replied. "Already, we have taken Jews out of any positions of influence in Germany in politics, economics, finance, academia, law, medicine, science and the arts. The question is how and when to do more. It is a matter of priorities. Unlike you and me, Himmler and Goebbels are not soldiers. They do not have the vision you do about the necessity for rearming Germany as quickly as possible. To do that requires foreign reserves that we need badly. The Jewish-inspired worldwide boycott against German exports last year has failed because of the Transfer Agreement with Jewish Palestine, the *Concordat* with the Roman Catholic Church, and our forbidding unauthorized violence against the Jews. New laws against the Jews may breath new life into the boycott."

Hitler took another sip of mineral water and gestured with his hand for the *Reichstag* President to continue. Göring always had a difficult time reading Hitler, but he decided to press on with his original argument, trusting that, if Hitler really disagreed, he would say so.

"What you have confided in me and *not* your *Reichswehr* generals is that you want Germany sufficiently rearmed in five years to prevail in a European war. To achieve that, we must continue to step up our rearmament efforts. To do that, we need foreign reserves to pay for it. Perhaps Schacht's so-called 'New Plan' for barter between Germany and Central and Eastern European countries will be sufficient to replace foreign reserves from our exports. Personally, I don't think so, but let's give him a year or two to see if he's right. If he's right, we can ignore the threat of a worldwide boycott and address the Jewish problem with new laws at that time. Until then, we need all the foreign reserves we can assemble.

The *Luftwaffe* is a good example. When we began to build new fighters and bombers last year, German aircraft engines were not powerful enough. We had to buy more modern aircraft engines from Britain, America and even France. Without foreign reserves to buy those engines, the *Luftwaffe* wouldn't be on the verge of becoming the largest air force in Europe. By next March we will be the largest, especially since Pratt & Whitney sold patents for its aircraft engines to BMW and Curtiss-Wright did the same with Fokker."

"You make good points, Hermann," Hitler said. "We can wait until next year to revisit the question of new laws against the Jew parasites. In the meantime, how do you define a Jew? Heinrich and Joseph have strongly held views on that. What's your response to them?"

Göring laughed and swallowed the rest of his lager. "Rudy! More beer!" he shouted and then turned his attention back to Hitler. "They're both idiots! You've read the Brown Pages. They embarrassed the German *Reich* when they conspired to kidnap, if not kill, the Scottish journalist McGary, the same woman both you and I sent wedding presents to last year. German Jews have been with us for hundreds of years. They've married into our best families. The majority of them are converts to Christianity. If we go back five generations—or even four—to find a Jew in the woodpile, so to speak, we'll end up with more Christians than real Jews defined as Jews. Take Himmler as an example. How much of an Aryan is he? No blue eyes like you or me, yet he's sending an expedition to Tibet to prove he has chicken farmer ancestors there. We could better spend the money on bombers for the *Luftwaffe!*" Goring said, slapping the low table in front of him and then taking another swallow of beer.

"Interesting," Hitler said, "but what about Goebbels? He says we need to do something about the Jews in order to keep the SA in check."

Just then, Rudy returned with another stein of lager for Göring. Hitler shook his head at Rudy's unspoken question for another mineral water and Göring continued.

"The SA is already in check. As for Goebbels, he wants a drastic definition of Jews so he can use it to blackmail UFA actresses into his bed with a threat to find a Jew hidden somewhere on their family trees. Frankly, we ought to pass a law sterilizing him and other clubfoots from passing on their clubfoot genes."

Hitler chuckled. "What does *Frau* Raeder think about defining who is a Jew? I've met her on several social occasions. She is really quite beautiful and she looks you in the eye and says what she thinks. She's one of the reasons I like her husband even though he's not a Nazi."

"She opposes criminalizing sex and marriage between Jews and Aryans, but as for defining Jews, she believes a person is a Jew if he or she has three Jewish grandparents, one of whom is the maternal grandmother. Alternatively, if someone is a practicing Jew with two Jewish grandparents including the maternal grandmother, then that person is a Jew. In my opinion, that's what the law should be."

"I think that's sound," Hitler said, "especially for German Jews. I'm not so sure about Jews of Polish origin, but I think we need to be consistent. So, we'll go with *Frau* Raeder's definition of a Jew and put off passing new laws about the Jews until the Party Congress in Nuremberg next year."

That went well, Göring thought as he settled into the backseat of his dark blue Mercedes limousine. So, Hitler was entranced by another pretty face, Hanna Raeder, the wife of the head of the German Navy who was constantly competing with the *Luftwaffe* for scarce supplies of steel.

It would be useful to know just what Raeder was planning. Hitler already had ordered wiretaps on him, but Göring wondered if there was more that could be done to ascertain just what the Navy's plans really were. Would Kurt von Sturm be up to seducing Hanna Raeder as well as Magda Goebbels? He would have to think about that.

64

Would You Prefer a Court Martial?

The White House
Washington, D.C
Wednesday, 10 October 1934

THE PRESIDENT had not been in a good mood for well over a week, ever since the appearance of Martha McGary's articles in the Hearst papers last week on new laws the Nazis were considering against the Jews began to appear. It was late in the afternoon—not quite 5:00 p.m.—on a bright, sunny day and Franklin Roosevelt badly needed a drink.

The McGary woman's articles were bad enough, especially the first three that revealed the Army's Military Intelligence Division had been paid by the Nazis to conduct legal research into race laws of American states and, worse, that the six lawyers who conducted the research—all ex-MID agents—had been killed, likely by gangsters. Hoover and the FBI were investigating this, but so far had come up with nothing more than McGary had—namely that a hitman for the New York gangster Owney Madden had been positively identified as the killer of one of the lawyers by the man's wife. Unfortunately, the wife had killed the hitman in self-defense so that was a dead end.

Worse news was sitting on his desk, a report from Jim Farley, the Postmaster General, Chairman of the Democratic Committee and the once and future manager of FDR's 1932 and 1936 Presidential campaigns. Roosevelt looked up from the report when he heard a knock on an open door to the Oval Office that led to the desk of his private secretary Margeurite 'Missy' LeHand.

Louis Howe stuck his large ugly head with its bulging, bloodshot eyes in the door. "Yes, Boss, you wanted to see me?"

"Come on in, Louie, I need a martini, maybe two or three. It must be five o'clock somewhere. I take it you've seen Farley's report on the reaction to those Hearst articles?"

"Yep. Based on what Emil Hurja has found in his survey of Democratic county chairmen across the country, the Blacks are sitting on their hands and the Jews are sitting on their wallets."

Hurja was the man at the Democratic Committee in charge of private polling and FDR had directed him—after McGary's second article last week on the Nazis paying MID—to gauge public opinion about the articles and what the various county chairmen were hearing.

"That about sums it up," Roosevelt said as he moved his wheelchair from behind his desk and rolled it with his powerful forearms over to a drinks trolley at the side of the Oval Office where he began to make a pitcher of martinis. He looked over his shoulder at Howe. "The question is what are we going to do about it?"

"I've been thinking about that, Frank," Howe replied. "There are three things we can do, one under the table and two more more or less above the table."

Roosevelt finished stirring the ice and gin in the pitcher. He popped an olive into the two stemmed martini glasses and poured each nearly to the rim. He handed a glass to Howe and each man took an appreciative sip.

"Ah, just what I needed," Roosevelt said. "Give me the underhanded option first."

"Simple. We bribe all the prominent black leaders in big cities to turn out the vote. We give them 'walking around' money that we promise to double after the elections if their city's Democratic vote totals for the Senate and House in 1934 exceed those in 1932. We do the same with all our county chairmen in Democratic states. This will give them an incentive to be 'creative' in turning out the vote. I don't especially care if its 'vote early and often' or the dead may rise again or just plain old ballot box stuffing. The people on the ground will know what works best for them."

"Good. I approve. Take money out of the funds left over from our 1932 campaign," FDR said before draining his martini and pouring two more. "Now, what are the other two things?"

"We need to get the Jews to re-open their checkbooks. So, we leak to Drew Pearson that, over the stong objections of the State Department, you have personally ordered the government to cease purchases of any German products so long as they are available elsewhere. We will suggest—and frankly this is true—that there is a strong anti-Semitic element at State. Pearson won't be able to resist reporting this. Then we get the Democratic National Committee to send copies of Pearson's 'Washington Merry-go-Round' column to every damn rabbi in the country."

"Excellent. Do it," FDR said. "What's # 3?"

"Someone has to walk the plank. We need a scapegoat and I vote for Marlborough. He's the idiot who got us into this mess in the first place. You've got to tell the country you're cleaning house at MID, starting at the top, by asking for Marlborough's resignation."

Roosevelt finished his second martini and poured a third. "I agree. Have him here first thing tomorrow morning."

The White House
Washington, D.C
Thursday, 11 October 1934

MAJOR GENERAL Leonard Marlborough was understandably nervous, being peremptorily ordered by that odious little dwarf, Louis Howe, to appear at precisely 9:45 a.m. in the Oval Office. He had been dreading such a summons for over a week, once the Hearst papers began running that series of articles on that damnable 'Prussian Memorandum'. He wondered why it had taken them over a week to do so.

Ushered into the Oval Office, FDR was seated behind his desk, trademark cigarette holder clutched firmly in his teeth. No one else was in the room.

"Have a seat, General," Roosevelt gestured to a straight-backed chair sitting all by itself in front of the President's desk. He felt like a schoolboy summoned to the Headmaster's office. The Presdient's use of 'General' rather than 'Leonard' signaled that it was going to be a formal meeting. Suddenly, a door that otherwise blended in with the curved wall opened and Louis Howe walked in followed by J. Edgar Hoover, the head of the FBI. Damn! Now, Marlborough was *really* worried.

"General, you've doubtless read the articles in the Hearst papers last week on this 'Prussian Memorandum' business?" FDR asked.

"Yes, Sir."

"Edgar, here, is particularly interested in last Wednesday's article, the murder of the six former MID agents who conducted the legal research for this 'Prussian Memorandum'. Have you read it?"

"Yes, Sir," Marlborough replied, thinking Yes, those were the loose ends you had that toad Howe tell us you wanted tied up. *Permanently.* He knew what was coming next.

"At my request, Edgar has his agents investigating those six murders. What do you know about them?"

Well, what I know, Marlborough thought, but did not say, is that your man Louis Howe told Harry Canfield that you thought those six former MID agents as well as two FBI agents and a German military attaché were loose ends to be tied up permanently; that Canfield engaged an assassin through Owney Madden to kill the six MID agents; and that Canfield took care of the FBI agents himself. So, nothing for it but to deny everything.

"Mr. President, I knew nothing about those murders until I read about them in the Hearst papers. I was as shocked as you undoubtedly were," Marlborough said and silently added *as you undoubtedly were not.*

"Is the Hearst papers' report accurate that the Nazi SS reimbursed MID for what you paid those six unfortunate men to conduct the legal research for this 'Prusssian Memorandum'?

"Yes, Mr. President," Marlborough replied.

"Louie, give the letter to the General," FDR said.

Marlborough watched as the emaciated little man pushed himself up from his chair beside Hoover and walked over to Roosevelt's desk where the President handed him a single sheet of heavy bond stationery. Howe than walked to the front of the desk and thrust the sheet at him. Marlborough took the letter and began to read. There was no letterhead, simply his own residence address in the top right hand corner. The contents were clear. He was to confess that the decision for MID to work for the Nazis was his and his alone; that no one else at MID knew what he was doing; and that neither FDR nor anyone else at the White House had any knowledge of this until the appearance of the articles in the Hearst papers last week. That was a damnable lie, Marlborough thought. The crippled bastard knew all about it a year ago and ordered a coverup!

Finally, Marlborough came to the last paragraph and did a double take. No, damnit! He wouldn't apologize for 'bringing disgrace upon the Army and his country'. He had been acting in good faith! Just last year at the President's direction, MID had worked with the SS to sabotage the worldwide boycott of German exports organized by that Jewish rabbi in Cleveland, Abba Hillel Silver. Yes, he would submit his resignation; he had expected that. Intelligence operations should never make headlines. But he would *never* waive all rights to his Army pension!

"I can't sign this letter, Mr. President. You and I both know it's not true. You will have my one-line resignation on your desk later today."

"No, Leonard," FDR said in a cold voice. "I will have your resignation on my desk *before* you leave this room. Sign that letter now or else you will face a secret court martial on charges of treason followed, I guarantee, by a firing squad. Would you prefer a court-martial?"

Marlborough sighed. He had no choice. Sure, he could blame the man most responsible—Harold fucking Hudson Canfield, III—but he had no way to prove it. He looked up as the little dwarf handed him a fountain pen. He took it, unscrewed the top, placed the letter on the President's desk and scrawled his name at the bottom, the sound of the pen's nib on the heavy paper seemed almost deafening to him as an honorable—at least to him—military career came to an ignominious end.

AFTER HOOVER and Marlborough left, Roosevelt looked at Howe. "Well, Louie, make sure Drew Pearson gets a copy of Marlborough's resignation from 'an undiscosed White House source'. Meanwhile, it looks like we are in need of a new Military Intelligence Director. Any ideas?"

"There's a Colonel Timothy O'Hanlon at MID. He's career military, good war record and his family is rich. He and his two brothers were big contributors to us in '32."

"I know him and his brothers. Good people, but I don't want anyone from MID who was there while all this was going on even if they knew nothing about it. Besides, I have it on good authority that it was O'Hanlon who hired Bourke Cockran's boy to investigate the deaths of those former MID agents. He's the journalist's husband and while the leaks about this 'Prussian Memorandum' all came from the Germans, we can't overlook the fact that Cockran's investigation may well have played a part, especially linking one murder to an Owney Madden hit man. How about that nice Navy chap from ONI? What's his name?"

"Canfield. Harold Hudson Canfield, III."

"Yeah, him," FDR said. "He was one you talked to about tying up the loose ends."

"He did a good job, better than Marlborough," Howe said. "He didn't leave any loose ends around from our side to give this story to Hearst. It's always good to have someone ruthless as an intelligence head."

"I agree. Get him in here this afternoon."

"You bet, Boss."

65

Camilla Always Lands on Her Feet

The White House
Washington, D.C
Wednesday, 10 October 1934

THE MEETING with the President at 5:00 p.m. surprised Canfield. Ever since that bitch McGary's articles appeared last week, he had expected to be called on the carpet along with Marlborough and Van Deman to explain to FDR what the hell had gone wrong. Canfield was fully prepared to throw the fucking Germans under the bus and claim—correctly—that any leaks had come from their side and that, in fact, every single 'loose end' from the American side had been dealt with. You could have knocked him over with a feather when he heard FDR's first words.

"Commander Canfield, so good of you to come on such short notice. It seems we have a vacancy in the Directorship of the Army's Military Intelligence Division. With all the bad publicity MID has received, I'm thinking we need a Navy man to go in there and clean house. You'd need to transfer your allegiance to a lesser branch of the Armed Services, but you'd also receive a promotion to the rank of Brigadier General. What do you say?" FDR asked as he rolled his wheel chair over to a drinks cart and began to make a pitcher of martinis. "One olive or two?"

"One, please. As to your offer I'm very flattered, Mr. President. Before I accept, there are several matters I would like to raise for discussion," Canfield said as he quickly began to think of ways to turn this new development to his financial advantage. There just might be a way for him to have his cake and eat it too. True, he really didn't need more money, but so far as he was concerned, you could never have too much money.

FDR gestured with his hand for Canfield to continue.

"I have several trust funds that own shares in aircraft and armaments companies who do a substantial amount of business with the U.S. government. I don't know which companies," he lied. In fact, Canfield knew, his trust owned *controlling* interests in seven U.S. aircraft and armaments companies. "Will that pose a problem?"

"Are they blind trusts?" FDR asked.

Not now, Canfield thought, but his lawyers could lock that empty barn door later. "Yes, Mr. President," he lied again.

"Then, I don't think it's a problem" FDR replied.

"I would have to resign, of course, as Executive Vice President of RVD International, but I have a sizeable ownership interest in RVD. Might I be permitted to retain that interest?"

"I don't see why not," FDR replied, "provided that you do not refer matters to it as your predecessor did. That would be a conflict of interest."

"I agree, Sir." And, Canfield thought, once the U.S. Senate confirmed his promotion to Brigadier General, he and his old ONI boss, the recently retired Rear Admiral Edwin Elliston, would form a new oufit along the lines of RVD International—'Bluewater Associates' had a nice ring to it—and hire ex-ONI agents exclusively. Work MID formerly farmed out to RVD would then go to Bluewater in which Canfield—or better yet, his wife—would be a silent partner.

"I believe you were recently in Germany. Do you have any knowledge of events there described in the articles in the Hearst papers last week?" FDR asked.

"Directly? No, Sir. I do have indirect knowledge because I was working with the Germans to plug their leaks to McGary. I'd rather not tell you what I know. Most of the time, it's better if you don't have specific information about any missions I might undertake. Like every President, you need to have 'plausible deniability'."

"Good point. What's the second matter?" the President asked.

"Except for sending my name to the Senate for my promotion to Brigadier General and my appointment to head MID, I'd like that to be the last time my name appears either in the newspapers or government records for that matter. Like the directors of the British MI-5 and MI-6, I wish only to be known by a single initial, in my case 'H'. Also, it would be very helpful if you would tell the press, off-the-record, that it would be in the best interests of national security if they never mentioned my name in print again. Is that something you could do?"

"Of course. That's an excellent idea!"

"Then I accept your offer, Mr.President, and I thank you for the trust you have shown in me," Canfield said and plucked the olive from his martini glass and popped it in his mouth. This would not be his first *nom de guerre* nor would it be the most lucrative one. Nevertheless, Canfield thought, it certainly had the potential to be the most useful one.

"You're most welcome. Say, Louie informs me that your wife is a Van Aken from Cleveland. Her father and I went to Harvard together and he is one of my largest campaign contributors. Please convey my best regards to your lovely wife."

"Thank you, Sir. I shall do so the next time I see her, but I confess I don't know when."

"Why's that?"

"My wife is still in Germany and I've not heard from her in over three weeks. I had to leave Germany suddenly for reasons best left unsaid. I fear the Nazis have arrested her, but the Germans tell our embassy they don't have her. If you could have our ambassador tell the German Foreign Office that she and her family are personal friends of yours, I'd greatly appreciate it."

"Of course. Louie, get on the phone to Cordell Hull and make it happen," FDR said.

"Thanks again, Mr. President. Camilla always lands on her feet, but it can't hurt to let the Nazis know she has friends in high places."

CAMILLA CANFIELD had indeed landed on her feet, her bare feet, as she stepped from a marble tub and wrapped a towel around her wet blonde hair. It was the only article of clothing on a glistening body still flushed pink from what she liked to think of as a little 'afternoon delight'. "How long are you going to keep me under house arrest?" she asked from the bathroom door of her suite at the *Hotel Kaiserhof*. "It's been over three weeks now."

"That depends," Walter Schellenberg replied as a naked Camilla Canfield paused for him to admire her body, something she knew he liked her to do. "How long do you want it to be?"

Camilla walked over to the bed where Schellenberg sat propped up by pillows, a sheet pulled up to his waist covering his own nakedness. She leaned over and gave him a long, lingering kiss. "I'm in no big hurry, but aren't you neglecting your official duties by spending so much time with me?"

"Let me worry about that," Schellenberg replied. "It's really your call. Just let me know when you'd like to leave."

As Schellenberg reached out and pulled her down on top of him, he had to admit, if only to himself, that arresting Camilla Canfield as an accomplice to her husband's crimes was one of his more clever decisions. He knew he was irresistibly attracted to older, smart, beautiful—and married—women like Marlene Dietrich, Mattie McGary and Camilla Canfield. If he couldn't have Marlene or Mattie in his bed—sadly, both were beyond his reach—Camilla was a perfect consolation prize.

After interrogating her husband in Bremerhaven, he began to think he might have a chance with Camilla provided her husband did something stupid. Which, in the event, he did.

His repeated attempts to intimidate or kill McGary were certainly stupid, especially when Canfield tried to cause an accident using a motorcar hired by his own company, RVD. Was all that enough to convict him? Schellenberg knew, as a lawyer, that it was mostly circumstantial evidence, but it would have been enough to arrest Canfield and keep him locked up for several weeks while Schellenberg made his play for the man's wife. Imagine Schellenberg's delight, therefore, when he discovered Canfield had done something else that was even more stupid—leaving his wife behind while he fled the country. That 'Good Luck' in his telegram to her was priceless.

It certainly made it easier to seduce Camilla when he placed her under arrest as her husband's accomplice, confiscated her passport, and put her up in a spacious suite at the *Kaiserhof* with an around-the-clock guard. He began the seduction by showing her (1) the Brown Pages transcript of her husband's telephone order to 'rough up' McGary in Berlin; (2) the Berlin Police report of the subsequent attempted rape of McGary by two RVD agents; (3) Canfield's telegram from Bremerhaven ordering McGary killed in Amsterdam; (4) the Brown Pages transcript of Himmler's call to Goebbels outlining Canfield's plan for a fatal 'accident' for McGary; (5) the Prussian State Police report about McGary's tampered brake lines; and (6) the license number of her husband's hired Mercedes SSK identified by a witness at the scene.

Schellenberg had seen from Camilla's shocked expression that she knew nothing of her husband's acrtivities. Still, he never let on that he believed her. Instead, he said that he would be around on a daily basis to continue his interrogation of her until he was satisfied, one way or another, of her guilt or innocence. He continued the seduction by telling her "Order anything you need from Room Service. The *Kaiserhof* has an excellent kitchen. Meanwhile, I'll see that an English language newspaper is delivered to your door every morning."

After that, he arrived at her suite every day at noon when he took her to lunch and dinner at Berlin's finest restaurants. In between meals, he served as a tour guide to Berlin, taking her shopping on *Unter den Linden* and the *Kurfurstendamm*; carriage rides through the *Tiergarten*; visits to the National Gallery and the *Kaiser-Friedrich* Museum; coffee at the *Café Krenzler* and *Café Bristol*; films at the *Ufa Palast* movie theatre; dancing at the elegant Casanova dance palace; and plays in the *Delphi-Palast* in the *Hardenbergstrasse*.

By the third day of this, his dutiful 'interrogation' of her had become a joke between them. At the end of the fourth day, they became lovers. In the weeks that followed, Schellenberg became quite fond of her, wholly apart from the sex and he gradually came to believe she felt the same for him.

Camilla's question was a good one. How long could he keep her in *Kaiserhof* luxury out of his SD funds? He had told his boss, Heydrich, of his plans with her and the lecherous bastard had approved. "Slip her one for me, Walter, and let me know if you get bored. I've never had an American before, let alone a beautiful blonde one." Still, there was a limit to Heydrich's good will and he wanted Camilla out of Germany before Heydrich insisted he 'share' her with him. He liked her far too much to subject her to the bed of that sadistic bastard.

"Well, my gutless husband said to travel first class," Camilla replied as she sat up and straddled his waist. "Which is more expensive, an ocean liner such as the *Europa*? Or an airship like the *Graf Bismarck*?"

"The airship," Schellenberg said, instantly aroused by her action. "It's a thousand *Reichsmarks* more than an ocean liner. You pay for the speed, two and a half days for the airship to cross the Atlantic versus five days by ocean liner."

"Good. It's settled then. When does the next zeppelin leave for America?"

"I'm not entirely certain," Schellenberg replied, "but I think it will be in approximately two weeks

"Then I'll stay under house arrest for another two weeks. Now, this evening, I'd like to dine again at Restaurant *Horcher*. And you must wear your black, silver-trimmed uniform with the knee high black leather boots. I love the jealous looks I get from the other women with their overweight Nazi escorts when I enter on your arm. By the way, have you read the *New York Herald* today?"

"No. Why?"

"Interesting little piece at the bottom of the fourth page. It seems my heroic husband has become a brigadier general and has been named as Director of the U.S. Army's Military Intelligence Division."

"Really? That *is* interesting," Schellenberg said and, his aroused condition notwithstanding, immediately began to think of ways he could turn that to his—or, rather, Germany's—advantage. Could he recruit Camilla as a double agent? He rather thought he could. She obviously had not forgiven her husband for abandoning her in Berlin. All he needed was to establish a secure means of communication between them, possibly a dead drop in Washington. He rather thought he could do that as well.

"As for tonight, of course we may go to *Horcher*," Schellenberg said with a smile. "Your wish, my beautiful prisoner, is my command. Besides, I have much to celebrate tonight."

"Oh? And what would that be?"

"I've never slept with the wife of a brigadier general or a spymaster. After dinner tonight, I intend to 'kill two birds with one stone' as you Americans say.

"Tonight? Why ever would you want to wait that long?" Camilla asked.

"Why ever indeed? When duty calls, never let it be said that an SS officer didn't rise to the challenge," he replied with a smile.

THE END

Historical Note

The Prussian Memorandum is a work of fiction but there are numerous historical persons, facts and elements that provide a foundation and framework for the story.

Winston Churchill. Churchill is accurately portrayed, given that his role occurs within a wholly fictitious adventure. During the 1930s, he did have his own informal intelligence network throughout England and Europe that regularly advised him of developments in Germany after Hitler became Chancellor. Those with only a casual knowledge of Winston Churchill may question his being cast as a key character in an historical thriller. They shouldn't. Saving the world from the revolutionary evil of Adolf Hitler tends to overshadow lesser accomplishments, but Churchill was a first-class athlete in his youth— an all-public school fencing champion, and a championship polo player, a sport he played into his 50s. His detractors — and there were many before he became Prime Minister in May 1940 — dismissed him as an "adventurer" and a "half-breed American." He was both of those things and more. In the late 1890s, he fought Islamic warriors on the Indian-Afghan border and in the Sudan, bloody no-quarter battles where he killed many men at close range. As a war correspondent, he escaped from a prison in South Africa during the Boer war in 1899 and made his way over hundreds of miles of enemy territory to freedom, an exploit that made him famous and led to his election to Parliament in 1900. He bagged a rare white rhino in Africa in 1908, drawing the admiration and envy of Theodore Roosevelt who tried to do the same but was not so fortunate. He became a seaplane pilot in the early 1910s after being appointed, at age 38, the First Lord of the

454 *Michael McMenamin & Kathleen McMenamin*

British Admiralty. Temporarily out of office for a time during the First World War, he commanded a battalion in the trenches in the bloody Ypres salient where Corporal Adolf Hitler also served and where both men drew sketches in their spare time of the same bombed-out Belgian church. Contrary to some views, Hitler was a talented artist, but Churchill was better, a gifted Impressionist whose works anonymously won awards in juried shows. He did not begin painting until age 41, but he produced over 400 oil paintings during his life. Despite being the grandson of a Duke and son of a Lord, Churchill was not a man of inherited wealth. From the outset, he always made his living as a writer of books, articles and essays. His first four books and speaking tours of England and North America in 1900 earned him over $1 million in current value by age 25. During the 1930s, he was the highest paid journalist in the world.

The Prussian Memorandum. Yes, there really was a 'Prussian Memorandum' and all quotes in the novel from it and the 5 June 1934 meeting of the German Commission on Criminal Law Reform are accurate. Sadly, it is true that in 1933, thirty American states prohibited marriage between whites and assorted 'coloreds' and Asians: Alabama, Arizona, Arkansas, California, Colorado, Delaware, Florida, Georgia, Idaho, Indiana, Kentucky, Louisiana, Maryland, Mississippi, Missouri, Montana, Nebraska, Nevada, North Carolina, North Dakota, Oklahoma, Oregon, South Carolina, South Dakota, Tennessee, Texas, Utah, Virginia, West Virginia and Wyoming. Having the legal research performed by American lawyers who were former MID agents is our invention as is the FBI bringing the Prussian Memorandum to the attention of FDR. Those who wish to know more about the Prussian Memorandum are referred to James Q. Whitman, *Hitler's American Model, The United States and the Making of Nazi Race Law.* Worse, in our opinion, was that the Nazis also adopted the eugenics laws of too many American states that provided for the involuntary sterilization of 'mental defectives'. By the time Hitler came to power, Germany had not involuntarily sterilized a single person. In the US, condoned by the Supreme Court in an opinion by Oliver Wendall Holmes, involuntary state sanctioned sterilizations were at 50,000 and counting.

FDR and Louis Howe. FDR and his 'fixer' Louis Howe are accurately portrayed in Chapters 1, 3, 64 and 65. Both opposed the Jewish-inspired worldwide anti-German boycott in 1933. FDR's bigoted internal monologue in Chapter 1 to the effect that America is a Protestant country and the Catholics and Jews are here on sufferance and, therefore, were to go along with anything FDR wanted is historically accurate. FDR actually made the statement in 1942 to the Irish Catholic Leo Crowley, FDR's Alien Property Custodian, who subsequently reported it to the Jewish Secretary of the Treasury, Henry Morgenthau, who included it in his diary entry for 27 January 1942. There is little doubt that FDR was an anti-Semite of a type common among upper class Protestants of the era, but there is no comparison between his anti-Semitism and that of Nazi Germany. While FDR made anti-Semitic comments in private, he never did so in public. The antipathy of both FDR and Howe to J. Edgar Hoover is accurately portrayed, although their characterization of him as 'That goddamned little fairy' is our invention. That all three men were ruthless political operators is historically accurate.

J. Edgar Hoover. Hoover's sexual orientation is unknown as is any proclivity of his for cross-dressing. While one lengthy Hoover biography by Anthony Summers in 2012 makes this claim, the credibility of his source has been questioned. Nevertheless, gossip about Hoover's sexuality was widespread in Washington during his tenure at the FBI, largely because he and his top assistant Clyde Tolson were both lifelong bachelors and by all accounts a devoted couple who lived together for over 40 years. Tolson was Hoover's sole heir upon his death.

The U.S. Army Military Intelligence Division (MID). General Ralph Van Deman, the founder of the Army's Military Intelligence Division in 1917, ran a private intelligence network in America during the 1930s with ex-MID agents who worked closely with MID, the

FBI, the Office of Naval Intelligence and local police departments to ferret out Bolsheviks and Bolshevik sympathizers. His successor as head of MID in the novel, General Leonard Marlborough, is our invention. His actual successor was General Marlborough Churchill, likely a far distant relative of Winston whose own American relatives came from his maternal grandfather Leonard Jerome. Anti-Semitism in MID and the U.S. Army officer corps generally in the 1930s is historically accurate and well documented. MID's collaboration with the SS in this novel and earlier McGary/Churchill novels is our invention. Those who wish to know more about anti-Semitism in the U.S. Army in the 1930s are referred to *The "Jewish Threat", Anti-Semitic Politics of the U.S. Army* by Joseph Bendersky.

Owney Madden, Mae West and The Cotton Club. Owney Madden is accurately portrayed as the ruthless gangster he was. He also owned many legitimate businesses, among them the Cotton Club, which is also accurately portrayed. Mae West was once Madden's mistress and she is accurately portrayed. Much of her dialogue in the novel are quotes attributed to her. While she is best known as a comedian, actress and writer in the motion picture industry, she first became famous on Broadway as a producer, director, actress and playwright. Owney Madden was an investor in many of her plays, including the first one *Sex* for which she was convicted in 1927 of "corrupting the morals of youth" and served eight days in jail.

The Blue Shirts in Ireland. General Eoin O'Duffy and the Army Comrades Association, aka, the "Blue Shirts" are accurately portrayed in Ch. 4 as is his interview with Mattie. General O'Duffy, in August 1933, did plan a parade of 30,000 Blue Shirts in Dublin in honor of Michael Collins, Arthur Griffin and Kevin O'Higgins that was to end on Leinster lawn in front of the Irish parliament where he and others would make speeches. De Valera banned the parade because he feared a *coup d'etat* and he was unsure whether the Irish Army would obey his orders to put it down. There were persistent rumors in 1934 that O'Duffy planned another parade in Dublin in September and wouldn't accept being banned this time.

Bella Fromm. Bella Fromm was a diplomatic correspondent for the Ullstein papers with many wide-ranging contacts among foreign diplomats As a liberal and a Jew, her position grew steadily worse after the Nazis came to power. In 1934, she sent her daughter to America. After 1934, she was legally forbidden to write under her own name and her articles appeared thereafter anonymously. She emigrated to America to join her daughter in 1938 where she wrote *Blood & Banquets, A Berlin Social Diary* about the social and political scene in Germany during the 1920s and 1930s.

Georg von Dohnanyi. Dohnanyi is a fictional character, but he is based on the real-life German lawyer Hans von Dohnanyi who worked in the Ministry of Justice and served on the German Commission on Criminal Law Reform. He later worked for the *Abwehr*—German Military Intelligence—and was an important member of the July 1944 Hitler assassination plot for which he was executed on 8 April 1945.

Admiral Erich Raeder. Admiral Raeder is accurately portrayed. He was not an anti-Semite and refused to dismiss Jewish naval officers. He did dismiss Reinhard Heydrich from the Navy in 1931 for impregnating the daughter of a major shipyard director. While Raeder did have a second wife, Erika, the lawyer Hanna Raeder as his second wife in the novel is our invention. Raeder was not a member of the Nazi Party in 1934 and he and his wife Erika did withdraw their only son from the Hitler youth.

Hermann Göring and the 'Brown Pages'. Hermann Göring was a genuine war hero, a fighter pilot ace in the Great War where he commanded the Richthofen squadron after the death of the famed 'Red Baron'and received the Blue Max, Imperial Germany's highest military honor. He kept lions for pets and, after Hitler, was the most popular Nazi with the German public who did refer to him affectionately as "*Unser* Hermann", i.e., "*Our* Hermann". He held all the offices mentioned in the novel and was every bit as ruthless toward his political enemies as we portray him. His hostility to Heinrich

Himmler and Joseph Goebbels is accurately portrayed. In the vipers' nest that was the Nazi hierarchy, no one trusted anyone. Likewise, Göring's wiretaps by the *Forschungsamt* or FA are accurately portrayed. The FA was Nazi Germany's most effective intelligence agency as it intercepted all international cables that crossed Germany and Göring did personally approve the wiretaps on over 500 telephones in Berlin alone. All intercepted cables and recorded telephone conversations were transcribed onto brown sheets of paper, hence "Brown Pages". Copies of these reports and transcripts went to the person requesting the wiretap as well as Göring himself.

As with all our characters who are actual historical persons, we attempt to portray them as they were during the period covered in the novel, i.e., 1934. Many, like Göring, became worse later on. Others, like Himmler and Goebbels, were so bad to begin with, it was difficult to become worse. While we have Göring come to Mattie's aid and rescue in this novel, it was based less on his good heart and more on his desire to stick it to his political enemies like Himmler and Goebbels.

Walter Schellenberg. Schellenberg is accurately portrayed. A young lawyer, he joined the Nazi Party and the SS after Hitler became Chancellor on 30 January 1933. He was a protégé of Reinhard Heydrich [the ruthless #2 man in the SS and author in 1942 of the 'Final Solution' for European Jews] and he eventually became head of the Foreign Intelligence Section of the SD. His financial reasons for joining the SS and his low opinion of Heydrich are accurately portrayed. He was one of the few leading Nazis who did not become worse after 1934. Despite his high rank, he was given the equivalent of a wrist slap at the Nuremberg trials, likely because of his secret efforts with the OSS to secure a negotiated peace with the Allies during World War II. His affair with Heydrich's wife Lina in Chapter 22 is not necessarily our invention. It may or may not have happened, but Heydrich suspected them of an affair and, at one point, he placed them both under surveillance.

Roland Freisler and the People's Court. Roland Freisler is accurately portrayed as the uniquely evil character he was. While having him as the Chairman of the German Commission on Criminal Law Reform is our invention, all of his statements at the 5 June 1934 meeting of the Commission where the Prussian Memorandum was discussed are accurate. He was a prisoner of war of the Russians in World War I where he learned to speak fluent Russian and, after the Bolshevik revolution in Russia, they subsequently made him the Commissar of the POW camp where he was held. Hitler appointed him Director of the Prussian Ministry of Justice in 1933. He served in the Ministry of Justice form 1934 to 1942 when he was named President of the People's Court and was known as the 'Hanging Judge' where death or life imprisonment were the sentences in 90% of the cases before him. Like Heydrich, he participated in the January 1942 Wannsee Conference where the plans for the destruction of European Jews—the Holocaust—were made. In 1943, he ordered the beheading of several members of the White Rose resistance group. Sadly, he did not die until 3 February 1945 during a bombing raid on Berlin by the US Army Air Force while presiding over a session of the People's Court. We typically try not to have actual historical persons die before their time in our historical novels, so having Freisler killed in 1934 in the novel is our invention. He is not widely known and, more importantly, we thought he deserved it.

Joseph Goebbels and Heinrich Himmler. Both Goebbels' and Himmler's anti-Semitism is accurately portrayed. Their joint funding of the legal research for the Prussian Memorandum is our invention. While superficially cordial, the antipathy each held for the other is accurately portrayed.

Adolf Hitler. Hitler is a difficult person to portray as a fictional character. As with Churchill and other historical characters in the novel, we have attempted to portray him as he was during 1934 in the months after he ordered the 30 June 1934 murder of his political opponents by the SS. While Hitler's virulent anti-Semitism is well documented, he was also a politician seeking to expand his appeal beyond the anti-Semites on which it was initially based. Hence, it is a fact that Hitler gave no anti-Semitic speeches after the Nazis became the second largest party in the *Reichstag* in August 1930 through the March 1933 *Reichstag* election. Anti-Semitism wasn't particularly popular in Weimar Germany beyond the Nazi core supporters. Hitler the politician knew he already had the anti-Semite vote and that attacking Jews in his speeches would not increase his vote totals whereas it might decrease them if other voters were turned off by bigoted rhetoric. After the single day anti-Jewish boycott on April 1, 1933, both Hitler and Göring attempted to suppress violence against the Jews, primarily because of the effect the worldwide anti-German boycott was having on the German economy. A mid-April 1933 letter from Rudolf Hess on behalf of Hitler prohibiting 'All boycotts of Jewish-owned department stores' because of the harm it was doing to the German economy was actually published in newspapers throughout Germany. Likewise, Hitler actually ordered a special subsidy in April 1933 to save Germany's second-largest department store chain, the Jewish-owned Hermann Tietz, from bankruptcy. As with Hitler choosing the most narrow definition of a Jew for the Nurenberg laws in 1935 rather than the radical Nazis' broader definition, being an anti-Semite was not incompatible with his being a pragmatist. The meeting between Hitler and Göring in Chapter 63 where Göring persuades Hitler to proceed with a more narrow definition of a Jew than that desired by Himmler and Goebbels is our invention, but the underlying rationale is historically accurate. The most 'moderate' definition of a Jew was Hitler's call and he did postpone for a year until September 1935 having the *Reichstag* pass what became known as the 'Nuremberg Laws' stripping German Jews of their citizenship and forbidding marriage and sexual relations between Jews and Aryans.

Beheading. Beheading was the form of capital punishment used in Germany for well over a century and was still used in the 1930s. There was only one *fallbeil* in Germany in 1933 when Hitler was appointed Chancellor and he did order the construction of 19 additional *fallbeil* because of a shortage of executioners. Prior to his taking power, 'Heads will roll' was a common Hitler campaign pledge and once in office, he kept his promise literally.

The R-100. The Vickers-built R-100 airship and its lavish interior are accurately described. It twice crossed the Atlantic. Its sister airship, the government-built R-101, crashed on its maiden voyage to India and brought to an end the British airship program. YouTube videos of both these airships are available. After the R-101 crash, the R-100 then was sold for its scrap value and not to the German Zeppelin Company as it is in the novel. We thought that to be a waste of a perfectly good airship so in our novels, we have the German Zeppelin Company purchase the R-100 and rechristen it as LZ-128, the *Graf Bismarck*. The idea of converting it to a German zeppelin occurred to us as a result of the Zeppelin Company's system of numbering its airships. The famed *Graf Zeppelin* that flew around the world in 1929 and safely logged millions of passenger miles on its regular route to South America was the LZ-127. The next zeppelin built, the ill-fated *Hindenburg*, was the LZ-129 whose commercial purpose was, like the *Graf Bismarck,* to fly between Europe and North America. So why was there no LZ-128? As we discovered, the LZ-128 was a zeppelin that never made it off the drawing boards. It was designed to have 150% of the lift capacity of the *Graf Zeppelin* and carry 26 passengers, twice that of the *Graf.* But the LZ-128 was never built. It was designed with hydrogen as its lifting agent and the crash of the R-101 caused its cancellation once the Zeppelin Company learned that most of the R-101's passengers survived the airship's crash and perished in the fires of the burning hydrogen. The Zeppelin Company then began work on the LZ-129, the *Hindenburg.* It is not widely known, but the LZ-129 was designed from the outset to use the inert, non-flammable helium gas on which the U.S. had a monopoly. The U.S. government refused to allow the Zeppelin Company to buy helium and thus is directly responsible for the *Hindenburg's* crash and loss of life. We gave the unused LZ-128 designation to the R-100.

Autogiros The Juan de la Cierva-designed autogiro was the next big thing in aviation when it was commercially introduced in the early

1930s. *Fortune* magazine devoted two articles to it in its March, 1931 edition, describing it as "a complex if not revolutionary addition to the science of aerodynamics." It flew and handled like an airplane but could take off and land in short spaces at safe, slow speeds. Lift was provided solely by the four blades of its huge hinged rotor, a common feature on today's helicopters.

Michael McMenamin
Kathleen McMenamin
April, 2020

About the Authors

Michael McMenamin is the co-author with his son Patrick of the first five of the six award winning 1930s era historical novels featuring Winston Churchill and his fictional Scottish goddaughter, the adventure-seeking Hearst photojournalist Mattie McGary. He is the co-author with his daughter **Kathleen McMenamin** of the sixth Mattie + Winston novel *The Liebold Protocol* and the novella *Appointment in Prague*. The first six novels in the series—*The DeValera Deception, The Parsifal Pursuit, The Gemini Agenda, The Berghof Betrayal, The Silver Mosaic and The Liebold Protocol*—received a total of 15 literary awards. He is currently at work with his daughter on the ninth Mattie + Winston historical adventure, *The Phoenix Project*.

Michael is also the author of the critically acclaimed *Becoming Winston Churchill, The Untold Story of Young Winston and His American Mentor* [Hardcover, Greenwood 2007; Paperback, Enigma 2009] and the co-author of *Milking the Public, Political Scandals of the Dairy Lobby from LBJ to Jimmy Carter* [Nelson Hall, 1980]. He is a contributing editor for *Finest Hour,* the quarterly journal of the International Churchill Society and for the libertarian magazine *Reason.* His work also has appeared in *The Churchills in Ireland, 1660-1965,* [Irish Academic Press, 2012] as well as two *Reason* anthologies, *Free Minds & Free Markets, Twenty Five Years of Reason* [Pacific Research Institute, 1993] and *Choice, the Best of Reason* [BenBella Books, 2004]. A full-time writer, he was formerly a First Amendment and Media Defense lawyer and a U.S. Army Counterintelligence Agent.

Kathleen McMenamin, the other half of the father-daughter writing team, has been editing her father's writing for longer than she cares to remember. She is the co-author with her father of the 2018 Mattie + Winston novella, *Appointment in Prague, A Mattie McGary + Winston Churchill World War II Adventure* and the sixth Mattie + Winston novel, *The Liebold Protocol.* She also is the co-author with her sister Kelly of the critically acclaimed *Organize Your Way: Simple*

Strategies for Every Personality [Sterling, 2017]. The two sisters are professional organizers, personality-type experts and the founders of *PixiesDidIt!* a   home   and   life   organization   business, www.pixiesdidit.com.

Kathleen is an honors graduate of Sarah Lawrence College and received an MFA in Creative Writing from New York University while she was with The Wendy Weill Agency. Prior to starting her own business, she was Senior Advertising and Promotion Coordinator for Bedford/St.Martin's. The novella *Appointment in Prague* was her second joint writing project with her father; *The Liebold Protocol* was her third; and *The Prussian Memorandum* is her fourth. Their first father-daughter writing project was "Bringing Home the First Amendment", a review of Nat Hentoff's *The Day They Came to Arrest the Book* in the August 1984 *Reason* magazine. While a teen-ager, she and her father would often take runs together, creating plots for adventure stories as they ran.

Acknowledgements

We owe a debt of gratitude to many people who helped bring *The Prussian Memorandum*, the eight Mattie McGary + Winston Churchill adventure, to light. **Dr. Gwen Minter, Ph.D**, who read several iterations, offered comments and corrections and proofread the final draft of the manuscript. Our biggest fan, **Chuck Rosenbaum,** who read and offered comments and corrections on the manuscript as did our good friend **Cindy Bowman** and, respectively, our wife and mother, **Carol Breckenridge**, who did the same and **Patrick McMenamin**, our son and brother, respectively. In addition, **Alexis Dragony**, Michael's assistant when he was still a practicing lawyer and who still comes to his aid when, as frequently happens, Word for Mac baffles him. Finally, our thanks to **Deborah Gordon** of First Edition Design Publishing for her creative cover designs for this novel as well as the earlier Mattie + Winston adventures by First Edition, *The Berghof Betrayal, the Silver Mosaic, Appointment in Prague* and *The Liebold Protocol.*

www.ingramcontent.com/pod-product-compliance
Lightning Source LLC
Chambersburg PA
CBHW020826030726
47496CB00001B/111